CHIMAMANDA NGOZI ADICHIE g
Purple Hibiscus, was published in 200
Prize. Her second novel, *Half of a Y*
Prize for Fiction. Her short-story collection,
was published to critical acclaim in 2009. She received a MacArthur Fellowship in 2009, and in 2010 appeared on the *New Yorker*'s list of the best 20 writers under 40. *Americanah* is her third novel.

From the reviews of *Americanah*:

'A tour de force . . . The artistry with which Adichie keeps her story moving, while animating the complex societies in which the characters live and work, is hugely impressive' Max Davidson, *Mail on Sunday*

'Adichie writes superb dialogue straight from the mouths of her people . . . Her breadth of vision is striking – and yet she never loses sight of the deepest psychological moments of her characters . . . This is a delicious, important novel from a writer with a great deal to say'
Diana Evans, *The Times*

'Brilliant . . . *Americanah* is an urgent and important book, further evidence that its author is a real talent who is out there, on the up and up'
David Annand, *Sunday Telegraph*

'In Adichie's able prose, social comedy mingles with cultural polemic under the umbrella of an exuberantly romantic love story . . . Here, in rich detail, is the immigrant experience' Sam Leith, *Financial Times*

'Impressive . . . an extremely thoughtful, subtly provocative exploration of structural inequality, of different kinds of oppression, of gender roles, of the idea of home. Subtle, but not afraid to pull its punches'
Alex Clark, *Guardian*

'Terrific on human interactions . . . Adichie's writing always has an elegant shimmer to it . . . wise, entertaining and unendingly perceptive'
Daneet Steffens, *Independent on Sunday*

'Rich and satisfying . . . has the same shape, and offers the same satisfactions, as *Persuasion*' Adam Kirsch, *Prospect*

'Hugely enjoyable . . . effortlessly tackles issues of race, class and belonging with compassion and wit, and you'll be gripped from the first page of this brilliantly evocative book' Anna Carey, *Irish Times*

'A brilliant novel: epic in scope, personal in resonance and with lots to say' Elizabeth Day, *Observer*

'[Adichie] is at once unsparing and compassionate in depicting the nuanced responses of her hero and heroine to the situations in which they find themselves. And her observations about race are fresh and incisive' Francine Prose, *Sunday Times*

'Joyful to read. But this is also an important book, and its strength and originality lie with the meticulous observation about race' *Economist*

'Superb . . . *Americanah* demonstrates that Adichie is starting to resemble her literary idol [Chinua Achebe] – fearlessly tackling weighty themes of race and identity, and ably challenging the West's ingrained perceptions of African life and culture. In short, then, she is a writer of huge talent who just keeps getting better' Malcolm Forbes, *Literary Review*

Also by Chimamanda Ngozi Adichie

The Thing Around Your Neck
Half of a Yellow Sun
Purple Hibiscus

Americanah

Chimamanda
Ngozi Adichie

FOURTH ESTATE • *London*

Fourth Estate
An imprint of HarperCollins*Publishers*
77–85 Fulham Palace Road
London W6 8JB
www.4thestate.co.uk

This Fourth Estate paperback edition published 2014

1

First published in Great Britain by Fourth Estate in 2013

Also published in the United States in 2013 by Alfred A. Knopf,
a division of Random House, Inc., New York,
and in Canada by Alfred A. Knopf Canada,
a division of Random House of Canada Limited, Toronto

A catalogue record for this book is
available from the British Library

ISBN 978-0-00-794568-9

Typeset in Requiem by Palimpsest Book Production Ltd, Falkirk, Stirlingshire,
Printed and bound in Great Britain by Clays Ltd, St Ives plc

This book is for our next generation, *ndi na-abia n'iru*: Toks, Chisom, Amaka, Chinedum, Kamsiyonna and Arinze.

For my wonderful father in this, his eightieth year.

And, as always, for Ivara.

Part 1

CHAPTER 1

Princeton, in the summer, smelled of nothing, and although Ifemelu liked the tranquil greenness of the many trees, the clean streets and stately homes, the delicately overpriced shops and the quiet, abiding air of earned grace, it was this, the lack of a smell, that most appealed to her, perhaps because the other American cities she knew well had all smelled distinctly. Philadelphia had the musty scent of history. New Haven smelled of neglect. Baltimore smelled of brine, and Brooklyn of sun-warmed garbage. But Princeton had no smell. She liked taking deep breaths here. She liked watching the locals who drove with pointed courtesy and parked their latest-model cars outside the organic grocery store on Nassau Street or outside the sushi restaurants or outside the ice cream shop that had fifty different flavours including red pepper or outside the post office where effusive staff bounded out to greet them at the entrance. She liked the campus, grave with knowledge, the Gothic buildings with their vine-laced walls, and the way everything transformed, in the half-light of night, into a ghostly scene. She liked, most of all, that in this place of affluent ease, she could pretend to be someone else, someone specially admitted into a hallowed American club, someone adorned with certainty.

But she did not like that she had to go to Trenton to braid her hair. It was unreasonable to expect a braiding salon in Princeton—the few black locals she had seen were so light-skinned and lank-haired she could not imagine them wearing braids—and yet as she waited at Princeton Junction station for the train, on an afternoon ablaze with heat, she wondered why there *was* no place where she could braid her hair. The chocolate bar in her handbag had melted. A few other people were waiting on the platform, all of them white and lean, in short, flimsy clothes. The man standing closest to her was eating an ice cream cone; she had always found it a little irresponsible, the eating of ice cream cones by grown-up American men, especially the eating of ice cream cones by grown-up American men in public. He turned to her and said, "About time," when the train finally creaked in, with the familiarity strangers adopt with each other after sharing in the disappointment of a public service. She smiled at him. The greying hair on the back of his head was swept forward, a comical arrangement to disguise his bald spot. He had to be an academic, but not in the humanities or he would be more self-conscious. A firm science like chemistry, maybe. Before, she would have said, "I know," that peculiar American expression that professed agreement rather than knowledge, and then she would have started a conversation with him, to see if he would say something she could use in her blog. People were flattered to be asked about themselves and if she said nothing after they spoke, it made them say more. They were conditioned to fill silences. If they asked what she did, she would say vaguely, "I write a lifestyle blog," because saying "I write an anonymous blog called *Raceteenth or Various Observations About American Blacks (Those Formerly Known as Negroes) by a Non-American Black*" would make them uncomfortable. She had said it, though, a few times. Once to a dreadlocked white man who sat next to her on the train, his hair like old twine ropes that ended in a blond fuzz, his tattered shirt worn with enough piety to convince her that he was a social warrior and might make a good guest blogger. "Race is totally overhyped these days, black people need to get over themselves, it's all about class now, the haves and the have-nots," he told her evenly, and she used it as the opening sentence of a post titled "Not All Dreadlocked White American Guys Are Down". Then there was the man from Ohio, who was squeezed next to her on a flight. A middle manager, she was sure, from his boxy suit and contrast collar. He wanted to know what she meant by "lifestyle blog", and she told him, expecting him to become reserved, or to end the conversation by saying something defensively bland like "The only race that matters is the human race." But he said, "Ever write about adoption? Nobody wants black babies in this country, and I don't mean biracial, I mean black. Even the black families don't want them."

He told her that he and his wife had adopted a black child and their neighbours looked at them as though they had chosen to become martyrs for a dubious cause. Her blog post about him, "Badly-Dressed White Middle Managers from Ohio Are Not Always What You Think", had received the highest number of comments for that month. She still wondered if he had read it. She hoped so. Often, she would sit in cafés, or airports, or train stations, watching strangers, imagining their lives, and wondering which of them were likely to have read her blog. Now her ex-blog. She had written the final post only days ago, trailed by two hundred and seventy-four comments so far. All those readers, growing month by month, linking and cross-posting, knowing so much more than she did; they had always frightened and exhilarated her. SapphicDerrida, one of the most frequent posters, wrote: *I'm a bit surprised by how personally I am taking this. Good luck as you pursue the unnamed "life change" but please come back to the blogosphere soon. You've used your irreverent, hectoring, funny and thought-provoking voice to create a space for real conversations about an important subject.* Readers like SapphicDerrida, who reeled off statistics and used words like "reify" in their comments, made Ifemelu nervous, eager to be fresh and to impress, so that she began, over time, to feel like a vulture hacking into the carcasses of people's stories for something she could use. Sometimes making fragile links to race. Sometimes not believing herself. The more she wrote, the less sure she became. Each post scraped off yet one more scale of self until she felt naked and false.

The ice-cream-eating man sat beside her on the train and, to discourage conversation, she stared fixedly at a brown stain near her feet, a spilled frozen Frappuccino, until they arrived at Trenton. The platform was crowded with black people, many of them fat, in short, flimsy clothes. It still startled her, what a difference a few minutes of train travel made. During her first year in America, when she took New Jersey Transit to Penn Station and then the subway to visit Aunty Uju in Flatlands, she was struck by how mostly slim white people got off at the stops in Manhattan and, as the train went further into Brooklyn, the people left were mostly black and fat. She had not thought of them as "fat", though. She had thought of them as "big", because one of the first things her friend Ginika told her was that "fat" in America was a bad word, heaving with moral judgement like "stupid" or "bastard", and not a mere description like "short" or "tall". So she had banished "fat" from her vocabulary. But "fat" came back to her last winter, after almost thirteen years, when a man in line behind her at the supermarket muttered, "Fat people don't need to be eating that shit," as she paid for her giant bag of Tostitos. She glanced at him, surprised, mildly offended, and thought it a perfect blog post, how this stranger had decided she was fat. She would file the post under the tag "race, gender and body size". But back home, as she stood and faced the mirror's truth, she realized that she had ignored, for too long, the new tightness of her clothes, the rubbing together of her inner thighs, the softer, rounder parts of her that shook when she moved. She *was* fat.

She said the word "fat" slowly, funnelling it back and forward, and thought about all the other things she had learned not to say aloud in America. She was fat. She was not curvy or big-boned; she was fat, it was the only word that felt true. And she had ignored, too, the cement in her soul. Her blog was doing well, with thousands of unique visitors each month, and she was earning good speaking fees, and she had a fellowship at Princeton and a relationship with Blaine—"You are the absolute love of my life," he'd written in her last birthday card—and yet there was cement in her soul. It had been there for a while, an early morning disease of fatigue, a bleakness and borderlessness. It brought with it amorphous longings, shapeless desires, brief imaginary glints of other lives she could be living, that over the months melded into a piercing homesickness. She scoured Nigerian websites, Nigerian profiles on Facebook, Nigerian blogs, and each click brought yet another story of a young person who had recently moved back home, clothed in American or British degrees, to start an investment company, a music production business, a fashion label, a magazine, a fast-food franchise. She looked at photographs of these men and women and felt the dull ache of loss, as though they had prised open her hand and taken something of hers. They were living her life. Nigeria became where she was supposed to be, the only place she could sink her roots in without the constant urge to tug them out and shake off the soil. And, of course, there was also Obinze. Her first love, her first lover, the only person with whom she had never felt the need to explain herself. He was now a husband and father, and they had not been in touch in years, yet she could not pretend that he was not a part of her homesickness, or that she did not often think of him, sifting through their past, looking for portents of what she could not name.

The rude stranger in the supermarket—who knew what problems *he* was wrestling with, haggard and thin-lipped as he was—had intended to offend her but had instead prodded her awake.

She began to plan and to dream, to apply for jobs in Lagos. She did not tell Blaine at first, because she wanted to finish her fellowship at Princeton, and then after her fellowship ended, she did not tell him because she wanted to give herself time to be sure. But as the weeks passed, she knew she would never be sure. So she told him that she was moving back home, and she added, "I have to," knowing he would hear in her words the sound of an ending.

"Why?" Blaine asked, almost automatically, stunned by her announcement. There they were, in his living room in New Haven, awash in soft jazz and daylight, and she looked at him, her good, bewildered man, and felt the day take on a sad, epic quality. They had lived together for three years, three years free of crease, like a smoothly ironed sheet, until their only fight, months ago, when Blaine's eyes froze with blame and he refused to speak to her. But they had survived that fight, mostly because of Barack Obama, bonding anew over their shared passion. On election night, before Blaine kissed her, his face wet with tears, he held her tightly as though Obama's victory was also their personal victory. And now here she was telling him it was over. "Why?" he asked. He taught ideas of nuance and complexity in his classes and yet he was asking her for a single reason, the *cause*. But she had not had a bold epiphany and there was no cause; it was simply that layer after layer of discontent had settled in her, and formed a mass that now propelled her. She did not tell him this, because it would hurt him to know she had felt that way for a while, that her relationship with him was like being content in a house but always sitting by the window and looking out.

"Take the plant," he said to her, on the last day she saw him, when she was packing the clothes she kept in his apartment. He looked defeated, standing slump-shouldered in the kitchen. It was his houseplant, hopeful green leaves rising from three bamboo stems, and when she took it, a sudden crushing loneliness lanced through her and stayed with her for weeks. Sometimes, she still felt it. How was it possible to miss something you no longer wanted? Blaine needed what she was unable to give and she needed what he was unable to give, and she grieved this, the loss of what could have been.

So here she was, on a day filled with the opulence of summer, about to braid her hair for the journey home. Sticky heat sat on her skin. There were people thrice her size on the Trenton platform and she looked admiringly at one of them, a woman in a very short skirt. She thought nothing of slender legs shown off in miniskirts—it was safe and easy, after all, to display legs of which the world approved—but the fat woman's act was about the quiet conviction that one shared only with oneself, a sense of rightness that others failed to see. Her decision to move back was similar; whenever she felt besieged by doubts, she would think of herself as standing valiantly alone, as almost heroic, so as to squash her uncertainty. The fat woman was co-coordinating a group of teenagers who looked sixteen and seventeen years old. They crowded around, a summer programme advertised on the front and back of their yellow T-shirts, laughing and talking. They reminded Ifemelu of her cousin Dike. One of the boys, dark and tall, with the leanly muscled build of an athlete, looked just like Dike. Not that Dike would ever wear those shoes that looked like espadrilles. Weak kicks, he would call them. It was a new one; he first used it a few days ago when he told her about going shopping with Aunty Uju. "Mom wanted to buy me these crazy shoes. Come on, Coz, you know I can't wear weak kicks!"

Ifemelu joined the taxi line outside the station. She hoped her driver would not be a Nigerian, because he, once he heard her accent, would either be aggressively eager to tell her that he had a master's degree, the taxi was a second job and his daughter was on the dean's list at Rutgers; or he would drive in sullen silence, giving her change and ignoring her "thank you", all the time nursing humiliation, that this fellow Nigerian, a small girl at that, who perhaps was a nurse or an accountant or even a doctor, was looking down on him. Nigerian taxi drivers in America were all convinced that they really were not taxi drivers. She was next in line. Her taxi driver was black and middle-aged. She opened the door and glanced at the back of the driver's seat. *Mervin Smith.* Not Nigerian, but you could never be too sure. Nigerians took on all sorts of names here. Even she had once been somebody else.

9

"How you doing?" the man asked.

She could tell right away, with relief, that his accent was Caribbean.

"I'm very well. Thank you." She gave him the address of Mariama African Hair Braiding. It was her first time at this salon—her regular one was closed because the owner had gone back to Côte d'Ivoire to get married—but it would look, she was sure, like all the other African hair braiding salons she had known: they were in the part of the city that had graffiti, dank buildings and no white people, they displayed bright signboards with names like Aisha and Fatima African Hair Braiding, they had radiators that were too hot in the winter and air conditioners that did not cool in the summer, and they were full of Francophone West African women braiders, one of whom would be the owner and speak the best English and answer the phone and be deferred to by the others. Often, there was a baby tied to someone's back with a piece of cloth. Or a toddler asleep on a wrapper spread over a battered sofa. Sometimes, older children stopped by. The conversations were loud and swift, in French or Wolof or Malinke, and when they spoke English to customers, it was broken, curious, as though they had not quite eased into the language itself before taking on a slangy Americanism. Words came out half-completed. Once a Guinean braider in Philadelphia had told Ifemelu, "Amma like, Oh Gad, Az someh." It took many repetitions for Ifemelu to understand that the woman was saying, "I'm like, Oh God, I was so mad."

Mervin Smith was upbeat and chatty. He talked, as he drove, about how hot it was, how rolling blackouts were sure to come.

"This is the kind of heat that kills old folks. If they don't have air conditioning, they have to go to the mall, you know. The mall is free air conditioning. But sometimes there's nobody to take them. People have to take care of the old folks," he said, his jolly mood unfazed by Ifemelu's silence.

"Here we are!" he said, parking in front of a shabby block. The salon was in the middle, between a Chinese restaurant called Happy Joy and a convenience store that sold lottery tickets. Inside, the room was thick with disregard, the paint peeling, the walls plastered with large posters of braided hairstyles and smaller posters that said QUICK TAX REFUND. Three women, all in T-shirts and knee-length shorts, were working on the hair of seated customers. A small TV mounted on a corner of the wall, the volume a little too loud, was showing a Nigerian film: a man beating his wife, the wife cowering and shouting, the poor audio quality jarring.

"Hi!" Ifemelu said.

They all turned to look at her but only one, who had to be the eponymous Mariama, said, "Hi. Welcome."

"I'd like to get braids."

"What kind of braids you want?"

Ifemelu said she wanted a medium kinky twist and asked how much it was.

"Two hundred," Mariama said.

"I paid one sixty last month." She had last braided her hair three months ago.

Mariama said nothing for a while, her eyes back on the hair she was braiding.

"So one sixty?" Ifemelu asked.

Mariama shrugged and smiled. "Okay, but you have to come back next time. Sit down. Wait for Aisha. She will finish soon." Mariama pointed at the smallest of the braiders, who had a skin condition, pinkish-cream whorls of discoloration on her arms and neck that looked worryingly infectious.

"Hi, Aisha," Ifemelu said.

Aisha glanced at Ifemelu, nodding ever so slightly, her face blank, almost forbidding in its expressionlessness. There was something strange about her.

Ifemelu sat close to the door; the fan on the chipped table was turned on high but did little for the stuffiness in the room. Next to the fan were combs, packets of hair attachments, magazines bulky with loose pages, piles of colourful DVDs. A broom was propped in one corner, near the candy dispenser and the rusty hair dryer that had not been used in a hundred years. On the TV screen, a father was beating two children, wooden punches that hit the air above their heads.

"No! Bad father! Bad man!" the other braider said, staring at the TV and flinching.

"You from Nigeria?" Mariama asked.

"Yes," Ifemelu said. "Where are you from?"

"Me and my sister Halima are from Mali. Aisha is from Senegal," Mariama said.

Aisha did not look up, but Halima smiled at Ifemelu, a smile that, in its warm knowingness, said welcome to a fellow African; she would not smile at an American in the same way. She was severely cross-eyed, pupils darting in opposite directions, so that Ifemelu felt thrown off-balance, not sure which of Halima's eyes was on her.

Ifemelu fanned herself with a magazine. "It's so hot," she said. At least, these women would not say to her "You're hot? But you're from Africa!"

"This heat wave is very bad. Sorry the air conditioner broke yesterday," Mariama said.

Ifemelu knew the air conditioner had not broken yesterday, it had been broken for much longer, perhaps it had always been broken; still she nodded and said that perhaps it had packed up from overuse. The phone rang. Mariama picked it up and after a minute said "Come now," the very words that had made Ifemelu stop making appointments with African hair braiding salons. Come now, they always said, and then you arrived to find two people waiting to get micro braids and still the owner would tell you "Wait, my sister is coming to help." The phone rang again and Mariama spoke in French, her voice rising, and she stopped braiding to gesture with her hand as she shouted into the phone. Then she unfolded a yellow Western Union form from her pocket and began reading out the numbers. "Trois! Cinq! Non, non, cinq!"

The woman whose hair she was braiding in tiny, painful-looking cornrows said sharply, "Come on! I'm not spending the whole day here!"

"Sorry, sorry," Mariama said. Still, she finished repeating the Western Union numbers before she continued braiding, the phone lodged between her shoulder and ear.

Ifemelu opened her novel, Jean Toomer's *Cane*, and skimmed a few pages. She had been meaning to read it for a while now, and imagined she would like it since Blaine did not. A precious performance, Blaine had called it, in that gently forbearing tone he used when they talked about novels, as though he was sure that she, with a little more time and a little more wisdom, would come to accept that the novels he liked were superior, novels written by young and youngish men and packed with *things*, a fascinating, confounding accumulation of brands and music and comic books and icons, with emotions skimmed over, and each sentence stylishly aware of its own stylishness. She had read many of them, because he recommended them, but they were like cotton candy that so easily evaporated from her tongue's memory.

She closed the novel; it was too hot to concentrate. She ate some melted chocolate, sent Dike a text to call her when he was finished with basketball practice, and fanned herself. She read the signs on the opposite wall—NO ADJUSTMENTS TO BRAIDS AFTER ONE WEEK. NO PERSONAL CHECKS. NO REFUNDS—but she carefully avoided looking at the corners of the room because she knew that clumps of mouldy newspapers would be stuffed beneath pipes and grime and things long rotten.

Finally, Aisha finished with her customer and asked what colour Ifemelu wanted for her hair attachments.

"Colour four."

"Not good colour," Aisha said promptly.

"That's what I use."

"It look dirty. You don't want colour one?"

"Colour one is too black, it looks fake," Ifemelu said, loosening her headwrap. "Sometimes I use colour two, but colour four is closest to my natural colour."

Aisha shrugged, a haughty shrug, as though it was not her problem if her customer did not have good taste. She reached into a cupboard, brought out two packets of attachments, checked to make sure they were both the same colour.

She touched Ifemelu's hair. "Why you don't have relaxer?"

"I like my hair the way God made it."

"But how you comb it? Hard to comb," Aisha said.

Ifemelu had brought her own comb. She gently combed her hair, dense, soft and tightly coiled, until it framed her head like a halo. "It's not hard to comb if you moisturize it properly," she said, slipping into the coaxing tone of the proselytizer that she used whenever she was trying to convince other black women about the merits of wearing their hair natural. Aisha snorted; she clearly could not understand why anybody would choose to suffer through combing natural hair, instead of simply relaxing it. She sectioned out Ifemelu's hair, plucked a little attachment from the pile on the table and began deftly to twist.

"It's too tight," Ifemelu said. "Don't make it tight." Because Aisha kept twisting to the end, Ifemelu thought that perhaps she had not understood, and so Ifemelu touched the offending braid and said, "Tight, tight."

Aisha pushed her hand away. "No. No. Leave it. It good."

"It's tight!" Ifemelu said. "Please loosen it."

Mariama was watching them. A flow of French came from her. Aisha loosened the braid.

"Sorry," Mariama said. "She doesn't understand very well."

But Ifemelu could see, from Aisha's face, that she understood very well. Aisha was simply a true market woman, immune to the cosmetic niceties of American customer service. Ifemelu imagined her working in a market in Dakar, like the braiders in Lagos who would blow their noses and wipe their hands on their wrappers, roughly jerk their customers' heads to position them better, complain about how full or how hard or how short the hair was, shout out to passing women, while all the time conversing too loudly and braiding too tightly.

"You know her?" Aisha asked, glancing at the television screen.

"What?"

Aisha repeated herself, and pointed at the actress on the screen.

"No," Ifemelu said.

"But you Nigerian."

"Yes, but I don't know her."

Aisha gestured to the pile of DVDs on the table. "Before, too much voodoo. Very bad. Now Nigeria film is very good. Big nice house!"

Ifemelu thought little of Nollywood films, with their exaggerated histrionics and their improbable plots, but she nodded in agreement because to hear "Nigeria" and "good" in the same sentence was a luxury, even coming from this strange Senegalese woman, and she chose to see in this an augury of her return home.

Everyone she had told she was moving back seemed surprised, expecting an explanation, and when she said she was doing it because she wanted to, puzzled lines would appear on foreheads.

"You are closing your blog and selling your condo to go back to Lagos and work for a magazine that doesn't pay that well," Aunty Uju had said and then repeated herself, as though to make Ifemelu see the gravity of her own foolishness. Only her old friend in Lagos, Ranyinudo, had made her return seem normal. "Lagos is now full of American returnees, so you better come back and join them. Every day you see them carrying a bottle of water as if they will die of heat if they are not drinking water every minute," Ranyinudo said. They had kept in touch, she and Ranyinudo, throughout the years. At first, they wrote infrequent letters, but as cybercafés opened, cell phones spread and Facebook flourished, they communicated more often. It was Ranyinudo who had told her, some years ago, that Obinze was getting married. "Meanwhile o, he has serious money now. See what you missed!" Ranyinudo had said. Ifemelu feigned indifference to this news. She had cut off contact with Obinze, after all, and so much time had passed, and she was newly in a relationship with Blaine, and happily easing herself into a shared life. But after she hung up, she thought endlessly of Obinze. Imagining him at his wedding left her with a feeling like sorrow, a faded sorrow. But she was pleased for him, she told herself, and to prove to herself that she was pleased for him, she decided to write to him. She was not sure if he still used his old address and she sent the e-mail half expecting that he would not reply, but he did. She did not write again, because she by then had acknowledged her own small, still-burning light. It was best to leave things alone. Last December, when Ranyinudo told her she had run into him at the Palms mall, with his baby daughter (and Ifemelu still could not picture this new sprawling, modern mall in Lagos; all that came to mind when she tried to was the cramped Mega Plaza she remembered)—"He was looking so *clean*, and his daughter is so fine," Ranyinudo said—Ifemelu felt a pang at all the changes that had happened in his life.

"Nigeria film very good now," Aisha said again.

"Yes," Ifemelu said enthusiastically. This was what she had become, a seeker of signs. Nigerian films were good, therefore her move back home would be good.

"You from Yoruba in Nigeria," Aisha said.

"No. I am Igbo."

"You Igbo?" For the first time, a smile appeared on Aisha's face, a smile that showed as much of her small teeth as her dark gums. "I think you Yoruba because you dark and Igbo fair. I have two Igbo men. Very good. Igbo men take care of women real good."

Aisha was almost whispering, a sexual suggestion in her tone, and in the mirror, the discoloration on her arms and neck became ghastly sores. Ifemelu imagined some bursting and oozing, others flaking. She looked away.

"Igbo men take care of women real good," Aisha repeated. "I want marry. They love me but they say the family want Igbo woman. Because Igbo marry Igbo always."

Ifemelu swallowed the urge to laugh. "You want to marry both of them?"

"No." Aisha made an impatient gesture. "I want marry one. But this thing is true? Igbo marry Igbo always?"

"Igbo people marry all kinds of people. My cousin's husband is Yoruba. My uncle's wife is from Scotland."

Aisha paused in her twisting, watching Ifemelu in the mirror, as though deciding whether to believe her.

"My sister say it is true. Igbo marry Igbo always," she said.

"How does your sister know?"

"She know many Igbo people in Africa. She sell cloth."

"Where is she?"

"In Africa."

"Where? In Senegal?"

"Benin."

"Why do you say Africa instead of just saying the country you mean?" Ifemelu asked.

Aisha clucked. "You don't know America. You say Senegal and American people, they say, Where is that? My friend from Burkina Faso, they ask her, your country in Latin America?" Aisha resumed twisting, a sly smile on her face, and then asked, as if Ifemelu could not possibly understand how things were done here, "How long you in America?"

Ifemelu decided then that she did not like Aisha at all. She wanted to curtail the conversation now, so that they would say only what they needed to say during the six hours it would take to braid her hair, and so she pretended not to have heard and instead brought out her phone. Dike had still not replied to her text. He always replied within minutes, or maybe he was still at basketball practice, or with his friends, watching some silly video on YouTube. She called him and left a long message, raising her voice, going on and on about his basketball practice and was it as hot up in Massachusetts and was he still taking Page to see the movie today. Then, feeling reckless, she composed an e-mail to Obinze and, without permitting herself to reread it, she sent it off. She had written that she was moving back to Nigeria and, even though she had a job waiting for her, even though her car was already on a ship bound for Lagos, it suddenly felt true for the first time. *I recently decided to move back to Nigeria.*

Aisha was not discouraged. Once Ifemelu looked up from her phone, Aisha asked again, "How long you in America?"

Ifemelu took her time putting her phone back into her bag. Years ago, she had been asked a similar question, at a wedding of one of Aunty Uju's friends, and she had said two years, which was the truth, but the jeer on the Nigerian's face had taught her that, to earn the prize of being taken seriously among Nigerians in America, among Africans in America, indeed among immigrants in America, she needed more years. Six years, she began to say when it was just three and a half. Eight years, she said when it was five. Now that it was thirteen years, lying seemed unnecessary but she lied anyway.

"Fifteen years," she said.

"Fifteen? That long time." A new respect slipped into Aisha's eyes. "You live here in Trenton?"

"I live in Princeton."

"Princeton." Aisha paused. "You student?"

"I've just finished a fellowship," she said, knowing that Aisha would not understand what a fellowship was, and in the rare moment that Aisha looked intimidated, Ifemelu felt a perverse pleasure. Yes, Princeton. Yes, the sort of place that Aisha could only imagine, the sort of place that would never have signs that said QUICK TAX REFUND; people in Princeton did not need quick tax refunds.

"But I'm going back home to Nigeria," Ifemelu added, suddenly remorseful. "I'm going next week."

"To see the family."

"No. I'm moving back. To live in Nigeria."

"Why?"

"What do you mean, why? Why not?"

"Better you send money back. Unless your father is big man? You have connections?"

"I've found a job there," she said.

"You stay in America fifteen years and you just go back to work?" Aisha smirked. "You can stay there?"

Aisha reminded her of what Aunty Uju had said, when she finally accepted that Ifemelu was serious about moving back—*Will you be able to cope?*—and the suggestion, that she was somehow irrevocably altered by America, had grown thorns on her skin. Her parents, too, seemed to think that she might not be able to "cope" with Nigeria. "At least you are now an American citizen, so you can always return to America," her father had said. Both of them had asked if Blaine would be coming with her, their question heavy with hope. It amused her how often they asked about Blaine now, since it had taken them a while to make peace with the idea of her black American boyfriend. She imagined them nursing quiet plans for her wedding; her mother would think of a caterer and colours, and her father would think of a distinguished friend he could ask to be the sponsor. Reluctant to flatten their hope, because it took so little to keep them hoping, which in turn kept them happy, she told her father, "We decided I will come back first and then Blaine will come after a few weeks."

"Splendid," her father said, and she said nothing else because it was best if things were simply left at splendid.

Aisha tugged a little too hard at her hair. "Fifteen years in America very long time," Aisha said, as though she had been pondering this. "You have boyfriend? You marry?"

"I'm also going back to Nigeria to see my man," Ifemelu said, surprising herself. *My man.* How easy it was to lie to strangers, to create with strangers the versions of our lives that we have imagined.

"Oh! Okay!" Aisha said, excited; Ifemelu had finally given her a comprehensible reason for wanting to move back. "You will marry?"

"Maybe. We'll see."

"Oh!" Aisha stopped twisting and stared at her in the mirror, a dead stare, and Ifemelu feared, for a moment, that the woman had clairvoyant powers and could tell she was lying.

"I want you see my men. I call them. They come and you see them. First I call Chijioke. He work cab driver. Then Emeka. He work security. You see them."

"You don't have to call them just to meet me."

"No. I call them. You tell them Igbo can marry not Igbo. They listen to you."

"No, really. I can't do that."

Aisha kept speaking as if she hadn't heard. "You tell them. They listen to you because you their Igbo sister. Any one is okay. I want marry."

Ifemelu looked at Aisha, a small, ordinary-faced Senegalese woman with patchwork skin who had two Igbo boyfriends, implausible as it seemed, and who was now insistent that Ifemelu should meet them and urge them to marry her. It would have made for a good blog post: "A Peculiar Case of a Non-American Black, or How the Pressures of Immigrant Life Can Make You Act Crazy."

CHAPTER 2

When Obinze first saw her e-mail, he was sitting in the back of his Range Rover in still Lagos traffic, his jacket slung over the front seat, a rusty-haired child beggar glued outside his window, a hawker pressing colourful CDs against the other window, the radio turned on low to the Pidgin English news on Wazobia FM, and the grey gloom of imminent rain all around. He stared at his BlackBerry, his body suddenly rigid. First, he skimmed the e-mail, instinctively wishing it were longer. *Ceiling,* kedu? *Hope all is well with work and family. Ranyinudo said she ran into you some time ago and that you now have a child! Proud Papa. Congratulations. I recently decided to move back to Nigeria. Should be in Lagos in a week. Would love to keep in touch. Take care. Ifemelu.*

He read it again slowly and felt the urge to smooth something, his trousers, his shaved-bald head. She had called him Ceiling. In the last e-mail from her, sent just before he got married, she had called him Obinze, apologized for her silence over the years, wished him happiness in sunny sentences and mentioned the black American she was living with. A gracious e-mail. He had hated it. He had hated it so much that he Googled the black American—and why should she give him the man's full name if not because she wanted him Googled?—a lecturer at Yale, and found it infuriating that she lived with a man who referred on his blog to friends as "cats", but it was the photo of the black American, oozing intellectual cool in distressed jeans and black-framed glasses, that had tipped Obinze over, made him send her a cold reply. *Thank you for the good wishes, I have never been happier in my life,* he'd written. He hoped she would write something mocking back—it was so unlike her, not to have been even vaguely tart in that first e-mail—but she did not write at all and when he e-mailed her again, after his honeymoon in Morocco, to say he wanted to keep in touch and wanted to talk sometime, she did not reply.

The traffic was moving. A light rain was falling. The child beggar ran along, his doe-eyed expression more theatrical, his motions frantic: bringing his hand to his mouth, again and again, fingertips pursed together. Obinze rolled down the window and held out a hundred-naira note. From the rear-view mirror, his driver, Gabriel, watched with grave disapproval.

"God bless you, oga!" the child beggar said.

"Don't be giving money to these beggars, sir," Gabriel said. "They are all rich. They are using begging to make big money. I heard about one that built a block of six flats in Ikeja!"

"So why are you working as a driver instead of a beggar, Gabriel?" Obinze asked, and laughed, a little too heartily. He wanted to tell Gabriel that his girlfriend from university had just e-mailed him, actually his girlfriend from university *and* secondary school. The first time she let him take off her bra, she lay on her back moaning softly, her fingers splayed on his head, and afterwards she said, "My eyes were open but I did not see the ceiling. This never happened before." Other girls would have pretended that they had never let another boy touch them, but not her, never her. There was a vivid honesty about her. She began to call what they did together *ceiling*, their warm entanglements on his bed when his mother was out, wearing only underwear, touching and kissing and sucking, hips moving in simulation. *I'm longing for ceiling*, she once wrote on the back of his geography notebook, and for a long time afterwards he could not look at that notebook without a gathering frisson, a sense of secret excitement. In university, when they finally stopped simulating, she began to call *him* Ceiling, in a playful way, in a suggestive way—but when they fought or when she retreated into moodiness, she called him Obinze. She had never called him The Zed, as his friends did. "Why do you call him Ceiling anyway?" his friend Okwudiba once asked her, on one of those languorous days after first semester exams. She had joined a group of his friends sitting around a filthy plastic table in a beer parlour off campus. She drank from her bottle of Maltina, swallowed, glanced at Obinze and said, "Because he is so tall his head touches the ceiling, can't you see?" Her deliberate slowness, the small smile that stretched her lips, made it clear that she wanted them to know that this was not why she called him Ceiling. And he was not tall. She kicked him under the table and he kicked her back, watching his laughing friends; they were all a little afraid of her and a little in love with her. Did she see the ceiling when the black American touched her? Had she used "ceiling" with other men? It upset him now to think that she might have. His phone rang and for a confused moment he thought it was Ifemelu calling from America.

"Darling, *kedu ebe I no*?" His wife, Kosi, always began her calls to him with those words: Where are you? He never asked where she was when he called her, but she would tell him, anyway: I'm just getting to the salon. I'm on Third Mainland Bridge. It was as if she needed the reassurance of their physicality when they were not together. She had a high, girlish voice. They were supposed to be at Chief's house for the party at seven-thirty and it was already past six.

He told her he was in traffic. "But it's moving, and we've just turned into Ozumba Mbadiwe. I'm coming."

On Lekki Expressway, the traffic moved swiftly in the waning rain and soon Gabriel was pressing the horn in front of the high black gates of his home. Mohammed, the gateman, wiry in his dirty white caftan, flung open the gates and raised a hand in greeting. Obinze looked at the tan colonnaded house. Inside was his furniture imported from Italy, his wife, his two-year-old daughter, Buchi, the nanny Christiana, his wife's sister Chioma, who was on a forced holiday because university lecturers were on strike yet again, and the new housegirl, Marie, who had been brought from Benin Republic after his wife decided that Nigerian housegirls were unsuitable. The rooms would all be cool, air-conditioner vents swaying quietly, and the kitchen would be fragrant with curry and thyme, and CNN would be on downstairs, while the television upstairs would be turned to Cartoon Network, and pervading it all would be the undisturbed air of well-being. He climbed out of the car. His gait was stiff, his legs difficult to lift. He had begun, in the past months, to feel bloated from all he had acquired—the family, the houses, the cars, the bank accounts—and would, from time to time, be overcome by the urge to prick everything with a pin, to deflate it all, to be free. He was no longer sure, he had in fact never been sure, whether he liked his life because he really did or whether he liked it because he was supposed to.

"Darling," Kosi said, opening the door before he got to it. She was all made-up, her complexion glowing, and he thought, as he often did, what a beautiful woman she was, eyes perfectly almond-shaped, a startling symmetry to her features. Her crushed-silk dress was cinched tightly at the waist and made her figure look very hourglassy. He hugged her, carefully avoiding her lips, painted pink and lined in a darker pink.

"Sunshine in the evening! *Asa! Ugo!*" he said. "Chief doesn't need to put on any lights at the party, once you arrive."

She laughed. The same way she laughed, with an open, accepting enjoyment of her own looks, when people asked her "Is your mother white? Are you a half-caste?" because she was so fair-skinned. It had always discomfited him, the pleasure she took in being mistaken for mixed-race.

"Daddy-daddy!" Buchi said, running to him in the slightly off-balance manner of toddlers. She was fresh from her evening bath, wearing her flowered pyjamas and smelling sweetly of baby lotion.

"Buch-buch! Daddy's Buch!" He swung her up, kissed her, nuzzled her neck and, because it always made her laugh, pretended to throw her down on the floor.

"Will you bathe or just change?" Kosi asked, following him upstairs, where she had laid out a blue caftan on his bed. He would have preferred a dress shirt or a simpler caftan instead of this, with its overly decorative embroidery, which Kosi had bought for an outrageous sum from one of those new pretentious fashion designers on The Island. But he would wear it to please her.

"I'll just change," he said.

"How was work?" she asked, in the vague, pleasant way that she always asked. He told her he was thinking about the new block of flats he had just completed in Parkview. He hoped Shell would rent it because the oil companies were always the best renters, never complaining about abrupt hikes, paying easily in American dollars so that nobody had to deal with the fluctuating naira.

"Don't worry," she said, and touched his shoulder. "God will bring Shell. We will be okay, darling."

The flats were in fact already rented by an oil company but he sometimes told her senseless lies such as this, because a part of him hoped she would ask a question or challenge him, though he knew she would not, because all she wanted was to make sure the conditions of their life remained the same, and how he made that happen she left entirely to him.

CHIEF'S PARTY WOULD bore him, as usual, but he went because he went to all of Chief's parties, and each time he parked in front of Chief's large compound, he remembered the first time he had come there, with his cousin Nneoma. He was newly back from England, had been in Lagos for only a week, but Nneoma was already grumbling about how he could not just lie around in her flat reading and moping.

"Ahn ahn! O *gini?* Are you the first person to have this problem? You have to get up and hustle. Everybody is hustling, Lagos is about hustling," Nneoma said. She had thick-palmed, capable hands and many business interests; she travelled to Dubai to buy gold, to China to buy women's clothing, and lately, she had become a distributor for a frozen chicken company. "I would have said you should come and help me in my business but no, you are too soft, you speak too much English. I need somebody with gra-gra," she said.

Obinze was still reeling from what had happened to him in England, still insulated in layers of his own self-pity, and to hear Nneoma's dismissive question—"Are you the first person to have this problem?"—upset him. She had no idea, this cousin who had grown up in the village, who looked at the world with stark and insensitive eyes. But slowly, he realized she was right; he was not the first and he would not be the last. He began applying for jobs listed in newspapers, but nobody called him for an interview, and his friends from school, who were now working at banks and mobile phone companies, began to avoid him, worried that he would thrust yet another CV into their hands.

One day, Nneoma said, "I know this very rich man, Chief. The man chased and chased me, eh, but I refused. He has a serious problem with women, and he can give somebody AIDS. But you know these men, the one woman that says no to them is the one that they don't forget. So from time to time, he will call me and sometimes I go and greet him. He even helped me with capital to start over my business after those children of Satan stole my money last year. He still thinks that one day I will agree for him. Ha, *o di egwu,* for where? I will take you to him. Once he is in a good mood, the man can be very generous. He knows everybody in this country. Maybe he will give us a note for a managing director somewhere."

A steward let them in; Chief was sitting on a gilded chair that looked like a throne, sipping cognac and surrounded by guests. He sprang up, a smallish man, high-spirited and ebullient. "Nneoma! Is this you? So you remember me today!" he said. He hugged Nneoma, moved back to look boldly at her hips outlined in her fitted skirt, her long weave falling to her shoulders. "You want to give me heart attack, eh?"

"How can I give you heart attack? What will I do without you?" Nneoma said playfully.

"You know what to do," Chief said, and his guests laughed, three guffawing, knowing men.

"Chief, this is my cousin, Obinze. His mother is my father's sister, the professor," Nneoma said. "She is the one that paid my school fees from beginning to end. If not for her, I don't know where I would be today."

"Wonderful, wonderful!" Chief said, looking at Obinze as though he was somehow responsible for this generosity.

"Good evening, sir," Obinze said. It surprised him that Chief was something of a fop, with his air of fussy grooming: nails manicured and shiny, black velvet slippers at his feet, a diamond cross around his neck. He had expected a larger man and a rougher exterior.

"Sit down. What can I offer you?"

Big Men and Big Women, Obinze would later learn, did not talk to people, they instead talked at people, and that evening Chief had talked and talked, pontificating about politics, while his guests crowed, "Exactly! You are correct, Chief! Thank you!" They were wearing the uniform of the Lagos youngish and wealthyish—leather slippers, jeans and open-neck tight shirts, all with familiar designer logos—but there was, in their manner, the ploughing eagerness of men in need.

After his guests left, Chief turned to Nneoma. "Do you know that song 'No One Knows Tomorrow'?" Then he proceeded to sing the song with childish gusto. *No one knows tomorrow! To-mor-row! No one knows tomorrow!* Another generous splash of cognac in his glass. "That is the one principle that this country is based on. The major principle. No one knows tomorrow. Remember those big bankers during Abacha's government? They thought they owned this country, and the next thing they knew, they were in prison. Look at that pauper who could not pay his rent before, then Babangida gave him an oil well, and now he has a private jet!" Chief spoke with a triumphant tone, mundane observations delivered as grand discoveries, while Nneoma listened and smiled and agreed. Her animation was exaggerated, as though a bigger smile and a quicker laugh, each ego-burnish shinier than the last, would ensure that Chief would help them. Obinze was amused by how obvious it seemed, how frank she was in her flirtations. But Chief merely gave them a case of red wine as a gift, and said vaguely to Obinze, "Come and see me next week."

Obinze visited Chief the next week and then the next; Nneoma told him to just keep hanging around until Chief did something for him. Chief's steward always served fresh pepper soup, deeply flavourful pieces of fish in a broth that made Obinze's nose run, cleared his head and somehow unclogged the future and filled him with hope, so that he sat contentedly, listening to Chief and his guests. They fascinated him, the unsubtle cowering of the almost rich in the presence of the rich, and the rich in the presence of the very rich; to have money, it seemed, was to be consumed by money. Obinze felt repulsion and longing; he pitied them, but he also imagined being like them. One day, Chief drank more cognac than usual, and talked haphazardly about people stabbing you in the back and small boys growing tails and ungrateful fools suddenly thinking they were sharp. Obinze was not sure what exactly had happened, but somebody had upset Chief, a gap had opened, and as soon as they were alone, he said, "Chief, if there is something I can help you do, please tell me. You can depend on me." His own words surprised him. He had stepped out of himself. He was high on pepper soup. This was what it meant to hustle. He was in Lagos and he had to hustle.

Chief looked at him, a long, shrewd look. "We need more people like you in this country. People from good families, with good home training. You are a gentleman, I see it in your eyes. And your mother is a professor. It is not easy."

Obinze half smiled, to seem humble in the face of this odd praise.

"You are hungry and honest, that is very rare in this country. Is that not so?" Chief asked.

"Yes," Obinze said, even though he was not sure whether he was agreeing about his having this quality or about the rarity of this quality. But it did not matter, because Chief sounded certain.

"Everybody is hungry in this country, even the rich men are hungry, but nobody is honest."

Obinze nodded, and Chief gave him another long look, before silently turning back to his cognac. On his next visit, Chief was his usual garrulous self.

"I was Babangida's friend. I was Abacha's friend. Now that the military has gone, Obasanjo is my friend," he said. "Do you know why? Is it because I am stupid?"

"Of course not, Chief," Obinze said.

"They said the National Farm Support Corporation is bankrupt and they're going to privatize it. Do you know this? No. How do I know this? Because I have friends. By the time you know it, I would have taken a position and I would have benefited from the arbitrage. That is our free market!" Chief laughed. "The corporation was set up in the sixties and it owns property everywhere. The houses are all rotten and termites are eating the roofs. But they are selling them. I'm going to buy seven properties for five million each. You know what they are listed for in the books? One million. You know what the real worth is? Fifty million." Chief paused to stare at one of his ringing mobile phones—four were placed on the table next to him—and then ignored it and leaned back on the sofa. "I need somebody to front this deal."

"Yes, sir, I can do that," Obinze said.

Later, Nneoma sat on her bed, excited for him, giving him advice while smacking her head from time to time; her scalp was itchy beneath her weave and this was the closest she could come to scratching.

"This is your opportunity! The Zed, shine your eyes! They call it a big-big name, evaluation consulting, but it is not difficult. You undervalue the properties and make sure it looks as if you are following due process. You acquire the property, sell off half to pay your purchase price and you are in business! You'll register your own company. Next thing, you'll build a house in Lekki and buy some cars and ask our hometown to give you some titles and your friends to put congratulatory messages in the newspapers for you and before you know, any bank you walk into, they will want to package a loan immediately and give it to you, because they think you no longer need the money! And after you register your own company, you must find a white man. Find one of your white friends in England. Tell everybody he is your General Manager. You will see how doors will open for you because you have an oyinbo General Manager. Even Chief has some white men that he brings in for show when he needs them. That is how Nigeria works. I'm telling you."

And it was, indeed, how it worked and still worked for Obinze. The ease of it had dazed him. The first time he took his offer letter to the bank, he had felt surreal saying "fifty" and "fifty-five" and leaving out the "million" because there was no need to state the obvious. It had startled him, too, how easy many other things became, how even just the semblance of wealth oiled his paths. He had only to drive to a gate in his BMW and the gatemen would salute and open it for him, without asking questions. Even the American embassy was different. He had been refused a visa years ago, when he was newly graduated and drunk with American ambitions, but with his new bank statements, he easily got a visa. On his first trip, at the airport in Atlanta, the immigration officer was chatty and warm, asking him, "So how much cash you got?" When Obinze said he didn't have much, the man looked surprised. "I see Nigerians like you declaring thousands and thousands of dollars all the time."

This was what he now was, the kind of Nigerian expected to declare a lot of cash at the airport. It brought to him a disorienting strangeness, because his mind had not changed at the same pace as his life, and he felt a hollow space between himself and the person he was supposed to be.

He still did not understand why Chief had decided to help him, to use him while overlooking, even encouraging, the astonishing collateral benefits. There was, after all, a trail of prostrating visitors to Chief's house, relatives and friends bringing other relatives and friends, their pockets full of requests and appeals. He sometimes wondered if Chief would one day ask something of him, the hungry and honest boy he had made big, and in his more melodramatic moments, he imagined Chief asking him to organize an assassination.

AS SOON AS they arrived at Chief's party, Kosi led the way around the room, hugging men and women she barely knew, calling the older ones "ma" and "sir" with exaggerated respect, basking in the attention her face drew but flattening her personality so that her beauty did not threaten. She praised a woman's hair, another's dress, a man's tie. She said "We thank God" often. When one woman asked her, in an accusing tone, "What cream do you use on your face? How can one person have this kind of perfect skin?" Kosi laughed graciously and promised to send the woman a text message with details of her skin-care routine.

Obinze had always been struck by how important it was to her to be a wholesomely agreeable person, to have no sharp angles sticking out. On Sundays, she would invite his relatives for pounded yam and onugbu soup and then watch over to make sure everyone was suitably overfed. *Uncle, you must eat o! There is more meat in the kitchen! Let me bring you another Guinness!* The first time he took her to his mother's house in Nsukka, just before they got married, she leaped up to help with serving the food, and when his mother made to clean up afterwards, she got up, offended, and said, "Mummy, how can I be here and you will be cleaning?" She ended every sentence she spoke to his uncles with "sir". She put ribbons in the hair of his cousins' daughters. There was something immodest about her modesty: it announced itself.

Now she was curtsying and greeting Mrs Akin-Cole, a famously old woman from a famously old family, who had the supercilious expression, eyebrows always raised, of a person used to receiving homage; Obinze often imagined her belching champagne bubbles.

"How is your child? Has she started school?" Mrs Akin-Cole asked. "You must send her to the French school. They are very good, very rigorous. Of course they teach in French but it can only be good for the child to learn another civilized language, since she already learns English at home."

"Okay, ma. I'll look at the French school," Kosi said.

"The French school is not bad, but I prefer Sidcot Hall. They teach the complete British curriculum," said another woman, whose name Obinze had forgotten. He knew she had made a lot of money during General Abacha's government. She had been a pimp, as the story went, providing young girls for the army officers who, in turn, gave her inflated supply contracts. Now, in her tight sequined dress that outlined the swell of her lower belly, she had become a certain kind of middle-aged Lagos woman, dried up by disappointments, blighted by bitterness, the sprinkle of pimples on her forehead smothered in heavy foundation.

"Oh, yes, Sidcot Hall," Kosi said. "It's already on top of my list because I know they teach the British curriculum."

Obinze would ordinarily not have said anything at all, just watched and listened, but today, for some reason, he said, "Didn't we all go to primary schools that taught the Nigerian curriculum?"

The women looked at him; their puzzled expressions implied that he could not possibly be serious. And in some ways, he was not. Of course he, too, wanted the best for his daughter. Sometimes, like now, he felt like an intruder in his new circle, of people who believed that the latest schools, the latest curriculums, would ensure the wholeness of their children. He did not share their certainties. He spent too much time mourning what could have been and questioning what should be.

When he was younger, he had admired people with moneyed childhoods and foreign accents, but he had come to sense an unvoiced yearning in them, a sad search for something they could never find. He did not want a well-educated child enmeshed in insecurities. Buchi would not go to the French school, of that he was sure.

"If you decide to disadvantage your child by sending her to one of these schools with half-baked Nigerian teachers, then you only have yourself to blame," Mrs Akin-Cole said. She spoke with the unplaceable foreign accent, British and American and something else all at once, of the wealthy Nigerian who did not want the world to forget how worldly she was, how her British Airways executive card was choking with miles.

"One of my friends, her son goes to a school on the mainland and do you know, they have only five computers in the whole school. Only five!" the other woman said. Obinze remembered her name now. Adamma.

Mrs Akin-Cole said, "Things have changed."

"I agree," Kosi said. "But I also see what Obinze is saying."

She was taking two sides at once, to please everyone; she always chose peace over truth, was always eager to conform. Watching her now as she talked to Mrs Akin-Cole, the gold shadow on her eyelids shimmering, he felt guilty about his thoughts. She was such a devoted woman, such a well-meaning, devoted woman. He reached out and held her hand.

"We'll go to Sidcot Hall and the French school, and also look at some Nigerian schools like Crown Day," Kosi said, and looked at him with a plea.

"Yes," he said, squeezing her hand. She would know it was an apology, and later, he would apologize properly. He should have kept quiet, left her conversation unruffled. She often told him that her friends envied her, and said he behaved like a foreign husband, the way he made her breakfast on weekends and stayed home every night. And, in the pride in her eyes, he saw a shinier, better version of himself. He was about to say something to Mrs Akin-Cole, something meaningless and mollifying, when he heard Chief's raised voice behind him: "But you know that as we speak, oil is flowing through illegal pipes and they sell it in bottles in Cotonou! Yes! Yes!"

Chief was upon them.

"My beautiful princess!" Chief said to Kosi, and hugged her, pressing her close; Obinze wondered if Chief had ever propositioned her. It would not surprise him. He had once been at Chief's house when a man brought his girlfriend to visit, and when she left the room to go to the toilet, Obinze heard Chief tell the man, "I like that girl. Give her to me and I will give you a nice plot of land in Ikeja."

"You look so well, Chief," Kosi said. "Ever young!"

"Ah, my dear, I try, I try." Chief jokingly tugged at the satin lapels of his black jacket. He did look well, spare and upright, unlike many of his peers who looked like pregnant men.

"My boy!" he said to Obinze.

"Good evening, Chief." Obinze shook his hand with both hands, bowing slightly. He watched the other men at the party bow, too, clustering around Chief, jostling to out-laugh one another when Chief made a joke.

The party was more crowded. Obinze looked up and saw Ferdinand, a stocky acquaintance of Chief's who had run for governor in the last elections, had lost and, as all losing politicians did, had gone to court to challenge the results. Ferdinand had a steely, amoral face; if one examined his hands, the blood of his enemies might be found crusted under his fingernails. Ferdinand's eyes met his and Obinze looked away. He was worried that Ferdinand would come over to talk about the shady land deal he had mentioned the last time they ran into each other, and so he mumbled that he was going to the toilet and slipped away from the group.

At the buffet table, he saw a young man looking with sad disappointment at the cold cuts and pastas. Obinze was drawn to his gaucheness; in the young man's clothes, and in the way that he stood, was an outsiderness he could not shield even if he had wanted to.

"There's another table on the other side with Nigerian food," Obinze told him, and the young man looked at him and laughed in gratitude. His name was Yemi and he was a newspaper journalist. Not surprising; pictures from Chief's parties were always splattered in the weekend papers.

Yemi had studied English at university and Obinze asked him what books he liked, keen to talk about something interesting at last, but he soon realized that, for Yemi, a book did not qualify as literature unless it had polysyllabic words and incomprehensible passages.

"The problem is that the novel is too simple, the man does not even use any big words," Yemi said.

It saddened Obinze that Yemi was so poorly educated and did not know that he was poorly educated. It made him want to be a teacher. He imagined himself standing in front of a class full of Yemis, teaching. It would suit him, the teaching life, as it had suited his mother. He often imagined other things he could have done, or that he could still do: teach in a university, edit a newspaper, coach professional table tennis.

"I don't know what your line of business is, sir, but I am always looking for a better job. I'm completing my master's now," Yemi said, in the manner of the true Lagosian who was always hustling, eyes eternally alert to the brighter and the better; Obinze gave him his card before going back to find Kosi.

"I was wondering where you were," she said.

"Sorry, I ran into somebody," Obinze said. He reached into his pocket to touch his BlackBerry. Kosi was asking if he wanted more food. He didn't. He wanted to go home. A rash eagerness had overcome him, to go into his study and reply to Ifemelu's e-mail, something he had unconsciously been composing in his mind. If she was considering coming back to Nigeria, then it meant she was no longer with the black American. But she might be bringing him with her; she was after all the kind of woman who would make a man easily uproot his life, the kind who, because she did not expect or ask for certainty, made a certain kind of sureness become possible. When she held his hand during their campus days, she would squeeze until both palms became slick with sweat, and she would say, teasing, "Just in case this is the last time we hold hands, let's really hold hands. Because a motorcycle or a car can kill us now, or I might see the real man of my dreams down the street and leave you or you might see the real woman of your dreams and leave me." Perhaps the black American would come back to Nigeria, too, clinging on to her. Still, he sensed, from the e-mail, that she was single. He brought out his BlackBerry to calculate the American time when it had been sent. Early afternoon. Her sentences had a hasty quality; he wondered what she had been doing then. And he wondered what else Ranyinudo had told her about him.

On the Saturday in December when he ran into Ranyinudo at the Palms mall, he was carrying Buchi in one arm, waiting at the entrance for Gabriel to bring the car around, and holding a bag with Buchi's biscuits in the other hand. "The Zed!" Ranyinudo called out. In secondary school she had been the bubbly tomboy, very tall and skinny and straightforward, not armed with the mysteriousness of girls. The boys had all liked her but never chased her, and they fondly called her Leave Me in Peace, because of how often she would say, whenever asked about her unusual name, "Yes, it is an Igbo name and it means 'leave us in peace', so you leave me in peace!" He was surprised at how chic she looked now, and how different, with her short spiky hair and tight jeans, her body full and curvy.

"The Zed—The Zed! Longest time! You don't ask about us again. Is this your daughter? Oh, bless! The other day I was with one of my friends, Dele. You know Dele from Hale Bank? He said you own that building near the Ace office in Banana Island? Congratulations. You've really done well o. And Dele said you are so humble."

He had been uncomfortable, with her overdone fussing, the deference that seeped subtly from her pores. He was, in her eyes, no longer The Zed from secondary school, and the stories of his wealth made her assume he had changed more than he possibly could have. People often told him how humble he was, but they did not mean real humility, it was merely that he did not flaunt his membership in the wealthy club, did not exercise the rights it brought—to be rude, to be inconsiderate, to be greeted rather than to greet—and because so many others like him exercised those rights, his choices were interpreted as humility. He did not boast, either, or speak about the things he owned, which made people assume he owned much more than he did. Even his closest friend Okwudiba often told him how humble he was, and it irked him slightly, because he wished Okwudiba would see that to call him humble was to make rudeness normal. Besides, humility had always seemed to him a specious thing, invented for the comfort of others; you were praised for humility by people because you did not make them feel any more lacking than they already did. It was honesty that he valued; he had always wished himself to be truly honest, and always feared that he was not.

In the car on the way home from Chief's party, Kosi said, "Darling, you must be hungry. You ate only that spring roll?"

"And suya."

"You need to eat. Thank God I asked Marie to cook," she said, and added, giggling, "Me, I should have respected myself and left those snails alone! I think I ate up to ten. They were so nice and peppery."

Obinze laughed, vaguely bored, but happy that she was happy.

MARIE WAS SLIGHT, and Obinze was not sure whether she was timid or whether her halting English made her seem so. She had been with them only a month. The last housegirl, brought by a relative of Gabriel's, was thickset and had arrived clutching a duffel bag. He was not there when Kosi looked through it—she did that routinely with all domestic help because she wanted to know what was being brought into her home—but he came out when he heard Kosi shouting, in that impatient, shrill manner she put on with domestic help to command authority, to ward off disrespect. The girl's bag was on the floor, open, clothing fluffing out. Kosi stood beside it, holding up, at the tips of her fingers, a packet of condoms.

"What is this for? Eh? You came to my house to be a prostitute?"

The girl looked down at first, silent, then she looked Kosi in the face and said quietly, "In my last job, my madam's husband was always forcing me."

Kosi's eyes bulged. She moved forward for a moment, as though to attack the girl in some way, and then stopped.

"Please carry your bag and go now-now," she said.

The girl shifted, looking a little surprised, and then she picked up her bag and turned to the door. After she left, Kosi said, "Can you believe the nonsense, darling? She came here with condoms and she actually opened her mouth to say that rubbish. Can you believe it?"

"Her former employer raped her so she decided to protect herself this time," Obinze said.

Kosi stared at him. "You feel sorry for her. You don't know these housegirls. How can you feel sorry for her?"

He wanted to ask, *How can you not?* But the tentative fear in her eyes silenced him. Her insecurity, so great and so ordinary, silenced him. She was worried about a housegirl whom it would never even occur to him to seduce. Lagos could do this to a woman married to a young and wealthy man; he knew how easy it was to slip into paranoia about housegirls, about secretaries, about *Lagos Girls,* those sophisticated monsters of glamour who swallowed husbands whole, slithering them down their jewelled throats. Still, he wished Kosi feared less, conformed less.

Some years ago, he had told her about an attractive banker who had come to his office to talk to him about opening an account, a young woman wearing a fitted shirt with an extra button undone, trying to hide the desperation in her eyes. "Darling, your secretary should not let any of these bank marketing girls come into your office!" Kosi had said, as though she seemed no longer to see him, Obinze, and instead saw blurred figures, classic types: a wealthy man, a female banker who had been given a target deposit amount, an easy exchange. Kosi expected him to cheat, and her concern was to minimize the possibilities he might have. "Kosi, nothing can happen unless I want it to. I will never want it to," he had said, in what was both a reassurance and a rebuke.

She had, in the years since they got married, grown an intemperate dislike of single women and an intemperate love of God. Before they got married, she went to service once a week at the Anglican church on the Marina, a Sunday tick-the-box routine that she did because she had been brought up that way, but after their wedding, she switched to the House of David because, as she told him, it was a Bible-believing church. Later, when he found out that the House of David had a special prayer service for Keeping Your Husband, he had felt unsettled. Just as he had when he once asked why her best friend from university, Elohor, hardly visited them, and Kosi said, "She's still single," as though that was a self-evident reason.

MARIE KNOCKED on his study door and came in with a tray of rice and fried plantains. He ate slowly. He put in a Fela CD and then started to write the e-mail on his computer; his BlackBerry keyboard would cramp his fingers and his mind. He had introduced Ifemelu to Fela at university. She had, before then, thought of Fela as the mad weed-smoker who wore underwear at his concerts, but she had come to love the Afrobeat sound and they would lie on his mattress in Nsukka and listen to it and then she would leap up and make swift, vulgar movements with her hips when the run-run-run chorus came on. He wondered if she remembered that. He wondered if she remembered how his cousin had sent mix tapes from abroad, and how he made copies for her at the famous electronics shop in the market where music blared all day long, ringing in your ears even after you had left. He had wanted her to have the music he had. She had never really been interested in Biggie and Warren G and Dr. Dre and Snoop Dogg, but Fela was different. On Fela, they had agreed.

He wrote and rewrote the e-mail, not mentioning his wife or using the first person plural, trying for a balance between earnest and funny. He did not want to alienate her. He wanted to make sure she would reply this time. He clicked Send and then minutes later checked to see if she had replied. He was tired. It was not a physical fatigue—he went to the gym regularly and felt better than he had in years—but a draining lassitude that numbed the margins of his mind. He got up and went out to the verandah; the sudden hot air, the roar of his neighbour's generator, the smell of diesel exhaust fumes brought a lightness to his head. Frantic winged insects flitted around the electric bulb. He felt, looking out at the muggy darkness farther away, as if he could float, and all he needed to do was to let himself go.

Part 2

CHAPTER 3

Mariama finished her customer's hair, sprayed it with sheen, and, after the customer left, she said, "I'm going to get Chinese."

Aisha and Halima told her what they wanted—General Tso's Chicken Very Spicy, Chicken Wings, Orange Chicken—with the quick ease of people saying what they said every day.

"You want anything?" Mariama asked Ifemelu.

"No, thanks," Ifemelu said.

"Your hair take long. You need food," Aisha said.

"I'm fine. I have a granola bar," Ifemelu said. She had some baby carrots in a Ziploc, too, although all she had snacked on so far was her melted chocolate.

"What bar?" Aisha asked.

Ifemelu showed her the bar, organic, one hundred per cent whole grain with real fruit.

"That not food!" Halima scoffed, looking away from the television.

"She here fifteen years, Halima," Aisha said, as if the length of years in America explained Ifemelu's eating of a granola bar.

"Fifteen? Long time," Halima said.

Aisha waited until Mariama left before pulling out her cell phone from her pocket. "Sorry, I make quick call," she said, and stepped outside. Her face had brightened when she came back; there was a smiling, even-featured prettiness, drawn out by that phone call, that Ifemelu had not earlier seen.

"Emeka work late today. So only Chijioke come to see you, before we finish," she said, as if she and Ifemelu had planned it all together.

"Look, you don't have to ask them to come. I won't even know what to tell them," Ifemelu said.

"Tell Chijioke Igbo can marry not Igbo."

"Aisha, I can't tell him to marry you. He will marry you if he wants to."

"They want marry me. But I am not Igbo!" Aisha's eyes glittered; the woman had to be a little mentally unstable.

"Is that what they told you?" Ifemelu asked.

"Emeka say his mother tell him if he marry American, she kill herself," Aisha said.

"That's not good."

"But me, I am African."

"So maybe she won't kill herself if he marries you."

Aisha looked blankly at her. "Your boyfriend mother want him to marry you?"

Ifemelu thought first of Blaine then she realized that Aisha, of course, meant her make-believe boyfriend.

"Yes. She keeps asking us when we will get married." She was amazed by her own fluidness, it was as if she had convinced even herself that she was not living on memories mildewed by thirteen years. But it could have been true; Obinze's mother had liked her, after all.

"Ah!" Aisha said, in well-meaning envy.

A man with dry, greying skin and a mop of white hair came in with a plastic tray of herbal potions for sale.

"No, no, no," Aisha said to him, palm raised as though to ward him off. The man retreated. Ifemelu felt sorry for him, hungry-looking in his worn dashiki, and wondered how much he could possibly make from his sales. She should have bought something.

"You talk Igbo to Chijioke. He listen to you," Aisha said. "You talk Igbo?"

"Of course I speak Igbo," Ifemelu said, defensive, wondering if Aisha was again suggesting that America had changed her. "Take it easy!" she added, because Aisha had pulled a tiny-toothed comb through a section of her hair.

"Your hair hard," Aisha said.

"It is not hard," Ifemelu said firmly. "You are using the wrong comb." And she pulled the comb from Aisha's hand and put it down on the table.

41

IFEMELU HAD GROWN UP in the shadow of her mother's hair. It was black-black, so thick it drank two containers of relaxer at the salon, so full it took hours under the hooded dryer, and, when finally released from pink plastic rollers, sprang free and full, flowing down her back like a celebration. Her father called it a crown of glory. "Is it your real hair?" strangers would ask, and then reach out to touch it reverently. Others would say "Are you from Jamaica?" as though only foreign blood could explain such bounteous hair that did not thin at the temples. Through the years of childhood, Ifemelu would often look in the mirror and pull at her own hair, separate the coils, will it to become like her mother's, but it remained bristly and grew reluctantly; braiders said it cut them like a knife.

One day, the year Ifemelu turned ten, her mother came home from work looking different. Her clothes were the same, a brown dress belted at the waist, but her face was flushed, her eyes unfocused. "Where is the big scissors?" she asked, and when Ifemelu brought it to her, she raised it to her head and, handful by handful, chopped off all her hair. Ifemelu stared, stunned. The hair lay on the floor like dead grass. "Bring me a big bag," her mother said. Ifemelu obeyed, feeling herself in a trance, with things happening that she did not understand. She watched her mother walk around their flat, collecting all the Catholic objects, the crucifixes hung on walls, the rosaries nested in drawers, the missals propped on shelves. Her mother put them all in the polythene bag, which she carried to the backyard, her steps quick, her faraway look unwavering. She made a fire near the rubbish dump, at the same spot where she burned her used sanitary pads, and first she threw in her hair, wrapped in old newspaper, and then, one after the other, the objects of faith. Dark grey smoke curled up into the air. From the verandah, Ifemelu began to cry because she sensed that something had happened, and the woman standing by the fire, splashing in more kerosene as it dimmed and stepping back as it flared, the woman who was bald and blank, was not her mother, could not be her mother.

When her mother came back inside, Ifemelu backed away, but her mother hugged her close.

"I am saved," she said. "Mrs Ojo ministered to me this afternoon during the children's break and I received Christ. Old things have passed away and all things have become new. Praise God. On Sunday we will start going to Revival Saints. It is a Bible-believing church and a living church, not like St Dominic's." Her mother's words were not hers. She spoke them too rigidly, with a demeanour that belonged to someone else. Even her voice, usually high-pitched and feminine, had deepened and curdled. That afternoon, Ifemelu watched her mother's essence take flight. Before, her mother said the rosary once in a while, crossed herself before she ate, wore pretty images of saints around her neck, sang Latin songs and laughed when Ifemelu's father teased her about her terrible pronunciation. She laughed, too, whenever he said, "I am an agnostic respecter of religion," and she would tell him how lucky he was to be married to her, because even though he went to church only for weddings and funerals, he would get into heaven on the wings of her faith. But, after that afternoon, her God changed. He became exacting. Relaxed hair offended Him. Dancing offended Him. She bartered with Him, offering starvation in exchange for prosperity, for a job promotion, for good health. She fasted herself bone-thin: dry fasts on weekends, and on weekdays, only water until evening. Ifemelu's father followed her with anxious eyes, urging her to eat a little more, to fast a little less, and he always spoke carefully, so that she would not call him the devil's agent and ignore him, as she had done with a cousin who was staying with them. "I am fasting for your father's conversion," she told Ifemelu often. For months, the air in their flat was like cracked glass. Everyone tiptoed around her mother, who had become a stranger, thin and knuckly and severe. Ifemelu worried that she would, one day, simply snap into two and die.

Then, on Easter Saturday, a dour day, the first quiet Easter Saturday in Ifemelu's life, her mother ran out of the kitchen and said, "I saw an angel!" Before, there would have been cooking and bustling, many pots in the kitchen and many relatives in the flat, and Ifemelu and her mother would have gone to night mass, and held up lit candles, singing in a sea of flickering flames, and then come home to continue cooking the big Easter lunch. But the flat was silent. Their relatives had kept away and lunch would be the usual rice and stew. Ifemelu was in the living room with her father, and when her mother said "I saw an angel!" Ifemelu saw exasperation in his eyes, a brief glimpse before it disappeared.

"What happened?" he asked, in the placating tone used for a child, as if humouring his wife's madness would make it go away quickly.

Her mother told them of a vision she had just had, a blazing appearance near the gas cooker of an angel holding a book trimmed in red thread, telling her to leave Revival Saints because the pastor was a wizard who attended nightly demonic meetings under the sea.

"You should listen to the angel," her father said.

And so her mother left the church and began to let her hair grow again, but stopped wearing necklaces and earrings because jewellery, according to the pastor at Miracle Spring, was ungodly, unbefitting a woman of virtue. Shortly afterwards, on the same day as the failed coup, while the traders who lived downstairs were crying because the coup would have saved Nigeria and market women would have been given cabinet positions, her mother saw another vision. This time, the angel appeared in her bedroom, above the wardrobe, and told her to leave Miracle Spring and join Guiding Assembly. Halfway through the first service Ifemelu attended with her mother, in a marble-floored convention hall, surrounded by perfumed people and the ricochet of rich voices, Ifemelu looked at her mother and saw that she was crying and laughing at the same time. In this church of surging hope, of thumping and clapping, where Ifemelu imagined a swirl of affluent angels above, her mother's spirit had found a home. It was a church full of the newly wealthy; her mother's small car, in the parking lot, was the oldest, with its dull paint and many scratches. If she worshipped with the prosperous, she said, then God would bless her as He had blessed them. She began to wear jewellery again, to drink her Guinness stout; she fasted only once a week and often said "*My* God tells me" and "*My* Bible says," as though other people's were not just different but misguided. Her response to a "Good morning" or a "Good afternoon" was a cheerful "God bless you!" Her God became genial and did not mind being commanded. Every morning, she woke the household up for prayers, and they would kneel on the scratchy carpet of the living room, singing, clapping, covering the day ahead with the blood of Jesus, and her mother's words would pierce the stillness of dawn: "God, my heavenly father, I command you to fill this day with blessings and prove to me that you are God! Lord, I am waiting on you for my prosperity! Do not let the evil one win, do not let my enemies triumph over me!" Ifemelu's father once said the prayers were delusional battles with imaginary traducers, yet he insisted that Ifemelu always wake up early to pray. "It keeps your mother happy," he told her.

In church, at testimony time, her mother was first to hurry to the altar. "I had catarrh this morning," she would start. "But as Pastor Gideon started to pray, it cleared. Now it is gone. Praise God!" The congregation would shout "Alleluia!" and other testimonies would follow. *I did not study because I was sick and yet I passed my exams with flying colours! I had malaria and prayed over it and was cured! My cough disappeared as Pastor started praying!* But always her mother went first, gliding and smiling, enclosed in salvation's glow. Later in the service, when Pastor Gideon would leap out in his sharp-shouldered suit and pointy shoes, and say, "Our God is not a poor God, amen? It is our portion to prosper, amen?" Ifemelu's mother would raise her arm high, heavenward, as she said, "Amen, Father Lord, amen."

Ifemelu did not think that God had given Pastor Gideon the big house and all those cars, he had of course bought them with money from the three collections at each service, and she did not think that God would do for all as He had done for Pastor Gideon, because it was impossible, but she liked that her mother ate regularly now. The warmth in her mother's eyes was back, and there was a new joy in her bearing, and she once again lingered at the dining table with her father after meals, and sang loudly while taking a bath. Her new church absorbed her but did not destroy her. It made her predictable and easy to lie to. "I am going to Bible study" and "I am going to Fellowship" were the easiest ways for Ifemelu to go out unquestioned during her teenage years. Ifemelu was uninterested in church, indifferent about making any religious effort, perhaps because her mother already made so much. Yet her mother's faith comforted her; it was, in her mind, a white cloud that moved benignly above her as she moved. Until The General came into their lives.

EVERY MORNING, Ifemelu's mother prayed for The General. She would say, "Heavenly father, I command you to bless Uju's mentor. May his enemies never triumph over him!" Or she would say, "We cover Uju's mentor with the precious blood of Jesus!" And Ifemelu would mumble something nonsensical instead of saying "Amen." Her mother said the word "mentor" defiantly, a thickness in her tone, as though the force of her delivery would truly turn The General into a mentor, and also remake the world into a place where young doctors could afford Aunty Uju's new Mazda, that green, glossy, intimidatingly streamlined car.

Chetachi, who lived upstairs, asked Ifemelu, "Your mum said Aunty Uju's mentor also gave her a loan for the car?"

"Yes."

"Eh! Aunty Uju is lucky o!" Chetachi said.

Ifemelu did not miss the knowing smirk on her face. Chetachi and her mother must have already gossiped about the car; they were envious, chattering people who visited only to see what others had, to size up new furniture or new electronics.

"God should bless the man o. Me I hope I will also meet a mentor when I graduate," Chetachi said. Ifemelu bristled at Chetachi's goading. Still, it was her mother's fault, to so eagerly tell the neighbours her mentor story. She should not have; it was nobody's business what Aunty Uju did. Ifemelu had overheard her telling somebody in the backyard, "You see, The General wanted to be a doctor when he was young, and so now he helps young doctors, God is really using him in people's lives." And she sounded sincere, cheerful, convincing. She believed her own words. Ifemelu could not understand this, her mother's ability to tell herself stories about her reality that did not even resemble her reality. When Aunty Uju first told them about her new job—"The hospital has no doctor vacancy but The General made them create one for me" were her words—Ifemelu's mother promptly said, "This is a miracle!"

Aunty Uju smiled, a quiet smile that held its peace; she did not, of course, think it was a miracle, but would not say so. Or maybe there *was* something of a miracle in her new job as consultant at the military hospital in Victoria Island, and her new house in Dolphin Estate, the cluster of duplexes that wore a fresh foreignness, some painted pink, others the blue of a warm sky, hemmed by a park with grass lush as a new rug and benches where people could sit—a rarity even on The Island. Only weeks before, she had been a new graduate and all her classmates were talking about going abroad to take the American medical exams or the British exams, because the other choice was to tumble into a parched wasteland of joblessness. The country was starved of hope, cars stuck for days in long, sweaty petrol lines, pensioners raising wilting placards demanding their pay, lecturers gathering to announce yet one more strike. But Aunty Uju did not want to leave; she had, for as long as Ifemelu could remember, dreamed of owning a private clinic, and she held that dream in a tight clasp.

"Nigeria will not be like this forever, I'm sure I will find part-time work and it will be tough, yes, but one day I will start my clinic, and on The Island!" Aunty Uju had told Ifemelu. Then she went to a friend's wedding. The bride's father was an air vice marshal, it was rumoured that the Head of State might attend, and Aunty Uju joked about asking him to make her medical officer at Aso Rock. He did not attend, but many of his generals did, and one of them asked his ADC to call Aunty Uju, to ask her to come to his car in the parking lot after the reception, and when she went to the dark Peugeot with a small flag flying from its front, and said, "Good afternoon, sir," to the man in the back, he told her, "I like you. I want to take care of you." Maybe there was a kind of miracle in those words, *I like you, I want to take care of you,* Ifemelu thought, but not in the way her mother meant it. "A miracle! God is faithful!" her mother said that day, eyes liquid with faith.

SHE SAID, in a similar tone, "The devil is a liar. He wants to start blocking our blessing, he will not succeed," when Ifemelu's father lost his job at the federal agency. He was fired for refusing to call his new boss Mummy. He came home earlier than usual, wracked with bitter disbelief, his termination letter in his hand, complaining about the absurdity of a grown man calling a grown woman Mummy because she had decided it was the best way to show her respect. "Twelve years of dedicated labour. It is unconscionable," he said. Her mother patted his back, told him God would provide another job and, until then, they would manage on her vice-principal salary. He went out job hunting every morning, teeth clenched and tie firmly knotted, and Ifemelu wondered if he just walked into random companies to try his luck, but soon he began to stay at home in a wrapper and singlet, lounging on the shabby sofa near the stereo. "You have not had a morning bath?" her mother asked him one afternoon, when she came back from work looking drained, clutching files to her chest, wet patches under her armpits. Then she added irritably, "If you have to call somebody Mummy to get your salary, you should have done so!"

He said nothing; for a moment, he seemed lost, shrunken and lost. Ifemelu felt sorry for him. She asked him about the book placed face down on his lap, a familiar-looking book that she knew he had read before. She hoped he would give her one of his long talks about something like the history of China, and she would half listen as always, while cheering him up. But he was in no mood for talk. He shrugged as though to say she could look at the book if she wanted to. Her mother's words too easily wounded him; he was too alert to her, his ears always pricked up at her voice, his eyes always rested on her. Recently, before he was fired, he had told Ifemelu, "Once I attain my promotion, I will buy your mother something truly memorable," and when she asked him what, he smiled and said, mysteriously, "It will unveil itself."

Looking at him as he sat mute on the sofa, she thought how much he looked like what he was, a man full of blanched longings, a middlebrow civil servant who wanted a life different from what he had, who had longed for more education than he was able to get. He talked often of how he could not go to university because he had to find a job to support his siblings, and how people he was cleverer than in secondary school now had doctorates. His was a formal, elevated English. Their house helps hardly understood him but were nevertheless very impressed. Once, their former house help, Jecinta, had come into the kitchen and started clapping quietly, and told Ifemelu, "You should have heard your father's big word now! O *di egwu!*" Sometimes Ifemelu imagined him in a classroom in the fifties, an overzealous colonial subject wearing an ill-fitting school uniform of cheap cotton, jostling to impress his missionary teachers. Even his handwriting was mannered, all curves and flourishes, with a uniform elegance that looked like something printed. He had scolded Ifemelu as a child for being recalcitrant, mutinous, intransigent, words that made her little actions seem epic and almost prideworthy. But his mannered English bothered her as she got older, because it was costume, his shield against insecurity. He was haunted by what he did not have—a postgraduate degree, an upper-middle-class life—and so his affected words became his armour. She preferred it when he spoke Igbo; it was the only time he seemed unconscious of his own anxieties.

Losing his job made him quieter, and a thin wall grew between him and the world. He no longer muttered "nation of intractable sycophancy" when the nightly news started on NTA, no longer held long monologues about how Babangida's government had reduced Nigerians to imprudent idiots, no longer teased her mother. And, most of all, he began to join in the morning prayers. He had never joined before; her mother had once insisted that he do so, before leaving to visit their hometown. "Let us pray and cover the roads with the blood of Jesus," she had said, and he replied that the roads would be safer, less slippery, if not covered with blood. Which had made her mother frown and Ifemelu laugh and laugh.

At least he still did not go to church. Ifemelu used to come home from church with her mother and find him sitting on the floor in the living room, sifting through his pile of LPs, and singing along to a song on the stereo. He always looked fresh, rested, as though being alone with his music had replenished him. But he hardly played music after he lost his job. They came home to find him at the dining table, bent over loose sheets of paper, writing letters to newspapers and magazines. And Ifemelu knew that, if given another chance, he would call his boss Mummy.

IT WAS a Sunday morning, early, and somebody was banging on the front door. Ifemelu liked Sunday mornings, the slow shifting of time, when she, dressed for church, would sit in the living room with her father while her mother got ready. Sometimes they talked, she and her father, and other times they were silent, a shared and satisfying silence, as they were that morning. From the kitchen, the hum of the refrigerator was the only sound to be heard, until the banging on the door. A rude interruption. Ifemelu opened it and saw the landlord standing there, a round man with bulging, reddened eyes who was said to start his day with a glass of harsh gin. He looked past Ifemelu at her father, and shouted, "It is now three months! I am still waiting for my money!" His voice was familiar to Ifemelu, the brassy shouting that always came from the flats of their neighbours, from somewhere else. But now he was here in their flat, and the scene jarred her, the landlord shouting at *their* door, and her father turning a steely, silent face to him. They had never owed rent before. They had lived in this flat all her life; it was cramped, the kitchen walls blackened by kerosene fumes, and she was embarrassed when her school friends came to visit, but they had never owed rent.

"A braggart of a man," her father said after the landlord left, and then he said nothing else. There was nothing else to say. They owed rent.

Her mother appeared, singing and heavily perfumed, her face dry and bright with powder that was one shade too light. She extended a wrist towards Ifemelu's father, her thin gold bracelet hung unclasped.

"Uju is coming after church to take us to see the house in Dolphin Estate," her mother said. "Will you follow us?"

"No," he said shortly, as though Aunty Uju's new life was a subject he would rather avoid.

"You should come," she said, but he did not respond, as he carefully snapped the bracelet around her wrist, and told her he had checked the water in her car.

"God is faithful. Look at Uju, to afford a house on The Island!" her mother said happily.

"Mummy, but you know Aunty Uju is not paying one kobo to live there," Ifemelu said.

Her mother glanced at her. "Did you iron that dress?"

"It doesn't need ironing."

"It is rumpled. *Ngwa,* go and iron it. At least there is light. Or change into something else."

Ifemelu got up reluctantly. "This dress is not rumpled."

"Go and iron it. There is no need to show the world that things are hard for us. Ours is not the worst case. Today is Sunday Work with Sister Ibinabo, so hurry up and let's go."

SISTER IBINABO WAS powerful, and because she pretended to wear her power lightly, it only made her more so. The pastor, it was said, did whatever she asked him. It was not clear why; some said she had started the church with him, others that she knew a terrible secret from his past, still others that she simply had more spiritual power than he did but could not be pastor because she was a woman. She could prevent pastoral approval of a marriage, if she wanted to. She knew everyone and everything and she seemed to be everywhere at the same time, with her weather-beaten air, as though life had tossed her around for a long time. It was difficult to tell how old she was, whether fifty or sixty, her body wiry, her face closed like a shell. She never laughed but often smiled the thin smile of the pious. The mothers were in reverent awe of her; they brought her small presents, they eagerly handed their daughters to her for Sunday Work. Sister Ibinabo, the saviour of young females. She was asked to talk to troubled and troublesome girls. Some mothers asked if their daughters could live with her, in the flat behind the church. But Ifemelu had always sensed, in Sister Ibinabo, a deep-sown, simmering hostility to young girls. Sister Ibinabo did not like them, she merely watched them and warned them, as though offended by what in them was still fresh and in her was long dried up.

"I saw you wearing tight trousers last Saturday," Sister Ibinabo said to a girl, Christie, in an exaggerated whisper, low enough to pretend it was a whisper but high enough for everyone to hear. "Everything is permissible but not everything is beneficial. Any girl that wears tight trousers wants to commit the sin of temptation. It is best to avoid it."

Christie nodded, humble, gracious, carrying her shame.

In the church back room, the two tiny windows did not let in much light, and so the electric bulb was always turned on during the day. Fund-raising envelopes were piled on the table, and next to them was a stack of coloured tissue, like fragile cloth. The girls began to organize themselves. Soon, some of them were writing on the envelopes, and others were cutting and curling pieces of tissue, gluing them into flower shapes, and stringing them together to form fluffy garlands. Next Sunday, at a special Thanksgiving service, the garlands would hang around the thick neck of Chief Omenka and the smaller necks of his family members. He had donated two new vans to the church.

"Join that group, Ifemelu," Sister Ibinabo said.

Ifemelu folded her arms, and as often happened when she was about to say something she knew was better unsaid, the words rushed up her throat. "Why should I make decorations for a thief?"

Sister Ibinabo stared in astonishment. A silence fell. The other girls looked on expectantly.

"What did you say?" Sister Ibinabo asked quietly, offering a chance for Ifemelu to apologize, to put the words back in her mouth. But Ifemelu felt herself unable to stop, her heart thumping, hurtling on a fast-moving path.

"Chief Omenka is a 419 and everybody knows it," she said. "This church is full of 419 men. Why should we pretend that this hall was not built with dirty money?"

"It is God's work," Sister Ibinabo said quietly. "If you cannot do God's work, then you should go. Go."

Ifemelu hurried out of the room, past the gate and towards the bus station, knowing that in minutes the story would reach her mother inside the main church building. She had ruined the day. They would have gone to see Aunty Uju's house and had a nice lunch. Now, her mother would be testy and prickly. She wished she had said nothing. She had, after all, joined in making garlands for other 419 men in the past, men who had special seats in the front row, men who donated cars with the ease of people giving away chewing gum. She had happily attended their receptions, she had eaten rice and meat and coleslaw, food tainted by fraud, and she had eaten knowing this and had not choked, and had not even considered choking. Yet something had been different today. When Sister Ibinabo was talking to Christie, with that poisonous spite she claimed was religious guidance, Ifemelu had looked at her and suddenly seen something of her own mother. Her mother was a kinder and simpler person, but like Sister Ibinabo, she was a person who denied that things were as they were. A person who had to spread the cloak of religion over her own petty desires. Suddenly, the last thing Ifemelu wanted was to be in that small room full of shadows. It had all seemed benign before, her mother's faith, all drenched in grace, and suddenly it no longer was. She wished, fleetingly, that her mother was not her mother, and for this she felt not guilt and sadness but a single emotion, a blend of guilt and sadness.

The bus stop was eerily empty, and she imagined all the people who would have been crowded here, now in churches, singing and praying. She waited for the bus, wondering whether to go home or somewhere else to wait for a while. It was best to go home, and face whatever she had to face.

HER MOTHER PULLED her ear, an almost-gentle tug, as though reluctant to cause real pain. She had done that since Ifemelu was a child. "I will beat you!" she would say, when Ifemelu did something wrong, but there was never any beating, only the limp ear pull. Now, she pulled it twice, once and then again to emphasize her words. "The devil is using you. You have to pray about this. Do not judge. Leave the judging to God!"

Her father said, "You must refrain from your natural proclivity towards provocation, Ifemelu. You have singled yourself out at school where you are known for insubordination and I have told you that it has already sullied your singular academic record. There is no need to create a similar pattern in church."

"Yes, Daddy."

When Aunty Uju arrived, Ifemelu's mother told her what had happened. "Go and give that Ifemelu a talking-to. You are the only person she will listen to. Ask her what I did to her that makes her want to embarrass me in the church like this. She insulted Sister Ibinabo! It is like insulting Pastor! Why must this girl be a troublemaker? I have been saying it since, that it would be better if she was a boy, behaving like this."

"Sister, you know her problem is that she doesn't always know when to keep her mouth shut. Don't worry, I will talk to her," Aunty Uju said, playing her role of pacifier, soothing her cousin's wife. She had always got along with Ifemelu's mother, the easy relationship between two people who carefully avoided conversations of any depth. Perhaps Aunty Uju felt gratitude to Ifemelu's mother for embracing her, accepting her status as the special resident relative. Growing up, Ifemelu did not feel like an only child because of the cousins, aunts and uncles who lived with them. There were always suitcases and bags in the flat; sometimes a relative or two would sleep on the floor of the living room for weeks. Most were her father's family, brought to Lagos to learn a trade or go to school or look for a job, so that the people back in the village would not mutter about their brother with only one child who did not want to help raise others. Her father felt an obligation to them, he insisted that everyone be home before eight p.m., made sure there was enough food to go around, and locked his bedroom door even when he went to the bathroom, because any of them could wander in and steal something. But Aunty Uju was different. Too clever to waste away in that backwater, he said. He called her his youngest sister although she was the child of his father's brother, and he had been more protective, less distant, with her. Whenever he came across Ifemelu and Aunty Uju curled up in bed talking, he would fondly say "You two." After Aunty Uju left to go to university in Ibadan, he told Ifemelu, almost wistfully, "Uju exerted a calming influence on you." He seemed to see, in their closeness, proof of his own good choice, as though he had knowingly brought a gift to his family, a buffer between his wife and daughter.

And so, in the bedroom, Aunty Uju told Ifemelu, "You should have just made the garland. I've told you that you don't have to say everything. You have to learn that. You don't have to *say* everything."

"Why can't Mummy like the things you get from The General without pretending they are from God?"

"Who says they are not from God?" Aunty Uju asked, and made a face, pulling her lips down at the sides. Ifemelu laughed.

According to the family legend, Ifemelu had been a surly three-year-old who screamed if a stranger came close, but the first time she saw Aunty Uju, thirteen and pimply faced, Ifemelu walked over and climbed into her lap and stayed there. She did not know if this had happened, or had merely become true from being told over and over again, a charmed tale of the beginning of their closeness. It was Aunty Uju who sewed Ifemelu's little-girl dresses and, as Ifemelu got older, they would pore over fashion magazines, choosing styles together. Aunty Uju taught her to mash an avocado and spread it on her face, to dissolve Robb in hot water and place her face over the steam, to dry a pimple with toothpaste. Aunty Uju brought her James Hadley Chase novels wrapped in newspaper to hide the near-naked women on the cover, hot-stretched her hair when she got lice from the neighbours, talked her through her first menstrual period, supplementing her mother's lecture that was full of biblical quotes about virtue but lacked useful details about cramps and pads. When Ifemelu met Obinze, she told Aunty Uju that she had met the love of her life, and Aunty Uju told her to let him kiss and touch but not to let him put it inside.

CHAPTER 4

The gods, the hovering deities who gave and took teenage loves, had decided that Obinze would go out with Ginika. Obinze was the new boy, a fine boy even if he was short. He had transferred from the university secondary school in Nsukka, and only days after, everyone knew of the swirling rumours about his mother. She had fought with a man, another professor at Nsukka, a real fight, punching and hitting, and she had won, too, even tearing his clothes, and so she was suspended for two years and had moved to Lagos until she could go back. It was an unusual story; market women fought, mad women fought, but not women who were professors. Obinze, with his air of calm and inwardness, made it even more intriguing. He was quickly admitted into the clan of swaggering, carelessly cool males, the Big Guys; he lounged in the corridors with them, stood with them at the back of the hall during assembly. None of them tucked in their shirts, and for this they always got into trouble, glamorous trouble, with the teachers, but Obinze came to school every day with his shirt neatly tucked in and soon all the Big Guys tucked in, too, even Kayode DaSilva, the coolest of them all.

Kayode spent every vacation in his parents' house in England, which looked large and forbidding in the photos Ifemelu had seen. His girlfriend, Yinka, was like him—she, too, went to England often and lived in Ikoyi and spoke with a British accent. She was the most popular girl in their form, her school bag made of thick monogrammed leather, her sandals always different from what anybody else had. The second most popular girl was Ginika, Ifemelu's close friend. Ginika did not go abroad often, and so did not have the air of *away* as Yinka did, but she had caramel skin and wavy hair that, when unbraided, fell down to her neck instead of standing Afro-like. Each year, she was voted Prettiest Girl in their form, and she would wryly say, "It's just because I'm a half-caste. How can I be finer than Zainab?"

And so it was the natural order of things, that the gods should match Obinze and Ginika. Kayode was throwing a hasty party in their guest quarters while his parents were away in London. He told Ginika, "I'm going to introduce you to my guy Zed at the party."

"He's not bad," Ginika said, smiling.

"I hope he did not get his mother's fighting genes o," Ifemelu teased. It was nice to see Ginika interested in a boy; almost all the Big Guys in school had tried with her and none had lasted long; Obinze seemed quiet, a good match.

Ifemelu and Ginika arrived together, the party still at its dawn, the dance floor bare, boys running around with cassette tapes, shyness and awkwardness still undissolved. Each time Ifemelu came to Kayode's house, she imagined what it was like to live here, in Ikoyi, in a gracious and gravelled compound, with servants who wore white.

"See Kayode with the new guy," Ifemelu said.

"I don't want to look," Ginika said. "Are they coming?"

"Yes."

"My shoes are so tight."

"You can dance in tight shoes," Ifemelu said.

The boys were before them. Obinze looked overdressed, in a thick corduroy jacket, while Kayode wore a T-shirt and jeans.

"Hey, babes!" Kayode said. He was tall and rangy, with the easy manner of the entitled. "Ginika, meet my friend Obinze, Zed, this is Ginika, the queen God made for you if you are ready to work for it!" He was smirking, already a little drunk, the golden boy making a golden match.

"Hi," Obinze said to Ginika.

"This is Ifemelu," Kayode said. "Otherwise known as Ifemsco. She's Ginika's right-hand man. If you misbehave, she will flog you."

They all laughed on cue.

"Hi," Obinze said. His eyes met Ifemelu's and held, and lingered.

Kayode was making small talk, telling Obinze that Ginika's parents were also university professors. "So both of you are book people," Kayode said. Obinze should have taken over and begun talking to Ginika, and Kayode would have left, and Ifemelu would have followed, and the will of the gods would have been fulfilled. But Obinze said little, and Kayode was left to carry the conversation, his voice getting boisterous, and from time to time he glanced at Obinze, as though to urge him on. Ifemelu was not sure when something happened, but in those moments, as Kayode talked, something strange happened. A quickening inside her, a dawning. She realized, quite suddenly, that she wanted to breathe the same air as Obinze. She became, also, acutely aware of the present, the now, Toni Braxton's voice from the cassette player, *be it fast or slow, it doesn't let go, or shake me,* the smell of Kayode's father's brandy, which had been sneaked out of the main house, and the tight white shirt that chafed at her armpits. Aunty Uju had made her tie it, in a loose bow, at her navel and she wondered now if it was truly stylish or if she looked silly.

The music stopped abruptly. Kayode said, "I'm coming," and left to find out what was wrong, and in the new silence, Ginika fiddled with the metal bangle that encircled her wrist.

Obinze's eyes met Ifemelu's again.

"Aren't you hot in that jacket?" Ifemelu asked. The question came out before she could restrain herself, so used was she to sharpening her words, to watching for terror in the eyes of boys. But he was smiling. He looked amused. He was not afraid of her.

"Very hot," he said. "But I'm a country bumpkin and this is my first city party so you have to forgive me." Slowly, he took his jacket off, green and padded at the elbows, under which he wore a long-sleeved shirt. "Now I'll have to carry a jacket around with me."

"I can hold it for you," Ginika offered. "And don't mind Ifem, the jacket is fine."

"Thanks, but don't worry. I should hold it, as punishment for wearing it in the first place." He looked at Ifemelu, eyes twinkling.

"I didn't mean it like that," Ifemelu said. "It's just that this room is so hot and that jacket looks heavy."

"I like your voice," he said, almost cutting her short.

And she, who was never at a loss, croaked, "My voice?"

"Yes."

The music had begun. "Let's dance?" he asked.

She nodded.

He took her hand and then smiled at Ginika, as though to a nice chaperone whose job was now done. Ifemelu thought Mills and Boon romances were silly, she and her friends sometimes enacted the stories, Ifemelu or Ranyinudo would play the man and Ginika or Priye would play the woman—the man would grab the woman, the woman would fight weakly, then collapse against him with shrill moans—and they would all burst out laughing. But in the filling-up dance floor of Kayode's party, she was jolted by a small truth in those romances. It was indeed true that because of a male, your stomach could tighten up and refuse to unknot itself, your body's joints could unhinge, your limbs fail to move to music, and all effortless things suddenly become leaden. As she moved stiffly, she saw Ginika in her side vision, watching them, her expression puzzled, mouth slightly slack, as though she did not quite believe what had happened.

"You actually said 'country bumpkin'," Ifemelu said, her voice high above the music.

"What?"

"Nobody says 'country bumpkin'. It's the kind of thing you read in a book."

"You have to tell me what books you read," he said.

He was teasing her, and she did not quite get the joke, but she laughed anyway. Later, she wished that she remembered every word they said to each other as they danced. She remembered, instead, feeling adrift. When the lights were turned off, and the blues dancing started, she wanted to be in his arms in a dark corner, but he said, "Let's go outside and talk."

They sat on cement blocks behind the guesthouse, next to what looked like the gateman's bathroom, a narrow stall which, when the wind blew, brought a stale smell. They talked and talked, hungry to know each other. He told her that his father had died when he was seven, and how clearly he remembered his father teaching him to ride a tricycle on a tree-lined street near their campus home, but sometimes he would discover, in panic, that he could not remember his father's face and a sense of betrayal would overwhelm him and he would hurry to examine the framed photo on their living room wall.

"Your mother never wanted to remarry?"

"Even if she wanted to, I don't think she would, because of me. I want her to be happy, but I don't want her to remarry."

"I would feel the same way. Did she really fight with another professor?"

"So you heard that story."

"They said it's why she had to leave Nsukka University."

"No, she didn't fight. She was on a committee and they discovered that this professor had misused funds and my mother accused him publicly and he got angry and slapped her and said he could not take a woman talking to him like that. So my mother got up and locked the door of the conference room and put the key in her bra. She told him she could not slap him back because he was stronger than her, but he would have to apologize to her publicly, in front of all the people who had seen him slap her. So he did. But she knew he didn't mean it. She said he did it in a kind of 'okay sorry if that's what you want to hear and just bring out the key' way. She came home that day really angry, and she kept talking about how things had changed and what did it mean that now somebody could just slap another person. She wrote circulars and articles about it, and the student union got involved. People were saying, Oh, why did he slap her when she's a widow, and that annoyed her even more. She said she should not have been slapped because she is a full human being, not because she doesn't have a husband to speak for her. So some of her female students went and printed Full Human Being on T-shirts. I guess it made her well-known. She's usually very quiet and doesn't have many friends."

"Is that why she came to Lagos?"

"No. She's been scheduled to do this sabbatical for a while. I remember the first time she told me we would go away for her two-year sabbatical, and I was excited because I thought it would be in America, one of my friend's dads had just gone to America, and then she said it was Lagos, and I asked her what was the point? We might as well just stay in Nsukka."

Ifemelu laughed. "But at least you can still get on a plane to come to Lagos."

"Yes, but we came by road," Obinze said, laughing. "But now I'm happy it was Lagos or I would not have met you."

"Or met Ginika," she teased.

"Stop it."

"Your guys will kill you. You're supposed to be chasing her."

"I'm chasing you."

She would always remember this moment, those words. *I'm chasing you.*

"I saw you in school some time ago. I even asked Kay about you," he said.

"Are you serious?"

"I saw you holding a James Hadley Chase, near the lab. And I said, Ah, correct, there is hope. She reads."

"I think I've read them all."

"Me too. What's your favourite?"

"*Miss Shumway Waves a Wand.*"

"Mine is *Want to Stay Alive?* I stayed up one night to finish it."

"Yes, I like that too."

"What about other books? Which of the classics do you like?"

"Classics, *kwa*? I just like crime and thrillers. Sheldon, Ludlum, Archer."

"But you also have to read proper books."

She looked at him, amused by his earnestness. "Aje-butter! University boy! That must be what your professor mother taught you."

"No, seriously." He paused. "I'll give you some to try. I love the American ones."

"You have to read proper books," she mimicked.

"What about poetry?"

"What's that last one we did in class, 'Ancient Mariner'? So boring."

Obinze laughed, and Ifemelu, uninterested in pursuing the subject of poetry, asked, "So what did Kayode say about me?"

"Nothing bad. He likes you."

"You don't want to tell me what he said."

"He said, 'Ifemelu is a fine babe but she is too much trouble. She can argue. She can talk. She never agrees. But Ginika is just a sweet girl.'" He paused, then added, "He didn't know that was exactly what I hoped to hear. I'm not interested in girls that are too nice."

"Ahn-ahn! Are you insulting me?" She nudged him, in mock anger. She had always liked this image of herself as too much trouble, as different, and she sometimes thought of it as a carapace that kept her safe.

"You know I'm not insulting you." He put an arm around her shoulders and pulled her to him gently; it was the first time their bodies had met and she felt herself stiffen. "I thought you were so fine, but not just that. You looked like the kind of person who will do something because you want to, and not because everyone else is doing it."

She rested her head against his and felt, for the first time, what she would often feel with him: a self-affection. He made her like herself. With him, she was at ease; her skin felt as though it was her right size. She told him how she very much wanted God to exist but feared He did not, how she worried that she should know what she wanted to do with her life but did not even know what she wanted to study at university. It seemed so natural, to talk to him about odd things. She had never done that before. The trust, so sudden and yet so complete, and the intimacy, frightened her. They had known nothing of each other only hours ago, and yet, there had been a knowledge shared between them in those moments before they danced, and now she could think only of all the things she yet wanted to tell him, wanted to do with him. The similarities in their lives became good omens: that they were both only children, their birthdays two days apart, and their hometowns in Anambra State. He was from Abba and she was from Umunnachi and the towns were minutes away from each other.

"Ahn-ahn! One of my uncles goes to your village all the time!" he told her. "I've been a few times with him. You people have terrible roads."

"I know Abba. The roads are worse."

"How often do you go to your village?"

"Every Christmas."

"Just once a year! I go very often with my mother, at least five times a year."

"But I bet I speak Igbo better than you."

"Impossible," he said, and switched to Igbo. "*Ama m atu inu.* I even know proverbs."

"Yes. The basic one everybody knows. A frog does not run in the afternoon for nothing."

"No. I know serious proverbs. *Akota ife ka ubi, e lee oba.* If something bigger than the farm is dug up, the barn is sold."

"Ah, you want to try me?" she asked, laughing. "*Acho afu adi ako n'akpa díbia.* The medicine man's bag has all kinds of things."

"Not bad," he said. "*E gbuo díke n'ogu uno, e luo na ogu agu, e lote ya.* If you kill a warrior in a local fight, you'll remember him when fighting enemies."

They traded proverbs. She could say only two more before she gave up, with him still raring to go.

"How do you know all that?" she asked, impressed. "Many guys won't even speak Igbo, not to mention knowing proverbs."

"I just listen when my uncles talk. I think my dad would have liked that."

They were silent. Cigarette smoke wafted up from the entrance of the guesthouse, where some boys had gathered. Party noises hung in the air: loud music, the raised voices and high laughter of boys and girls, all of them looser and freer than they would be the next day.

"Aren't we going to kiss?" she asked.

He seemed startled. "Where did that come from?"

"I'm just asking. We've been sitting here for so long."

"I don't want you to think that is all I want."

"What about what I want?"

"What do you want?"

"What do you think I want?"

"My jacket?"

She laughed. "Yes, your famous jacket."

"You make me shy," he said.

"Are you serious? Because *you* make *me* shy."

"I don't believe anything makes you shy," he said.

They kissed, pressed their foreheads together, held hands. His kiss was enjoyable, almost heady; it was nothing like her ex-boyfriend Mofe, whose kisses she had thought too salivary.

When she told Obinze this some weeks later—she said, "So where did you learn to kiss? Because it's nothing like my ex-boyfriend's salivary fumbling"—he laughed and repeated "salivary fumbling!" and then told her that it was not technique, but emotion. He had done what her ex-boyfriend had done but the difference, in this case, was love.

"You know it was love at first sight for both of us," he said.

"For both of us? Is it by force? Why are you speaking for me?"

"I'm just stating a fact. Stop struggling."

They were sitting side by side on a desk in the back of his almost empty classroom. The end-of-break bell began to ring, jangling and discordant.

"Yes, it's a fact," she said.

"What?"

"I love you." How easily the words came out, how loudly. She wanted him to hear and she wanted the boy sitting in front, bespectacled and studious, to hear and she wanted the girls gathered in the corridor outside to hear.

"Fact," Obinze said, with a grin.

Because of her, he had joined the debate club, and after she spoke, he clapped the loudest and longest, until her friends said, "Obinze, please, it is enough." Because of him, she joined the sports club and watched him play football, sitting by the touchline and holding his bottle of water. But it was table tennis that he loved, sweating and shouting as he played, glistening with energy, smashing the small white ball, and she marvelled at his skill, how he seemed to stand too far away from the table and yet managed to get the ball. He was already the undefeated school champion, as he had been, he told her, in his former school. When she played with him, he would laugh and say, "You don't win by hitting the ball with anger o!" Because of her, his friends called him "woman wrapper". Once, as he and his friends talked about meeting after school to play football, one of them asked, "Has Ifemelu given you permission to come?" And Obinze swiftly replied, "Yes, but she said I have only an hour." She liked that he wore their relationship so boldly, like a brightly coloured shirt. Sometimes she worried that she was too happy. She would sink into moodiness, and snap at Obinze, or be distant. And her joy would become a restless thing, flapping its wings inside her, as though looking for an opening to fly away.

CHAPTER 5

After Kayode's party, Ginika was stilted; an alien awkwardness grew between them.

"You know I didn't think it would happen that way," Ifemelu told her.

"Ifem, he was looking at you from the beginning," Ginika said, and then, to show that she was fine with it all, she teased Ifemelu about stealing her guy without even trying. Her breeziness was forced, laid on thickly, and Ifemelu felt burdened with guilt, and with a desire to overcompensate. It seemed wrong, that her close friend Ginika, pretty, pleasant, popular Ginika with whom she had never quarrelled, was reduced to pretending that she did not care, even though a wistfulness underlined her tone whenever she talked about Obinze. "Ifem, will you have time for us today or is it Obinze all the way?" she would ask.

And so when Ginika came to school one morning, her eyes red and shadowed, and told Ifemelu, "My popsie said we are going to America next month," Ifemelu felt almost relieved. She would miss her friend, but Ginika's leaving forced them both to wring out their friendship and lay it out newly fresh to dry, to return to where they used to be. Ginika's parents had been talking for a while about resigning from the university and starting over in America. Once, while visiting, Ifemelu had heard Ginika's father say, "We are not sheep. This regime is treating us like sheep and we are starting to behave as if we are sheep. I have not been able to do any real research in years, because every day I am organizing strikes and talking about unpaid salary and there is no chalk in the classrooms." He was a small, dark man, smaller-looking and darker-looking beside Ginika's large, ash-haired mother, with an undecided air about him, as though he was always dithering between choices. When Ifemelu told her own parents that Ginika's family was finally leaving, her father sighed and said, "At least they are fortunate to have that option," and her mother said, "They are blessed."

But Ginika complained and cried, painting images of a sad, friendless life in a strange America. "I wish I could live with you people while they go," she told Ifemelu. They had gathered at Ginika's house, Ifemelu, Ranyinudo, Priye and Tochi, and were in her bedroom, picking through the clothes she would not be taking with her.

"Ginika, just make sure you can still talk to us when you come back," Priye said.

"She'll come back and be a serious Americanah like Bisi," Ranyinudo said.

They roared with laughter, at that word "Americanah", wreathed in glee, the fourth syllable extended, and at the thought of Bisi, a girl in the form below them, who had come back from a short trip to America with odd affectations, pretending she no longer understood Yoruba, adding a slurred *r* to every English word she spoke.

"But, Ginika, seriously, I would give anything to be you right now," Priye said. "I don't understand why you don't want to go. You can always come back."

At school, friends gathered around Ginika. They all wanted to take her out to the tuck shop, and to see her after school, as though her impending departure had made her even more desirable. Ifemelu and Ginika were lounging in the corridor, during short break, when the Big Guys joined them: Kayode, Obinze, Ahmed, Emenike and Osahon.

"Ginika, where in America are you going?" Emenike asked. He was awed by people who went abroad. After Kayode came back from a trip to Switzerland with his parents, Emenike had bent down to caress Kayode's shoes, saying "I want to touch them because they have touched snow."

"Missouri," Ginika said. "My dad got a teaching job there."

"Your mother is an American, *abi*? So you have an American passport?" Emenike asked.

"Yes. But we haven't travelled since I was in primary three."

"American passport is the coolest thing," Kayode said. "I would exchange my British passport tomorrow."

"Me too," Yinka said.

"I very nearly had one o," Obinze said. "I was eight months old when my parents took me to America. I keep telling my mum that she should have gone earlier and had me there!"

"Bad luck, man," Kayode said.

"I don't have a passport. Last time we travelled, I was on my mum's passport," Ahmed said.

"I was on my mum's until primary three, then my dad said we needed to get our own passports," Osahon said.

"I've never gone abroad but my father has promised that I will go for university. I wish I could just apply for my visa now instead of waiting to finish school," Emenike said. After he spoke, a hushed silence followed.

"Don't leave us now, wait until you finish," Yinka finally said, and she and Kayode burst out laughing. The others laughed, too, even Emenike himself, but there was, underneath their laughter, a barbed echo. They knew he was lying, Emenike who made up stories of rich parents that everyone knew he didn't have, so immersed in his need to invent a life that was not his. The conversation ebbed, changed to the mathematics teacher who did not know how to solve simultaneous equations. Obinze took Ifemelu's hand and they drifted away. They did that often, slowly detaching themselves from their friends, to sit in a corner by the library or take a walk on the green behind the laboratories. As they walked, she wanted to tell Obinze that she didn't know what it meant to "be on your mother's passport", that her mother didn't even have a passport. But she said nothing, walking beside him in silence. He fitted here, in this school, much more than she did. She was popular, always on every party list, and always announced, during assembly, as one of the "first three" in her class, yet she felt sheathed in a translucent haze of difference. She would not be here if she had not done so well on the entrance examination, if her father had not been determined that she would go to "a school that builds both character and career". Her primary school had been different, full of children like her, whose parents were teachers and civil servants, who took the bus and did not have drivers. She remembered the surprise on Obinze's face, a surprise he had quickly shielded, when he asked, "What's your phone number?" and she replied, "We don't have a phone."

He was holding her hand now, squeezing gently. He admired her for being outspoken and different, but he did not seem able to see beneath that. To be here, among people who had gone abroad, was natural for him. He was fluent in the knowledge of foreign things, especially of American things. Everybody watched American films and exchanged faded American magazines, but he knew details about American presidents from a hundred years ago. Everybody watched American shows, but he knew about Lisa Bonet leaving *The Cosby Show* to go and do *Angel Heart* and Will Smith's huge debts before he was signed to do *The Fresh Prince of Bel Air.* "You look like a black American" was his ultimate compliment, which he told her when she wore a nice dress, or when her hair was done in large braids. Manhattan was his zenith. He often said "It's not as if this is Manhattan" or "Go to Manhattan and see how things are." He gave her a copy of *Huckleberry Finn*, the pages creased from his thumbing, and she started reading it on the bus home but stopped after a few chapters. The next morning, she put it down on his desk with a decided thump. "Unreadable nonsense," she said.

"It's written in different American dialects," Obinze said.

"And so what? I still don't understand it."

"You have to be patient, Ifem. If you really get into it, it's very interesting and you won't want to stop reading."

"I've already stopped reading. Please keep your proper books and leave me with the books I like. And by the way, I still win when we play Scrabble, Mr Read Proper Books."

Now, she slipped her hand from his as they walked back to class. Whenever she felt this way, panic would slice into her at the slightest thing, and mundane events would become arbiters of doom. This time, Ginika was the trigger; she was standing near the staircase, her backpack on her shoulder, her face gold-streaked in the sunlight, and suddenly Ifemelu thought how much Ginika and Obinze had in common. Ginika's house at the University of Lagos, the quiet bungalow, the yard crowned by bougainvillea hedges, was perhaps like Obinze's house in Nsukka, and she imagined Obinze realizing how better suited Ginika was for him, and then this joy, this fragile, glimmering thing between them, would disappear.

OBINZE TOLD HER, one morning after assembly, that his mother wanted her to visit.

"Your mother?" she asked him, agape.

"I think she wants to meet her future daughter-in-law."

"Obinze, be serious!"

"I remember in primary six, I took this girl to the send-off party and my mum dropped both of us off and gave the girl a handkerchief. She said, 'A lady always needs a handkerchief.' My mother can be strange, *sha.* Maybe she wants to give you a handkerchief."

"Obinze Maduewesi!"

"She's never done this before but then I've never had a serious girlfriend before. I think she just wants to see you. She said you should come to lunch."

Ifemelu stared at him. What sort of mother in her right mind asked her son's girlfriend to visit? It was odd. Even the expression "come to lunch" was something people said in books. If you were Boyfriend and Girlfriend, you did not visit each other's homes; you registered for after-school lessons, for French Club, for anything that could mean seeing each other outside school. Her parents did not, of course, know about Obinze. Obinze's mother's invitation frightened and excited her; for days, she worried about what to wear.

"Just be yourself," Aunty Uju told her and Ifemelu replied, "How can I just be myself? What does that even mean?"

On the afternoon she visited, she stood outside the door of their flat for a while before she pressed the bell, suddenly and wildly hoping that they had gone out. Obinze opened the door.

"Hi. My mum just came back from work."

The living room was airy, the walls free of photographs except for a turquoise painting of a long-necked woman in a turban.

"That's the only thing that is ours. Everything else came with the flat," Obinze said.

"It's nice," she mumbled.

"Don't be nervous. Remember, she wants you here," Obinze whispered, just before his mother appeared. She looked like Onyeka Onwenu, the resemblance was astounding: a full-nosed, full-lipped beauty, her round face framed by a low Afro, her faultless complexion the deep brown of cocoa. Onyeka Onwenu's music had been one of the luminous joys of Ifemelu's childhood, and had remained undimmed in the aftermath of childhood. She would always remember the day her father came home with the new album *In the Morning Light*; Onyeka Onwenu's face on it was a revelation, and for a long time she traced that photo with her finger. The songs, each time her father played them, made their flat festive, turned him into a looser person who sang along with songs steeped in femaleness, and Ifemelu would guiltily fantasize about him being married to Onyeka Onwenu instead of to her mother. When she greeted Obinze's mother with a "Good afternoon, ma," she almost expected her, in response, to break into song in a voice as peerless as Onyeka Onwenu's. But she had a low, murmuring voice.

"What a beautiful name you have. Ifemelunamma," she said.

Ifemelu stood tongue-tied for seconds. "Thank you, ma."

"Translate it," she said.

"Translate?"

"Yes, how would you translate your name? Did Obinze tell you I do some translation? From the French. I am a lecturer in literature, not English literature, mind you, but literatures in English, and my translating is something I do as a hobby. Now translating your name from Igbo to English might be Made-in-Good-Times or Beautifully Made, or what do you think?"

Ifemelu could not think. There was something about the woman that made her want to say intelligent things, but her mind was blank.

"Mummy, she came to greet you, not to translate her name," Obinze said, with a playful exasperation.

"Do we have a soft drink to offer our guest? Did you bring out the soup from the freezer? Let's go to the kitchen," his mother said. She reached out and picked off a piece of lint from his hair, and then hit his head lightly. Their fluid, bantering rapport made Ifemelu uncomfortable. It was free of restraint, free of the fear of consequences; it did not take the familiar shape of a relationship with a parent. They cooked together, his mother stirring the soup, Obinze making the garri, while Ifemelu stood by drinking a Coke. She had offered to help, but his mother had said, "No, my dear, maybe next time," as though she did not just let anyone help in her kitchen. She was pleasant and direct, even warm, but there was a privacy about her, a reluctance to bare herself completely to the world, the same quality as Obinze. She had taught her son the ability to be, even in the middle of a crowd, somehow comfortably inside himself.

"What are your favourite novels, Ifemelunamma?" his mother asked. "You know Obinze will only read American books? I hope you're not that foolish."

"Mummy, you're just trying to force me to like this book." He gestured to the book on the kitchen table, Graham Greene's *The Heart of the Matter.* "My mother reads this book twice a year. I don't know why," he said to Ifemelu.

"It is a wise book. The human stories that matter are those that endure. The American books you read are lightweights." She turned to Ifemelu. "This boy is too besotted with America."

"I read American books because America is the future, Mummy. And remember that your husband was educated there."

"That was when only dullards went to school in America. American universities were considered to be at the same level as British secondary schools then. I did a lot of brushing-up on that man after I married him."

"Even though you left your things in his flat so that his other girlfriends would stay away?"

"I've told you not to pay any attention to your uncle's false stories."

Ifemelu stood there mesmerized. Obinze's mother, her beautiful face, her air of sophistication, her wearing a white apron in the kitchen, was not like any other mother Ifemelu knew. Here, her father would seem crass, with his unnecessary big words, and her mother provincial and small.

"You can wash your hands at the sink," Obinze's mother told her. "I think the water is still running."

They sat at the dining table, eating garri and soup, Ifemelu trying hard to be, as Aunty Uju had said, "herself", although she was no longer sure what "herself" was. She felt undeserving, unable to sink with Obinze and his mother into their atmosphere.

"The soup is very sweet, ma," she said politely.

"Oh, Obinze cooked it," his mother said. "Didn't he tell you that he cooks?"

"Yes, but I didn't think he could make soup, ma," Ifemelu said.

Obinze was smirking.

"Do you cook at home?" his mother asked.

Ifemelu wanted to lie, to say that she cooked and loved cooking, but she remembered Aunty Uju's words. "No, ma," she said. "I don't like cooking. I can eat Indomie noodles day and night."

His mother laughed, as though charmed by the honesty, and when she laughed, she looked like a softer-faced Obinze. Ifemelu ate her food slowly, thinking how much she wanted to remain there with them, in their rapture, forever.

THEIR FLAT SMELLED of vanilla on weekends, when Obinze's mother baked. Slices of mango glistening on a pie, small brown cakes swelling with raisins. Ifemelu stirred the batter and peeled the fruit; her own mother did not bake, their oven housed cockroaches.

"Obinze just said 'trunk', ma. He said it's in the trunk of your car," she said. In their America–Britain jousting, she always sided with his mother.

"Trunk is a part of a tree and not a part of a car, my dear son," his mother said. When Obinze pronounced "schedule" with the *k* sound, his mother said, "Ifemelunamma, please tell my son I don't speak American. Could he say that in English?"

On weekends, they watched films on video. They sat in the living room, eyes on the screen, and Obinze said, "Mummy, *chelu*, let's hear," when his mother, from time to time, gave her commentary on the plausibility of a scene, or the foreshadowing, or whether an actor was wearing a wig. One Sunday, midway into a film, his mother left for the pharmacy, to buy her allergy medicine. "I'd forgotten they close early today," she said. As soon as her car engine started, a dull revving, Ifemelu and Obinze hurried to his bedroom and sank onto his bed, kissing and touching, their clothing rolled up, shifted aside, pulled halfway. Their skin warm against each other. They left the door and the window louvres open, both of them alert to the sound of his mother's car. In a sluice of seconds, they were dressed, back in the living room, Play pressed on the video recorder.

Obinze's mother walked in and glanced at the TV. "You were watching this scene when I left," she said quietly. A frozen silence fell, even from the film. Then the sing-song cries of a beans hawker floated in through the window.

"Ifemelunamma, please come," his mother said, turning to go inside.

Obinze got up, but Ifemelu stopped him. "No, she called me."

His mother asked her to come inside her bedroom, asked her to sit on the bed.

"If anything happens between you and Obinze, you are both responsible. But Nature is unfair to women. An act is done by two people but if there are any consequences, one person carries it alone. Do you understand me?"

"Yes." Ifemelu kept her eyes averted from Obinze's mother, firmly fixed on the black-and-white linoleum on the floor.

"Have you done anything serious with Obinze?"

"No."

"I was once young. I know what it is like to love while young. I want to advise you. I am aware that, in the end, you will do what you want. My advice is that you wait. You can love without making love. It is a beautiful way of showing your feelings but it brings responsibility, great responsibility, and there is no rush. I will advise you to wait until you are at least in the university, wait until you own yourself a little more. Do you understand?"

"Yes," Ifemelu said. She did not know what "own yourself a little more" meant.

"I know you are a clever girl. Women are more sensible than men, and you will have to be the sensible one. Convince him. Both of you should agree to wait so that there is no pressure."

Obinze's mother paused and Ifemelu wondered if she had finished. The silence rang in her head.

"Thank you, ma," Ifemelu said.

"And when you want to start, I want you to come and see me. I want to know that you are being responsible."

Ifemelu nodded. She was sitting on Obinze's mother's bed, in the woman's bedroom, nodding and agreeing to tell her when she started having sex with her son. Yet she felt the absence of shame. Perhaps it was Obinze's mother's tone, the evenness of it, the normalness of it.

"Thank you, ma," Ifemelu said again, now looking at Obinze's mother's face, which was open, no different from what it usually was. "I will."

She went back to the living room. Obinze seemed nervous, perched on the edge of the centre table. "I'm so sorry. I'm going to talk to her about this when you leave. If she wants to talk to anybody, it should be me."

"She said I should never come here again. That I am misleading her son."

Obinze blinked. "What?"

Ifemelu laughed. Later, when she told him what his mother had said, he shook his head. "We have to tell her when we start? What kind of rubbish is that? Does she want to buy condoms for us? What is wrong with that woman?"

"But who told you we are ever going to start anything?"

CHAPTER 6

During the week, Aunty Uju hurried home to shower and wait for The General and, on weekends, she lounged in her nightdress, reading or cooking or watching television, because The General was in Abuja with his wife and children. She avoided the sun and used creams in elegant bottles, so that her complexion, already naturally light, became lighter, brighter, and took on a sheen. Sometimes, as she gave instructions to her driver, Sola, or her gardener, Baba Flower, or her two house helps, Inyang who cleaned and Chikodili who cooked, Ifemelu would remember Aunty Uju, the village girl brought to Lagos so many years ago, who Ifemelu's mother mildly complained was so parochial she kept touching the walls, and what was it with all those village people who could not stand on their feet without reaching out to smear their palm on a wall? Ifemelu wondered if Aunty Uju ever looked at herself with the eyes of the girl she used to be. Perhaps not. Aunty Uju had steadied herself into her new life with a lightness of touch, more consumed by The General himself than by her new wealth.

The first time Ifemelu saw Aunty Uju's house in Dolphin Estate, she did not want to leave. The bathroom fascinated her, with its hot water tap, its gushing shower, its pink tiles. The bedroom curtains were made of raw silk, and she told Aunty Uju, "Ahn-ahn, it's a waste to use this material as a curtain! Let's sew a dress with it." The living room had glass doors that slid noiselessly open and noiselessly shut. Even the kitchen was air-conditioned. She wanted to live there. It would impress her friends; she imagined them sitting in the small room just off the living room, which Aunty Uju called the TV room, watching programmes on satellite. And so she asked her parents if she could stay with Aunty Uju during the week. "It's closer to school, I won't need to take two buses. I can go on Mondays and come home on Fridays," Ifemelu said. "I can also help Aunty Uju in the house."

"My understanding is that Uju has sufficient help," her father said.

"It is a good idea," her mother said to her father. "She can study well there, at least there will be light every day. No need for her to study with kerosene lamps."

"She can visit Uju after school and on weekends. But she is not going to live there," her father said.

Her mother paused, taken aback by his firmness. "Okay," she said, with a helpless glance at Ifemelu.

For days, Ifemelu sulked. Her father often indulged her, giving in to what she wanted, but this time he ignored her pouts, her deliberate silences at the dinner table. He pretended not to notice when Aunty Uju brought them a new television. He settled back in his well-worn sofa, reading his well-worn book, while Aunty Uju's driver put down the brown Sony carton. Ifemelu's mother began to sing a church song—"the Lord has given me victory, I will lift him higher"—which was often sung at collection time.

"The General bought more than I needed in the house. There was nowhere to put this one," Aunty Uju said, a general statement made to nobody in particular, a way of shrugging off thanks. Ifemelu's mother opened the carton, gently stripped away the Styrofoam packaging.

"Our old one doesn't even show anything any more," she said, although they all knew that it still did.

"Look at how slim it is!" she added. "Look!"

Her father raised his eyes from the book. "Yes, it is," he said, and then lowered his gaze.

THE LANDLORD CAME AGAIN. He barged past Ifemelu into the flat, into the kitchen, and reached up to the electric meter, yanking off the fuse, cutting off what little electricity they had.

After he left, Ifemelu's father said, "What ignominy. To ask us for two years' rent. We have been paying one year."

"But even that one year, we have not paid," her mother said, and in her tone was the slightest of accusations.

"I've spoken to Akunne about a loan," her father said. He disliked Akunne, his almost-cousin, the prosperous man from their hometown to whom everyone took their problems. He called Akunne a lurid illiterate, a money-miss-road.

"What did he say?"

"He said I should come and see him next Friday." His fingers were unsteady; he was struggling, it seemed, to suppress emotions. Ifemelu hastily looked away, hoping he had not seen her watching him, and asked him if he could explain a difficult question in her homework. To distract him, to make it seem that life could happen again.

HER FATHER WOULD NOT ask Aunty Uju for help, but if Aunty Uju presented him with the money, he would not refuse. It was better than being indebted to Akunne. Ifemelu told Aunty Uju how the landlord banged on their door, a loud, unnecessary banging for the benefit of the neighbours, while hurling insults at her father. "Are you not a real man? Pay me my money. I will throw you out of this flat if I don't get that rent by next week!"

As Ifemelu mimicked the landlord, a wan sadness crossed Aunty Uju's face. "How can that useless landlord embarrass Brother like this? I'll ask Oga to give me the money."

Ifemelu stopped. "You don't have money?"

"My account is almost empty. But Oga will give it to me. And do you know I have not been paid a salary since I started work? Every day, there is a new story from the accounts people. The trouble started with my position that does not officially exist, even though I see patients every day."

"But doctors are on strike," Ifemelu said.

"The military hospitals still pay. Not that my pay will be enough for the rent, *sha*."

"You don't have money?" Ifemelu asked again, slowly, to clarify, to be sure. "Ahn-ahn, Aunty, but how can you not have money?"

"Oga never gives me big money. He pays all the bills and he wants me to ask for everything I need. Some men are like that."

Ifemelu stared. Aunty Uju, in her big pink house with the wide satellite dish blooming from its roof, her generator brimming with diesel, her freezer stocked with meat, and she did not have money in her bank account.

"Ifem, don't look as if somebody died!" Aunty Uju laughed, her wry laugh. She looked suddenly small and bewildered among the detritus of her new life, the fawn-coloured jewel case on the dressing table, the silk robe thrown across the bed, and Ifemelu felt frightened for her.

"HE EVEN GAVE ME a little more than I asked for," Aunty Uju told Ifemelu the next weekend, with a small smile, as though amused by what The General had done. "We'll go to the house from the salon so I can give it to Brother."

It startled Ifemelu, how much a relaxer retouching cost at Aunty Uju's hair salon; the haughty hairdressers sized up each customer, eyes swinging from head to shoes, to decide how much attention she was worth. With Aunty Uju, they hovered and grovelled, curtsying deeply as they greeted her, overpraising her handbag and shoes. Ifemelu watched, fascinated. It was here, at a Lagos salon, that the different ranks of imperial femaleness were best understood.

"Those girls, I was waiting for them to bring out their hands and beg you to shit so they could worship that too," Ifemelu said, as they left the salon.

Aunty Uju laughed and patted the silky hair extensions that fell to her shoulders: Chinese weave-on, the latest version, shiny and straight as straight could be; it never tangled.

"You know, we live in an ass-licking economy. The biggest problem in this country is not corruption. The problem is that there are many qualified people who are not where they are supposed to be because they won't lick anybody's ass, or they don't know which ass to lick or they don't even know how to lick an ass. I'm lucky to be licking the right ass." She smiled. "It's just luck. Oga said I was well brought up, that I was not like all the Lagos girls who sleep with him on the first night and the next morning give him a list of what they want him to buy. I slept with him on the first night but I did not ask for anything, which was stupid of me now that I think of it, but I did not sleep with him because I wanted something. Ah, this thing called power. I was attracted to him even with his teeth like Dracula. I was attracted to his power."

Aunty Uju liked to talk about The General, different versions of the same stories repeated and savoured. Her driver had told her—she swayed his loyalty by arranging his wife's prenatal visits and his baby's immunizations—that The General asked for details of where she went and how long she stayed, and each time Aunty Uju told Ifemelu the story, she would end with a sigh, "Does he think I can't see another man without him knowing, if I wanted to? But I don't want to."

They were in the cold interior of the Mazda. As the driver backed out of the gates of the salon compound, Aunty Uju gestured to the gateman, rolled down her window and gave him some money.

"Thank you, madam!" he said, and saluted.

She had slipped naira notes to all the salon workers, to the security men outside, to the policemen at the road junction.

"They're not paid enough to afford school fees for even one child," Aunty Uju said.

"That small money you gave him will not help him pay any school fees," Ifemelu said.

"But he can buy a little extra something and he will be in a better mood and he won't beat his wife this night," Aunty Uju said. She looked out of the window and said, "Slow down, Sola," so that she could get a good look at an accident on Osborne Road; a bus had hit a car, the front of the bus and the back of the car were now mangled metal, and both drivers were shouting in each other's faces, buffered by a gathering crowd. "Where do they come from? These people that appear once there is an accident?" Aunty Uju leaned back in her seat. "Do you know I have forgotten what it feels like to be in a bus? It is so easy to get used to all this."

"You can just go to Falomo now and get on a bus," Ifemelu said.

"But it won't be the same. It's never the same when you have other choices." Aunty Uju looked at her. "Ifem, stop worrying about me."

"I'm not worrying."

"You've been worrying since I told you about my account."

"If somebody else was doing this, you would say she was stupid."

"I would not even advise you to do what I'm doing." Aunty Uju turned back to the window. "He'll change. I'll make him change. I just need to go slowly."

At the flat, Aunty Uju handed Ifemelu's father a plastic bag swollen with cash. "It's rent for two years, Brother," she said, with an embarrassed casualness, and then made a joke about the hole in his singlet. She did not look him in the face as she spoke and he did not look her in the face as he thanked her.

THE GENERAL HAD yellowed eyes, which suggested to Ifemelu a malnourished childhood. His solid, thickset body spoke of fights that he had started and won, and the buck-teeth that gaped through his lips made him seem vaguely dangerous. Ifemelu was surprised by the gleeful coarseness of him. "I'm a village man!" he said happily, as though to explain the drops of soup that landed on his shirt and on the table while he ate, or his loud burping afterwards. He arrived in the evenings, in his green uniform, holding a gossip magazine or two, while his ADC, at an obsequious pace behind him, brought his briefcase and put it on the dining table. He rarely left with the gossip magazines; copies of *Vintage People* and *Prime People* and *Lagos Life* littered Aunty Uju's house, with their blurry photos and garish headlines.

"If I tell you what these people do, eh," Aunty Uju would say to Ifemelu, tapping at a magazine photo with her French-manicured nail. "Their real stories are not even in the magazines. Oga has the real gist." Then she would talk about the man who had sex with a top general to get an oil bloc, the military administrator whose children were fathered by somebody else, the foreign prostitutes flown in weekly for the Head of State. She repeated the stories with affectionate amusement, as though she thought The General's keenness on raunchy gossip was a charming and forgivable indulgence. "Do you know he is afraid of injections? A whole General Officer Commanding and if he sees a needle, he is afraid!" Aunty Uju said, in the same tone. It was, to her, an endearing detail. Ifemelu could not think of The General as endearing, with his loud, boorish manner, the way he reached out to slap Aunty Uju's backside as they went upstairs, saying, "All this for me? All this for me?" and the way he talked and talked, never acknowledging an interruption, until he finished a story. One of his favourites, which he often told Ifemelu while drinking Star beer after dinner, was the story of how Aunty Uju was different. He told it with a self-congratulatory tone, as if her difference reflected his own good taste. "The first time I told her I was going to London and asked what she wanted, she gave me a list. Before I looked at it, I said I already know what she wants. Is it not perfume, shoes, bag, watch and clothes? I know Lagos girls. But you know what was in it? One perfume and four books! I was shocked. *Chai.* I spent one good hour in that bookshop in Piccadilly. I bought her twenty books! Which Lagos babe do you know that will be asking for books?"

Aunty Uju would laugh, suddenly girlish and pliant. Ifemelu would smile dutifully. She thought it undignified and irresponsible, this old married man telling her stories; it was like showing her his unclean underwear. She tried to see him through Aunty Uju's eyes, a man of wonders, a man of worldly excitements, but she could not. She recognized the lightness of being, the joyfulness that Aunty Uju had on weekdays; it was how she felt when she was looking forward to seeing Obinze after school. But it seemed wrong, a waste, that Aunty Uju should feel this for The General. Aunty Uju's ex-boyfriend, Olujimi, was different, nice-looking and smooth-voiced; he glistened with a quiet polish. They had been together for most of university and when you saw them, you saw why they were together. "I outgrew him," Aunty Uju said.

"Don't you outgrow and move on to something better?" Ifemelu asked. And Aunty Uju laughed as though it was really a joke.

On the day of the coup, a close friend of The General's called Aunty Uju to ask if she was with him. There was tension; some army officers had already been arrested. Aunty Uju was not with The General, did not know where he was, and she paced upstairs and then downstairs, worried, making phone calls that yielded nothing. Soon she began to heave, struggling to breathe. Her panic had turned into an asthma attack. She was gasping, shaking, piercing her arm with a needle, trying to inject herself with medicine, drops of blood staining the bedcovers, until Ifemelu ran down the street to bang on the door of a neighbour whose sister was also a doctor. Finally, The General called to say that he was fine, the coup had failed and all was well with the Head of State; Aunty Uju's trembling stopped.

ON A MUSLIM HOLIDAY, one of those two-day holidays when non-Muslims in Lagos said "Happy Sallah" to whoever they assumed to be a Muslim, often gatemen from the north, and NTA showed footage after footage of men slaughtering rams, The General promised to visit; it would be the first time he spent a public holiday with Aunty Uju. She was in the kitchen the entire morning supervising Chikodili, singing loudly from time to time, being a little too familiar with Chikodili, a little too quick to laugh with her. Finally, the cooking done and the house smelling of spices and sauces, Aunty Uju went upstairs to shower.

"Ifem, please come and help me trim my hair down there. Oga said it disturbs him!" Aunty Uju said, laughing, and then lay on her back, legs spread and held high, an old gossip magazine beneath her, while Ifemelu worked with a shaving stick. Ifemelu had finished and Aunty Uju was coating an exfoliating mask on her face when The General called to say he could no longer come. Aunty Uju, her face ghoulish, covered in chalk-white paste except for the circles of skin around her eyes, hung up and walked into the kitchen and began to put the food in plastic containers for the freezer. Chikodili looked on in confusion. Aunty Uju worked feverishly, jerking the freezer compartment, slamming the cupboard, and as she pushed back the pot of jollof rice, the pot of egusi soup fell off the cooker. Aunty Uju stared at the yellowish-green sauce spreading across the kitchen floor as though she did not know how it had happened. She turned to Chikodili and screamed, "Why are you looking like a mumu? Come on, clean it up!"

Ifemelu was watching from the kitchen entrance. "Aunty, the person you should be shouting at is The General."

Aunty Uju stopped, her eyes bulging and enraged. "Is it me you are talking to like that? Am I your agemate?"

Aunty Uju charged at her. Ifemelu had not expected Aunty Uju to hit her, yet when the slap landed on the side of her face, making a sound that seemed to her to come from far away, finger-shaped welts rising on her cheek, she was not surprised. They stared at each other.

Aunty Uju opened her mouth as though to say something and then she closed it and turned and walked upstairs, both of them aware that something between them was now different. Aunty Uju did not come downstairs until evening, when Adesuwa and Uche came to visit. She called them "my friends in quotes". "I'm going to the salon with my friends in quotes," she would say, a wan laughter in her eyes. She knew they were her friends only because she was The General's mistress. But they amused her. They visited her insistently, comparing notes on shopping and travel, asking her to go to parties with them. It was strange what she knew and did not know about them, she once told Ifemelu. She knew that Adesuwa owned land in Abuja, given to her when she dated the Head of State, and that a famously wealthy Hausa man had bought Uche's boutique in Surulere, but she did not know how many siblings either of them had or where their parents lived or whether they had gone to university.

Chikodili let them in. They wore embroidered caftans and spicy perfume, their Chinese weaves hanging down to their backs, their conversation lined with a hard-edged worldliness, their laughter short and scornful. *I told him he must buy it in my name o. Ah, I knew he would not bring the money unless I said somebody was sick. No now, he doesn't know I opened the account.* They were going to a Sallah party in Victoria Island and had come to take Aunty Uju.

"I don't feel like going," Aunty Uju told them, while Chikodili served orange juice, a carton on a tray, two glasses placed beside it.

"Ahn-ahn. Why now?" Uche asked.

"Serious big men are coming," Adesuwa said. "You never know if you will meet somebody."

"I don't want to meet anybody," Aunty Uju said, and there was quiet, as though each of them had to catch their breath, Aunty Uju's words a gale that tore through their assumptions. She was supposed to want to meet men, to keep her eyes open; she was supposed to see The General as an option that could be bettered. Finally, one of them, Adesuwa or Uche, said, "This your orange juice is the cheap brand o! You don't buy Just Juice any more?" A lukewarm joke, but they laughed to ease the moment away.

After they left, Aunty Uju came over to the dining table, where Ifemelu sat reading.

"Ifem, I don't know what got into me. *Ndo.*" She held Ifemelu's wrist, then ran her hand, almost meditatively, over the embossed title of Ifemelu's Sidney Sheldon novel. "I must be mad. He has a beer belly and Dracula teeth and a wife and children and he's old."

For the first time, Ifemelu felt older than Aunty Uju, wiser and stronger than Aunty Uju, and she wished that she could wrest Aunty Uju away, shake her into a clear-eyed self, who would not lay her hopes on The General, slaving and shaving for him, always eager to fade his flaws. It was not as it should be. Ifemelu felt a small gratification to hear, later, Aunty Uju shouting on the phone. "Nonsense! You knew you were going to Abuja from the beginning so why let me waste my time preparing for you!"

The cake a driver delivered the next morning, with "I'm sorry my love" written on it in blue frosting, had a bitter aftertaste but Aunty Uju kept it in the freezer for months.

AUNTY UJU'S PREGNANCY came like a sudden sound in a still night. She arrived at the flat wearing a sequined bou-bou that caught the light, glistening like a flowing celestial presence, and said that she wanted to tell Ifemelu's parents about it before they heard the gossip. "*Adi m ime*," she said simply.

Ifemelu's mother burst into tears, loud dramatic cries, looking around, as though she could see, lying around her, the splintered pieces of her own story. "My God, why have you forsaken me?"

"I did not plan this, it happened," Aunty Uju said. "I fell pregnant for Olujimi in university. I had an abortion and I am not doing it again." The word "abortion", blunt as it was, scarred the room, because they all knew that what Ifemelu's mother did not say was that surely there were ways to take care of this. Ifemelu's father put his book down and picked it up again. He cleared his throat. He soothed his wife.

"Well, I cannot ask about the man's intentions," he said finally to Aunty Uju. "So I should ask what your own intentions are."

"I will have the baby."

He waited to hear more, but Aunty Uju said nothing else, and so he sat back, assailed. "You are an adult. This is not what I hoped for you, Obianuju, but you are an adult."

Aunty Uju went over and sat on the arm of his sofa. She spoke in a low, pacifying voice, stranger for being formal, but saved from falseness by the soberness of her face. "Brother, this is not what I hoped for myself either, but it has happened. I am sorry to disappoint you, after everything you have done for me, and I beg you to forgive me. But I will make the best of this situation. The General is a responsible man. He will take care of his child."

Ifemelu's father shrugged wordlessly. Aunty Uju put an arm around him, as though it were he who needed comforting.

LATER, Ifemelu would think of the pregnancy as symbolic. It marked the beginning of the end and made everything else seem rapid, the months rushing past, time hurtling forward. There was Aunty Uju, dimpled with exuberance, her face aglow, her mind busy with plans as her belly curved outwards. Every few days, she came up with a new girl's name for the baby. "Oga is happy," she said. "He is happy to know that he can still score a goal at his age, old man like him!" The General came more often, even on some weekends, bringing her hot water bottles, herbal pills, things he had heard were good for pregnancy.

He told her, "Of course you will deliver abroad," and asked which she preferred, America or England. He wanted England, so that he could travel with her; the Americans had barred entry to high-ranking members of the military government. But Aunty Uju chose America, because her baby could still have automatic citizenship there. The plans were made, a hospital picked, a furnished condo rented in Atlanta. "What is a condo, anyway?" Ifemelu asked. And Aunty Uju shrugged and said, "Who knows what Americans mean? You should ask Obinze, he will know. At least it is a place to live. And Oga has people there who will help me." Aunty Uju was dampened only when her driver told her that The General's wife had heard about the pregnancy and was furious; there had, apparently, been a tense family meeting with his relatives and hers. The General hardly spoke about his wife but Aunty Uju knew enough: a lawyer who had given up working to raise their four children in Abuja, a woman who looked portly and pleasant in newspaper photographs. "I wonder what she is thinking," Aunty Uju said sadly, musingly. While she was in America, The General had one of the bedrooms repainted a brilliant white. He bought a cot, its legs like delicate candles. He bought stuffed toys, and too many teddy bears. Inyang propped them in the cot, lined some up on a shelf and, perhaps because she thought nobody would notice, she took one teddy bear to her room in the back. Aunty Uju had a boy. She sounded high and elated over the phone. "Ifem, he has so much hair! Can you imagine? What a waste!"

She called him Dike, after her father, and gave him her surname, which left Ifemelu's mother agitated and sour.

"The baby should have his father's name, or is the man planning to deny his child?" Ifemelu's mother asked, as they sat in their living room, still digesting the news of the birth.

"Aunty Uju said it was just easier to give him her name," Ifemelu said. "And is he behaving like a man that will deny his child? Aunty told me he's even talking about coming to pay her bride price."

"God forbid," Ifemelu's mother said, almost spitting the words out, and Ifemelu thought of all those fervent prayers for Aunty Uju's mentor. Her mother, when Aunty Uju came back, stayed in Dolphin Estate for a while, bathing and feeding the gurgling, smooth-skinned baby, but she faced The General with a cold officiousness. She answered him in monosyllables, as though he had betrayed her by breaking the rules of her pretence. A relationship with Aunty Uju was acceptable, but such flagrant proof of the relationship was not. The house smelled of baby powder. Aunty Uju was happy. The General held Dike often, suggesting that perhaps he needed to be fed again or that a doctor needed to see the rash on his neck.

FOR DIKE'S FIRST BIRTHDAY PARTY, The General brought a live band. They set up in the front garden, near the generator house, and stayed until the last guests left, all of them slow and sated, taking food wrapped in foil. Aunty Uju's friends came, and The General's friends came, too, their expressions determined, as though to say that no matter the circumstances, their friend's child was their friend's child. Dike, newly walking, tottered around in a suit and red bow tie, while Aunty Uju followed him, trying to get him to be still for a few moments with the photographer. Finally, tired, he began to cry, yanking at his bow tie, and The General picked him up and carried him around. It was the image of The General that would endure in Ifemelu's mind, Dike's arms around his neck, his face lit up, his front teeth jutting out as he smiled, saying, "He looks like me o, but thank God he took his mother's teeth."

The General died the next week, in a military plane crash. "On the same day, the very same day, that the photographer brought the pictures from Dike's birthday," Aunty Uju would often say, in telling the story, as though this held some particular significance.

It was a Saturday afternoon, Obinze and Ifemelu were in the TV room, Inyang was upstairs with Dike, Aunty Uju was in the kitchen with Chikodili when the phone rang. Ifemelu picked it up. The voice on the other end, The General's ADC, crackled through a bad connection, but was still clear enough to give her details: the crash happened a few miles outside Jos, the bodies were charred, there were already rumours that the Head of State had engineered it to get rid of officers who he feared were planning a coup. Ifemelu held the phone too tightly, stunned. Obinze went with her to the kitchen, and stood by Aunty Uju as Ifemelu repeated the ADC's words.

"You are lying," Aunty Uju said. "It is a lie."

She marched towards the phone, as though to challenge it, too, and then she slid to the floor, a boneless, bereft sliding, and began to weep. Ifemelu held her, cradled her, all of them unsure of what to do, and the silence in between her sobs seemed too silent. Inyang brought Dike downstairs.

"Mama?" Dike said, looking puzzled.

"Take Dike upstairs," Obinze told Inyang.

There was banging on the gate. Two men and three women, relatives of The General, had bullied Adamu to open the gate, and now stood at the front door, shouting. "Uju! Pack your things and get out now! Give us the car keys!" One of the women was skeletal, agitated and red-eyed, and as she shouted—"Common harlot! God forbid that you will touch our brother's property! Prostitute! You will never live in peace in this Lagos!"—she pulled her headscarf from her head and tied it tightly around her waist, in preparation for a fight. At first, Aunty Uju said nothing, staring at them, standing still at the door. Then she asked them to leave in a voice hoarse from tears, but the relatives' shouting intensified, and so Aunty Uju turned to go back indoors. "Okay, don't go," she said. "Just stay there. Stay there while I go and call my boys from the army barracks."

Only then did they leave, telling her, "We are coming back with our own boys." Only then did Aunty Uju begin to sob again. "I have nothing. Everything is in his name. Where will I take my son to now?"

She picked up the phone from its cradle and then stared at it, uncertain whom to call.

"Call Uche and Adesuwa," Ifemelu said. *They* would know what to do.

Aunty Uju did, pressing the speaker button, and then leaned against the wall.

"You have to leave immediately. Make sure you clear the house, take everything," Uche said. "Do it fast-fast before his people come back. Arrange a tow van and take the generator. Make sure you take the generator."

"I don't know where to find a van," Aunty Uju mumbled, with a helplessness foreign to her.

"We're going to arrange one for you, fast-fast. You have to take that generator. That is what will pay for your life until you gather yourself. You have to go somewhere for a while, so that they don't give you trouble. Go to London or America. Do you have American visa?"

"Yes."

Ifemelu would remember the final moments in a blur, Adamu saying there was a journalist from *City People* at the gate, Ifemelu and Chikodili stuffing clothes in suitcases, Obinze carrying things out to the van, Dike stumbling around and chortling. The rooms upstairs had grown unbearably hot; the air conditioners had suddenly stopped working, as though they had decided, in unison, to pay tribute to the end.

CHAPTER 7

Obinze wanted to go to the University of Ibadan because of a poem.

He read the poem to her, J. P. Clark's "Ibadan", and he lingered on the words "running splash of rust and gold".

"Are you serious?" she asked him. "Because of this poem?"

"It's so beautiful."

Ifemelu shook her head, in mocking, exaggerated incredulity. But she, too, wanted to go to Ibadan, because Aunty Uju had gone there. They filled out their JAMB forms together, sitting at the dining table while his mother hovered around, saying, "Are you using the right pencil? Cross-check everything. I have heard of the most unlikely mistakes that you will not believe."

Obinze said, "Mummy, we are more likely to fill it out without mistakes if you stop talking."

"At least you should make Nsukka your second choice," his mother said. But Obinze did not want to go to Nsukka, he wanted to escape the life he had always had, and Nsukka, to Ifemelu, seemed remote and dusty. And so they both agreed to make the University of Lagos their second choice.

The next day, Obinze's mother collapsed in the library. A student found her spread on the floor like a rag, a small bump on her head, and Obinze told Ifemelu, "Thank God we haven't submitted our JAMB forms."

"What do you mean?"

"My mum is returning to Nsukka at the end of this session. I have to be near her. The doctor said this thing will keep happening." He paused. "We can see each other during long weekends. I will come to Ibadan and you come to Nsukka."

"You're a joker," she told him. "*Biko*, I'm changing to Nsukka as well."

The change pleased her father. It was heartening, he said, that she would go to university in Igboland, since she had lived her whole life in the west. Her mother was downcast. Ibadan was only an hour away, but Nsukka meant a day's journey on the bus.

"It's not a day, Mummy, just seven hours," Ifemelu said.

"And what is the difference between that and a day?" her mother asked.

Ifemelu was looking forward to being away from home, to the independence of owning her own time, and she felt comforted that Ranyinudo and Tochi were going to Nsukka too. So was Emenike, who asked Obinze if they could be room-mates, in the boys' quarters of Obinze's house. Obinze said yes. Ifemelu wished he had not. "There's just something about Emenike," she said. "But anyway, as long as he goes away when we are busy with ceiling."

Later, Obinze would ask, half seriously, if Ifemelu thought his mother's fainting had been deliberate, a plot to keep him close. For a long time, he spoke wistfully of Ibadan, until he visited the campus, for a table tennis tournament, and returned to tell her, sheepishly, "Ibadan reminded me of Nsukka."

TO GO TO NSUKKA was to finally see Obinze's home, a bungalow resting in a compound filled with flowers. Ifemelu imagined him growing up, riding his bicycle down the sloping street, returning home from primary school with his bag and water bottle. Still, Nsukka disoriented her. She thought it too slow, the dust too red, the people too satisfied with the smallness of their lives. But she would come to love it, a hesitant love at first. From the window of her hostel room, where four beds were squashed into a space for two, she could look out to the entrance of Bello Hall. Tall gmelina trees swayed in the wind, and underneath them were hawkers, guarding trays of bananas and groundnuts, and okadas all parked close to each other, the motorcyclists talking and laughing, but each of them alert to customers. She put up bright blue wallpaper in her corner and because she had heard stories of room-mate squabbles—one final-year student, it was said, had poured kerosene into the drawer of the first-year student for being what was called "saucy"—she felt fortunate about her room-mates. They were easy-going and soon she was sharing with them and borrowing from them the things that easily ran out, toothpaste and powdered milk and Indomie noodles and hair pomade. Most mornings, she woke up to the rumbling murmur of voices in the corridor, the Catholic students saying the rosary, and she would hurry to the bathroom, to collect water in her bucket before the tap stopped, to squat over the toilet before it became unbearably full. Sometimes, when she was too late, and the toilets already swirled with maggots, she would go to Obinze's house, even if he was not there, and once the house help Augustina opened the front door, she would say, "Tina-Tina, how now? I came to use the toilet."

She often ate lunch in Obinze's house, or they would go to town, to Onyekaozulu, and sit on wooden benches in the dimness of the restaurant, eating, on enamel plates, the tenderest of meats and the tastiest of stews. She spent some nights in Obinze's boys' quarters, lounging on his mattress on the floor, listening to music. Sometimes she would dance in her underwear, wiggling her hips, while he teased her about having a small bottom: "I was going to say shake it, but there's nothing to shake."

University was bigger and baggier, there was room to hide, so much room; she did not feel as though she did not belong because there were many options for belonging. Obinze teased her about how popular she already was, her room busy during the first-year rush, final-year boys dropping by, eager to try their luck, even though a large photo of Obinze hung above her pillow. The boys amused her. They came and sat on her bed and solemnly offered to "show her around campus", and she imagined them saying the same words in the same tone to the first-year girl in the next room. One of them, though, was different. His name was Odein. He came to her room, not as part of the first-year rush but to talk to her room-mates about the students' union, and after that, he would come by to visit her, to say hello, sometimes bringing a pack of suya, hot and spicy, wrapped in oil-stained newspaper. His activism surprised Ifemelu—he seemed a little too urbane, a little too cool, to be in the students' union government—but also impressed her. He had thick, perfectly shaped lips, the lower the same size as the upper, lips that were both thoughtful and sensual, and as he spoke—"If the students are not united, nobody will listen to us"—Ifemelu imagined kissing him, in a way that she imagined doing something she knew she never would. It was because of him that she joined the demonstration, and convinced Obinze to join, too. They chanted "No Light! No Water!" and "VC is a Goat!" and found themselves carried along with the roaring crowd that settled, finally, in front of the vice chancellor's house. Bottles were broken, a car was set on fire, and then the vice chancellor came out, diminutive, encased between security men, and spoke in pastel tones.

Later, Obinze's mother said, "I understand the students' grievances, but we are not the enemy. The military is the enemy. They have not paid our salary in months. How can we teach if we cannot eat?" And, still later, the news spread around campus of a strike by lecturers, and students gathered in the hostel foyer, bristling with the known and the unknown. It was true, the hall rep confirmed the news, and they all sighed, contemplating this sudden unwanted break, and returned to their rooms to pack; the hostel would be closed the next day. Ifemelu heard a girl close by say, "I don't have ten kobo for transport to go home."

THE STRIKE LASTED too long. The weeks crawled past. Ifemelu was restless, antsy; every day she listened to the news, hoping to hear that the strike was over. Obinze called her at Ranyinudo's house; she would arrive minutes before he was due to call and sit by the grey rotary phone, waiting for it to ring. She felt cut away from him, each of them living and breathing in separate spheres, he bored and spiritless in Nsukka, she bored and spiritless in Lagos, and everything curdled in lethargy. Life had become a turgid and suspended film. Her mother asked if she wanted to join the sewing class at church, to keep her occupied, and her father said that this, the unending university strike, was why young people became armed robbers. The strike was nationwide, and all her friends were home, even Kayode was home, back on holiday from his

American university. She visited friends and went to parties, wishing Obinze lived in Lagos. Sometimes Odein, who had a car, would pick her up and take her where she needed to go. "That your boyfriend is lucky," he told her, and she laughed, flirting with him. She still imagined kissing him, sloe-eyed and thick-lipped Odein.

One weekend, Obinze visited and stayed with Kayode.

"What is going on with this Odein?" Obinze asked her.

"What?"

"Kayode said he took you home after Osahon's party. You didn't tell me."

"I forgot."

"You forgot."

"I told you he picked me up the other day, didn't I?"

"Ifem, what is going on?"

She sighed. "Ceiling, it's nothing. I'm just curious about him. Nothing is ever going to happen. But I am curious. You get curious about other girls, don't you?"

He was looking at her, his eyes fearful. "No," he said coldly. "I don't."

"Be honest."

"I am being honest. The problem is you think everyone is like you. You think you're the norm but you're not."

"What do you mean?"

"Nothing. Just forget it."

He did not want to talk about it any further, but the air between them was marred, and remained disturbed for days, even after he went back home, so that when the strike ended ("The lecturers have called it off! Praise God!" Chetachi shouted from their flat one morning) and Ifemelu returned to Nsukka, they were tentative with each other for the first few days, their conversations on tiptoe, their hugs abridged.

It surprised Ifemelu, how much she had missed Nsukka itself, the routines of unhurried pace, friends gathered in her room until past midnight, the inconsequential gossip told and retold, the stairs climbed slowly up and down as though in a gradual awakening, and each morning whitened by the harmattan. In Lagos, the harmattan was a mere veil of haze, but in Nsukka, it was a raging, mercurial presence; the mornings were crisp, the afternoons ashen with heat and the nights unknown. Dust whirls would start in the far distance, very pretty to look at as long as they were far away, and swirl until they coated everything brown. Even eyelashes. Everywhere, moisture would be greedily sucked up; the wood laminate on tables would peel off and curl, pages of exercise books would crackle, clothes would dry minutes after being hung out, lips would crack and bleed, and Robb and Mentholatum kept within reach, in pockets and handbags. Skin would be shined with Vaseline, while the forgotten bits—between the fingers or at the elbows—turned a dull ash. The tree branches would be stark and, with their leaves fallen, wear a kind of proud desolation. The church bazaars would leave the air redolent, smoky from mass cooking. Some nights, the heat lay thick like a towel. Other nights, a sharp cold wind would descend, and Ifemelu would abandon her hostel room and, snuggled next to Obinze on his mattress, listen to the whistling pines howling outside, in a world suddenly fragile and breakable.

OBINZE'S MUSCLES WERE ACHING. He lay on his belly, and Ifemelu straddled him, massaging his back and neck and thighs with her fingers, her knuckles, her elbows. He was painfully taut. She stood on him, placed one foot gingerly on the back of a thigh, and then the other. "Does it feel okay?"

"Yes." He groaned in pleasure-pain. She pressed down slowly, his skin warm under the soles of her feet, his tense muscles unknotting. She steadied herself with a hand on the wall, and dug her heels deeper, moving inch by inch while he grunted, "Ah! Ifem, yes, just there. Ah!"

"You should stretch after playing ball, mister man," she said, and then she was lying on his back, tickling his underarms and kissing his neck.

"I have a suggestion for a better kind of massage," he said. When he undressed her, he did not stop, as usual, at her underwear. He pulled it down and she raised her legs to aid him.

"Ceiling," she said, half-certain. She did not want him to stop, but she had imagined this differently, assumed they would make a carefully planned ceremony of it.

"I'll come out," he said.

"You know it doesn't always work."

"If it doesn't work, then we'll welcome Junior."

"Stop it."

He looked up. "But, Ifem, we're going to get married anyway."

"Look at you. I might meet a rich handsome man and leave you."

"Impossible. We'll go to America when we graduate and raise our fine children."

"You'll say anything now because your brain is between your legs."

"But my brain is always there!"

They were both laughing, and then the laughter stilled, gave way to a new, strange graveness, a slippery joining. It felt, to Ifemelu, like a weak copy, a floundering imitation of what she had imagined it would be. After he pulled away, jerking and gasping and holding himself, a discomfort nagged at her. She had been tense through it all, unable to relax. She had imagined his mother watching them; the image had forced itself onto her mind, and it had, even more oddly, been a double image, of his mother and Onyeka Onwenu, both watching them with unblinking eyes. She knew she could not possibly tell Obinze's mother what had happened, even though she had promised to, and had believed then that she would. But now she could not see how. What would she say? What words would she use? Would Obinze's mother expect details? She and Obinze should have planned it better; that way, she would know how to tell his mother. The unplannedness of it all had left her a little shaken, and also a little disappointed. It seemed somehow as though it had not been worth it after all.

When, a week or so later, she woke up in pain, a sharp stinging on her side and a great, sickening nausea pervading her body, she panicked. Then she vomited and her panic grew.

"It's happened," she told Obinze. "I'm pregnant." They had met, as usual, in front of the Ekpo refectory after their morning lecture. Students milled around. A group of boys were smoking and laughing close by and for a moment, their laughter seemed directed at her.

Obinze's brows wrinkled. He did not seem to understand what she was saying. "But, Ifem, it can't be. It's too early. Besides, I came out."

"I told you it doesn't work!" she said. He suddenly seemed young, a confused small boy looking helplessly at her. Her panic grew. On an impulse, she hailed a passing okada and jumped on the back and told the motorcyclist that she was going to town.

"Ifem, what are you doing?" Obinze asked. "Where are you going?"

"To call Aunty Uju," she said.

Obinze got on the next okada and was soon speeding behind her, past the university gates and to the NITEL office, where Ifemelu gave the man behind the peeling counter a piece of paper with Aunty Uju's American number. On the phone, she spoke in code, making it up as she went along, because of the people standing there, some waiting to make their own calls, others merely loitering, but all listening, with unabashed and open interest, to the conversations of others.

"Aunty, I think what happened to you before Dike came has happened to me," Ifemelu said. "We ate the food a week ago."

"Just last week? How many times?"

"Once."

"Ifem, calm down. I don't think you're pregnant. But you need to do a test. Don't go to the campus medical centre. Go to town, where nobody will know you. But calm down first. It will be okay, *inugo*?"

Later, Ifemelu sat on a rickety chair in the waiting room of the lab, stony and silent, ignoring Obinze. She was angry with him. It was unfair, she knew, but she was angry with him. As she went into the dirty toilet with a small container the lab girl had given her, he had asked, already getting up, "Should I come with you?" and she snapped, "Come with me for what?" And she wanted to slap the lab girl. A yellow-faced beanpole of a girl who sneered and shook her head when Ifemelu first said, "Pregnancy test," as though she could not believe she was encountering one more case of immorality. Now, she was watching them, smirking and humming insouciantly.

"I have the result," she said after a while, holding the unsealed paper, her expression disappointed because it was negative. Ifemelu was too stunned, at first, to be relieved, and then she needed to urinate again.

"People should respect themselves and live like Christians to avoid trouble," the lab girl said as they left.

That evening, Ifemelu vomited again. She was in Obinze's room, lying down and reading, still frosty towards him, when a rush of salty saliva filled her mouth and she leaped up and ran to the toilet.

"It must be something I ate," she said. "That yam pottage I bought from Mama Owerre."

Obinze went inside the main house and came back to say his mother was taking her to the doctor's. It was late evening, his mother did not like the young doctor who was on call at the medical centre in the evenings, and so she drove to Dr Achufusi's house. As they passed the primary school with its trimmed hedges of whistling pine, Ifemelu suddenly imagined that she was indeed pregnant, and the girl had used expired test chemicals in that dingy lab. She blurted out, "We had sex, Aunty. Once." She felt Obinze tense. His mother looked at her in the rear-view mirror. "Let us see the doctor first," she said. Dr Achufusi, an avuncular and pleasant man, pressed at Ifemelu's side and announced, "It's your appendix, very inflamed. We should get it out quickly." He turned to Obinze's mother. "I can schedule her for tomorrow afternoon."

"Thank you so much, Doctor," Obinze's mother said.

In the car, Ifemelu said, "I've never had surgery, Aunty."

"It's nothing," Obinze's mother said briskly. "Our doctors here are very good. Get in touch with your parents and tell them not to worry. We will take care of you. After they discharge you, you can stay in the house until you feel strong."

Ifemelu called her mother's colleague, Aunty Bunmi, and gave her a message, as well as Obinze's home phone number, to pass on to her mother. That evening, her mother called; she sounded short of breath.

"God is in control, my precious," her mother said. "Thank God for this your friend. God will bless her and her mother."

"It's him. A boy."

"Oh." Her mother paused. "Please thank them. God bless them. We will take the first bus tomorrow morning to Nsukka."

Ifemelu remembered a nurse cheerfully shaving her pubic hair, the rough scratch of the razor blade, the smell of antiseptic. Then there was a blankness, an erasure of her mind, and when she emerged from it, groggy and still swaying on the edge of memory, she heard her parents talking to Obinze's mother. Her mother was holding her hand. Later, Obinze's mother would ask them to stay in her house, there was no point wasting money on a hotel. "Ifemelu is like a daughter to me," she said.

Before they returned to Lagos, her father said, with that intimidated awe he had in the face of the well-educated, "She has BA London First Class." And her mother said, "Very respectful boy, that Obinze. He has good home training. And their hometown is not far from us."

OBINZE'S MOTHER WAITED a few days, perhaps for Ifemelu to regain her strength, before she called them and asked them to sit down and turn the TV off.

"Obinze and Ifemelu, people make mistakes, but some mistakes can be avoided."

Obinze remained silent. Ifemelu said, "Yes, Aunty."

"You must always use a condom. If you want to be irresponsible, then wait until you are no longer in my care." Her tone had hardened, become censorious. "If you make the choice to be sexually active, then you must make the choice to protect yourself. Obinze, you should take your pocket money and buy condoms. Ifemelu, you too. It is not my concern if you are embarrassed. You should go into the pharmacy and buy them. You should never ever let the boy be in charge of your own protection. If he does not want to use it, then he does not care enough about you and you should not be there. Obinze, you may not be the person who will get pregnant but if it happens it will change your entire life and you cannot undo it. And please, both of you, keep it between both of you. Diseases are everywhere. AIDS is real."

They were silent.

"Did you hear me?" Obinze's mother asked.

"Yes, Aunty," Ifemelu said.

"Obinze?" his mother said.

"Mummy, I've heard you," Obinze said, adding, sharply, "I'm not a small boy!" Then he got up and stalked out of the room.

CHAPTER 8

Strikes now were common. In the newspapers, university lecturers listed their complaints, the agreements that were trampled in the dust by government men whose own children were schooling abroad. Campuses were emptied, classrooms drained of life. Students hoped for short strikes, because they could not hope to have no strike at all. Everyone was talking about leaving. Even Emenike had left for England. Nobody knew how he managed to get a visa. "So he didn't even tell you?" Ifemelu asked Obinze, and Obinze said, "You know how Emenike is." Ranyinudo, who had a cousin in America, applied for a visa but was rejected at the embassy by a black American who she said had a cold and was more interested in blowing his nose than in looking at her documents. Sister Ibinabo started the Student Visa Miracle Vigil on Fridays, a gathering of young people, each one holding out an envelope with a visa application form, on which Sister Ibinabo laid a hand of blessing. One girl, already in her final year at the University of Ife, got an American visa the first time she tried, and gave a tearful, excited testimony in church. "Even if I have to start from the beginning in America, at least I know when I will graduate," she said.

One day, Aunty Uju called. She no longer called frequently; before, she would call Ranyinudo's house if Ifemelu was in Lagos, or Obinze's house if Ifemelu was at school. But her calls had dried up. She was working three jobs, not yet qualified to practise medicine in America. She talked about the exams she had to take, various steps meaning various things that Ifemelu did not understand. Whenever Ifemelu's mother suggested asking Aunty Uju to send them something from America—multivitamins, shoes—Ifemelu's father would say no, they had to let Uju find her feet first, and her mother would say, a hint of slyness in her smile, that four years was long enough to find one's feet.

"Ifem, *kedu*?" Aunty Uju asked. "I thought you would be in Nsukka. I just called Obinze's house."

"We're on strike."

"Ahn-ahn! The strike hasn't ended?"

"No, that last one ended, we went back to school and then they started another one."

"What is this kind of nonsense?" Aunty Uju said. "Honestly, you should come and study here, I am sure you can easily get a scholarship. And you can help me take care of Dike. I'm telling you, the small money I make is all going to his babysitter. And by God's grace, by the time you come, I will have passed all my exams and started my residency." Aunty Uju sounded enthusiastic but vague; until she voiced it, she had not given the idea much thought.

Ifemelu might have left it at that, a formless idea floated but allowed to sink again, if not for Obinze. "You should do it, Ifem," he said. "You have nothing to lose. Take the SATs and try for a scholarship. Ginika can help you apply to schools. Aunty Uju is there, so at least you have a foundation to start with. I wish I could do the same but I can't just get up and go. It's better for me to finish my first degree and then come to America for graduate school. International students can get funding and financial aid for graduate school."

Ifemelu did not quite grasp what it all meant, but it sounded correct because it came from him, the America expert, who so easily said "graduate school" instead of "postgraduate school". And so she began to dream. She saw herself in a house from *The Cosby Show*, in a school with students holding notebooks miraculously free of wear and crease. She took the SATs at a Lagos centre, packed with thousands of people, all bristling with their own American ambitions. Ginika, who had just graduated from college, applied to schools on her behalf, calling to say, "I just wanted you to know I'm focusing on the Philadelphia area because I went here," as though Ifemelu knew where Philadelphia was. To her, America was America.

The strike ended. Ifemelu returned to Nsukka, eased back into campus life, and from time to time, she dreamed of America. When Aunty Uju called to say that there were acceptance letters and a scholarship offer, she stopped dreaming. She was too afraid to hope, now that it seemed possible.

"Make small-small braids that will last long, it's very expensive to make hair here," Aunty Uju told her.

"Aunty, let me get the visa first!" Ifemelu said.

She applied for a visa, convinced that a rude American would reject her application, it was what happened so often, after all, but the grey-haired woman wearing a St Vincent de Paul pin on her lapel smiled at her and said, "Pick up your visa in two days. Good luck with your studies."

On the afternoon that she picked up her passport, the pale-toned visa on the second page, she organized that triumphant ritual that signalled the start of a new life overseas: the division of personal property among friends. Ranyinudo, Priye and Tochi were in her bedroom, drinking Coke, her clothes in a pile on the bed, and the first thing they all reached for was her orange dress, her favourite dress, a gift from Aunty Uju; the A-line flair and neck-to-hem zipper had always made her feel both glamorous and dangerous. It makes things easy for me, Obinze would say, before he slowly began to unzip it. She wanted to keep the dress, but Ranyinudo said, "Ifem, you know you'll have any kind of dress you want in America and next time we see you, you will be a serious Americanah."

Her mother said Jesus told her in a dream that Ifemelu would prosper in America. Her father pressed a slender envelope into her hand, saying, "I wish I had more," and she realized, with sadness, that he must have borrowed it. In the face of the enthusiasm of others, she suddenly felt flaccid and afraid.

"Maybe I should stay and finish here," she told Obinze.

"Ifem, no, you should go. Besides, you don't even like geology. You can study something else in America."

"But the scholarship is partial. Where will I find the money to pay the balance? I can't work with a student visa."

"You can do work-study at school. You'll find a way. Seventy-five per cent off your tuition is a big deal."

She nodded, riding the wave of his faith. She visited his mother to say goodbye.

"Nigeria is chasing away its best resources," Obinze's mother said resignedly, hugging her.

"Aunty, I will miss you. Thank you so much for everything."

"Stay well, my dear, and do well. Write to us. Make sure you keep in touch."

Ifemelu nodded, tearful. As she left, already parting the curtain at the front door, Obinze's mother said, "And make sure you and Obinze have a plan. Have a plan." Her words, so unexpected and so right, lifted Ifemelu's spirits. Their plan became this: he would come to America the minute he graduated. He would find a way to get a visa. Perhaps, by then, she would be able to help with his visa.

In the following years, even after she was no longer in touch with him, she would sometimes remember his mother's words—*make sure you and Obinze have a plan*—and feel comforted.

CHAPTER 9

Mariama returned carrying oil-stained brown paper bags from the Chinese restaurant, trailing the smells of grease and spice into the stuffy salon.

"The film finished?" She glanced at the blank TV screen, and then flipped through the pile of DVDs to select another.

"Excuse me, please, to eat," Aisha said to Ifemelu. She perched on a chair at the back and ate fried chicken wings with her fingers, her eyes on the TV screen. The new film began with trailers, jaggedly cut scenes interspersed with flashes of light. Each ended with a male Nigerian voice, theatrical and loud, saying "Grab your copy now!" Mariama ate standing up. She said something to Halima.

"I finish first and eat," Halima replied in English.

"You can go ahead and eat if you want to," Halima's customer said, a young woman with a high voice and a pleasant manner.

"No, I finish. Just small more," Halima said. Her customer's head had only a tuft of hair left in front, sticking up like animal fur, while the rest was done in neat micro braids that fell to her neck.

"I have a hour before I have to go pick up my daughters," the customer said.

"How many you have?" Halima asked.

"Two," the customer said. She looked about seventeen. "Two beautiful girls."

The new film had started. The grinning face of a middle-aged actress filled the screen.

"Oh-oh, yes! I like her!" Halima said. "Patience! She don't take any nonsense!"

"You know her?" Mariama asked Ifemelu, pointing at the TV screen.

"No," Ifemelu said. Why did they insist on asking if she knew Nollywood actors? The entire room smelled too strongly of food. It made the stuffy air rank with oiliness, and yet it also made her slightly hungry. She ate some of her carrots. Halima's customer tilted her head this way and that in front of the mirror and said, "Thank you so much, it's gorgeous!"

After she left, Mariama said, "Very small girl and already she has two children."

"Oh oh oh, these people," Halima said. "When a girl is thirteen already she knows all the positions. Never in Afrique!"

"Never!" Mariama agreed.

They looked at Ifemelu for her agreement, her approval. They expected it, in this shared space of their Africanness, but Ifemelu said nothing and turned a page of her novel. They would, she was sure, talk about her after she left. That Nigerian girl, she feels very important because of Princeton. Look at her food bar, she does not eat real food any more. They would laugh with derision, but only a mild derision, because she was still their African sister, even if she had briefly lost her way. A new smell of oiliness flooded the room when Halima opened her plastic container of food. She was eating and talking to the television screen. "Oh, stupid man! She will take your money!"

Ifemelu brushed away at some sticky hair on her neck. The room was seething with heat. "Can we leave the door open?" she asked.

Mariama opened the door, propped it with a chair. "This heat is really bad."

EACH HEAT WAVE reminded Ifemelu of her first, the summer she arrived. It was summer in America, she knew this, but all her life she had thought of "overseas" as a cold place of wool coats and snow, and because America was "overseas", and her illusions so strong they could not be fended off by reason, she bought the thickest sweater she could find in Tejuosho market for her trip. She wore it for the journey, zipping it all the way up in the humming interior of the plane and then unzipping it as she left the airport building with Aunty Uju. The sweltering heat alarmed her, as did Aunty Uju's old Toyota hatchback, with a patch of rust on its side and peeling fabric on the seats. She stared at buildings and cars and signboards, all of them matt, disappointingly matt; in the landscape of her imagination, the mundane things in America were covered in a high-shine gloss. She was startled, most of all, by the teenage boy in a baseball cap standing near a brick wall, face down, body leaning forward, hands between his legs. She turned to look again.

"See that boy!" she said. "I didn't know people do things like this in America."

"You didn't know people pee in America?" Aunty Uju asked, barely glancing at the boy before turning back to a traffic light.

"Ahn-ahn, Aunty! I mean that they do it outside. Like that."

"They don't. It's not like back home where everybody does it. He can get arrested for that, but this is not a good neighbourhood anyway," Aunty Uju said shortly. There was something different about her. Ifemelu had noticed it right away at the airport, her roughly braided hair, her ears bereft of earrings, her quick casual hug, as if it had been weeks rather than years since they had last seen each other.

"I'm supposed to be with my books now," Aunty Uju said, eyes focused on the road. "You know my exam is coming."

Ifemelu had not known that there was yet another exam; she had thought Aunty Uju was waiting for a result. But she said, "Yes, I know."

Their silence was full of stones. Ifemelu felt like apologizing, although she was not quite sure what she would be apologizing for. Perhaps Aunty Uju regretted her presence, now that she was here, in Aunty Uju's wheezing car.

Aunty Uju's cell phone rang. "Yes, this is Uju." She pronounced it *you-joo* instead of *oo-joo.*

"Is that how you pronounce your name now?" Ifemelu asked afterwards.

"It's what they call me."

Ifemelu swallowed the words "Well, that isn't your name." Instead she said in Igbo, "I did not know it would be so hot here."

"We have a heat wave, the first one this summer," Aunty Uju said, as though *heat wave* was something Ifemelu was supposed to understand. She had never felt a heat quite so *hot.* An enveloping, uncompassionate heat. Aunty Uju's door handle, when they arrived at her one-bedroom apartment, was warm to the touch. Dike sprang up from the carpeted floor of the living room, scattered with toy cars and action figures, and hugged her as though he remembered her. "Alma, this is my cousin!" he said to his babysitter, a pale-skinned, tired-faced woman with black hair held in a greasy ponytail. If Ifemelu had met Alma in Lagos, she would have thought of her as white, but she would learn that Alma was Hispanic, an American category that was, confusingly, both an ethnicity and a race, and she would remember Alma when, years later, she wrote a blog post titled "Understanding America for the Non-American Black: What Hispanic Means".

> Hispanic means the frequent companions of American blacks in poverty rankings, Hispanic means a slight step above American blacks in the American race ladder, Hispanic means the chocolate-skinned woman from Peru, Hispanic means the indigenous people of Mexico. Hispanic means the biracial-looking folks from the Dominican Republic. Hispanic means the paler folks from Puerto Rico. Hispanic also means the blond, blue-eyed guy from Argentina. All you need to be is Spanish-speaking but not from Spain and voilà, you're a race called Hispanic.

But that afternoon, she hardly noticed Alma, or the living room furnished only with a couch and a TV, or the bicycle lodged in a corner, because she was absorbed by Dike. The last time she saw him, on the day of Aunty Uju's hasty departure from Lagos, he had been a one-year-old, crying unendingly at the airport as though he understood the upheaval his life had just undergone, and now here he was, a first grader with a seamless American accent and a hyper-happiness about him; the kind of child who could never stay still and who never seemed sad.

"Why do you have a sweater? It's too hot for a sweater!" he said, chortling, still holding on to her in a drawn-out hug. She laughed. He was so small, so innocent, and yet there was a precociousness about him, but it was a sunny one; he did not nurse dark intentions about the adults in his world. That night, after he and Aunty Uju got into bed and Ifemelu settled on a blanket on the floor, he said, "How come she has to sleep on the floor, Mom? We can all fit in," as though he could sense how Ifemelu felt. There was nothing *wrong* with the arrangement—she had, after all, slept on mats when she visited her grandmother in the village—but this was America at last, glorious America at last, and she had not expected to bed on the floor.

"I'm fine, Dike," she said.

He got up and brought her his pillow. "Here. It's soft and comfy."

Aunty Uju said, "Dike, come and lie down. Let your aunty sleep."

Ifemelu could not sleep, her mind too alert to the newness of things, and she waited to hear Aunty Uju's snoring before she slipped out of the room and turned on the kitchen light. A fat cockroach was perched on the wall near the cabinets, moving slightly up and down as though breathing heavily. If she had been in their Lagos kitchen, she would have found a broom and killed it, but she left the American cockroach alone and went and stood by the living room window. Flatlands, Aunty Uju said this section of Brooklyn was called. The street below was poorly lit, bordered not by leafy trees but by closely parked cars, nothing like the pretty street on *The Cosby Show*. Ifemelu stood there for a long time, her body unsure of itself, overwhelmed by a sense of newness. But she felt, also, a frisson of expectation, an eagerness to discover America.

"I THINK it's better if you take care of Dike for the summer and save me babysitting money and then start looking for a job when you get to Philadelphia," Aunty Uju said the next morning. She had woken Ifemelu up, giving brisk instructions about Dike, saying she would go to the library to study after work. Her words tumbled out. Ifemelu wished she would slow down a little.

"You can't work with your student visa, and work-study is rubbish, it pays nothing, and you have to be able to cover your rent and the balance of your tuition. Me, you can see I am working three jobs and yet it's not easy. I talked to one of my friends, I don't know if you remember Ngozi Okonkwo? She's now an American citizen and she has gone back to Nigeria for a while, to start a business. I begged her and she agreed to let you work with her Social Security card."

"How? I'll use her name?" Ifemelu asked.

"Of course you'll use her name," Aunty Uju said, eyebrows raised, as though she had barely stopped herself from asking if Ifemelu was stupid. There was a small white blob of face cream on her hair, caught at the root of a braid, and Ifemelu was going to tell her to wipe it off but she changed her mind, saying nothing, and watched Aunty Uju hurry to the door. She felt singed by Aunty Uju's reproach. It was as if, between them, an old intimacy had quite suddenly lapsed. Aunty Uju's impatience, that new prickliness in her, made Ifemelu feel that there were things she should already know but, through some personal failing of hers, did not know. "There's corned beef so you can make sandwiches for lunch," Aunty Uju had said, as though those words were perfectly normal and did not require a humorous preamble about how Americans ate bread for lunch. But Dike didn't want a sandwich. After he had shown her all his toys, and they had watched some episodes of *Tom and Jerry*, with him laughing, thrilled, because she had watched them all before in Nigeria and so told him what would happen before it did, he opened the refrigerator and pointed at what he wanted her to make him. "Hot dogs." Ifemelu examined the curiously long sausages and then began to open cupboards to look for some oil.

"Mommy says I have to call you Aunty Ifem. But you're not my aunt. You're my cousin."

"So call me Cousin."

"Okay, Coz," Dike said, and laughed. His laughter was so warm, so open. She had found the vegetable oil.

"You don't need oil," Dike said. "You just cook the hot dog in water."

"Water? How can a sausage be cooked in water?"

"It's a hot dog, not a sausage."

Of course it was a sausage, whether or not they called it the ludicrous name of "hot dog", and so she fried two in a little oil as she was used to doing with Satis sausages. Dike looked on in horror. She turned the stove off. He backed away and said "Ugh." They stood looking at each other, between them a plate with a bun and two shrivelled hot dogs. She knew then that she should have listened to him.

"Can I have a peanut butter and jelly sandwich instead?" Dike asked. She followed his instructions for the sandwich, cutting off the bread crusts, layering on the peanut butter first, stifling her laughter at how closely he watched her, as though she just might decide to fry the sandwich.

When, that evening, Ifemelu told Aunty Uju about the hot dog incident, Aunty Uju said with none of the amusement Ifemelu had expected, "They are not sausages, they are hot dogs."

"It's like saying that a bikini is not the same thing as underwear. Would a visitor from space know the difference?"

Aunty Uju shrugged; she was sitting at the dining table, a medical textbook open in front of her, eating a hamburger from a rumpled paper bag. Her skin dry, her eyes shadowed, her spirit bleached of colour. She seemed to be staring at, rather than reading, the book.

AT THE GROCERY STORE, Aunty Uju never bought what she needed; instead she bought what was on sale and made herself need it. She would take the colourful flyer at the entrance of Key Food, and go looking for the sale items, aisle after aisle, while Ifemelu wheeled the cart and Dike walked along.

"Mommy, I don't like that. Get the blue one," Dike said, as Aunty Uju put cartons of cereal in the cart.

"It's buy one, get one free," Aunty Uju said.

"It doesn't taste good."

"It tastes just like your regular cereal, Dike."

"No." Dike took a blue carton from the shelf and hurried ahead to the checkout counter.

"Hi, little guy!" The cashier was large and cheerful, her cheeks reddened and peeling from sunburn. "Helping Mommy out?"

"Dike, put it back," Aunty Uju said, with the nasal, sliding accent she put on when she spoke to white Americans, in the presence of white Americans, in the hearing of white Americans. *Pooh-reet-back.* And with the accent emerged a new persona, apologetic and self-abasing. She was overeager with the cashier. "Sorry, sorry," she said as she fumbled to get her debit card from her wallet. Because the cashier was watching, Aunty Uju let Dike keep the cereal but in the car she grabbed his left ear and twisted it, yanked it.

"I have told you, do not ever take anything in the grocery! Do you hear me? Or do you want me to slap you before you hear?"

Dike pressed his palm to his ear.

Aunty Uju turned to Ifemelu. "This is how children like to misbehave in this country. Jane was even telling me that her daughter threatens to call the police when she beats her. Imagine. I don't blame the girl, she has come to America and learned about calling the police."

Ifemelu rubbed Dike's knee. He did not look at her. Aunty Uju was driving a little too fast.

DIKE CALLED OUT from the bathroom, where he had been sent to brush his teeth before bed.

"Dike, *I mechago*?" Ifemelu asked.

"Please don't speak Igbo to him," Aunty Uju said. "Two languages will confuse him."

"What are you talking about, Aunty? We spoke two languages growing up."

"This is America. It's different."

Ifemelu held her tongue. Aunty Uju closed her medical book and stared ahead at nothing. The television was off and the sound of water running came from the bathroom.

"Aunty, what is it?" Ifemelu asked. "What is wrong?"

"What do you mean? Nothing is wrong." Aunty Uju sighed. "I failed my last exam. I got the result just before you came."

"Oh." Ifemelu was watching her.

"I've never failed an exam in my life. But they weren't testing actual knowledge, they were testing our ability to answer tricky multiple-choice questions that have nothing to do with real medical knowledge." She stood up and went to the kitchen. "I'm tired. I am so tired. I thought by now things would be better for me and Dike. It's not as if anybody was helping me and I just could not believe how quickly money went. I was studying and working three jobs. I was doing retail at the mall, and a research assistantship, and I even did some hours at Burger King."

"It will get better," Ifemelu said, helplessly. She knew how hollow she sounded. Nothing was familiar. She was unable to comfort Aunty Uju because she did not know how. When Aunty Uju spoke about her friends who had come to America earlier and passed their exams—Nkechi in Maryland had sent her the dining set, Kemi in Indiana bought her the bed, Ozavisa had sent crockery and clothes from Hartford—Ifemelu said, "God bless them," and the words felt bulky and useless in her mouth.

She had assumed, from Aunty Uju's calls home, that things were not too bad, although she realized now that Aunty Uju had always been vague, mentioning "work" and "exam" without details. Or perhaps it was because she had not asked for details, had not expected to understand details. And she thought, watching her, how the old Aunty Uju would never have worn her hair in such scruffy braids. She would never have tolerated the ingrown hair that grew like raisins on her chin, or worn trousers that gathered bulkily between her legs. America had subdued her.

CHAPTER 10

That first summer was Ifemelu's summer of waiting; the real America, she felt, was just around the next corner she would turn. Even the days, sliding one into the other, languorous and limpid, the sun lingering until very late, seemed to be waiting. There was a stripped-down quality to her life, a kindling starkness, without parents and friends and home, the familiar landmarks that made her who she was. And so she waited, writing Obinze long, detailed letters, calling him once in a while—calls kept brief because Aunty Uju said she could not waste the phone card—and spending time with Dike. He was a mere child, but she felt, with him, a kinship close to friendship; they watched his favourite cartoon shows together, *Rugrats* and *Franklin*, and they read books together, and she took him out to play with Jane's children. Jane lived in the next apartment. She and her husband, Marlon, were from Grenada and spoke in a lyrical accent as though just about to break into song. "They are like us; he has a good job and he has ambition and they spank their children," Aunty Uju had said approvingly.

Ifemelu and Jane laughed when they discovered how similar their childhoods in Grenada and Nigeria had been, with Enid Blyton books and Anglophile teachers and fathers who worshipped the BBC World Service. She was only a few years older than Ifemelu. "I married very young. Everybody wanted Marlon, so how could I say no?" she said, half teasing. They would sit together on the front steps of the building and watch Dike and Jane's children, Elizabeth and Junior, ride their bicycles to the end of the street and then back, Ifemelu often calling out to Dike not to go any farther, the children shouting, the concrete sidewalks gleaming in the hot sun, and the summer lull disrupted by the occasional rise and fall of loud music from passing cars.

"Things must still be very strange for you," Jane said.

Ifemelu nodded. "Yes."

An ice cream van drove into the street, and with it a tinkling melody.

"You know, this is my tenth year here and I feel as if I'm still settling in," Jane said. "The hardest thing is raising my kids. Look at Elizabeth, I have to be very careful with her. If you are not careful in this country, your children become what you don't know. It's different back home because you can control them. Here, no." Jane wore an air of harmlessness, with her plain face and jiggly arms, but there was, beneath her ready smile, an icy watchfulness.

"How old is she? Ten?" Ifemelu asked.

"Nine and already trying to be a drama queen. We pay good money for her to go to private school because the public schools here are useless. Marlon says we'll move to the suburbs soon so they can go to better schools. Otherwise she will start behaving like these black Americans."

"What do you mean?"

"Don't worry, you will understand with time," Jane said, and got up to get some money for the children's ice cream.

Ifemelu looked forward to sitting outside with Jane, until the evening Marlon came back from work and told Ifemelu in a hasty whisper, after Jane went in to get some lemonade for the children, "I've been thinking about you. I want to talk to you." She did not tell Jane. Jane would never hold Marlon responsible for anything, her light-skinned, hazel-eyed Marlon whom everyone wanted, and so Ifemelu began to avoid both of them, to design elaborate board games that she and Dike could play indoors.

Once, she asked Dike what he had done in school before summer, and he said, "Circles." They would sit on the floor in a circle and share their favourite things.

She was appalled. "Can you do division?"

He looked at her strangely. "I'm only in first grade, Coz."

"When I was your age I could do simple division."

The conviction lodged in her head that American children learned nothing in elementary school, and it hardened when he told her that his teacher sometimes gave out homework coupons; if you got a homework coupon, then you could skip one day of homework. Circles, homework coupons, what foolishness would she next hear? And so she began to teach him mathematics—she called it "maths" and he called it "math" and so they agreed not to shorten the word. She could not think, now, of that summer without thinking of long division, of Dike's brows furrowed in confusion as they sat side by side at the dining table, of her swings from bribing him to shouting at him. Okay, try it one more time and you can have ice cream. You're not going to play unless you get them all right. Later, when he was older, he would say that he found mathematics easy because of her summer of torturing him. "You must mean summer of tutoring," she would say in what became a familiar joke that, like comfort food, they would reach for from time to time.

It was, also, her summer of eating. She enjoyed the unfamiliar—the McDonald's hamburgers with the brief tart crunch of pickles, a new taste that she liked on one day and disliked on the next, the wraps Aunty Uju brought home, wet with piquant dressing, and the bologna and pepperoni that left a film of salt in her mouth. She was disoriented by the blandness of fruits, as though Nature had forgotten to sprinkle some seasoning on the oranges and the bananas, but she liked to look at them, and to touch them; because bananas were so big, so evenly yellow, she forgave them their tastelessness. Once, Dike said, "Why are you doing that? Eating a banana with peanuts?"

"That's what we do in Nigeria. Do you want to try?"

"No," he said firmly. "I don't think I like Nigeria, Coz."

Ice cream was, fortunately, a taste unchanged. She scooped straight from the buy-one-get-one-free giant tubs in the freezer, globs of vanilla and chocolate, while staring at the television. She followed shows she had watched in Nigeria—*The Fresh Prince of Bel Air, A Different World*—and discovered new shows she had not known—*Friends, The Simpsons*—but it was the commercials that captivated her. She ached for the lives they showed, lives full of bliss, where all problems had sparkling solutions in shampoos and cars and packaged foods, and in her mind they became the real America, the America she would only see when she moved to school in the autumn. At first, the evening news puzzled her, a litany of fires and shootings, because she was used to NTA news, where self-important army officers cut ribbons or gave speeches. But as she watched day after day, images of men being hauled off in handcuffs, distraught families in front of charred, smouldering houses, the wreckage of cars crashed in police chases, blurred videos of armed robberies in shops, her puzzlement ripened to worry. She panicked when there was a sound by the window, when Dike went too far down the street on his bicycle. She stopped taking out the trash after dark, because a man with a gun might be lurking outside. Aunty Uju said, laughing shortly, "If you keep watching television, you will think these things happen all the time. Do you know how much crime happens in Nigeria? Is it because we don't report it like they do here?"

CHAPTER 11

Aunty Uju came home dry-faced and tense, the streets dark and Dike already in bed, to ask "Do I have mail? Do I have mail?" the question always repeated, her entire being at a perilous edge, about to tip over. Some nights, she would talk on the phone for a long time, her voice hushed, as though she were protecting something from the world's prying gaze. Finally, she told Ifemelu about Bartholomew. "He is an accountant, divorced, and he is looking to settle down. He is from Eziowelle, very near us."

Ifemelu, floored by Aunty Uju's words, could only say, "Oh, okay," and nothing else. "What does he do?" and "Where is he from?" were the questions her own mother would ask, but when had it started to matter to Aunty Uju that a man was from a hometown close to theirs?

One Saturday, Bartholomew visited from Massachusetts. Aunty Uju cooked peppered gizzards, powdered her face and stood by the living room window, waiting to see his car pull in. Dike watched her, playing half-heartedly with his action figures, confused but also excited because he could sense her expectation. When the doorbell rang, she told Dike, urgently, "Behave well!"

Bartholomew wore khaki trousers pulled up high on his belly, and spoke with an American accent filled with holes, mangling words until they were impossible to understand. Ifemelu sensed, from his demeanour, a deprived rural upbringing that he tried to compensate for with his American affectation, his gonnas and wannas.

He glanced at Dike, and said, almost indifferently, "Oh, yes, your boy. How are you doing?"

"Good," Dike mumbled.

It irked Ifemelu that Bartholomew was not interested in the son of the woman he was courting, and did not bother to pretend that he was. He was jarringly unsuited for, and unworthy of, Aunty Uju. A more intelligent man would have realized this and tempered himself, but not Bartholomew. He behaved grandiosely, like a special prize that Aunty Uju was fortunate to have, and Aunty Uju humoured him. Before he tasted the gizzards, he said, "Let me see if this is any good."

Aunty Uju laughed and in her laughter was a certain assent, because his words "Let me see if this is any good" were about her being a good cook, and therefore a good wife. She had slipped into the rituals, smiling a smile that promised to be demure to him but not to the world, lunging to pick up his fork when it slipped from his hand, serving him more beer. Quietly, Dike watched from the dining table, his toys untouched. Bartholomew ate gizzards and drank beer. He talked about Nigerian politics with the fervid enthusiasm of a person who followed it from afar, who read and reread articles on the Internet. "Kudirat's death will not be in vain, it will only galvanize the democratic movement in a way that even her life did not! I just wrote an article about this issue online in *Nigerian Village*." Aunty Uju nodded while he talked, agreeing with everything he said. Often, silence gaped between them. They watched television, a drama, predictable and filled with brightly shot scenes, one of which featured a young girl in a short dress.

"A girl in Nigeria will never wear that kind of dress," Bartholomew said. "Look at that. This country has no moral compass."

Ifemelu should not have spoken, but there was something about Bartholomew that made silence impossible, the exaggerated caricature that he was, with his back-shaft haircut unchanged since he came to America thirty years ago and his false, overheated moralities. He was one of those people who, in his village back home, would be called "lost". *He went to America and got lost,* his people would say. *He went to America and refused to come back.*

"Girls in Nigeria wear dresses much shorter than that o," Ifemelu said. "In secondary school, some of us changed in our friends' houses so our parents wouldn't know."

Aunty Uju turned to her, eyes narrow with warning. Bartholomew looked at her and shrugged, as though she was not worth responding to. Dislike simmered between them. For the rest of the afternoon, he ignored her. He would, in the future, often ignore her. Later, she read his online posts on *Nigerian Village*, all of them sour-toned and strident, under the moniker "Igbo Massachusetts Accountant", and it surprised her how profusely he wrote, how actively he pursued airless arguments.

He had not been back to Nigeria in years and perhaps he needed the consolation of those online groups, where small observations flared and blazed into attacks, personal insults flung back and forth. Ifemelu imagined the writers, Nigerians in bleak houses in America, their lives deadened by work, nursing their careful savings throughout the year so that they could visit home in December for a week, when they would arrive bearing suitcases of shoes and clothes and cheap watches, and see, in the eyes of their relatives, brightly burnished images of themselves. Afterwards they would return to America to fight on the Internet over their mythologies of home, because home was now a blurred place between here and there, and at least online they could ignore the awareness of how inconsequential they had become.

Nigerian women came to America and became wild, Igbo Massachusetts Accountant wrote in one post; it was an unpleasant truth but one that had to be said. What else accounted for the high divorce rates among Nigerians in America and the low rates among Nigerians in Nigeria? Delta Mermaid replied that women simply had laws protecting them in America and the divorce rates would be just as high if those laws were in Nigeria. Igbo Massachusetts Accountant's rejoinder: *You have been brainwashed by the West. You should be ashamed to call yourself a Nigerian.* In response to Eze Houston, who wrote that Nigerian men were cynical when they went back to Nigeria looking for nurses and doctors to marry, only so that the new wives would earn money for them back in America, Igbo Massachusetts Accountant wrote, *What is wrong with a man wanting financial security from his wife? Don't women want the same thing?*

After he left that Saturday, Aunty Uju asked Ifemelu, "What did you think?"

"He uses bleaching creams."

"What?"

"Couldn't you see? His face is a funny colour. He must be using the cheap ones with no sunscreen. What kind of man bleaches his skin, *biko*?"

Aunty Uju shrugged, as though she had not noticed the greenish-yellow tone of the man's face, worse at his temples.

"He's not bad. He has a good job." She paused. "I'm not getting any younger. I want Dike to have a brother or a sister."

"In Nigeria, a man like him would not even have the courage to talk to you."

"We are not in Nigeria, Ifem."

Before Aunty Uju went into the bedroom, tottering under her many anxieties, she said, "Please just pray that it will work."

Ifemelu did not pray, but even if she did, she could not bear praying for Aunty Uju to be with Bartholomew. It saddened her that Aunty Uju had settled merely for what was familiar.

BECAUSE OF OBINZE, Manhattan intimidated Ifemelu. The first time she took the subway from Brooklyn to Manhattan, her palms sweaty, she walked the streets, watching, absorbing. A sylph-like woman running in high heels, her short dress floating behind her, until she tripped and almost fell, a pudgy man coughing and spitting on the kerb, a girl dressed all in black raising a hand for the taxis that sliced past. The endless skyscrapers taunted the sky, but there was dirt on the building windows. The dazzling imperfection of it all calmed her. "It's wonderful but it's not heaven," she told Obinze. She could not wait until he, too, saw Manhattan. She imagined them both walking hand in hand, like the American couples she saw, lingering at a shop window, pausing to read menus taped on restaurant doors, stopping at a food cart to buy cold bottles of iced tea. "Soon," he said in his letter. They said "soon" to each other often, and "soon" gave their plan the weight of something real.

FINALLY, Aunty Uju's result came. Ifemelu brought in the envelope from the mailbox, so slight, so ordinary, *United States Medical Licensing Examination* printed on it in even script, and held it in her hand for a long time, willing it to be good news. She raised it up as soon as Aunty

Uju walked indoors. Aunty Uju gasped. "Is it thick? Is it thick?" she asked.

"What? *Gini*?" Ifemelu asked.

"Is it thick?" Aunty Uju asked again, letting her handbag slip to the floor and moving forward, her hand outstretched, her face savage with hope. She took the envelope and shouted, "I made it!" and then opened it to make sure, peering at the thin sheet of paper. "If you fail, they send you a thick envelope so that you can reregister."

"Aunty! I knew it! Congratulations!" Ifemelu said.

Aunty Uju hugged her, both of them leaning into each other, hearing each other's breathing, and it brought to Ifemelu a warm memory of Lagos.

"Where's Dike?" Aunty Uju asked, as though he was not already in bed when she came home from her second job. She went into the kitchen, stood under the bright ceiling light and looked, again, at the result, her eyes wet. "So I will be a family physician in this America," she said, almost in a whisper. She opened a can of Coke and left it undrunk.

Later, she said, "I have to take my braids out for my interviews and relax my hair. Kemi told me that I shouldn't wear braids to the interview. If you have braids, they will think you are unprofessional."

"So there are no doctors with braided hair in America?" Ifemelu asked.

"I have told you what they told me. You are in a country that is not your own. You do what you have to do if you want to succeed."

There it was again, the strange naïveté with which Aunty Uju had covered herself like a blanket. Sometimes, while having a conversation, it would occur to Ifemelu that Aunty Uju had deliberately left behind something of herself, something essential, in a distant and forgotten place. Obinze said it was the exaggerated gratitude that came with immigrant insecurity. Obinze, so like him to have an explanation. Obinze, who anchored her through that summer of waiting—his steady voice over the phone, his long letters in blue airmail envelopes—and who understood, as summer was ending, the new gnawing in her stomach. She wanted to start school, to find the real America, and yet there was that gnawing in her stomach, an anxiety, and a new, aching nostalgia for the Brooklyn summer that had become familiar: children on bicycles, sinewy black men in tight white tank tops, ice cream vans tinkling, loud music from roofless cars, sun shining into night, and things rotting and smelling in the humid heat. She did not want to leave Dike—the mere thought brought a sense of treasure already lost—and yet she wanted to leave Aunty Uju's apartment, and begin a life in which she alone determined the margins.

Dike had once told her, wistfully, about his friend who had gone to Coney Island and come back with a picture taken on a steep, sliding ride, and so she surprised him on the weekend before she left, saying "We're going to Coney Island!" Jane had told her what train to take, what to do, how much it would cost. Aunty Uju said it was a good idea, but gave her no money to add to what she had. As she watched Dike on the rides, screaming, terrified and thrilled, a little boy entirely open to the world, she did not mind what she had spent. They ate hot dogs and milkshakes and cotton candy. "I can't wait until I don't have to come with you to the girls' bathroom," he told her, and she laughed and laughed. On the train back, he was tired and sleepy. "Coz, this was the bestest day ever with you," he said, resting against her.

The bittersweet glow of an ending limbo overcame her days later when she kissed Dike goodbye—once then twice and three times, while he cried, a child so unused to crying, and she bit back her own tears and Aunty Uju said over and over that Philadelphia was not very far away. Ifemelu rolled her suitcase to the subway, took it to the Forty-second Street terminal and got on a bus to Philadelphia. She sat by the window—somebody had stuck a blob of chewed gum on the pane—and spent long minutes looking again at the Social Security card and driver's licence that belonged to Ngozi Okonkwo. Ngozi Okonkwo was at least ten years older than she was, with a narrow face, eyebrows that started as little balls before loping into arcs, and a jaw shaped like the letter *V*.

"I don't even look like her at all," Ifemelu had said when Aunty Uju gave her the card.

"All of us look alike to white people," Aunty Uju said.

"Ahn-ahn, Aunty!"

"I'm not joking. Amara's cousin came last year and she doesn't have her papers yet, so she has been working with Amara's ID. You remember Amara? Her cousin is very fair and slim. They do not look alike at all. Nobody noticed. She works as a home health aide in Virginia. Just make sure you always remember your new name. I have a friend who forgot and one of her co-workers called her and called her and she was blank. Then they became suspicious and reported her to immigration."

CHAPTER 12

There was Ginika, standing in the small, crowded bus terminal, wearing a miniskirt and a tube top that covered her chest but not her midriff, and waiting to scoop Ifemelu up and into the real America. Ginika was much thinner, half her old size, and her head looked bigger, balanced on a long neck that brought to mind a vague, exotic animal. She extended her arms, as though urging a child into an embrace, laughing, calling out, "Ifemsco! Ifemsco!" and Ifemelu was taken back, for a moment, to secondary school: an image of gossiping girls in their blue-and-white uniforms, felt berets perched on their heads, crowded in the school corridor. She hugged Ginika. The theatrics of their holding each other close, disengaging and then holding each other close again, made her eyes fill, to her mild surprise, with tears.

"Look at you!" Ginika said, gesturing, jangling the many silver bangles around her wrist. "Is it really you?"

"When did *you* stop eating and start looking like a dried stockfish?" Ifemelu asked.

Ginika laughed, took the suitcase and turned to the door. "Come on, let's go. I'm parked illegally."

The green Volvo was at the corner of a narrow street. An unsmiling woman in uniform, ticket booklet in hand, was stumping towards them when Ginika jumped in and started the car. "Close!" she said, laughing. A homeless man in a grubby T-shirt, pushing a trolley filled with bundles, had stopped just by the car, as though to rest briefly, staring ahead at nothing, and Ginika glanced at him as she eased the car into the street. They drove with the windows down. Philadelphia was the smell of the summer sun, of burnt asphalt, of sizzling meat from food carts tucked into street corners, foreign brown men and women hunched inside. Ifemelu would come to like the gyros from those carts, flatbread and lamb and dripping sauces, as she would come to love Philadelphia itself. It did not raise the spectre of intimidation as Manhattan did; it was intimate but not provincial, a city that might yet be kind to you. Ifemelu saw women on the sidewalks going to lunch from work, wearing sneakers, proof of their American preference for comfort over elegance, and she saw young couples clutching each other, kissing from time to time as if they feared that, if they unclasped their hands, their love would dissolve, melt into nothingness.

"I borrowed my landlord's car. I didn't want to come get you in my shit-ass car. I can't believe it, Ifemsco. You're in America!" Ginika said. There was a metallic, unfamiliar glamour in her gauntness, her olive skin, her short skirt that had risen up, barely covering her crotch, her straight-straight hair that she kept tucking behind her ears, blonde streaks shiny in the sunlight.

"We're entering University City, and that's where Wellson campus is, shay you know? We can go for you to see the school first and then we can go to my place, out in the suburbs, and after we can go to my friend's place in the evening. She's doing a get-together." Ginika had lapsed into Nigerian English, a dated, overcooked version, eager to prove how unchanged she was. She had, with a strenuous loyalty, kept in touch through the years: calling and writing letters and sending books and shapeless trousers she called slacks. And now she was saying "shay you know" and Ifemelu did not have the heart to tell her that nobody said "shay" any more.

Ginika recounted anecdotes about her own early experiences in America, as though they were all filled with subtle wisdom that Ifemelu would need.

"If you see how they laughed at me in high school when I said that somebody was boning for me. Because boning here means to have sex! So I had to keep explaining that in Nigeria it means carrying face. And can you imagine 'half-caste' is a bad word here? In freshman year, I was telling a bunch of my friends about how I was voted prettiest girl in school back home. Remember? I should never have won. Zainab should have won. It was just because I was a half-caste. There's even more of that here. There's some shit you'll get from white people in this country that I won't get. But anyway, I was telling them about back home and how all the boys were chasing me because I was a half-caste, and they said I was dissing myself. So now I say biracial, and I'm supposed to be offended when somebody says half-caste. I've met a lot of people here with white mothers and they are so full of issues, eh. I didn't know I was even supposed to *have* issues until I came to America. Honestly, if anybody wants to raise biracial kids, do it in Nigeria."

"Of course. Where all the boys chase the half-caste girls."

"Not *all* the boys, by the way." Ginika made a face. "Obinze had better hurry up and come to the US, before somebody will carry you away. You know you have the kind of body they like here."

"What?"

"You're thin with big breasts."

"Please, I'm not thin. I'm slim."

"Americans say 'thin'. Here 'thin' is a good word."

"Is that why you stopped eating? All your bum has gone. I always wished I had a bum like yours," Ifemelu said.

"Do you know I started losing weight almost as soon as I came? I was even close to anorexia. The kids at my high school called me Pork. You know at home when somebody tells you that you lost weight, it means something bad. But here somebody tells you that you lost weight and you say thank you. It's just different here," Ginika said, a little wistfully, as though she, too, were new to America.

Later, Ifemelu watched Ginika at her friend Stephanie's apartment, a bottle of beer poised at her lips, her American-accented words sailing out of her mouth, and was struck by how like her American friends Ginika had become. Jessica, the Japanese American, beautiful and animated, playing with the emblemed key of her Mercedes. Pale-skinned Teresa, who had a loud laugh and wore diamond studs and shabby, worn-out shoes. Stephanie, the Chinese American, her hair a perfect swingy bob that curved inwards at her chin, who from time to time reached into her monogrammed bag to get her cigarettes and step out for a smoke. Hari, coffee-skinned and black-haired and wearing a tight T-shirt, who said, "I am Indian, not Indian American," when Ginika introduced Ifemelu. They all laughed at the same things and said "Gross!" about the same things; they were well choreographed. Stephanie announced that she had home-made beer in her fridge and everyone chanted "Cool!" Then Teresa said, "Can I have the regular beer, Steph?" in the small voice of a person afraid to offend. Ifemelu sat on a lone armchair at the end of the room, drinking orange juice, listening to them talk. *That company is so evil. Oh my God, I can't believe there's so much sugar in this stuff. The Internet is totally going to change the world.* She heard Ginika ask, "Did you know they use something from animal bones to make that breath mint?" and the others groaned. There were codes Ginika knew, ways of being that she had mastered. Unlike Aunty Uju, Ginika had come to America with the flexibility and fluidness of youth, the cultural cues had seeped into her skin, and now she went bowling, and knew what Tobey Maguire was about, and found double-dipping gross. Bottles and cans of beer were piling up. They all lounged in glamorous lassitude on the sofa, and on the rug, while heavy rock, which Ifemelu thought was unharmonious noise, played on the CD player. Teresa drank the fastest, rolling each empty can of beer on the wood floor, while the others laughed with an enthusiasm that puzzled Ifemelu because it really was not that funny. How did they know when to laugh, what to laugh about?

GINIKA WAS BUYING a dress for a dinner party, hosted by the lawyers she was interning with.

"You should get some things, Ifem."

"I'm not spending ten kobo of my money unless I have to."

"Ten cents."

"Ten cents."

"I'll give you a jacket and bedding stuff, but at least you need tights. The cold is coming."

"I'll manage," Ifemelu said. And she would. If she needed to, she would wear all her clothes at the same time, in layers, until she found a job. She was terrified to spend money.

"Ifem, I'll pay for you."

"It's not as if you are earning much."

"At least I am earning some," Ginika quipped.

"I really hope I find a job soon."

"You will, don't worry."

"I don't understand how anybody will believe I'm Ngozi Okonkwo."

"Don't show them the licence when you go to an interview. Just show the Social Security card. Maybe they won't even ask. Sometimes they don't for small jobs like that."

Ginika led the way into a clothing store, which Ifemelu thought too fevered; it reminded her of a nightclub, disco music playing loudly, the interior shadowy, and the salespeople, two thin-armed young women in all black, moving up and down too swiftly. One was chocolate-skinned, her long black weave highlighted with auburn, the other was white, inky hair floating behind her as she came up to them.

"Hi, ladies, how are you? Is there anything I can help you with?" she asked in a tinkly, sing-song voice. She pulled clothes off hangers and unfurled them from shelves to show Ginika. Ifemelu was looking at the price tags, converting them to naira, exclaiming, "Ahn-ahn! How can this thing cost this much?" She picked up and carefully examined some of the clothes, to find out what each was, underwear or blouse, shirt or dress, and sometimes she was still not certain.

"This literally just came in," the salesperson said of a sparkly dress, as though divulging a big secret, and Ginika said, "Oh my God, really?" with a great excitement. Under the too-bright lighting of the fitting room, Ginika tried on the dress, walking on tiptoe. "I love it."

"But it's shapeless," Ifemelu said. It looked, to her, like a boxy sack on which a bored person had haphazardly stuck sequins.

"It's postmodern," Ginika said.

Watching Ginika preen in front of the mirror, Ifemelu wondered whether she, too, would come to share Ginika's taste for shapeless dresses, whether this was what America did to you.

At the checkout, the blonde cashier asked, "Did anybody help you?"

"Yes," Ginika said.

"Chelcy or Jennifer?"

"I'm sorry, I don't remember her name." Ginika looked around, to point at her helper, but both young women had disappeared into the fitting rooms at the back.

"Was it the one with long hair?" the cashier asked.

"Well, both of them had long hair."

"The one with dark hair?"

Both of them had dark hair.

Ginika smiled and looked at the cashier and the cashier smiled and looked at her computer screen, and two damp seconds crawled past before she cheerfully said, "It's okay, I'll figure it out later and make sure she gets her commission."

As they walked out of the store, Ifemelu said, "I was waiting for her to ask 'Was it the one with two eyes or the one with two legs?' Why didn't she just ask 'Was it the black girl or the white girl?' "

Ginika laughed. "Because this is America. You're supposed to pretend that you don't notice certain things."

GINIKA ASKED Ifemelu to stay with her, to save on rent, but her apartment was too far away, at the end of the Main Line, and the commuter train, taken every day into Philadelphia, would cost too much. They looked at apartments together in West Philadelphia, Ifemelu surprised by the rotting cabinets in the kitchen, the mouse that dashed past an empty bedroom.

"My hostel in Nsukka was dirty but there were no rats o."

"It's a mouse," Ginika said.

Ifemelu was about to sign a lease—if saving money meant living with mice, then so be it—when Ginika's friend told them of a room for rent, a great deal, as college life went. It was in a four-bedroom apartment with mouldy carpeting, above a pizza store on Powelton Avenue, on the corner where drug addicts sometimes dropped crack pipes, miserable pieces of twisted metal that glinted in the sun. Ifemelu's room was the cheapest, the smallest, facing the scuffed brick walls of the next building. Dog hair floated around. Her room-mates, Jackie, Elena and Allison, looked almost interchangeable, all small-boned and slim-hipped, their chestnut hair ironed straight, their lacrosse sticks piled in the narrow hallway. Elena's dog ambled about, large and black, like a shaggy donkey; once in a while, a mound of dog shit appeared at the bottom of the stairs and Elena would scream "You're in big trouble now, buddy!" as though performing for the room-mates, playing a role whose lines everyone knew. Ifemelu wished the dog were kept outside, which was where dogs belonged. When Elena asked why Ifemelu had not petted her dog, or scratched his head in the week since she moved in, she said, "I don't like dogs."

"Is that like a cultural thing?"

"What do you mean?"

"I mean like I know in China they eat cat meat and dog meat."

"My boyfriend back home loves dogs. I just don't."

"Oh," Elena said, and looked at her, brows furrowed, as Jackie and Allison had earlier looked at her when she said she had never gone bowling, as though wondering how she could have turned out a normal human being without ever having gone bowling. She was standing at the periphery of her own life, sharing a fridge and a toilet, a shallow intimacy, with people she did not know at all. People who lived in exclamation points. "Great!" they said often. "That's great!" People who did not scrub in the shower; their shampoos and conditioners and gels were cluttered in the bathroom, but there was not a single sponge, and this, the absence of a sponge, made them seem unreachably alien to her. (One of her earliest memories was of her mother, a bucket of water between them in the bathroom, saying to her, "*Ngwa*, scrub between your legs very well, very well . . . ," and Ifemelu had applied a little too much vigour with the loofah, to show her mother just how clean she could get herself, and for a few days afterwards had hobbled around with her legs spread wide.) There was something unquestioning about her room-mates' lives, an assumption of certainty that fascinated her, so that they often said, "Let's go get some," about whatever it was they needed—more beer, pizza, buffalo wings, liquor—as though this getting was not an act that required money. She was used, at home, to people first asking "Do you have money?" before they made such plans. They left pizza boxes on the kitchen table, and the kitchen itself in casual disarray for days, and on weekends their friends gathered in the living room, with packs of beer stacked in the refrigerator and streaks of dried urine on the toilet seat.

"We're going to a party. Come with us, it'll be fun!" Jackie said, and Ifemelu pulled on her slim-fitting trousers and a halter-neck blouse borrowed from Ginika.

"Won't you get dressed?" she asked her room-mates before they left, all of them wearing slouchy jeans, and Jackie said, "We *are* dressed. What are you talking about?" with a laugh that suggested yet another foreign pathology had emerged. They went to a fraternity house on Chestnut Street, where everyone stood around drinking vodka-rich punch from plastic cups, until Ifemelu accepted that there would be no dancing; to party here was to stand around and drink. They were all a jumble of frayed fabric and slack collars, the students at the party, all their clothes looked determinedly worn. (Years later, a blog post would read: *When it comes to dressing well, American culture is so self-fulfilled that it has not only disregarded this courtesy of self-presentation, but has turned that disregard into a virtue. "We are too superior/busy/cool/not-uptight to bother about how we look to other people, and so we can wear pajamas to school and underwear to the mall."*) As they got drunker and drunker, some lay limp on the floor and others took felt-tipped pens and began to write on the exposed skin of the fallen. *Suck me off. Go Sixers.*

"Jackie said you're from Africa?" a boy in a baseball cap asked her.

"Yes."

"That's really cool!" he said, and Ifemelu imagined telling Obinze about this, the way she would mimic the boy. Obinze pulled every strand of story from her, going over details, asking questions, and sometimes he would laugh, the sound echoing down the line. She had told him how Allison had said, "Hey, we're getting a bite to eat. Come with us!" and she thought it was an invitation and that, as with invitations back home, Allison or one of the others would buy her meal. But when the waitress brought the bill, Allison carefully began to untangle how many drinks each person had ordered and who had the calamari appetizer, to make sure nobody paid for anybody else. Obinze had found this very funny, finally saying, "That's America for you!"

It was, to her, funny only in retrospect. She had struggled to hide her bafflement at the boundaries of hospitality, and also at this business of tipping—paying an extra fifteen or twenty per cent of your bill to the waitress—which was suspiciously like bribing, a forced and efficient bribing system.

CHAPTER 13

At first, Ifemelu forgot that she was someone else. In an apartment in South Philadelphia, a tired-faced woman opened the door and led her into a strong stench of urine. The living room was dark, unaired, and she imagined the whole building steeped in months, even years, of accumulated urine, and herself working every day in this urine cloud. From inside the apartment, a man was groaning, deep and eerie sounds; they were the groans of a person for whom groaning was the only choice left, and they frightened her.

"That's my dad," the woman said, looking at her with keen assessing eyes. "Are you strong?"

The advertisement in the *City Paper* had stressed strong. *Strong Home Health Aide. Pays cash.*

"I'm strong enough to do the job," Ifemelu said, and fought the urge to back out of the apartment and run and run.

"That's a pretty accent. Where are you from?"

"Nigeria."

"Nigeria. Isn't there a war going on there?"

"No."

"Can I see your ID?" the woman asked, and then, glancing at the licence, added, "How do you pronounce your name again?"

"Ifemelu."

"What?"

Ifemelu almost choked. "Ngozi. You hum the *N*."

"Really." The woman, with her air of unending exhaustion, seemed too tired to question the two different pronunciations. "Can you live in?"

"Live in?"

"Yes. Live here with my dad. There's a spare bedroom. You would do three nights a week. You'd need to clean him up in the morning." The woman paused. "You *are* pretty slight. Look, I've two more people to interview and I'll get back to you."

"Okay. Thank you." Ifemelu knew she would not get the job and for this she was grateful.

She repeated "I'm Ngozi Okonkwo" in front of the mirror before her next interview, at the Seaview restaurant. "Can I call you Goz?" the manager asked after they shook hands, and she said yes, but before she said yes, she paused, the slightest and shortest of pauses, but still a pause. And she wondered if that was why she did not get the job.

Later Ginika said, "You could have just said Ngozi is your tribal name and Ifemelu is your jungle name and throw in one more as your spiritual name. They'll believe all kinds of shit about Africa."

Ginika laughed, a sure throaty laugh. Ifemelu laughed, too, although she did not fully understand the joke. And she had the sudden sensation of fogginess, of a milky web through which she tried to claw. Her autumn of half blindness had begun, the autumn of puzzlements, of experiences she had knowing there were slippery layers of meaning that eluded her.

THE WORLD WAS WRAPPED in gauze; she could see the shapes of things but not clearly enough, never enough. She told Obinze that there were things she should know how to do but didn't, details she should have corralled into her space but hadn't. And he reminded her of how quickly she was adapting, his tone always calm, always consoling. She applied to be a waitress, hostess, bartender, cashier, and then waited for job offers that never came, and for this she blamed herself. It had to be that she was not doing something right; and yet she did not know what it might be. Autumn had come, wet and grey-skied. Her meagre bank account was leaking money. The cheapest sweaters from Ross still startled with their high cost, bus and train tickets added up, and groceries punctured holes in her bank balance, even though she stood guard at the checkout, watching the electronic display and saying, "Please stop. I won't be taking the rest," when it got to thirty dollars. Each day, there seemed to be a letter for her on the kitchen table, and inside the envelope was a tuition bill, and words printed in capital letters: *YOUR RECORDS WILL BE FROZEN UNLESS PAYMENT IS RECEIVED BY THE DATE AT THE BOTTOM OF THIS NOTICE.*

It was the boldness of the capital letters more than the words that frightened her. She worried about the possible consequences, a vague but constant worry. She did not imagine a police arrest for not paying her school fees, but what did happen if you did not pay your school fees in America? Obinze told her nothing would happen, suggested she speak to the bursar about getting on a payment plan so that she would at least have taken some action. She called Obinze often, with cheap phone cards she bought from the crowded store of a gas station on Lancaster Avenue, and just scratching off the metallic dust, to reveal the numbers printed beneath, flooded her with anticipation: to hear Obinze's voice again. He calmed her. With him, she could feel whatever she felt, and she did not have to force some cheer into her voice, as she did with her parents, telling them she was very fine, very hopeful to get a waitress job, settling down very well with her classes.

The highlight of her days was talking to Dike. His voice, higher-pitched on the phone, warmed her as he told her what had happened on his TV show, how he had just beaten a new level on Game Boy. "When are you coming to visit, Coz?" he asked often. "I wish you were taking care of me. I don't like going to Miss Brown's. Her bathroom is stinky."

She missed him. Sometimes she told him things she knew he would not understand, but she told him anyway. She told him about her professor who sat on the grass at lunch to eat a sandwich, the one who asked her to call him by his first name, Al, the one who wore a studded leather jacket and had a motorcycle. On the day she got her first piece of junk mail, she told him, "Guess what? I got a letter today." That credit card preapproval, with her name correctly spelled and elegantly italicized, had roused her spirits, made her a little less invisible, a little more present. Somebody knew her.

CHAPTER 14

And then there was Cristina Tomas. Cristina Tomas with her rinsed-out look, her washy blue eyes, faded hair and pallid skin, Cristina Tomas seated at the front desk with a smile, Cristina Tomas wearing whitish tights that made her legs look like death. It was a warm day, Ifemelu had walked past students sprawled on green lawns; cheery balloons were clustered below a WELCOME FRESHMEN sign.

"Good afternoon. Is this the right place for registration?" Ifemelu asked Cristina Tomas, whose name she did not then know.

"Yes. Now. Are. You. An. International. Student?"

"Yes."

"You. Will. First. Need. To. Get. A. Letter. From. The. International. Students. Office."

Ifemelu half smiled in sympathy, because Cristina Tomas had to have some sort of illness that made her speak so slowly, lips scrunching and puckering, as she gave directions to the international students office. But when Ifemelu returned with the letter, Cristina Tomas said, "I. Need. You. To. Fill. Out. A. Couple. Of. Forms. Do. You. Understand. How. To. Fill. These. Out?" and she realized that Cristina Tomas was speaking like that because of *her*, her foreign accent, and she felt for a moment like a small child, lazy-limbed and drooling.

"I speak English," she said.

"I bet you do," Cristina Tomas said. "I just don't know how *well*."

Ifemelu shrank. In that strained, still second when her eyes met Cristina Tomas's before she took the forms, she shrank. She shrank like a dried leaf. She had spoken English all her life, led the debating society in secondary school, and always thought the American twang inchoate; she should not have cowered and shrunk, but she did. And in the following weeks, as autumn's coolness descended, she began to practise an American accent.

SCHOOL IN AMERICA was easy, assignments sent in by e-mail, classrooms air-conditioned, professors willing to give make-up tests. But she was uncomfortable with what the professors called "participation", and did not see why it should be part of the final grade; it merely made students talk and talk, class time wasted on obvious words, hollow words, sometimes meaningless words. It had to be that Americans were taught, from elementary school, to always *say something* in class, no matter what. And so she sat stiff-tongued, surrounded by students who were all folded easily on their seats, all flush with knowledge, not of the subject of the classes, but of how to *be* in the classes. They never said "I don't know." They said, instead, "I'm not sure," which did not give any information but still suggested the possibility of knowledge. And they ambled, these Americans, they walked without rhythm. They avoided giving direct instructions: they did not say "Ask somebody upstairs"; they said "You might want to ask somebody upstairs." When you tripped and fell, when you choked, when misfortune befell you, they did not say "Sorry." They said "Are you okay?" when it was obvious that you were not. And when you said "Sorry" to them when they choked or tripped or encountered misfortune, they replied, eyes wide with surprise, "Oh, it's not your fault." And they overused the word "excited", a professor excited about a new book, a student excited about a class, a politician on TV excited about a law; it was altogether too much excitement. Some of the expressions she heard every day astonished her, jarred her, and she wondered what Obinze's mother would make of them. *You shouldn't of done that. There is three things. I had a apple. A couple days. I want to lay down.* "These Americans cannot speak English o," she told Obinze. On her first day at school, she had visited the health centre, and had stared a little too long at the bin filled with free condoms in the corner. After her physical, the receptionist told her, "You're all set!" and she, blank, wondered what "You're all set" meant until she assumed it had to mean that she had done all she needed to.

She woke up every day worrying about money. If she bought all the textbooks she needed, she would not have enough to pay her rent, and so she borrowed textbooks during class and made feverish notes which, reading them later, sometimes confused her. Her new class friend, Samantha, a thin woman who avoided the sun, often saying "I burn easily," would, from time to time, let her take a textbook home. "Keep it until tomorrow and make notes if you need to," she would say. "I know how tough things can be, that's why I dropped out of college years ago to work." Samantha was older, and a relief to befriend, because she was not a slack-jawed eighteen-year-old as so many others in her communications major were. Still, Ifemelu never kept the books for more than a day, and sometimes refused to take them home. It stung her, to have to beg. Sometimes after classes, she would sit on a bench in the quad and watch the students walking past the large grey sculpture in the middle; they all seemed to have their lives in the shape that they wanted, they could have jobs if they wanted to have jobs, and above them, small flags fluttered serenely from lampposts.

SHE HUNGERED to understand everything about America, to wear a new, knowing skin right away: to support a team at the Super Bowl, understand what a Twinkie was and what sports "lockouts" meant, measure in ounces and square feet, order a "muffin" without thinking that it really was a cake, and say "I 'scored' a deal" without feeling silly.

Obinze suggested she read American books, novels and histories and biographies. In his first e-mail to her—a cybercafé had just opened in Nsukka—he gave her a list of books. *The Fire Next Time* was the first. She stood by the library shelf and skimmed the opening chapter, braced for boredom, but slowly she moved to a couch and sat down and kept reading until three-quarters of the book was gone, then she stopped and took down every James Baldwin title on the shelf. She spent her free hours in the library, so wondrously well lit; the sweep of computers, the large, clean, airy reading spaces, the welcoming brightness of it all, seemed like a sinful decadence. She was used, after all, to reading books with pages missing, fallen off while passing through too many hands. And now to be in a cavalcade of books with healthy spines. She wrote to Obinze about the books she read, careful, sumptuous letters that opened, between them, a new intimacy; she had begun, finally, to grasp the power books had over him. His longing for Ibadan because of "Ibadan" had puzzled her; how could a string of words make a person ache for a place he did not know? But in those weeks when she discovered the rows and rows of books with their leathery smell and their promise of pleasures unknown, when she sat, knees tucked underneath her, on an armchair in the lower level or at a table upstairs with the fluorescent light reflecting off the book's pages, she finally understood. She read the books on Obinze's list but also, randomly, pulled out book after book, reading a chapter before deciding which she would speed-read in the library and which she would check out. And as she read, America's mythologies began to take on meaning, America's tribalisms—race, ideology and region—became clear. And she was consoled by her new knowledge.

"YOU KNOW you said 'excited'?" Obinze asked her one day, his voice amused. "You said you were excited about your media class."

"I did?"

New words were falling out of her mouth. Columns of mist were dispersing. Back home, she would wash her underwear every night and hang it in a discreet corner of the bathroom. Now that she piled them up in a basket and threw them into the washing machine on Friday evenings, she had come to see this, the heaping of dirty underwear, as normal. She spoke up in class, buoyed by the books she read, thrilled that she could disagree with professors and get, in return, not a scolding about being disrespectful but an encouraging nod.

"We watch films in class," she told Obinze. "They talk about films here as if films are as important as books. So we watch films and then we write a response paper and almost everybody gets an A. Can you imagine? These Americans are not serious o."

In her honours history seminar, Professor Moore, a tiny, tentative woman with the emotionally malnourished look of someone who did not have friends, showed some scenes from *Roots*, the images bright on the board of the darkened classroom. When she turned off the projector, a ghostly white patch hovered on the wall for a moment before disappearing. Ifemelu had first watched *Roots* on video with Obinze and his mother, sunk into sofas in their living room in Nsukka. As Kunta Kinte was being flogged into accepting his slave name, Obinze's mother got up abruptly, so abruptly she almost tripped on a leather pouffe, and left the room, but not before Ifemelu saw her reddened eyes. It startled her, that Obinze's mother, fully hemmed into her self-containment, her intense privacy, could cry watching a film. Now, as the window blinds were raised and the classroom once again plunged into light, Ifemelu remembered that Saturday afternoon, and how she had felt lacking, watching Obinze's mother, and wishing that she, too, could cry.

"Let's talk about historical representation in film," Professor Moore said.

A firm, female voice from the back of the class, with a non-American accent, asked, "Why was 'nigger' bleeped out?"

And a collective sigh, like a small wind, swept through the class.

"Well, this was a recording from network television and one of the things I wanted us to talk about is how we represent history in popular culture and the use of the N-word is certainly an important part of that," Professor Moore said.

"It makes no sense to me," the firm voice said. Ifemelu turned. The speaker's natural hair was cut as low as a boy's and her pretty face, wide-foreheaded and fleshless, reminded Ifemelu of the East Africans who always won long-distance races on television.

"I mean, 'nigger' is a word that exists. People use it. It is part of America. It has caused a lot of pain to people and I think it is insulting to bleep it out."

"Well," Professor Moore said, looking around, as though for help.

It came from a gravelly voice in the middle of the class. "Well, it's because of the pain that word has caused that you *shouldn't* use it!" *Shouldn't* sailed astringently into the air, the speaker an African American girl wearing bamboo hoop earrings.

"Thing is, each time you say it, the word hurts African Americans," a pale, shaggy-haired boy in front said.

Ifemelu raised her hand; Faulkner's *Light in August*, which she had just read, was on her mind. "I don't think it's always hurtful. I think it depends on the intent and also on who is using it."

A girl next to her, face flushing bright red, burst out, "No! The word is the same for whoever says it."

"That is nonsense." The firm voice again. A voice unafraid. "If my mother hits me with a stick and a stranger hits me with a stick, it's not the same thing."

Ifemelu looked at Professor Moore to see how the word "nonsense" had been received. She did not seem to have noticed; instead, a vague terror was freezing her features into a smirk-smile.

"I agree it's different when African Americans say it, but I don't think it should be used in films, because that way people who shouldn't use it can use it and hurt other people's feelings," a light-skinned African American girl said, the last of the four black people in class, her sweater an unsettling shade of fuchsia.

"But it's like being in denial. If it was used like that, then it should be represented like that. Hiding it doesn't make it go away." The firm voice.

"Well, if you all hadn't sold us, we wouldn't be talking about any of this," the gravelly-voiced African American girl said, in a lowered tone that was, nonetheless, audible.

The classroom was wrapped in silence. Then rose that voice again. "Sorry, but even if no Africans had been sold by other Africans, the transatlantic slave trade would still have happened. It was a European enterprise. It was about Europeans looking for labour for their plantations."

Professor Moore interrupted in a small voice. "Okay, now let's talk about the ways in which history can be sacrificed for entertainment."

After class, Ifemelu and the firm voice drifted towards each other.

"Hi. I'm Wambui. I'm from Kenya. You're Nigerian, right?" She had a formidable air; a person who went about setting everyone and everything right in the world.

"Yes. I'm Ifemelu."

They shook hands. They would, in the next weeks, ease into a lasting friendship. Wambui was the president of the African Students Association.

"You don't know about ASA? You must come to the next meeting on Thursday," she said.

The meetings were held in the basement of Wharton Hall, a harshly lit, windowless room, paper plates, pizza cartons and soda bottles piled on a metal table, folding chairs arranged in a limp semi-circle. Nigerians, Ugandans, Kenyans, Ghanaians, South Africans, Tanzanians, Zimbabweans, one Congolese and one Guinean sat around eating, talking, fuelling spirits, and their different accents formed meshes of solacing sounds. They mimicked what Americans told them: *You speak such good English. How bad is AIDS in your country? It's so sad that people live on less than a dollar a day in Africa.* And they themselves mocked Africa, trading stories of absurdity, of stupidity, and they felt safe to mock, because it was mockery born of longing, and of the heartbroken desire to see a place made whole again. Here, Ifemelu felt a gentle, swaying sense of renewal. Here, she did not have to explain herself.

WAMBUI HAD TOLD everyone that Ifemelu was looking for a job. Dorothy, the girly Ugandan with long braids who worked as a waitress in Center City, said her restaurant was hiring. But first, Mwombeki, the Tanzanian double major in engineering and political science, looked over Ifemelu's résumé and asked her to delete the three years of university in Nigeria: American employers did not like lower-level employees to be too educated. Mwombeki reminded her of Obinze, that ease about him, that quiet strength. At meetings, he made everyone laugh. "I got a good primary education because of Nyerere's socialism," Mwombeki said often. "Otherwise I would be in Dar right now, carving ugly giraffes for tourists." When two new students came for the first time, one from Ghana and the other from Nigeria, Mwombeki gave them what he called the welcome talk.

"Please do not go to Kmart and buy twenty pairs of jeans because each costs five dollars. The jeans are not running away. They will be there tomorrow at an even more reduced price. You are now in America: do not expect to have hot food for lunch. That African taste must be abolished. When you visit the home of an American with some money, they will offer to show you their house. Forget that in your house back home, your father would throw a fit if anyone came close to his bedroom. We all know that the living room was where it stopped and, if absolutely necessary, then the toilet. But please smile and follow the American and see the house and make sure you say you like everything. And do not be shocked by the indiscriminate touching of American couples. Standing in line at the cafeteria, the girl will touch the boy's arm and the boy will put his arm around her shoulder and they will rub shoulders and back and rub rub rub but please do not imitate this behaviour."

They were all laughing. Wambui shouted something in Swahili.

"Very soon you will start to adopt an American accent, because you don't want customer service people on the phone to keep asking you 'What? What?' You will start to admire Africans who have perfect American accents, like our brother here, Kofi. Kofi's parents came from Ghana when he was two years old, but do not be fooled by the way he sounds. If you go to their house, they eat kenkey every day. His father slapped him when he got a C in a class. There's no American nonsense in that house. He goes back to Ghana every year. We call people like Kofi American African, not African American, which is what we call our brothers and sisters whose ancestors were slaves."

"It was a B minus, not a C," Kofi quipped.

"Try and make friends with our African American brothers and sisters in a spirit of true pan-Africanism. But make sure you remain friends with fellow Africans, as this will help you keep your perspective. Always attend African Students Association meetings, but if you must, you can also try the Black Student Union. Please note that in general, African Americans go to the Black Student Union and Africans go to the African Students Association. Sometimes it overlaps but not a lot. The Africans who go to BSU are those with no confidence who are quick to tell you 'I am *originally* from Kenya' even though Kenya just pops out the minute they open their mouths. The African Americans who come to our meetings are the ones who write poems about Mother Africa and think every African is a Nubian queen. If an African American calls you a Mandingo or a booty scratcher, he is insulting you for being African. Some will ask you annoying questions about Africa, but others will connect with you. You will also find that you might make friends more easily with other internationals, Koreans, Indians, Brazilians, whatever, than with Americans both black and white. Many of the internationals understand the trauma of trying to get an American visa and that is a good place to start a friendship."

There was more laughter, Mwombeki himself laughing loudly, as though he had not heard his own jokes before.

Later, as Ifemelu left the meeting, she thought of Dike, wondered which he would go to in college, ASA or BSU, and what he would be considered, American African or African American. He would have to choose what he was, or rather, what he was would be chosen for him.

IFEMELU THOUGHT the interview at the restaurant where Dorothy worked had gone well. It was for a hostess position, and she wore her nice shirt, smiled warmly, shook hands firmly. The manager, a chortling woman full of a seemingly uncontrollable happiness, told her, "Great! Wonderful to talk to you! You'll hear from me soon!" And so when, that evening, her phone rang, she snatched it up, hoping it was a job offer.

"Ifem, *kedu*?" Aunty Uju said.

Aunty Uju called too often to ask if she had found a job. "Aunty, you will be the first person I will call when I do," Ifemelu had said during the last call, only yesterday, and now Aunty Uju was calling again.

"Fine," Ifemelu said, and was about to add, "I have not found anything yet," when Aunty Uju said, "Something happened with Dike."

"What?" Ifemelu asked.

"Miss Brown told me that she saw him in a closet with a girl. The girl is in third grade. Apparently they were showing each other their private parts."

There was a pause.

"Is that all?" Ifemelu asked.

"What do you mean, is that all? He is not yet seven years old! What type of thing is this? Is this what I came to America for?"

"We actually read something about this in one of my classes the other day. It's normal. Children are curious about things like that at an early age, but they don't really understand it."

"Normal *kwa*? It's not normal at all."

"Aunty, we were all curious as children."

"Not at seven years old! Tufiakwa! Where did he learn that from? It is that day care he goes to. Since Alma left and he started going to Miss Brown, he has changed. All those wild children with no home training, he is learning rubbish from them. I've decided to move to Massachusetts at the end of this term."

"Ahn-ahn!"

"I'll finish my residency there and Dike will go to a better school and better day care. Bartholomew is moving from Boston to a small town, Warrington, to start his business, so it will be a new beginning for both of us. The elementary school there is very good. And the local doctor is looking for a partner because his practice is growing. I've spoken to him and he is interested in my joining him when I finish."

"You're leaving New York to go to a village in Massachusetts? Can you just leave residency like that?"

"Of course. My friend Olga, the one from Russia? She is leaving, too, but she will have to repeat a year in her new programme. She wants to practise dermatology and most of our patients here are black and she said skin diseases look different on black skin and she knows she will not end up practising in a black area, so she wants to go where the patients will be white. I don't blame her. It's true my programme is higher ranked, but sometimes job opportunities are better in smaller places. Besides, I don't want Bartholomew to think I am not serious. I'm not getting any younger. I want to start trying."

"You're really going to marry him."

Aunty Uju said with mock exasperation, "Ifem, I thought we had passed that stage. Once I move, we'll go to court and get married, so that he can act as Dike's legal parent."

Ifemelu heard the beep-beep of an incoming call. "Aunty, let me call you back," she said, and switched over without waiting for Aunty Uju's response. It was the restaurant manager.

"I'm sorry, Ngozi," she said, "but we decided to hire a more qualified person. Good luck!"

Ifemelu put the phone down and thought of her mother, how she often blamed the devil. *The devil is a liar. The devil wants to block us.* She stared at the phone, and then at the bills on her table, a tight, suffocating pressure rising inside her chest.

CHAPTER 15

The man was short, his body a glut of muscles, his hair thinning and sun-bleached. When he opened the door, he looked her over, mercilessly sizing her up, and then he smiled and said, "Come on in. My office is in the basement." Her skin prickled, an unease settling over her. There was something venal about his thin-lipped face; he had the air of a man to whom corruption was familiar.

"I'm a pretty busy guy," he said, gesturing to a chair in his cramped home office that smelled slightly of damp.

"I assumed so from the advertisement," Ifemelu said. *Female personal assistant for busy sports coach in Ardmore, communication and interpersonal skills required.* She sat on the chair, perched really, suddenly thinking that, from reading a *City Paper* ad, she was now alone with a strange man in the basement of a strange house in America. Hands thrust deep in his jeans pockets, he walked back and forth with short quick steps, talking about how much in demand he was as a tennis coach, and Ifemelu thought he might trip on the stacks of sports magazines on the floor. She felt dizzy just watching him. He spoke as quickly as he moved, his expression uncannily alert; his eyes stayed wide and unblinking for too long.

"So here's the deal. There are two positions, one for office work and the other for help relaxing. The office position has already been filled. She started yesterday, she goes to Bryn Mawr, and she'll spend the whole week just clearing up my backlog of stuff. I bet I have some unopened cheques in there somewhere." He withdrew a hand to gesture towards his messy desk. "Now what I need is help to relax. If you want the job you have it. I'd pay you a hundred dollars a day, with the possibility of a raise, and you'd work as needed, no set schedule."

A hundred dollars, almost enough for her monthly rent. She

shifted on the chair. "What exactly do you mean by 'help to relax'?"

She was watching him, waiting for his explanation. It began to bother her, thinking of how much she had paid for the suburban train ticket.

"Look, you're not a kid," he said. "I work so hard I can't sleep. I can't relax. I don't do drugs, so I figured I need help to relax. You can give me a massage, help me relax, you know. I had somebody doing it before, but she's just moved to Pittsburgh. It's a great gig, at least she thought so. Helped her with a lot of her college debt." He had said this to many other women, she could tell, from the measured pace with which the words came out. He was not a kind man. She did not know exactly what he meant, but whatever it was, she regretted that she had come.

She stood up. "Can I think about this and give you a call?"

"Of course." He shrugged, shoulders thick with sudden irritability, as though he could not believe she did not recognize her good fortune. As he let her out, he shut the door quickly, not responding to her final "Thank you." She walked back to the station, mourning the train fare. The trees were awash with colour, red and yellow leaves tinted the air golden, and she thought of the words she had recently read somewhere: *Nature's first green is gold*. The crisp air, fragrant and dry, reminded her of Nsukka during the harmattan season, and brought with it a sudden stab of homesickness, so sharp and so abrupt that it filled her eyes with tears.

EACH TIME she went to a job interview, or made a phone call about a job, she told herself that this would, finally, be her day; this time, the waitress, hostess, babysitter position would be hers, but even as she wished herself well, there was already a gathering gloom in a far corner of her mind. "What am I doing wrong?" she asked Ginika, and Ginika told her to be patient, to have hope. She typed and retyped her résumé, invented past waitressing experience in Lagos, wrote Ginika's name as an employer whose children she had babysat, gave the name of Wambui's landlady as a reference, and, at each interview, she smiled warmly and shook hands firmly, all the things that were suggested in a book she had read about interviewing for American jobs. Yet there was no job. Was it her foreign accent? Her lack of experience? But her African friends all had jobs, and college students got jobs all the time with no experience. Once, she went to a gas station near Chestnut Street and a large Mexican man said, with his eyes on her chest, "You're here for the attendant position? You can work for me in another way." Then, with a smile, the leer never leaving his eyes, he told her the job was taken. She began to think more about her mother's devil, to imagine how the devil might have a hand here. She added and subtracted endlessly, determining what she would need and not need, cooking rice and beans each week, and heating up small portions in the microwave for lunch and dinner. Obinze offered to send her some money. His cousin had visited from London and given him some pounds. He would change it to dollars in Enugu.

"How can you be sending me money from Nigeria? It should be the other way around," she said. But he sent it to her anyway, a little over a hundred dollars carefully sealed in a card.

GINIKA WAS BUSY, working long hours at her internship and studying for her law school exams, but she called often to check up on Ifemelu's job searching, and always with that upbeat voice, as though to urge Ifemelu towards hope. "This woman I did an internship with her charity, Kimberly, called me to say her babysitter is leaving and she's looking. I told her about you and she'd like to meet you. If she hires you, she'll pay cash under the table so you won't have to use that fake name. When do you finish tomorrow? I can come and take you to her for an interview."

"If I get this job, I will give you my first month's salary," Ifemelu said, and Ginika laughed.

Ginika parked in the circular driveway of a house that announced its wealth, the stone exterior solid and overbearing, four white pillars rising portentously at the entrance. Kimberly opened the front door. She was slim and straight, and raised both hands to push her thick golden hair away from her face, as though one hand could not possibly tame all that hair.

"How nice to meet you," she said to Ifemelu, smiling, as they shook hands, her hand small, bony-fingered, fragile. In her gold sweater belted at an impossibly tiny waist, with her gold hair, in gold flats, she looked improbable, like sunlight.

"This is my sister Laura, who's visiting. Well, we visit each other almost every day! Laura practically lives next door. The kids are in the Poconos until tomorrow, with my mother. I thought it would be best to do this when they're not here anyway."

"Hi," Laura said. She was as thin and straight and blonde as Kimberly. Ifemelu, describing them to Obinze, would say that Kimberly gave the impression of a tiny bird with fine bones, easily crushed, while Laura brought to mind a hawk, sharp-beaked and dark-minded.

"Hello, I'm Ifemelu."

"What a beautiful name," Kimberly said. "Does it mean anything? I love multicultural names because they have such wonderful meanings, from wonderful rich cultures." Kimberly was smiling the kindly smile of people who thought "culture" the unfamiliar colourful reserve of colourful people, a word that always had to be qualified with "rich". She would not think Norway had a "rich culture".

"I don't know what it means," Ifemelu said, and sensed rather than saw a small amusement on Ginika's face.

"Would you like some tea?" Kimberly asked, leading the way into a kitchen of shiny chrome and granite and affluent empty space. "We're tea drinkers, but of course there are other choices."

"Tea is great," Ginika said.

"And you, Ifemelu?" Kimberly asked. "I know I'm mauling your name but it really is such a beautiful name. Really beautiful."

"No, you said it properly. I'd like some water or orange juice, please." Ifemelu would come to realize later that Kimberly used "beautiful" in a peculiar way. "I'm meeting my beautiful friend from graduate school," Kimberly would say, or "We're working with this beautiful woman on the inner-city project," and always, the women she referred to would turn out to be quite ordinary-looking, but always black. One day, late that winter, when she was with Kimberly at the huge kitchen table, drinking tea and waiting for the children to be brought back from an outing with their grandmother, Kimberly said, "Oh, look at this beautiful woman," and pointed at a plain model in a magazine whose only distinguishing feature was her very dark skin. "Isn't she just stunning?"

"No, she isn't." Ifemelu paused. "You know, you can just say 'black'. Not every black person is beautiful."

Kimberly was taken aback, something wordless spread on her face and then she smiled, and Ifemelu would think of it as the moment they became, truly, friends. But on that first day, she liked Kimberly, her breakable beauty, her purplish eyes full of the expression Obinze often used to describe the people he liked: *obi ocha.* A clean heart. Kimberly asked Ifemelu questions about her experience with children, listening carefully as though what she wanted to hear was what might be left unsaid.

"She doesn't have CPR certification, Kim," Laura said. She turned to Ifemelu. "Are you willing to take the course? It's very important if you are going to have children in your care."

"I'm willing to."

"Ginika said you left Nigeria because college professors are always on strike there?" Kimberly asked.

"Yes."

Laura nodded knowingly. "Horrible, what's going on in African countries."

"How are you finding the US so far?" Kimberly asked.

Ifemelu told her about the vertigo she had felt the first time she went to the supermarket; in the cereal aisle, she had wanted to get cornflakes, which she was used to eating back home, but suddenly confronted by a hundred different cereal boxes, in a swirl of colours and images, she had fought dizziness. She told this story because she thought it was funny; it appealed harmlessly to the American ego.

Laura laughed. "I can see how you'd be dizzy!"

"Yes, we're really about excess in this country," Kimberly said. "I'm sure back home you ate a lot of wonderful organic food and vegetables, but you're going to see it's different here."

"Kim, if she was eating all of this wonderful organic food in Nigeria, why would she come to the US?" Laura asked. As children, Laura must have played the role of the big sister who exposed the stupidity of the little sister, always with kindness and good cheer, and preferably in the company of adult relatives.

"Well, even if they had very little food, I'm just saying it was probably all organic vegetables, none of the Frankenfood we have here," Kimberly said. Ifemelu sensed, between them, the presence of spiky thorns floating in the air.

"You haven't told her about television," Laura said. She turned to Ifemelu. "Kim's kids do supervised TV, only PBS. So if she hired you, you would need to be completely present and monitor what goes on, especially with Morgan."

"Okay."

"I don't have a babysitter," Laura said, her "I" glowing with righteous emphasis. "I'm a full-time, hands-on mom. I thought I would return to work when Athena turned two, but I just couldn't bear to let her go. Kim is really hands-on, too, but she's busy sometimes, she does wonderful work with her charity, and so I'm always worried about the babysitters. The last one, Martha, was wonderful, but we did wonder whether the one before her, what was her name again, let Morgan watch inappropriate shows. I don't do any television at all with my daughter. I think there's too much violence. I might let her do a few cartoons when she's a little older."

"But there's violence in cartoons, too," Ifemelu said.

Laura looked annoyed. "It's cartoon. Kids are traumatized by the real thing."

Ginika glanced at Ifemelu, a knitted-brow look that said: Just leave it alone. In primary school, Ifemelu had watched the firing squad that killed Lawrence Anini, fascinated by the mythologies around his armed robberies, how he wrote warning letters to newspapers, fed the poor with what he stole, turned himself into air when the police came. Her mother had said, "Go inside, this is not for children," but half-heartedly, after Ifemelu had already seen most of the shooting anyway, Anini's body roughly tied to a pole, jerking as the bullets hit him, before slumping against the criss-cross of rope. She thought about this now, how haunting and yet how ordinary it had seemed.

"Let me show you the house, Ifemelu," Kimberly said. "Did I say it right?"

They walked from room to room—the daughter's room with pink walls and a frilly bedcover, the son's room with a set of drums, the den with a piano, its polished wooden top crowded with family photographs.

"We took that in India," Kimberly said. They were standing by an empty rickshaw, wearing T-shirts, Kimberly with her golden hair tied back, her tall and lean husband, her small blond son and older red-haired daughter, all holding water bottles and smiling. They were always smiling in the photos they took, while sailing and hiking and visiting tourist spots, holding each other, all easy limbs and white teeth. They reminded Ifemelu of television commercials, of people whose lives were lived always in flattering light, whose messes were still aesthetically pleasing.

"Some of the people we met had nothing, absolutely nothing, but they were so happy," Kimberly said. She extracted a photograph from the crowded back of the piano, of her daughter with two Indian women, their skin dark and weathered, their smiles showing missing teeth. "These women were so wonderful," she said.

Ifemelu would also come to learn that, for Kimberly, the poor were blameless. Poverty was a gleaming thing; she could not conceive of poor people being vicious or nasty, because their poverty had canonized them, and the greatest saints were the foreign poor.

"Morgan loves that, it's Native American. But Taylor says it's scary!" Kimberly pointed to a small piece of sculpture amid the photographs.

"Oh." Ifemelu suddenly did not remember which was the boy and which the girl; both names, Morgan and Taylor, sounded to her like surnames.

Kimberly's husband came home just before Ifemelu left.

"Hello! Hello!" he said, gliding into the kitchen, tall and tanned and tactical. Ifemelu could tell, from the longish length, the near-perfect waves that grazed his collar, that he took fastidious care of his hair.

"You must be Ginika's friend from Nigeria," he said, smiling, brimming with his awareness of his own charm. He looked people in the eye not because he was interested in them but because he knew it made them feel that he was interested in them.

With his appearance, Kimberly became slightly breathless. Her voice changed; she spoke now in the high-pitched voice of the self-consciously female. "Don, honey, you're early," she said as they kissed.

Don looked into Ifemelu's eyes and told her how he had nearly visited Nigeria, just after Shagari was elected, when he worked as a consultant to an international development agency, but the trip fell through at the last minute and he had felt bad because he had been hoping to go to the shrine and see Fela perform. He mentioned Fela casually, intimately, as though it was something they had in common, a secret they shared. There was, in his storytelling, an expectation of successful seduction. Ifemelu stared at him, saying little, refusing to be ensnared, and feeling strangely sorry for Kimberly. To be saddled with a sister like Laura and a husband like this.

"Don and I are involved with a really good charity in Malawi, actually Don is much more involved than I am." Kimberly looked at Don, who made a wry face and said, "Well, we do our best but we know very well that we're not messiahs."

"We really should plan a trip to visit. It's an orphanage. We've never been to Africa. I would love to do something with my charity in Africa."

Kimberly's face had softened, her eyes misted over, and for a moment Ifemelu was sorry to have come from Africa, to be the reason that this beautiful woman, with her bleached teeth and bounteous hair, would have to dig deep to feel such pity, such hopelessness. She smiled brightly, hoping to make Kimberly feel better.

"I'm interviewing one more person and then I'll let you know, but I really think you're a great fit for us," Kimberly said, leading Ifemelu and Ginika to the front door.

"Thank you," Ifemelu said. "I would love to work for you."

The next day, Ginika called and left a message, her tone low. "Ifem, I'm so sorry. Kimberly hired somebody else but she said she'll keep you in mind. Something will work out soon, don't worry too much. I'll call later."

Ifemelu wanted to fling the phone away. *Keep her in mind.* Why would Ginika even repeat such an empty expression, "keep her in mind"?

IT WAS late autumn, the trees had grown antlers, dried leaves were sometimes trailed into the apartment, and the rent was due. Her room-mates' cheques were on the kitchen table, one on top of the other, all of them pink and bordered by flowers. She thought it unnecessarily decorative, to have flowered cheques in America; it almost took away from the seriousness of a cheque. Beside the cheques was a note, in Jackie's childish writing: *Ifemelu, we're almost a week late for rent.* Writing a cheque would leave her account empty. Her mother had given her a small jar of Mentholatum the day before she left Lagos, saying, "Put this in your bag, for when you will be cold." She rummaged now in her suitcase for it, opened and sniffed it, rubbing some under her nose. The scent made her want to weep. The answering machine was blinking but she did not check it because it would be yet another variation of Aunty Uju's message. "Has anyone called you back? Have you tried the nearby McDonald's and Burger King? They don't always advertise but they might be hiring. I can't send you anything until next month. My own account is empty, honestly to be a resident doctor is slave labour."

Newspapers were strewn on the floor, job listings circled in ink. She picked one up and flipped through, looking at advertisements she had already seen. ESCORTS caught her eye again. Ginika had said to her, "Forget that escort thing. They say it isn't prostitution but it is, and the worst thing is that you get maybe a quarter of what you earn because the agency takes the rest. I know this girl who did it in freshman year." Ifemelu read the advertisement and thought, again, of calling, but she didn't, because she was hoping that the last interview she went for, a waitress position in a little restaurant that didn't pay a salary, only tips, would come through. They had said they would call her by the end of the day if she got the job; she waited until very late but they did not call.

AND THEN Elena's dog ate her bacon. She had heated up a slice of bacon on a paper towel, put it on the table and turned to open the fridge. The dog swallowed the bacon and the paper towel. She stared at the empty space where her bacon had been, and then she stared at the dog, its expression smug, and all the frustrations of her life boiled up in her head. A dog eating her bacon, a dog eating her bacon while she was jobless.

"Your dog just ate my bacon," she told Elena, who was slicing a banana at the other end of the kitchen, the pieces falling into her cereal bowl.

"You just hate my dog."

"You should train him better. He shouldn't eat people's food from the kitchen table."

"You better not kill my dog with voodoo."

"What?"

"Just kidding!" Elena said. Elena was smirking, her dog's tail wagging, and Ifemelu felt acid in her veins; she moved towards Elena, hand raised and ready to explode on Elena's face, before she caught herself with a jolt, stopped and turned and went upstairs. She sat on her bed and hugged her knees to her chest, shaken by her own reaction, how quickly her fury had risen. Downstairs, Elena was screaming on the phone: "I swear to God, bitch just tried to hit me!" Ifemelu had wanted to slap her dissolute room-mate not because a slobbering dog had eaten her bacon but because she was at war with the world, and woke up each day feeling bruised, imagining a horde of faceless people who were all against her. It terrified her, to be unable to visualize tomorrow. When her parents called and left a voice message, she saved it, unsure if that would be the last time she would hear their voices. To be here, living abroad, not knowing when she could go home again, was to watch love become anxiety. If she called her mother's friend Aunty Bunmi and the phone rang to the end, with no answer, she panicked, worried that perhaps her father had died and Aunty Bunmi did not know how to tell her.

LATER, Allison knocked on her door. "Ifemelu? Just wanted to remind you, your rent cheque isn't on the table. We're already really late."

"I know. I'm writing it." She lay face up on her bed. She didn't want to be the room-mate who had rent problems. She hated that Ginika had bought her groceries last week. She could hear Jackie's raised voice from downstairs. "What are we supposed to do? We're not her fucking parents."

She brought out her chequebook. Before she wrote the cheque, she called Aunty Uju to speak to Dike. Then, refreshed by his innocence, she called the tennis coach in Ardmore.

"When can I start working?" she asked.

"Want to come over right now?"

"Okay," she said.

She shaved her underarms, dug out the lipstick she had not worn since the day she left Lagos, most of it left smeared on Obinze's neck at the airport. What would happen with the tennis coach? He had said "massage", but his manner, his tone, had dripped suggestion. Perhaps he was one of those white men she had read about, with strange tastes, who wanted women to drag a feather over their back or urinate on them. She could certainly do that, urinate on a man for a hundred dollars. The thought amused her, and she smiled a small wry smile. Whatever happened, she would approach it looking her best, she would make it clear to him that there were boundaries she would not cross. She would say, from the beginning, "If you expect sex, then I can't help you." Or perhaps she would say it more delicately, more suggestively. "I'm not comfortable going too far." She might be imagining too much; he might just want a massage.

When she arrived at his house, his manner was brusque. "Come on up," he said, and led the way to his bedroom, bare but for a bed and a large painting of a tomato soup can on the wall. He offered her something to drink, in a perfunctory way that suggested he expected her to say no, and then he took off his shirt and lay on the bed. Was there no preface? She wished he had done things a little more slowly. Her own words had deserted her.

"Come over here," he said. "I need to be warm."

She should leave now. The power balance was tilted in his favour, had been tilted in his favour since she walked into his house. She should leave. She stood up.

"I can't have sex," she said. Her voice felt squeaky, unsure of itself. "I can't have sex with you," she repeated.

"Oh no, I don't expect you to," he said, too quickly.

She moved slowly towards the door, wondering if it was locked, if he had locked it, and then she wondered if he had a gun.

"Just come here and lie down," he said. "Keep me warm. I'll touch you a little bit, nothing you'll be uncomfortable with. I just need some human contact to relax."

There was, in his expression and tone, a complete assuredness; she felt defeated. How sordid it all was, that she was here with a stranger who already knew she would stay. He knew she would stay because she had come. She was already here, already tainted. She took off her shoes and climbed into his bed. She did not want to be here, did not want his active finger between her legs, did not want his sigh-moans in her ear, and yet she felt her body rousing to a sickening wetness. Afterwards, she lay still, coiled and deadened. He had not forced her. She had come here on her own. She had lain on his bed, and when he placed her hand between his legs, she had curled and moved her fingers. Now, even after she had washed her hands, holding the crisp, slender hundred-dollar bill he had given her, her fingers still felt sticky; they no longer belonged to her.

"Can you do twice a week? I'll cover your train fare," he said, stretching and dismissive; he wanted her to leave.

She said nothing.

"Shut the door," he said, and turned his back to her.

She walked to the train, feeling heavy and slow, her mind choked with mud, and, seated by the window, she began to cry. She felt like a small ball, adrift and alone. The world was a big, big place and she was so tiny, so insignificant, rattling around emptily. Back in her apartment, she washed her hands with water so hot that it scalded her fingers, and a small soft welt flowered on her thumb. She took off all her clothes and squashed them into a rumpled ball that she threw at a corner, staring at it for a while. She would never again wear those clothes, never even touch them. She sat naked on her bed and looked at her life, in this tiny room with the mouldy carpet, the hundred-dollar bill on the table, her body rising with loathing. She should never have gone there. She should have walked away. She wanted to shower, to scrub herself, but she could not bear the thought of touching her own body, and so she put on her nightdress, gingerly, to touch as little of herself as possible. She imagined packing her things, somehow buying a ticket and going back to Lagos. She curled on her bed and cried, wishing she could reach into herself and yank out the memory of what had just happened. Her voicemail light was blinking. It was probably Obinze. She could not bear to think of him now. She thought of calling Ginika. Finally, she called Aunty Uju.

"I went to work for a man in the suburbs today. He paid me a hundred dollars."

"Ehn? That's very good. But you have to keep looking for something permanent. I've just realized I have to buy health insurance for Dike because the one this new hospital in Massachusetts offers is nonsense, it does not cover him. I am still in shock by how much I have to pay."

"Won't you ask me what I did, Aunty? Won't you ask me what I did before the man paid me a hundred dollars?" Ifemelu asked, a new anger sweeping over her, treading itself through her fingers so that they shook.

"What did you do?" Aunty Uju asked flatly.

Ifemelu hung up. She pressed New on her machine. The first message was from her mother, speaking quickly to reduce the cost of the call: "Ifem, how are you? We are calling to see how you are. We have not heard from you in a while. Please send a message. We are well. God bless you."

Then Obinze's voice, his words floating into the air, into her head. "I love you, Ifem," he said, at the end, in that voice that seemed suddenly so far away, part of another time and place. She lay rigid on her bed. She could not sleep, she could not distract herself. She began to think about killing the tennis coach. She would hit him on the head over and over with an axe. She would plunge a knife into his muscled chest. He lived alone, he probably had other women coming to his room to spread their legs for his stubby finger with its bitten-back nail. Nobody would know which of them had done it. She would leave the knife sunk in his chest and then search his drawers for his bundle of one-hundred-dollar bills, so that she could pay her rent and her tuition.

That night, it snowed, her first snow, and in the morning, she watched the world outside her window, the parked cars made lumpy, misshapen, by layered snow. She was bloodless, detached, floating in a world where darkness descended too soon and everyone walked around burdened by coats, and flattened by the absence of light. The days drained into one another, crisp air turning to freezing air, painful to inhale. Obinze called many times but she did not pick up her phone. She deleted his voice messages unheard and his e-mails unread, and she felt herself sinking, sinking quickly, and unable to pull herself up.

SHE WOKE UP torpid each morning, slowed by sadness, frightened by the endless stretch of day that lay ahead. Everything had thickened. She was swallowed, lost in a viscous haze, shrouded in a soup of nothingness. Between her and what she should feel, there was a gap. She cared about nothing. She wanted to care, but she no longer knew how; it had slipped from her memory, the ability to care. Sometimes she woke up flailing and helpless, and she saw, in front of her and behind her and all around her, an utter hopelessness. She knew there was no point in being here, in being alive, but she had no energy to think concretely of how she could kill herself. She lay in bed and read books and thought of nothing. Sometimes she forgot to eat and other times she waited until midnight, her room-mates in their rooms, before heating up her food, and she left the dirty plates under her bed, until greenish mould fluffed up around the oily remnants of rice and beans. Often, in the middle of eating or reading, she would feel a crushing urge to cry and the tears would come, the sobs hurting her throat. She had turned off the ringer of her phone. She no longer went to class. Her days were stilled by silence and snow.

ALLISON WAS BANGING on her door again. "Are you there? Phone call! She says it's an emergency, for God's sake! I know you're there, I heard you flush the toilet a minute ago!"

The flat, dulled banging, as though Allison was hitting the door with an open palm rather than a knuckle, unnerved Ifemelu. "She's not opening," she heard Allison say, and then, just when she thought Allison had left, the banging resumed. She got up from her bed, where she had been lying and taking turns reading two novels chapter by chapter, and with leaden feet moved to the door. She wanted to walk quickly, normally, but she could not. Her feet had turned into snails. She unlocked the door. With a glare, Allison thrust the phone in her hand.

"Thanks," she said, limply, and added, in a lower mumble, "Sorry."

Even talking, making words rise up her throat and out of her mouth, exhausted her.

"Hello?" she said into the phone.

"Ifem! What's going on? What's happening to you?" Ginika asked.

"Nothing," she said.

"I've been so worried about you. Thank God I found your roommate's number! Obinze has been calling me. He's worried out of his mind," Ginika said. "Even Aunty Uju called to ask if I had seen you."

"I've been busy," Ifemelu said vaguely.

There was a pause. Ginika's tone softened. "Ifem, I'm here, you know that, right?"

Ifemelu wanted to hang up and return to her bed. "Yes."

"I have good news. Kimberly called me to ask for your phone number. The babysitter she hired just left. She wants to hire you. She wants you to start on Monday. She said she wanted you from the beginning but Laura talked her into hiring the other person. So, Ifem, you have a job! Cash! Under the table! Ifemsco, this is great. She'll pay you two-fifty a week, more than the old babysitter. And pure cash under the table! Kimberly is a really great person. I'm coming tomorrow to take you over there to see her."

Ifemelu said nothing, struggling to understand. Words took so long to form meaning.

The next day, Ginika knocked and knocked on her door before Ifemelu finally opened, and saw Allison standing on the landing at the back, watching curiously.

"We're late already, get dressed," Ginika said, firmly, authoritatively, with no room for dissent. Ifemelu pulled on a pair of jeans. She felt Ginika watching her. In the car, Ginika's rock music filled the silence between them. They were on Lancaster Avenue, just about to cross over from West Philadelphia, with boarded-up buildings and hamburger wrappers strewn around, and into the spotless, tree-filled suburbs of the Main Line, when Ginika said, "I think you're suffering from depression."

Ifemelu shook her head and turned to the window. Depression was what happened to Americans, with their self-absolving need to turn everything into an illness. She was not suffering from depression; she was merely a little tired and a little slow. "I don't have depression," she said. Years later, she would blog about this: "On the Subject of Non-American Blacks Suffering from Illnesses Whose Names They Refuse to Know." A Congolese woman wrote a long comment in response: She had moved to Virginia from Kinshasa and, months into her first semester of college, begun to feel dizzy in the morning, her heart pounding as though in flight from her, her stomach fraught with nausea, her fingers tingling. She went to see a doctor. And even though she checked "yes" to all the symptoms on the card the doctor gave her, she refused to accept the diagnosis of panic attacks because panic attacks happened only to Americans. Nobody in Kinshasa had panic attacks. It was not even that it was called by another name, it was simply not called at all. Did things begin to exist only when they were named?

"Ifem, this is something a lot of people go through, and I know it's not been easy for you adjusting to a new place and still not having a job. We don't talk about things like depression in Nigeria but it's real. You should see somebody at the health centre. There's always therapists."

Ifemelu kept her face to the window. She felt, again, that crushing desire to cry, and she took a deep breath, hoping it would pass. She wished she had told Ginika about the tennis coach, taken the train to Ginika's apartment on that day, but now it was too late, her self-loathing had hardened inside her. She would never be able to form the sentences to tell her story.

"Ginika," she said. "Thank you." Her voice was hoarse. The tears had come, she could not control them. Ginika stopped at a gas station, gave her a tissue and waited for her sobs to die down before she started the car and drove to Kimberly's house.

CHAPTER 16

Kimberly called it a signing bonus. "Ginika told me you've had some challenges," Kimberly said. "Please don't refuse."

It would not have occurred to Ifemelu to refuse the cheque; now she could pay some bills, send something home to her parents. Her mother liked the shoes she sent, tasselled and tapering, the kind she could wear to church. "Thank you," her mother said, and then sighing heavily over the phone line, she added, "Obinze came to see me."

Ifemelu was silent.

"Whatever problem you have, please discuss it with him," her mother said.

Ifemelu said, "Okay," and began to talk about something else. When her mother said there had been no light for two weeks, it seemed suddenly foreign to her, and home itself a distant place. She could no longer remember what it felt like to spend an evening in candlelight. She no longer read the news on Nigeria.com because each headline, even the most unlikely ones, somehow reminded her of Obinze.

At first, she gave herself a month. A month to let her self-loathing seep away, then she would call Obinze. But a month passed and still she kept Obinze sealed in silence, gagged her own mind so that she would think of him as little as possible. She still deleted his e-mails unread. Many times she started to write to him, she crafted e-mails, and then stopped and discarded them. She would have to tell him what happened, and she could not bear the thought of telling him what happened. She felt shamed; she had failed. Ginika kept asking what was wrong, why she had shut out Obinze, and she said it was nothing, she just wanted some space, and Ginika gaped at her in disbelief. *You just want some space?*

Early in the spring, a letter arrived from Obinze. Deleting his e-mails took a click, and after the first click, the others were easier because she could not imagine reading the second if she had not read the first. But a letter was different. It brought to her the greatest sorrow she had ever felt. She sank to her bed, holding the envelope in her hand; she smelled it, stared at his familiar handwriting. She imagined him at his desk in his boys' quarters, near his small humming refrigerator, writing in that calm manner of his. She wanted to read the letter, but she could not get herself to open it. She put it on her table. She would read it in a week; she needed a week to gather her strength. She would reply, too, she told herself. She would tell him everything. But a week later, the letter still lay there. She placed a book on top of it, then another book, and one day it was swallowed beneath files and books. She would never read it.

TAYLOR WAS EASY, a childish child, the playful one who was sometimes so naïve that Ifemelu guiltily thought him stupid. But Morgan, only three years older, already wore the mourning demeanour of a teenager. She read many grades above her level, was steeped in enrichment classes and watched adults with a hooded gaze, as though privy to the darkness that lurked in their lives. At first, Ifemelu disliked Morgan, responding to what she thought was Morgan's own disturbingly full-grown dislike. She was cool, sometimes even cold, to Morgan during her first weeks with them, determined not to indulge this spoilt silken child with a dusting of burgundy freckles on her nose, but she had come, with the passing months, to care for Morgan, an emotion she was careful not to show to Morgan. Instead she was firm and neutral, staring back when Morgan stared. Perhaps it was why Morgan did what Ifemelu asked. She would do it coldly, indifferently, grudgingly, but she would do it. She routinely ignored her mother. And with her father, her brooding watchfulness sharpened into poison. Don would come home and sweep into the den, expecting that everything would stop because of him. And everything did stop, except for whatever Morgan was doing. Kimberly, fluttery and ardent, would ask how his day was, scrambling to please, as though she could not quite believe that he had again come home to her. Taylor would hurl himself into Don's arms. And Morgan would look up from the TV or a book or a game to watch him, as though she saw through him, while Don pretended not to squirm under her piercing eyes. Sometimes Ifemelu wondered. Was it Don? Was he cheating and had Morgan found out? Cheating was the first thing anyone would think of with a man like Don, with that lubricious aura of his. But he might be satisfied with suggestiveness alone; he would flirt outrageously but not do more, because an affair would require some effort and he was the kind of man who took but did not give.

Ifemelu thought often of that afternoon early in her babysitting: Kimberly was out, Taylor was playing and Morgan reading in the den. Suddenly, Morgan put down her book, calmly walked upstairs and ripped off the wallpaper in her room, pushed down her dresser, yanked off her bedcovers, tore down the curtains, and was on her knees pulling and pulling and pulling at the strongly glued carpet when Ifemelu ran in and stopped her. Morgan was like a small, steel robot, writhing to be let free, with a strength that frightened Ifemelu. Perhaps the child would end up being a serial murderer, like those women on television crime documentaries, standing half-naked on dark roads to lure truck drivers and then strangle them. When finally Ifemelu let go, slowly loosening her grip on a quietened Morgan, Morgan went back downstairs to her book.

Later, Kimberly, in tears, asked her, "Honey, please tell me what's wrong."

And Morgan said, "I'm too old for all that pink stuff in my room."

Now, Kimberly took Morgan twice a week to a therapist in Bala Cynwyd. Both she and Don were more tentative towards her, more cowering under her denouncing stare.

When Morgan won an essay contest at school, Don came home with a present for her. Kimberly anxiously stood at the bottom of the stairs while Don went up to present the gift, wrapped in sparkly paper. He came down moments later.

"She wouldn't even look at it. She just got up and went into the bathroom and stayed there," he said. "I left it on the bed."

"It's okay, honey, she'll come around," Kimberly said, hugging him, rubbing his back.

Later, Kimberly, sotto voce, told Ifemelu, "Morgan's really hard on him. He tries so hard and she won't let him in. She just won't."

"Morgan doesn't let anyone in," Ifemelu said. Don needed to remember that Morgan, and not he, was the child.

"She listens to you," Kimberly said, a little sadly.

Ifemelu wanted to say, "I don't give her too many choices," because she wished Kimberly would not be so sheer in her yieldingness; perhaps Morgan just needed to feel that her mother could push back. Instead she said, "That's because I'm not her family. She doesn't love me and so she doesn't feel all these complicated things for me. I'm just a nuisance at best."

"I don't know what I'm doing wrong," Kimberly said.

"It's a phase. It will pass, you'll see." She felt protective of Kimberly, she wanted to shield Kimberly.

"The only person she really cares about is my cousin Curt. She adores him. If we have family gatherings, she'll brood unless Curt is there. I'll see if he can come visit and talk to her."

LAURA HAD BROUGHT a magazine.

"Look at this, Ifemelu," she said. "It isn't Nigeria, but it's close. I know celebrities can be flighty but she seems to be doing good work."

Ifemelu and Kimberly looked at the page together: a thin white woman, smiling at the camera, holding a dark-skinned African baby in her arms, and all around her, little dark-skinned African children were spread out like a rug. Kimberly made a sound, a hmmm, as though she was unsure how to feel.

"She's stunning too," Laura said.

"Yes, she is," Ifemelu said. "And she's just as skinny as the kids, only that her skinniness is by choice and theirs is not by choice."

A pop of loud laughter burst out from Laura. "You *are* funny! I love how sassy you are!"

Kimberly did not laugh. Later, alone with Ifemelu, she said, "I'm sorry Laura said that. I've never liked that word 'sassy'. It's the kind of word that's used for certain people and not for others." Ifemelu shrugged and smiled and changed the subject. She did not understand why Laura looked up so much information about Nigeria, asking her about 419 scams, telling her how much money Nigerians in America sent back home every year. It was an aggressive, unaffectionate interest; strange indeed, to pay so much attention to something you did not like. Perhaps it was really about Kimberly, and Laura was in some distorted way aiming at her sister by saying things that would make Kimberly launch into apologies. It seemed too much work for too little gain, though. At first, Ifemelu thought Kimberly's apologizing sweet, even if unnecessary, but she had begun to feel a flash of impatience, because Kimberly's repeated apologies were tinged with self-indulgence, as though she believed that she could, with apologies, smooth all the scalloped surfaces of the world.

A FEW MONTHS into her babysitting, Kimberly asked her, "Would you consider living in? The basement is really a one-bedroom apartment with a private entrance. It would be rent-free, of course."

Ifemelu was already looking for a studio apartment, eager to leave her room-mates now that she could afford to, and she did not want to be further enmeshed in the lives of the Turners, yet she considered saying yes, because she heard a plea in Kimberly's voice. In the end, she decided she could not live with them. When she said no, Kimberly offered her the use of their spare car. "It'll make it much easier for you to get here after your classes. It's an old thing. We were going to give it away. I hope it doesn't stop you on the road," she said, as if the Honda, only a few years old, its body unmarked, could possibly stop on the road.

"You really shouldn't trust me to take your car home. What if I don't come back one day?" Ifemelu said.

Kimberly laughed. "It's not worth very much."

"You do have an American licence?" Laura asked. "I mean, you can drive legally in this country?"

"Of course she can, Laura," Kimberly said. "Why would she accept the car if she couldn't?"

"I'm just checking," Laura said, as though Kimberly could not be depended upon to ask the necessary tough questions of non-American citizens. Ifemelu watched them, so alike in their looks, and both unhappy people. But Kimberly's unhappiness was inward, unacknowledged, shielded by her desire for things to be as they should, and also by hope: she believed in other people's happiness because it meant that she, too, might one day have it. Laura's unhappiness was different, spiky, she wished that everyone around her were unhappy because she had convinced herself that she would always be.

"Yes, I have an American licence," Ifemelu said, and then she began to talk about the safe-driving course she had taken in Brooklyn, before she got her licence, and how the instructor, a thin white man with matted hair the colour of straw, had cheated. In the dark basement room full of foreigners, the entrance of which was an even darker flight of narrow stairs, the instructor had collected all the cash payments before he showed the safe-driving film on the wall projector. From time to time, he made jokes that nobody understood and chuckled to himself. Ifemelu was a little suspicious of the film: how could a car driving so slowly have caused that amount of damage in an accident, leaving the driver's neck broken? Afterwards, he gave out the test questions. Ifemelu found them easy, quickly shading in the answers in pencil. A small South Asian man beside her, perhaps fifty years old, kept glancing over at her, his eyes pleading, while she pretended not to understand that he wanted her help. The instructor collected the papers, brought out a clay-coloured eraser and began to wipe out some of the answers and to shade in others. Everybody passed. Many of them shook his hand, said "Thank you, thank you" in a wide range of accents before they shuffled out. Now they could apply for American driver's licences. Ifemelu told the story with a false openness, as though it was merely a curiosity for her, and not something she had chosen to goad Laura.

"It was a strange moment for me, because until then I thought nobody in America cheated," Ifemelu said.

Kimberly said, "Oh my goodness."

"This happened in Brooklyn?" Laura asked.

"Yes."

Laura shrugged, as though to say that it would, of course, happen in Brooklyn but not in the America in which she lived.

AT ISSUE WAS an orange. A round, flame-coloured orange that Ifemelu had brought with her lunch, peeled and quartered and enclosed in a Ziploc bag. She ate it at the kitchen table, while Taylor sat nearby writing in his homework sheet.

"Would you like some, Taylor?" she asked, and offered him a piece.

"Thanks," he said. He put it into his mouth. His face crumpled. "It's bad! It's got stuff in it!"

"Those are the seeds," she said, looking at what he had spat into his hand.

"The seeds?"

"Yes, the orange seeds."

"Oranges don't have stuff in them."

"Yes, they do. Throw that in the trash, Taylor. I'm going to put the learning video in for you."

"Oranges don't have stuff in them," he repeated.

All his life, he had eaten oranges without seeds, oranges grown to look perfectly orange and to have faultless skin and no seeds, so at eight years old he did not know that there was such a thing as an orange with seeds. He ran into the den to tell Morgan about it. She looked up from her book, raised a slow, bored hand and tucked her red hair behind her ear.

"Of course oranges have seeds. Mom just buys the seedless variety. Ifemelu didn't get the right kind." She gave Ifemelu one of her accusatory glares.

"The orange is the right one for me, Morgan. I grew up eating oranges with seeds," Ifemelu said, turning on the video.

"Okay." Morgan shrugged. With Kimberly she would have said nothing, only glowered.

The doorbell rang. It had to be the carpet cleaner. Kimberly and Don were hosting a cocktail party fund-raiser the next day, for a friend of theirs about whom Don had said, "It's just an ego trip for him running for Congress, he won't even come close," and Ifemelu was surprised that he seemed to recognize the ego of others, while blinded in the fog of his own. She went to the door. A burly, red-faced man stood there, carrying cleaning equipment, something slung over his shoulder, something else that looked like a lawn mower propped at his feet.

He stiffened when he saw her. First surprise flitted over his features, then it ossified to hostility.

"You need a carpet cleaned?" he asked, as if he did not care, as if she could change her mind, as if he wanted her to change her mind. She looked at him, a taunt in her eyes, prolonging a moment loaded with assumptions: he thought she was a homeowner, and she was not what he had expected to see in this grand stone house with the white pillars.

"Yes," she said finally, suddenly tired. "Mrs Turner told me you were coming."

It was like a conjuror's trick, the swift disappearance of his hostility. His face sank into a grin. She, too, was the help. The universe was once again arranged as it should be.

"How are you doing? Know where she wants me to start?" he asked.

"Upstairs," she said, letting him in, wondering how all that cheeriness could have existed earlier in his body. She would never forget him, bits of dried skin stuck to his chapped, peeling lips, and she would begin the blog post "Sometimes in America, Race Is Class" with the story of his dramatic change, and end with: *It didn't matter to him how much money I had. As far as he was concerned I did not fit as the owner of that stately house because of the way I looked. In America's public discourse, "Blacks" as a whole are often lumped with "Poor Whites." Not Poor Blacks and Poor Whites. But Blacks and Poor Whites. A curious thing indeed.*

Taylor was excited. "Can I help? Can I help?" he asked the carpet cleaner.

"No thanks, buddy," the man said. "I got it."

"I hope he doesn't start in my room," Morgan said.

"Why?" Ifemelu asked.

"I just don't want him to."

IFEMELU WANTED to tell Kimberly about the carpet cleaner, but Kimberly might become flustered and apologize for what was not her fault as she often, too often, apologized for Laura.

It was discomfiting to observe how Kimberly lurched, keen to do the right thing and not knowing what the right thing was. If she told Kimberly about the carpet cleaner, there was no telling how she would respond—laugh, apologize, snatch up the phone to call the company and complain.

And so, instead, she told Kimberly about Taylor and the orange.

"He really thought seeds meant it was bad? How funny."

"Morgan of course promptly set him right," Ifemelu said.

"Oh, she would."

"When I was a little girl my mother used to tell me that an orange would grow on my head if I swallowed a seed. I had many anxious mornings of going to look in the mirror. At least Taylor won't have that childhood trauma."

Kimberly laughed.

"Hello!" It was Laura, coming in through the back door with Athena, a tiny wisp of a child with hair so thin that her pale scalp gaped through. A waif. Perhaps Laura's blended vegetables and strict diet rules had left the child malnourished.

Laura put a vase on the table. "This will look terrific tomorrow."

"It's lovely," Kimberly said, bending to kiss Athena's head. "That's the caterer's menu. Don thinks the hors d'oeuvre selection is too simple. I'm not sure."

"He wants you to add more?" Laura said, scanning the menu.

"He just thought it was a little simple, he was very sweet about it."

In the den, Athena began to cry. Laura went to her and, soon enough, a string of negotiations followed: "Do you want this one, sweetheart? The yellow or the blue or the red? Which do you want?"

Just give her one, Ifemelu thought. To overwhelm a child of four with choices, to lay on her the burden of making a decision, was to deprive her of the bliss of childhood. Adulthood, after all, already loomed, where she would have to make grimmer and grimmer decisions.

"She's been grumpy today," Laura said, coming back into the kitchen, Athena's crying quelled. "I took her to her follow-up from the ear infection and she's been an absolute bear all day. Oh, and I met the most charming Nigerian man today. We get there and it turns out a new doctor has just joined the practice and he's Nigerian and he came by and said hello to us. He reminded me of you, Ifemelu. I read on the Internet that Nigerians are the most educated immigrant group in this country. Of course, it says nothing about the millions who live on less than a dollar a day back in your country, but when I met the doctor I thought of that article and of you and other privileged Africans who are here in this country." Laura paused and Ifemelu, as she often did, felt that Laura had more to say but was holding back. It felt strange, to be called privileged. Privileged was people like Kayode DaSilva, whose passport sagged with the weight of visa stamps, who went to London for summer and to Ikoyi Club to swim, who could casually get up and say "We're going to Frenchies for ice cream."

"I've never been called privileged in my life!" Ifemelu said. "It feels good."

"I think I'll switch and have him be Athena's doctor. He was wonderful, so well-groomed and well-spoken. I haven't been very satisfied with Dr Bingham since Dr Hoffman left, anyway." Laura picked up the menu again. "In graduate school I knew a woman from Africa who was just like this doctor, I think she was from Uganda. She was wonderful, and she didn't get along with the African American woman in our class at all. She didn't have all those issues."

"Maybe when the African American's father was not allowed to vote because he was black, the Ugandan's father was running for parliament or studying at Oxford," Ifemelu said.

Laura stared at her, made a mocking confused face. "Wait, did I miss something?"

"I just think it's a simplistic comparison to make. You need to understand a bit more history," Ifemelu said.

Laura's lips sagged. She staggered, collected herself.

"Well, I'll get my daughter and then go find some history books from the library, if I can figure out what they look like!" Laura said, and marched out.

Ifemelu could almost hear Kimberly's heart beating wildly.

"I'm sorry," Ifemelu said.

Kimberly shook her head and murmured, "I know Laura can be challenging," her eyes on the salad she was mixing.

Ifemelu hurried upstairs to Laura.

"I'm sorry. I was rude just now and I apologize." But she was sorry only because of Kimberly, the way she had begun to mix the salad as though to reduce it to a pulp.

"It's fine," Laura sniffed, smoothing her daughter's hair, and Ifemelu knew that for a long time afterwards, she would not unwrap from herself the pashmina of the wounded.

APART FROM a stiff "Hi", Laura did not speak to her at the party the next day. The house filled with the gentle murmur of voices, guests raising wineglasses to their lips. They were similar, all of them, their clothes nice and safe, their sense of humour nice and safe, and, like other upper-middle-class Americans, they used the word "wonderful" too often. "You'll come and help out with the party, won't you, please?" Kimberly had asked Ifemelu, as she always did of their gatherings. Ifemelu was not sure how she helped out, since the events were catered and the children went to bed early, but she sensed, beneath the lightness of Kimberly's invitation, something close to a need. In some small way that she did not entirely understand, her presence seemed to steady Kimberly. If Kimberly wanted her there, then she would be there.

"This is Ifemelu, our babysitter and my friend," Kimberly introduced her to guests.

"You're so beautiful," a man told her, smiling, his teeth jarringly white. "African women are gorgeous, especially Ethiopians."

A couple spoke about their safari in Tanzania. "We had a wonderful tour guide and we're now paying for his first daughter's education." Two women spoke about their donations to a wonderful charity in Malawi that built wells, a wonderful orphanage in Botswana, a wonderful microfinance cooperative in Kenya. Ifemelu gazed at them. There was a certain luxury to charity that she could not identify with and did not have. To take "charity" for granted, to revel in this charity towards people whom one did not know—perhaps it came from having had yesterday and having today and expecting to have tomorrow. She envied them this.

A petite woman in a severe pink jacket said, "I'm chair of the board of a charity in Ghana. We work with rural women. We're always interested in African staff, we don't want to be the NGO that won't use local labour. So if you're ever looking for a job after graduation and want to go back and work in Africa, give me a call."

"Thank you." Ifemelu wanted, suddenly and desperately, to be from the country of people who gave and not those who received, to be one of those who had and could therefore bask in the grace of having given, to be among those who could afford copious pity and empathy. She went out to the deck in search of fresh air. Over the hedge, she could see the Jamaican nanny of the neighbours' children, walking down the driveway, the one who always evaded Ifemelu's eyes, and did not like to say hello. Then she noticed a movement on the other end of the deck. It was Don. There was something furtive about him and she felt rather than saw that he had just ended a cell phone conversation.

"Great party," he told her. "It's just an excuse for Kim and me to have friends over. Roger is totally out of his league and I've told him that, no chance in hell . . ."

Don kept talking, his voice too larded in bonhomie, her dislike clawing at her throat. She and Don did not talk like this. It was too much information, too much talk. She wanted to tell him that she had heard nothing of his phone conversation, if there had been anything at all to hear, that she knew nothing and that she did not want to know.

"They must be wondering where you are," she said.

"Yes, we must go back," he said, as though they had come out together. Back inside, Ifemelu saw Kimberly standing in the middle of the den, slightly apart from her circle of friends; she had been looking around for Don and when she saw him, her eyes rested on him, and her face became soft, and shorn of worry.

IFEMELU LEFT the party early; she wanted to speak to Dike before his bedtime. Aunty Uju picked up the phone.

"Has Dike slept?" Ifemelu asked.

"He's brushing his teeth," she said, and then in a lower voice, she added, "He was asking me about his name again."

"What did you tell him?"

"The same thing. You know, he never asked me this kind of thing before we moved here."

"Maybe it's having Bartholomew in the picture, and the new environment. He's used to having you to himself."

"This time he didn't ask why he has my name, he asked if he has my name because his father did not love him."

"Aunty, maybe it's time to tell him you were not a second wife," Ifemelu said.

"I was practically a second wife." Aunty Uju sounded defiant, even petulant, clenching her fist tightly around her own story. She had told Dike that his father was in the military government, that she was his second wife, and that they had given him her surname to protect him, because some people in the government, not his father, had done some bad things.

"Okay, here's Dike," Aunty Uju said, in a normal tone.

"Hey, Coz! You should have seen my soccer game today!" Dike said.

"How come you score all the great goals when I'm not there? Are these goals in your dreams?" Ifemelu asked.

He laughed. He still laughed easily, his sense of humour whole, but since the move to Massachusetts, he was no longer transparent. Something had filmed itself around him, making him difficult to read, his head perennially bent towards his Game Boy, looking up once in a while to view his mother, and the world, with a weariness too heavy for a child. His grades were falling. Aunty Uju threatened him more often. The last time Ifemelu visited, Aunty Uju told him, "I will send you back to Nigeria if you do that again!" speaking Igbo as she did to him only when she was angry, and Ifemelu worried that it would become for him the language of strife.

Aunty Uju, too, had changed. At first, she had sounded curious, expectant about her new life. "This place is so *white*," she said. "Do you know I went to the drugstore to quickly buy lipstick, because the mall is thirty minutes away, and all the shades were too pale! But they can't carry what they can't sell! At least this place is quiet and restful, and I feel safe drinking the tap water, something I will never even try in Brooklyn."

Slowly, over the months, her tone soured.

"Dike's teacher said he is aggressive," she told Ifemelu one day, after she had been called to come in and see the principal. "Aggressive, of all things. She wants him to go to what they call special ed, where they will put him in a class alone and bring somebody who is trained to deal with mental children to teach him. I told the woman that it is not my son, it is her father who is aggressive. Look at him, just because he looks different, when he does what other little boys do, it becomes aggression. Then the principal told me, 'Dike is just like one of us, we don't see him as different at all.' What kind of pretending is that? I told him to look at my son. There are only two of them in the whole school. The other child is a half-caste, and so fair that if you look from afar you will not even know that he is black. My son sticks out, so how can you tell me that you don't see any difference? I refused completely that they should put him in a special class. He is brighter than all of them combined. They want to start now to mark him. Kemi warned me about this. She said they tried to do it to her son in Indiana."

Later, Aunty Uju's complaints turned to her residency programme, how slow and small it was, medical records still handwritten and kept in dusty files, and then when she finished her residency, she complained about the patients who thought they were doing her a favour by seeing her. She hardly mentioned Bartholomew; it was as though she lived only with Dike in the Massachusetts house by the lake.

CHAPTER 17

Ifemelu decided to stop faking an American accent on a sunlit day in July, the same day she met Blaine. It was convincing, the accent. She had perfected, from careful watching of friends and newscasters, the blurring of the *t*, the creamy roll of the *r*, the sentences starting with "So", and the sliding response of "Oh really", but the accent creaked with consciousness, it was an act of will. It took an effort, the twisting of lip, the curling of tongue. If she were in a panic, or terrified, or jerked awake during a fire, she would not remember how to produce those American sounds. And so she resolved to stop, on that summer day, the weekend of Dike's birthday. Her decision was prompted by a telemarketer's call. She was in her apartment on Spring Garden Street, the first that was truly hers in America, hers alone, a studio with a leaky faucet and a noisy heater. In the weeks since she moved in, she had felt light-footed, cloaked in well-being, because she opened the fridge knowing that everything in it was hers and she cleaned the bathtub knowing she would not find tufts of disconcertingly foreign room-mate hair in the drain. "Officially two blocks away from the real hood" was how the apartment super, Jamal, had put it, when he told her to expect to hear gunshots from time to time, but although she had opened her window every evening, straining and listening, all she heard were the sounds of late summer, music from passing cars, the high-spirited laughter of playing children, the shouting of their mothers.

On that July morning, her weekend bag already packed for Massachusetts, she was making scrambled eggs when the phone rang. The caller ID showed "unknown" and she thought it might be a call from her parents in Nigeria. But it was a telemarketer, a young, male American who was offering better long-distance and international phone rates. She always hung up on telemarketers, but there was something about his voice that made her turn down the stove and hold on to the receiver, something poignantly young, untried, untested, the slightest of tremors, an aggressive customer-service friendliness that was not aggressive at all; it was as though he was saying what he had been trained to say but was mortally worried about offending her.

He asked how she was, how the weather was in her city, and told her it was pretty hot in Phoenix. Perhaps it was his first day on the job, his telephone piece poking uncomfortably in his ear while he half hoped that the people he was calling would not be home to pick up. Because she felt strangely sorry for him, she asked whether he had rates better than fifty-seven cents a minute to Nigeria.

"Hold on while I look up Nigeria," he said, and she went back to stirring her eggs.

He came back and said his rates were the same, but wasn't there another country that she called? Mexico? Canada?

"Well, I call London sometimes," she said. Ginika was there for the summer.

"Okay, hold on while I look up France," he said.

She burst out laughing.

"Something funny over there?" he asked.

She laughed harder. She had opened her mouth to tell him, bluntly, that what was funny was that he was selling international telephone rates and did not know where London was, but something held her back, an image of him, perhaps eighteen or nineteen, overweight, pink-faced, awkward around girls, keen on video games, and with no knowledge of the roiling contradictions that were the world. So she said, "There's a hilarious old comedy on TV."

"Oh, really?" he said, and he laughed too. It broke her heart, his greenness, and when he came back on to tell her the France rates, she thanked him and said they were better than the rates she already had and that she would think about switching carriers.

"When is a good time to call you back? If that's okay . . ." he said. She wondered whether they were paid on commission. Would his pay cheque be bigger if she did switch her phone company? Because she would, as long as it cost her nothing.

"Evenings," she said.

"May I ask who I'm talking to?"

"My name is Ifemelu."

He repeated her name with exaggerated care. "Is it a French name?"

"No. Nigerian."

"That where your family came from?"

"Yes." She scooped the eggs onto a plate. "I grew up there."

"Oh, really? How long have you been in the US?"

"Three years."

"Wow. Cool. You sound totally American."

"Thank you."

Only after she hung up did she begin to feel the stain of a burgeoning shame spreading all over her, for thanking him, for crafting his words "You sound American" into a garland that she hung around her own neck. Why was it a compliment, an accomplishment, to sound American? She had won; Cristina Tomas, pallid-faced Cristina Tomas under whose gaze she had shrunk like a small, defeated animal, would speak to her normally now. She had won, indeed, but her triumph was full of air. Her fleeting victory had left in its wake a vast, echoing space, because she had taken on, for too long, a pitch of voice and a way of being that was not hers. And so she finished eating her eggs and resolved to stop faking the American accent. She first spoke without the American accent that afternoon at Thirtieth Street Station, leaning towards the woman behind the Amtrak counter.

"Could I have a round-trip to Haverhill, please? Returning Sunday afternoon. I have a Student Advantage card," she said, and felt a rush of pleasure from giving the *t* its full due in "advantage", from not rolling her *r* in "Haverhill". This was truly her; this was the voice with which she would speak if she were woken up from a deep sleep during an earthquake. Still, she resolved that if the Amtrak woman responded to her accent by speaking too slowly as though to an idiot, then she would put on her Mr Agbo Voice, the mannered, overcareful pronunciations she had learned during debate meetings in secondary school when the bearded Mr Agbo, tugging at his frayed tie, played BBC recordings on his cassette player and then made all the students pronounce words over and over until he beamed and cried "Correct!" She would also affect, with the Mr Agbo Voice, a slight raising of her eyebrows in what she imagined was a haughty foreigner pose. But there was no need to do any of these because the Amtrak woman spoke normally. "Can I see an ID, miss?"

And so she did not use her Mr Agbo Voice until she met Blaine.

The train was crowded. The seat next to Blaine was the only empty one in that car, as far as she could see, and the newspaper and bottle of juice placed on it seemed to be his. She stopped, gesturing towards the seat, but he kept his gaze levelly ahead. Behind her, a woman was pulling along a heavy suitcase and the conductor was announcing that all personal belongings had to be moved from free seats and Blaine saw her standing there—how could he possibly not see her?—and still he did nothing. So her Mr Agbo Voice emerged. "Excuse me. Are these yours? Could you possibly move them?"

She placed her bag on the overhead rack and settled onto the seat, stiffly, holding her magazine, her body aligned towards the aisle and away from him. The train had begun to move when he said, "I'm really sorry I didn't see you standing there."

His apologizing surprised her, his expression so earnest and sincere that it seemed as though he had done something more offensive. "It's okay," she said, and smiled.

"How are you?" he asked.

She had learned to say "Good-how-are-you?" in that sing-song American way, but now she said, "I'm well, thank you."

"My name's Blaine," he said, and extended his hand.

He looked tall. A man with skin the colour of gingerbread and the kind of lean, proportioned body that was perfect for a uniform, any uniform. She knew right away that he was African American, not Caribbean, not African, not a child of immigrants from either place. She had not always been able to tell. Once she had asked a taxi driver, "So where are you from?" in a knowing, familiar tone, certain that he was from Ghana, and he said "Detroit" with a shrug. But the longer she spent in America, the better she had become at distinguishing, sometimes from looks and gait, but mostly from bearing and demeanour, that fine-grained mark that culture stamps on people. She felt confident about Blaine: he was a descendant of the black men and women who had been in America for hundreds of years.

"I'm Ifemelu, it's nice to meet you," she said.

"Are you Nigerian?"

"I am, yes."

"Bourgie Nigerian," he said, and smiled. There was a surprising and immediate intimacy to his teasing her, calling her privileged.

"Just as bourgie as you," she said. They were on firm flirting territory now. She looked him over quietly, his light-coloured khakis and navy shirt, the kind of outfit that was selected with the right amount of thought; a man who looked at himself in the mirror but did not look for too long. He knew about Nigerians, he told her, he was an assistant professor at Yale, and although his interest was mostly in southern Africa, how could he not know about Nigerians when they were everywhere?

"What is it, one in every five Africans is Nigerian?" he asked, still smiling. There was something both ironic and gentle about him. It was as if he believed that they shared a series of intrinsic jokes that did not need to be verbalized.

"Yes, we Nigerians get around. We have to. There are too many of us and not enough space," she said, and it struck her how close to each other they were, separated only by the single armrest. He spoke the kind of American English that she had just given up, the kind that made race pollsters on the telephone assume that you were white and educated.

"So is southern Africa your discipline?" she asked.

"No. Comparative politics. You can't do just Africa in political science graduate programmes in this country. You can compare Africa to Poland or Israel, but focusing on Africa itself? They don't let you do that."

His use of "they" suggested an "us", which would be the both of them. His nails were clean. He was not wearing a wedding band. She began to imagine a relationship, both of them waking up in the winter, cuddling in the stark whiteness of the morning light, drinking English Breakfast tea; she hoped he was one of those Americans who liked tea. His juice, the bottle stuffed in the pouch in front of him, was organic pomegranate. A plain brown bottle with a plain brown label, both stylish and salutary. No chemicals in the juice and no ink wasted on decorative labels. Where had he bought it? It was not the sort of thing that was sold at the train station. Perhaps he was vegan and distrusted large corporations and shopped only at farmers' markets and brought his own organic juice from home. She had little patience for Ginika's friends, most of whom were like that, their righteousness made her feel both irritated and lacking, but she was prepared to forgive Blaine's pieties. He was holding a hardcover library book whose title she could not see and had stuffed his *New York Times* next to the juice bottle. When he glanced at her magazine, she wished she had brought out the Esiaba Irobi book of poems that she planned to read on the train back. He would think that she read only shallow fashion magazines. She felt the sudden and unreasonable urge to tell him how much she loved the poetry of Yusef Komunyakaa, to redeem herself. First, she shielded, with her palm, the bright red lipstick on the cover model's face. Then, she reached forward and pushed the magazine into the pouch in front of her and said, with a slight sniff, that it was absurd how women's magazines forced images of small-boned, small-breasted white women on the rest of the multi-boned, multi-ethnic world of women to emulate.

"But I keep reading them," she said. "It's like smoking, it's bad for you but you do it anyway."

"Multi-boned and multi-ethnic," he said, amused, his eyes warm with unabashed interest; it charmed her that he was not the kind of man who, when he was interested in a woman, cultivated a certain cool, pretended indifference.

"Are you a grad student?" he asked.

"I'm a junior at Wellson."

Did she imagine it or did his face fall, in disappointment, in surprise? "Really? You seem more mature."

"I am. I'd done some college in Nigeria before I left to come here." She shifted on her seat, determined to get back on firm flirting ground. "You, on the other hand, look too young to be a professor. Your students must be confused about who the professor is."

"I think they're probably confused about a lot of stuff. This is my second year of teaching." He paused. "Are you thinking of graduate school?"

"Yes, but I'm worried I will leave grad school and no longer be able to speak English. I know this woman in grad school, a friend of a friend, and just listening to her talk is scary. The semiotic dialectics of intertextual modernity. Which makes no sense at all. Sometimes I feel that they live in a parallel universe of academia speaking academese instead of English and they don't really know what's happening in the real world."

"That's a pretty strong opinion."

"I don't know how to have any other kind."

He laughed, and it pleased her to have made him laugh.

"But I hear you," he said. "My research interests include social movements, the political economy of dictatorships, American voting rights and representation, race and ethnicity in politics, and campaign finance. That's my classic spiel. Much of which is bullshit anyway. I teach my classes and I wonder if any of it matters to the kids."

"Oh, I'm sure it does. I'd love to take one of your classes." She had spoken too eagerly. It had not come out as she wanted. She had cast herself, without meaning to, in the role of a potential student. He seemed keen to change the direction of the conversation; perhaps he did not want to be her teacher either. He told her he was going back to New Haven after visiting friends in Washington, DC. "So where are you headed?" he asked.

"Warrington. A bit of a drive from Boston. My aunt lives there."

"So do you ever come up to Connecticut?"

"Not much. I've never been to New Haven. But I've gone to the malls in Stamford and Clinton."

"Oh, yes, malls." His lips turned down slightly at the sides.

"You don't like malls?"

"Apart from being soulless and bland? They're perfectly fine."

She had never understood the quarrel with malls, with the notion of finding exactly the same shops in all of them; she found malls quite comforting in their sameness. And with his carefully chosen clothes, surely he had to shop somewhere?

"So do you grow your own cotton and make your own clothes?" she asked.

He laughed, and she laughed too. She imagined both of them, hand in hand, going to the mall in Stamford, she teasing him, reminding him of this conversation on the day they met, and raising her face to kiss him. It was not in her nature to talk to strangers on public transportation—she would do it more often when she started her blog a few years later—but she talked and talked, perhaps because of the newness of her own voice. The more they talked, the more she told herself that this was no coincidence; there was a significance to her meeting this man on the day that she returned her voice to herself. She told him, with the suppressed laughter of a person impatient for the punchline of her own joke, about the telemarketer who thought that London was in France. He did not laugh, but instead shook his head.

"They don't train these telemarketer folks well at all. I bet he's a temp with no health insurance and no benefits."

"Yes," she said, chastened. "I felt kind of sorry for him."

"So my department moved buildings a few weeks ago. Yale hired professional movers and told them to make sure to put everything from each person's old office in the exact same spot in the new office. And they did. All my books were shelved in the right position. But you know what I noticed later? Many of the books had their spines upside down." He was looking at her, as though to experience a shared revelation, and for a blank moment, she was not sure what the story was about.

"Oh. The movers couldn't read," she said finally.

He nodded. "There was just something about it that totally killed me . . ." He let his voice trail away.

She began to imagine what he would be like in bed: he would be a kind, attentive lover for whom emotional fulfilment was just as important as ejaculation, he would not judge her slack flesh, he would wake up even-tempered every morning. She hastily looked away, afraid that he might have read her mind, so startlingly clear were the images there.

"Would you like a beer?" he asked.

"A beer?"

"Yes. The café car serves beers. You want one? I'm going to get one."

"Yes. Thank you."

She stood up, self-consciously, to let him pass and hoped she would smell something on him, but she didn't. He did not wear cologne. Perhaps he had boycotted cologne because the makers of cologne did not treat their employees well. She watched him walk up the aisle, knowing that he knew that she was watching him. The beer offer had pleased her. She had worried that all he drank was organic pomegranate juice, but now the thought of organic pomegranate juice was pleasant if he drank beer as well. When he came back with the beers and plastic cups, he poured hers with a flourish that, to her, was thick with romance. She had never liked beer. Growing up, it had been male alcohol, gruff and inelegant. Now, sitting next to Blaine, laughing as he told her about the first time he got truly drunk in his freshman year, she realized that she could like beer. The grainy fullness of beer.

He talked about his undergraduate years: the stupidity of eating a semen sandwich during his fraternity initiation, constantly being called Michael Jordan in China the summer of his junior year when he travelled through Asia, his mother's death from cancer the week after he graduated.

"A semen sandwich?"

"They masturbated into a piece of pita bread and you had to take a bite, but you didn't have to swallow."

"Oh God."

"Well, hopefully you do stupid things when you're young so you don't do them when you're older," he said.

When the conductor announced that the next stop was New Haven, Ifemelu felt a stab of loss. She tore out a page from her magazine and wrote her phone number. "Do you have a card?" she asked.

He touched his pockets. "I don't have any with me."

There was silence while he gathered his things. Then the screeching of the train brakes. She sensed, and hoped she was wrong, that he did not want to give her his number.

"Well, will you write your number then, if you remember it?" she asked. A lame joke. The beer had pushed those words out of her mouth.

He wrote his number on her magazine. "You take care," he said. He touched her shoulder lightly as he left and there was something in his eyes, something both tender and sad, that made her tell herself that she had been wrong to sense reluctance from him. He already missed her. She moved to his seat, revelling in the warmth his body had left in its wake, and watched through the window as he walked along the platform.

When she arrived at Aunty Uju's house, the first thing she wanted to do was call him. But she thought it was best to wait a few hours.

After an hour, she said fuck it and called. He did not answer. She left a message. She called back later. No answer. She called and called and called. No answer. She called at midnight. She did not leave messages. The whole weekend she called and called and he never picked up the phone.

WARRINGTON WAS a somnolent town, a town contented with itself; winding roads cut through thick woods—even the main road, which the residents did not want widened for fear that it would bring in foreigners from the city, was winding and narrow—sleepy homes were shielded by trees, and on weekends the blue lake was stippled with boats. From the dining room window of Aunty Ụju's house, the lake shimmered, a blueness so tranquil that it held the gaze. Ifemelu stood by the window while Aunty Uju sat at the table drinking orange juice and airing her grievances like jewels. It had become a routine of Ifemelu's visits: Aunty Uju collected all her dissatisfactions in a silk purse, nursing them, polishing them, and then on the Saturday of Ifemelu's visit, while Bartholomew was out and Dike upstairs, she would spill them out on the table, and turn each one this way and that, to catch the light.

Sometimes she told the same story twice. How she had gone to the public library the other day, had forgotten to bring out the unreturned book from her handbag, and the guard told her, "You people never do anything right." How she walked into an examining room and a patient asked "Is the doctor coming?" and when she said she was the doctor the patient's face changed to fired clay.

"Do you know, that afternoon she called to transfer her file to another doctor's office! Can you imagine?"

"What does Bartholomew think about all this?" Ifemelu gestured to take in the room, the view of the lake, the town.

"That one is too busy chasing business. He leaves early and comes home late every day. Sometimes Dike doesn't even set eyes on him for a whole week."

"I'm surprised you're still here, Aunty," Ifemelu said quietly, and by "here" they both knew that she did not merely mean Warrington.

"I want another child. We've been trying." Aunty Uju came and stood beside her, by the window.

There was the clatter of footsteps on the wooden stairs, and Dike came into the kitchen, in a faded T-shirt and shorts, holding his Game Boy. Each time Ifemelu saw him, he seemed to her to have grown taller and to have become more reserved.

"Are you wearing that shirt to camp?" Aunty Uju asked him.

"Yes, Mom," he said, his eyes on the flickering screen in his hand.

Aunty Uju got up to check the oven. She had agreed this morning, his first of summer camp, to make him chicken nuggets for breakfast.

"Coz, we're still playing soccer later, right?" Dike asked.

"Yes," Ifemelu said. She took a chicken nugget from his plate and put it in her mouth. "Chicken nuggets for breakfast is strange enough, but is this chicken or just plastic?"

"Spicy plastic," he said.

She walked him to the bus and watched him get on, the pale faces of the other children at the window, the bus driver waving to her too cheerfully. She was standing there waiting when the bus brought him back that afternoon. There was a guardedness on his face, something close to sadness.

"What's wrong?" she asked, her arm around his shoulder.

"Nothing," he said. "Can we play soccer now?"

"After you tell me what happened."

"Nothing happened."

"I think you need some sugar. You'll probably have too much tomorrow, with your birthday cake. But let's get a cookie."

"Do you bribe the kids you babysit with sugar? Man, they're lucky."

She laughed. She brought out the packet of Oreos from the fridge.

"Do you play soccer with the kids you babysit?" he asked.

"No," she said, even though she played once in a while with Taylor, kicking the ball back and forth in their oversized, wooded backyard. Sometimes, when Dike asked her about the children she cared for, she indulged his childish interest, telling him about their toys and their lives, but she was careful not to make them seem important to her.

"So how was camp?"

"Good." A pause. "My group leader, Haley? She gave sunscreen to everyone but she wouldn't give me any. She said I didn't need it."

She looked at his face, which was almost expressionless, eerily so. She did not know what to say.

"She thought that because you're dark you don't need sunscreen. But you do. Many people don't know that dark people also need sunscreen. I'll get you some, don't worry." She was speaking too fast, not sure that she was saying the right thing, or what the right thing to say was, and worried because this had upset him enough that she had seen it on his face.

"It's okay," he said. "It was kind of funny. My friend Danny was laughing about it."

"Why did your friend think it was funny?"

"Because it was!"

"You wanted her to give you the sunscreen, too, right?"

"I guess so," he said with a shrug. "I just want to be regular."

She hugged him. Later, she went to the store and bought him a big bottle of sunscreen, and the next time she visited, she saw it lying on his dresser, forgotten and unused.

Understanding America for the Non-American Black: American Tribalism

In America, tribalism is alive and well. There are four kinds—class, ideology, region, and race. First, class. Pretty easy. Rich folk and poor folk.

Second, ideology. Liberals and conservatives. They don't merely disagree on political issues, each side believes the other is evil. Intermarriage is discouraged and on the rare occasion that it happens, is considered remarkable. Third, region. The North and the South. The two sides fought a civil war and tough stains from that war remain. The North looks down on the South while the South resents the North. Finally, race. There's a ladder of racial hierarchy in America. White is always on top, specifically White Anglo-Saxon Protestant, otherwise known as WASP, and American Black is always on the bottom, and what's in the middle depends on time and place. (Or as that marvelous rhyme goes: if you're white, you're all right; if you're brown, stick around; if you're black, get back!) Americans assume that everyone will get their tribalism. But it takes a while to figure it all out. So in undergrad, we had a visiting speaker and a classmate whispers to another, "Oh my God, he looks so Jewish," with a shudder, an actual shudder. Like Jewish was a bad thing. I didn't get it. As far as I could see, the man was white, not much different from the classmate herself. Jewish to me was something vague, something biblical. But I learned quickly. You see, in America's ladder of races, Jewish is white but also some rungs below white. A bit confusing, because I knew this straw-haired, freckled girl who said she was Jewish. How can Americans tell who is Jewish? How did the classmate know the guy was Jewish? I read somewhere how American colleges used to ask applicants for their mother's surnames, to make sure they weren't Jewish because they wouldn't admit Jewish people. So maybe that's how to tell? From people's names? The longer you are here, the more you start to get it.

CHAPTER 18

Mariama's new customer was wearing jeans shorts, the denim glued to her backside, and sneakers the same bright pink shade as her top. Large hoop earrings grazed her face. She stood in front of the mirror, describing the kind of cornrows she wanted.

"Like a zigzag with a parting at the side right here, but you don't add the hair at the beginning, you add it when you get to the ponytail," she said, speaking slowly, over-enunciating. "You understand me?" she added, already convinced, it seemed, that Mariama did not.

"I understand," Mariama said quietly. "You want to see a photo? I have that style in my album."

The album was flipped through and, finally, the customer was satisfied and seated, frayed plastic hoisted around her neck, her chair height adjusted, and Mariama all the time smiling a smile full of things restrained.

"This other braider I went to the last time," the customer said. "She was African, too, and she wanted to burn my damned hair! She brought out this lighter and I'm going, Shontay White, don't let that woman bring that thing close to your hair. So I ask her, What's that for? She says, I want to clean your braids, and I go, What? Then she tries to show me, she tries to run the lighter over one braid and I went all crazy on her."

Mariama shook her head. "Oh, that's bad. Burning is not good. We don't do that."

A customer came in, her hair covered in a bright yellow headwrap. "Hi," she said. "I'd like to get braids."

"What kind of braids you want?" Mariama asked.

"Just regular box braids, medium size."

"You want it long?" Mariama asked.

"Not too long, maybe shoulder length?"

"Okay. Please sit down. She will do it for you," Mariama said, gesturing to Halima, who was sitting at the back, her eyes on the television. Halima stood up and stretched, for a little too long, as though to register her reluctance.

The woman sat down and gestured to the pile of DVDs. "You sell Nigerian films?" she asked Mariama.

"I used to but my supplier went out of business. You want to buy?"

"No. You just seem to have a lot of them."

"Some of them are real nice," Mariama said.

"I can't watch that stuff. I guess I'm biased. In my country, South Africa, Nigerians are known for stealing credit cards and doing drugs and all kinds of crazy stuff. I guess the films are kind of like that too."

"You're from South Africa? You don't have accent!" Mariama exclaimed.

The woman shrugged. "I've been here a long time. It doesn't make much of a difference."

"No," Halima said, suddenly animated, standing behind the woman. "When I come here with my son they beat him in school because of African accent. In Newark. If you see my son face? Purple like onion. They beat, beat, beat him. Black boys beat him like this. Now accent go and no problems."

"I'm sorry to hear that," the woman said.

"Thank you." Halima smiled, enamoured of the woman because of this extraordinary feat, an American accent. "Yes, Nigeria very corrupt. Worst corrupt country in Africa. Me, I watch the film but no, I don't go to Nigeria!" She half waved her palm in the air.

"I cannot marry a Nigerian and I won't let anybody in my family marry a Nigerian," Mariama said, and darted Ifemelu an apologetic glance. "Not all but many of them do bad things. Even killing for money."

"Well, I don't know about that," the customer said, in a half-heartedly moderate tone.

Aisha looked on, sly and quiet. Later, she whispered to Ifemelu, her expression suspicious, "You here fifteen years, but you don't have American accent. Why?"

Ifemelu ignored her and, once again, opened Jean Toomer's *Cane*. She stared at the words and wished suddenly that she could turn back time and postpone this move back home. Perhaps she had been hasty. She should not have sold her condo. She should have accepted *Letterly* magazine's offer to buy her blog and keep her on as a paid blogger. What if she got back to Lagos and realized what a mistake it was to move back? Even the thought that she could always return to America did not comfort her as much as she wished it to.

The film had ended, and in the new noiselessness of the room, Mariama's customer said, "This one's rough," touching one of the thin cornrows that zigzagged over her scalp, her voice louder than it needed to be.

"No problem. I will do it again," Mariama said. She was agreeable, and smooth-tongued, but Ifemelu could tell that she thought her customer was a troublemaker, and there was nothing wrong with the cornrow, but this was a part of her new American self, this fervour of customer service, this shiny falseness of surfaces, and she had accepted it, embraced it. When the customer left, she might shrug out of that self and say something to Halima and to Aisha about Americans, how spoilt and childish and entitled they were, but when the next customer came, she would become, again, a faultless version of her American self.

Her customer said, "It's cute," as she paid Mariama, and shortly after she left, a young white woman came in, soft-bodied and tanned, her hair held back in a loose ponytail.

"Hi!" she said.

Mariama said "Hi," and then waited, wiping her hands over and over the front of her shorts.

"I wanted to get my hair braided? You can braid my hair, right?"

Mariama smiled an overly eager smile. "Yes. We do every kind of hair. Do you want braids or cornrows?" She was furiously cleaning the chair now. "Please sit."

The woman sat down and said she wanted cornrows. "Kind of like Bo Derek in the movie? You know that movie *10*?"

"Yes, I know," Mariama said. Ifemelu doubted that she did.

"I'm Kelsey," the woman announced as though to the whole room. She was aggressively friendly. She asked where Mariama was from, how long she had been in America, if she had children, how her business was doing.

"Business is up and down but we try," Mariama said.

"But you couldn't even have this business back in your country, right? Isn't it wonderful that you get to come to the US and now your kids can have a better life?"

Mariama looked surprised. "Yes."

"Are women allowed to vote in your country?" Kelsey asked.

A longer pause from Mariama. "Yes."

"What are you reading?" Kelsey turned to Ifemelu.

Ifemelu showed her the cover of the novel. She did not want to start a conversation. Especially not with Kelsey. She recognized in Kelsey the nationalism of liberal Americans who copiously criticized America but did not like you to do so; they expected you to be silent and grateful, and always reminded you of how much better than wherever you had come from America was.

"Is it good?"

"Yes."

"It's a novel, right? What's it about?"

Why did people ask "What is it about?" as if a novel had to be about only one thing. Ifemelu disliked the question; she would have disliked it even if she did not feel, in addition to her depressed uncertainty, the beginning of a headache. "It may not be the kind of book you would like if you have particular tastes. He mixes prose and verse."

"You have a great accent. Where are you from?"

"Nigeria."

"Oh. Cool." Kelsey had slender fingers; they would be perfect for advertising rings. "I'm going to Africa in the fall. Congo and Kenya and I'm going to try and see Tanzania too."

"That's nice."

"I've been reading books to get ready. Everybody recommended *Things Fall Apart*, which I read in high school. It's very good but sort of quaint, right? I mean like it didn't help me understand modern Africa. I've just read this great book, *A Bend in the River.* It made me truly understand how modern Africa works."

Ifemelu made a sound, halfway between a snort and a hum, but said nothing.

"It's just so honest, the most honest book I've read about Africa," Kelsey said.

Ifemelu shifted. Kelsey's knowing tone grated. Her headache was getting worse. She did not think the novel was about Africa at all. It was about Europe, or the longing for Europe, about the battered self-image of an Indian man born in Africa, who felt so wounded, so diminished, by not having been born European, a member of a race which he had elevated for their ability to create, that he turned his imagined personal insufficiencies into an impatient contempt for Africa; in his knowing haughty attitude to the African, he could become, even if only fleetingly, a European. She leaned back on her seat and said this in measured tones. Kelsey looked startled; she had not expected a mini-lecture. Then, she said kindly, "Oh, well, I see why you would read the novel like that."

"And I see why *you* would read it like you did," Ifemelu said.

Kelsey raised her eyebrows, as though Ifemelu was one of those slightly unbalanced people who were best avoided. Ifemelu closed her eyes. She had the sensation of clouds gathering over her head. She felt faint. Perhaps it was the heat. She had ended a relationship in which she was not unhappy, closed a blog she enjoyed, and now she was chasing something she could not articulate clearly, even to herself. She could have blogged about Kelsey, too, this girl who somehow believed that she was miraculously neutral in how she read books, while other people read emotionally.

"You want to use hair?" Mariama asked Kelsey.

"Hair?"

Mariama held up a pack of the attachments in a see-through plastic wrapping. Kelsey's eyes widened, and she glanced quickly around, at the pack from which Aisha took small sections for each braid, at the pack that Halima was only just unwrapping.

"Oh my God. So that's how it's done. I used to think African American women with braided hair had such full hair!"

"No, we use attachments," Mariama said, smiling.

"Maybe next time. I think I'll just do my own hair today," Kelsey said.

Her hair did not take long, seven cornrows, the too-fine hair already slackening in the plaits. "It's great!" she said afterwards.

"Thank you," Mariama said. "Please come back again. I can do another style for you next time."

"Great!"

Ifemelu watched Mariama in the mirror, thinking of her own new American selves. It was with Curt that she had first looked in the mirror and, with a flush of accomplishment, seen someone else.

CURT LIKED to say that it was love at first laugh. Whenever people asked how they met, even people they hardly knew, he would tell the story of how Kimberly had introduced them, he the cousin visiting from Maryland, she the Nigerian babysitter whom Kimberly talked so much about, and how taken he was by her deep voice, by the braid that had escaped from her rubber band. But it was when Taylor dashed into the den, wearing a blue cape and underwear, shouting, "I am Captain Underpants!" and she threw back her head and laughed, that he had fallen in love. Her laugh was so vibrant, shoulders shaking, chest heaving; it was the laugh of a woman who, when she laughed, really laughed. Sometimes when they were alone and she laughed, he would say teasingly, "That's what got me. And you know what I thought? If she laughs like that, I wonder how she does *other things*." He told her, too, that she had known he was smitten—how could she not know?—but pretended not to because she didn't want a white man. In truth, she did not notice his interest. She had always been able to sense the desire of men, but not Curt's, not at first. She still thought of Blaine, saw him walking along the platform at the New Haven train station, an apparition that filled her with a doomed yearning. She had not merely been attracted to Blaine, she had been arrested by Blaine, and in her mind he had become the perfect American partner that she would never have. Still, she had had other crushes since then, minor compared to that strike on the train, and had only just emerged from a crush on Abe in her ethics class, Abe who was white, Abe who liked her well enough, who thought her smart and funny, even attractive, but who did not see her as female. She was curious about Abe, interested in Abe, but all the flirting she did was, to him, merely niceness: Abe would hook her up with his black friend, if he had a black friend. She was invisible to Abe. This crushed her crush, and perhaps also made her overlook Curt. Until one afternoon when she was playing catch with Taylor, who threw the ball high, too high, and it fell into the thicket near the neighbour's cherry tree.

"I think we've lost that one," Ifemelu said. The week before, a Frisbee had disappeared in there. Curt rose from the patio chair (he had been watching her every move, he told her later) and bounded into the bush, almost diving, as though into a pool, and emerged with the yellow ball.

"Yay! Uncle Curt!" Taylor said. But Curt did not give Taylor the ball; instead he held it out to Ifemelu. She saw in his eyes what he wanted her to see. She smiled and said, "Thank you." Later in the kitchen, after she had put in a video for Taylor and was drinking a glass of water, he said, "This is where I ask you to dinner, but at this point, I'll take anything I can get. May I buy you a drink, an ice cream, a meal, a movie ticket? This evening? This weekend before I go back to Maryland?"

He was looking at her with wonder, his head slightly lowered, and she felt an unfurling inside her. How glorious it was, to be so wanted, and by this man with the rakish metal band around his wrist and the cleft-chinned handsomeness of models in department store catalogues. She began to like him because he liked her. "You eat so delicately," he told her on their first date, at an Italian restaurant in Old City. There was nothing particularly delicate about her raising a fork to her mouth but she liked that he thought that there was.

"So, I'm a rich white guy from Potomac, but I'm not nearly as much of an asshole as I'm supposed to be," he said, in a way that made her feel he had said that before, and that it had been received well when he did. "Laura always says my mom is richer than God, but I'm not sure she is."

He talked about himself with such gusto, as though determined to tell her everything there was to know, and all at once. His family had been hoteliers for a hundred years. He went to college in California to escape them. He graduated and travelled through Latin America and Asia. Something began to pull him homewards, perhaps his father's death, perhaps his unhappiness with a relationship. So he moved, a year ago, back to Maryland, started a software business just so that he would not be in the family business, bought an apartment in Baltimore, and went down to Potomac every Sunday to have brunch with his mother. He talked about himself with an uncluttered simplicity, assuming that she enjoyed his stories simply because he enjoyed them himself. His boyish enthusiasm fascinated her. His body was firm as they hugged good night in front of her apartment.

"I'm about to move in for a kiss in exactly three seconds," he said. "A real kiss that can take us places, so if you don't want that to happen, you might want to back off right now."

She did not back off. The kiss was arousing in the way that unknown things are arousing. Afterwards he said, with urgency, "We have to tell Kimberly."

"Tell Kimberly what?"

"That we're dating."

"We are?"

He laughed, and she laughed, too, although she had not been joking. He was open and gushing; cynicism did not occur to him. She felt charmed and almost helpless in the face of this, carried along by him; perhaps they were indeed dating after one kiss since he was so sure that they were.

Kimberly's greeting to her the next day was "Hello there, lovebird."

"So you'll forgive your cousin for asking out the help?" Ifemelu asked.

Kimberly laughed and then, in an act that both surprised and moved Ifemelu, Kimberly hugged her. They moved apart awkwardly. Oprah was on the TV in the den and she heard the audience erupt in applause.

"Well," Kimberly said, looking a little startled by the hug herself. "I just wanted to say I'm really . . . happy for you both."

"Thank you. But it's only been one date and there has been no consummation."

Kimberly giggled and for a moment it felt as though they were high school girlfriends gossiping about boys. Ifemelu sometimes sensed, underneath the well-oiled sequences of Kimberly's life, a flash of regret not only for things she longed for in the present but for things she had longed for in the past.

"You should have seen Curt this morning," Kimberly said. "I've never seen him like this! He's really excited."

"About what?" Morgan asked. She was standing by the kitchen entrance, her prepubescent body stiff with hostility. Behind her, Taylor was trying to straighten the legs of a small plastic robot.

"Well, honey, you're going to have to ask Uncle Curt."

Curt came into the kitchen, smiling shyly, his hair slightly wet, wearing a fresh, light cologne. "Hey," he said. He had called her at night to say he couldn't sleep. "This is really corny but I am so full of you, it's like I'm *breathing* you, you know?" he had said, and she thought that the romance novelists were wrong and it was men, not women, who were the true romantics.

"Morgan is asking why you seem so excited," Kimberly said.

"Well, Morg, I'm excited because I have a new girlfriend, somebody really special who you might know."

Ifemelu wished Curt would remove the arm he had thrown around her shoulder; they were not announcing their engagement, for goodness' sake. Morgan was staring at them. Ifemelu saw Curt through her eyes: the dashing uncle who travelled the world and told all the really funny jokes at Thanksgiving dinner, the cool one young enough to get her, but old enough to try and make her mother get her.

"Ifemelu is your girlfriend?" Morgan asked.

"Yes," Curt said.

"That's disgusting," Morgan said, looking genuinely disgusted.

"Morgan!" Kimberly said.

Morgan turned and stalked off upstairs.

"She has a crush on Uncle Curt, and now the babysitter steps onto her turf. It can't be easy," Ifemelu said.

Taylor, who seemed happy both with the news and with having straightened out the robot's legs, said, "Are you and Ifemelu going to get married and have a baby, Uncle Curt?"

"Well, buddy, right now we are just going to be spending a lot of time together, to get to know each other."

"Oh, okay," Taylor said, slightly dampened, but when Don came home, Taylor ran into his arms and said, "Ifemelu and Uncle Curt are going to get married and have a baby!"

"Oh," Don said.

His surprise reminded Ifemelu of Abe in her ethics class: Don thought she was attractive and interesting, and thought Curt was attractive and interesting, but it did not occur to him to think of both of them, together, entangled in the delicate threads of romance.

CURT HAD NEVER been with a black woman; he told her this after their first time, in his penthouse apartment in Baltimore, with a self-mocking toss of his head, as if this were something he should have done long ago but had somehow neglected.

"Here's to a milestone, then," she said, pretending to raise a glass.

Wambui once said, after Dorothy introduced them to her new Dutch boyfriend at an ASA meeting, "I can't do a white man, I'd be scared to see him naked, all that paleness. Unless maybe an Italian with a serious tan. Or a Jewish guy, dark Jewish." Ifemelu looked at Curt's pale hair and pale skin, the rust-coloured moles on his back, the fine sprinkle of golden chest hair, and thought how strongly, at this moment, she disagreed with Wambui.

"You are so sexy," she said.

"You are *sexier.*"

He told her he had never been so attracted to a woman before, had never seen a body so beautiful, her perfect breasts, her perfect butt. It amused her, that he considered a perfect butt what Obinze called a flat ass, and she thought her breasts were ordinary big breasts, already with a downward slope. But his words pleased her, like an unnecessary lavish gift. He wanted to suck her finger, to lick honey from her nipple, to smear ice cream on her belly, as though it was not enough simply to lie bare skin to bare skin.

Later, when he wanted to do impersonations—"How about you be Foxy Brown," he said—she thought it endearing, his ability to act, to lose himself so completely in character, and she played along, humouring him, pleased by his pleasure, although it puzzled her that this could be so exciting to him. Often, naked beside him, she found herself thinking of Obinze. She struggled not to compare Curt's touch to his. She had told Curt about her secondary school boyfriend Mofe, but she said nothing about Obinze. It felt a sacrilege to discuss Obinze, to refer to him as an "ex", that flippant word that said nothing and meant nothing. With each month of silence that passed between them, she felt the silence itself calcify, and become a hard and hulking statue, impossible to defeat. She still, often, began to write to him, but always she stopped, always she decided not to send the e-mails.

WITH CURT, she became, in her mind, a woman free of knots and cares, a woman running in the rain with the taste of sun-warmed strawberries in her mouth. "A drink" became a part of the architecture of her life, mojitos and martinis, dry whites and fruity reds. She went hiking with him, kayaking, camping near his family's vacation home, all things she would never have imagined herself doing before. She was lighter and leaner; she was Curt's Girlfriend, a role she slipped into as into a favourite, flattering dress. She laughed more because he laughed so much. His optimism blinded her. He was full of plans. "I have an idea!" he said often. She imagined him as a child surrounded by too many brightly coloured toys, always being encouraged to carry out "projects", always being told that his mundane ideas were wonderful.

"Let's go to Paris tomorrow!" he said one weekend. "I know it's totally unoriginal but you've never been and I love that I get to show you Paris!"

"I just can't get up and go to Paris. I have a Nigerian passport. I need to apply for a visa, with bank statements and health insurance and all sorts of proof that I won't stay and become a burden to Europe."

"Yeah, I forgot about that. Okay, we'll go next weekend. We'll get the visa stuff done this week. I'll get a copy of my bank statement tomorrow."

"Curtis," she said, a little sternly, to make him be reasonable, but standing there looking down at the city from so high up, she was already caught in the whirl of his excitement. He was upbeat, relentlessly so, in a way that only an American of his kind could be, and there was an infantile quality to this that she found admirable and repulsive. One day, they took a walk on South Street, because she had never seen what he told her was the best part of Philadelphia, and he slipped his hand into hers as they wandered past tattoo parlours and groups of boys with pink hair. Near Condom Kingdom, he ducked into a tiny tarot shop, pulling her along. A woman in a black veil told them, "I see light and long-term happiness ahead for you two," and Curt said, "So do we!" and gave her an extra ten dollars. Later, when his ebullience became a temptation to Ifemelu, an unrelieved sunniness that made her want to strike at it, to crush it, this would be one of her best memories of Curt, as he was in the tarot shop on South Street on a day filled with the promise of summer: so handsome, so happy, a true believer. He believed in good omens and positive thoughts and happy endings to films, a trouble-free belief, because he had not considered them deeply before choosing to believe; he just simply believed.

CHAPTER 19

Curt's mother had a bloodless elegance, her hair shiny, her complexion well-preserved, her tasteful and expensive clothes made to look tasteful and expensive; she seemed like the kind of wealthy person who did not tip well. Curt called her "Mother", which had a certain formality, an archaic ring. On Sundays, they had brunch with her. Ifemelu enjoyed the Sunday ritual of those meals in the ornate hotel dining room, full of nicely dressed people, silver-haired couples with their grandchildren, middle-aged women with brooches pinned on their lapels. The only other black person was a stiffly dressed waiter. She ate fluffy eggs and thinly sliced salmon and crescents of fresh melon, watching Curt and his mother, both blindingly golden-haired. Curt talked, while his mother listened, rapt. She adored her son—the child born late in life when she wasn't sure she could still have children, the charmer, the one whose manipulations she always gave in to. He was her adventurer who would bring back exotic species—he had dated a Japanese girl, a Venezuelan girl—but would, with time, settle down properly. She would tolerate anybody he liked, but she felt no obligation for affection.

"I'm Republican, our whole family is. We are very anti-welfare but we did very much support civil rights. I just want you to know the kind of Republicans we are," she told Ifemelu when they first met, as though it was the most important thing to get out of the way.

"And would you like to know what kind of Republican I am?" Ifemelu asked.

His mother first looked surprised, and then her face stretched into a tight smile. "You're funny," she said.

Once, his mother told Ifemelu, "Your lashes are pretty," abrupt, unexpected words, and then sipped her Bellini, as though she had not heard Ifemelu's surprised "Thank you."

On the drive back to Baltimore, Ifemelu said, "Lashes? She must have really tried hard to find something to compliment!"

Curt laughed. "Laura says my mother doesn't like beautiful women."

ONE WEEKEND, Morgan visited.

Kimberly and Don wanted to take the children to Florida, but Morgan refused to go. So Curt asked her to spend the weekend in Baltimore. He planned a boating trip, and Ifemelu thought he should have some time alone with Morgan. "You're not coming, Ifemelu?" Morgan asked, looking deflated. "I thought we were all going *together.*" The word "together" said with more animation than Ifemelu had ever heard from Morgan. "Of course I'm coming," she said. As she put on mascara and lip gloss, Morgan watched.

"Come here, Morg," she said, and she ran the lip gloss over Morgan's lips. "Smack your lips. Good. Now why are you so pretty, Miss Morgan?" Morgan laughed. On the pier, Ifemelu and Curt walked along, each holding Morgan's hand, Morgan happy to have her hands held, and Ifemelu thought, as she sometimes fleetingly did, of being married to Curt, their life engraved in comfort, he getting along with her family and friends and she with his, except for his mother. They joked about marriage. Since she first told him about bride price ceremonies, that Igbo people did them before the wine-carrying and church wedding, he joked about going to Nigeria to pay her bride price, arriving at her ancestral home, sitting with her father and uncles, and insisting he get her for free. And she joked, in return, about walking down the aisle in a church in Virginia, to the tune of "Here Comes the Bride", while his relatives stared in horror and asked one another, in whispers, why the help was wearing the bride's dress.

THEY WERE CURLED UP on the couch, she reading a novel, he watching sports. She found it endearing, how absorbed he was in his games, eyes small and still in concentration. During commercial breaks, she teased him: Why did American football have no inherent logic, just overweight men jumping on top of one another? And why did baseball players spend so much time spitting and then making sudden incomprehensible runs? He laughed and tried to explain, yet again, the meaning of home runs and touchdowns, but she was uninterested, because understanding meant she could no longer tease him, and so she glanced back at her novel, ready to tease him again at the next break.

The couch was soft. Her skin was glowing. At school, she took extra credits and raised her GPA. Outside the tall living room windows, the Inner Harbor spread out below, water gleaming and lights twinkling. A sense of contentment overwhelmed her. That was what Curt had given her, this gift of contentment, of ease. How quickly she had become used to their life, her passport filled with visa stamps, the solicitousness of flight attendants in first-class cabins, the feathery bed linen in the hotels they stayed in and the little things she hoarded: jars of preserves from the breakfast tray, little vials of conditioner, woven slippers, even face towels if they were especially soft. She had slipped out of her old skin. She almost liked winter, the glittering coat of frosted ice on the tops of cars, the lush warmth of the cashmere sweaters Curt bought her. In stores, he did not look first at the prices of things. He bought her groceries and textbooks, sent her gift certificates for department stores, took her shopping himself. He asked her to give up babysitting; they could spend more time together if she didn't have to work every day. But she refused. "I have to have a job," she said.

She saved money, sent more home. She wanted her parents to move to a new flat. There had been an armed robbery in the block of flats next to theirs.

"Something bigger in a better neighbourhood," she said.

"We are okay here," her mother said. "It is not too bad. They built a new gate in the street and banned okadas after six p.m., so it is safe."

"A gate?"

"Yes, near the kiosk."

"Which kiosk?"

"You don't remember the kiosk?" her mother asked. Ifemelu paused. A sepia tone to her memories. She could not remember the kiosk.

Her father had, finally, found a job, as the deputy director of human resources in one of the new banks. He bought a mobile phone. He bought new tyres for her mother's car. Slowly, he was easing back into his monologues about Nigeria.

"One could not describe Obasanjo as a good man, but it must be conceded that he has done some good things in the country; there is a flourishing spirit of entrepreneurship," he said.

It felt strange to call them directly, to hear her father's "Hello?" after the second ring, and when he heard her voice, he raised his, almost shouting, as he always did with international calls. Her mother liked to take the phone out to the verandah, to make sure the neighbours overheard: *"Ifem, how is the weather in America?"*

Her mother asked breezy questions and accepted breezy replies. "Everything is going well?" and Ifemelu had no choice but to say yes. Her father remembered classes she'd mentioned, and asked about specifics. She chose her words, careful not to say anything about Curt. It was easier not to tell them about Curt.

"What are your employment prospects?" her father asked. Her graduation was approaching, her student visa expiring.

"I have been assigned to a career counsellor, and I'm meeting her next week," she said.

"All graduating students have a counsellor assigned to them?"

"Yes."

Her father made a sound, of admiring respect. "America is an organized place, and job opportunities are rife there."

"Yes. They have placed many students in good jobs," Ifemelu said. It was untrue, but it was what her father expected to hear. The career services office, an airless space, piles of files sitting forlornly on desks, was known to be full of counsellors who reviewed résumés and asked you to change the font or format and gave you outdated contact information for people who never called you back. The first time Ifemelu went there, her counsellor, Ruth, a caramel-skinned African American woman, asked, "What do you really want to do?"

"I want a job."

"Yes, but what kind?" Ruth asked, slightly incredulous.

Ifemelu looked at her résumé on the table. "I'm a communications major, so anything in communications, the media."

"Do you have a passion, a dream job?"

Ifemelu shook her head. She felt weak, for not having a passion, not being sure what she wanted to do. Her interests were vague and varied, magazine publishing, fashion, politics, television; none of them had a firm shape. She attended the school career fair, where students wore awkward suits and serious expressions, and tried to look like adults worthy of real jobs. The recruiters, themselves not long out of college, the young who had been sent out to catch the young, told her about "opportunity for growth" and "good fit" and "benefits", but they all became noncommittal when they realized she was not an American citizen, that they would, if they hired her, have to descend into the dark tunnel of immigration paperwork. "I should have majored in engineering or something," she told Curt. "Communications majors are a dime a dozen."

"I know some people my dad did business with, they might be able to help," Curt said. And, not long afterwards, he told her she had an interview at an office in downtown Baltimore, for a position in public relations. "All you need to do is ace the interview and it's yours," he said. "So I know folks in this other bigger place, but the good thing about this one is they'll get you a work visa *and* start your green card process."

"What? How did you do it?"

He shrugged. "Made some calls."

"Curt. Really. I don't know how to thank you."

"I have some ideas," he said, boyishly pleased.

It was good news, and yet a soberness wrapped itself around her. Wambui was working three jobs under the table to raise the five thousand dollars she would need to pay an African American man for a green-card marriage, Mwombeki was desperately trying to find a company that would hire him on his temporary visa, and here she was, a pink balloon, weightless, floating to the top, propelled by things outside of herself. She felt, in the midst of her gratitude, a small resentment: that Curt could, with a few calls, rearrange the world, have things slide into the spaces that he wanted them to.

When she told Ruth about the interview in Baltimore, Ruth said, "My only advice? Lose the braids and straighten your hair. Nobody says this kind of stuff but it matters. We want you to get that job."

Aunty Uju had said something similar in the past, and she had laughed then. Now, she knew enough not to laugh. "Thank you," she said to Ruth.

Since she came to America, she had always braided her hair with long extensions, always alarmed at how much it cost. She wore each style for three months, even four months, until her scalp itched unbearably and the braids sprouted fuzzily from a bed of new growth. And so it was a new adventure, relaxing her hair. She removed her braids, careful to leave her scalp unscratched, to leave undisturbed the dirt that would protect it. Relaxers had grown in their range, boxes and boxes in the "ethnic hair" section of the drugstore, faces of smiling black women with impossibly straight and shiny hair, beside words like "botanical" and "aloe" that promised gentleness. She bought one in a green carton. In her bathroom, she carefully smeared the protective gel around her hairline before she began to slather the creamy relaxer on her hair, section by section, her fingers in plastic gloves. The smell reminded her of chemistry lab in secondary school, and so she forced open the bathroom window, which was often jammed. She timed the process carefully, washing off the relaxer in exactly twenty minutes, but her hair remained kinky, its denseness unchanged. The relaxer did not take. That was the word—"take"—that the hairdresser in West Philadelphia used. "Girl, you need a professional," the hairdresser said as she reapplied another relaxer. "People think they're saving money by doing it at home but they're really not."

Ifemelu felt only a slight burning, at first, but as the hairdresser rinsed out the relaxer, Ifemelu's head bent backwards against a plastic sink, needles of stinging pain shot up from different parts of her scalp, down to different parts of her body, back up to her head.

"Just a little burn," the hairdresser said. "But look how pretty it is. Wow, girl, you've got the white-girl swing!"

Her hair was hanging down rather than standing up, straight and sleek, parted at the side and curving to a slight bob at her chin. The verve was gone. She did not recognize herself. She left the salon almost mournfully; while the hairdresser had flat-ironed the ends, the smell of burning, of something organic dying which should not have died, had made her feel a sense of loss. Curt looked uncertain when he saw her.

"Do you like it, babe?" he asked.

"I can see you don't," she said.

He said nothing. He reached out to stroke her hair, as though doing so might make him like it.

She pushed him away. "Ouch. Careful. I have a bit of relaxer burn."

"What?"

"It's not too bad. I used to get it all the time in Nigeria. Look at this."

She showed him a keloid behind her ear, a small enraged swelling of skin, which she got after Aunty Uju straightened her hair with a hot comb in secondary school. "Pull back your ear," Aunty Uju often said, and Ifemelu would hold her ear, tense and unbreathing, terrified that the red-hot comb fresh from the stove would burn her but also excited by the prospect of straight, swingy hair. And one day it did burn her, as she moved slightly and Aunty Uju's hand moved slightly and the hot metal singed the skin behind her ear.

"Oh my God," Curt said, his eyes wide. He insisted on gently looking at her scalp to see how much she had been hurt. "Oh my God."

His horror made her more concerned than she would ordinarily have been. She had never felt so close to him as she did then, sitting still on the bed, her face sunk in his shirt, the scent of fabric softener in her nose, while he gently parted her newly straightened hair.

"Why do you have to do this? Your hair was gorgeous braided. And when you took out the braids the last time and just kind of let it be? It was even more gorgeous, so full and cool."

"My full and cool hair would work if I were interviewing to be a backup singer in a jazz band, but I need to look professional for this interview, and professional means straight is best but if it's going to be curly then it has to be the white kind of curly, loose curls or, at worst, spiral curls but never kinky."

"It's so fucking *wrong* that you have to do this."

At night, she struggled to find a comfortable position on her pillow. Two days later, there were scabs on her scalp. Three days later, they oozed pus. Curt wanted her to see a doctor and she laughed at him. It would heal, she told him, and it did. Later, after she breezed through the job interview, and the woman shook her hand and said she would be a "wonderful fit" in the company, she wondered if the woman would have felt the same way had she walked into that office wearing her thick, kinky, God-given halo of hair, the Afro.

She did not tell her parents how she got the job; her father said, "I have no doubt that you will excel. America creates opportunities for people to thrive. Nigeria can indeed learn a lot from them," while her mother began to sing when Ifemelu said that, in a few years, she could become an American citizen.

Understanding America for the Non-American Black: What Do WASPs Aspire To?

Professor Hunk has a visiting professor colleague, a Jewish guy with a thick accent from the kind of European country where most people drink a glass of antisemitism at breakfast. So Professor Hunk was talking about civil rights and Jewish guy says, "The blacks have not suffered like the Jews." Professor Hunk replies, "Come on, is this the oppression olympics?"

Jewish guy did not know this, but "oppression olympics" is what smart liberal Americans say, to make you feel stupid and to make you shut up. But there IS an oppression olympics going on. American racial minorities—blacks, Hispanics, Asians, and Jews—all get shit from white folks, different kinds of shit, but shit still. Each secretly believes that it gets the worst shit. So, no, there is no United League of the Oppressed. However, all the others think they're better than blacks because, well, they're not black. Take Lili, for example, the coffee-skinned, black-haired and Spanish-speaking woman who cleaned my aunt's house in a New England town. She had a great hauteur. She was disrespectful, cleaned poorly, made demands. My aunt believed Lili didn't like working for black people. Before she finally fired her, my aunt said, "Stupid woman, she thinks she's white." So whiteness is the thing to aspire to. Not everyone does, of course (please, commenters, don't state the obvious) but many minorities have a conflicted longing for WASP whiteness or, more accurately, for the privileges of WASP whiteness. They probably don't really like pale skin but they certainly like walking into a store without some security dude following them. Hating Your Goy and Eating One Too, as the great Philip Roth put it. So if everyone in America aspires to be WASPs, then what do WASPs aspire to? Does anyone know?

CHAPTER 20

Ifemelu came to love Baltimore—for its scrappy charm, its streets of faded glory, its farmers' market that appeared on weekends under the bridge, bursting with green vegetables and plump fruit and virtuous souls—although never as much as her first love, Philadelphia, that city that held history in its gentle clasp. But when she arrived in Baltimore knowing she was going to live there, and not merely visiting Curt, she thought it forlorn and unlovable. The buildings were joined to one another in faded slumping rows, and on shabby corners, people were hunched in puffy jackets, black and bleak people waiting for buses, the air around them hazed in gloom. Many of the drivers outside the train station were Ethiopian or Punjabi.

Her Ethiopian taxi driver said, "I can't place your accent. Where are you from?"

"Nigeria."

"Nigeria? You don't look African at all."

"Why don't I look African?"

"Because your blouse is too tight."

"It is not too tight."

"I thought you were from Trinidad or one of those places." He was looking in the rear-view with disapproval and concern. "You have to be very careful or America will corrupt you." When, years later, she wrote the blog post "On the Divisions Within the Membership of Non-American Blacks in America", she wrote about the taxi driver, but she wrote of it as the experience of someone else, careful not to let on whether she was African or Caribbean, because her readers did not know which she was.

She told Curt about the taxi driver, how his sincerity had infuriated her and how she had gone to the station bathroom to see if her pink long-sleeved blouse *was* too tight. Curt laughed and laughed. It became one of the many stories he liked to tell friends. *She actually went to the bathroom to look at her blouse!* His friends were like him, sunny and wealthy people who existed on the glimmering surface of things. She liked them, and sensed that they liked her. To them, she was interesting, unusual in the way she bluntly spoke her mind. They expected certain things of her, and forgave certain things from her, because she was foreign. Once, sitting with them in a bar, she heard Curt talking to Brad, and Curt said "blowhard". She was struck by the word, by the irredeemable Americanness of it. Blowhard. It was a word that would never occur to her. To understand this was to realize that Curt and his friends would, on some level, never be fully knowable to her.

She got an apartment in Charles Village, a one-bedroom with old wood floors, although she might as well have been living with Curt; most of her clothes were in his walk-in closet lined with mirrors. Now that she saw him every day, no longer just on weekends, she saw new layers of him, how difficult it was for him to be still, simply still without thinking of what next to do, how used he was to stepping out of his trousers and leaving them on the floor for days, until the cleaning woman came. Their lives were full of plans he made—Cozumel for one night, London for a long weekend—and she sometimes took a taxi on Friday evenings after work to meet him at the airport.

"Isn't this great?" he would ask her, and she would say yes, it was great. He was always thinking of what else to *do* and she told him that it was rare for her, because she had grown up not doing, but being. She added quickly, though, that she liked it all, because she did like it and she knew, too, how much he needed to hear that. In bed, he was anxious.

"Do you like that? Do you enjoy me?" he asked often. And she said yes, which was true, but she sensed that he did not always believe her, or that his belief lasted only so long before he would need to hear her affirmation again. There was something in him, lighter than ego but darker than insecurity, that needed constant buffing, polishing, waxing.

AND THEN her hair began to fall out at the temples. She drenched it in rich, creamy conditioners, and sat under steamers until water droplets ran down her neck. Still, her hairline shifted further backwards each day.

"It's the chemicals," Wambui told her. "Do you know what's in a relaxer? That stuff can kill you. You need to cut your hair and go natural."

Wambui's hair was now in short locs, which Ifemelu did not like; she thought them sparse and dull, unflattering to Wambui's pretty face.

"I don't want dreads," she said.

"It doesn't have to be dreads. You can wear an Afro, or braids like you used to. There's a lot you can do with natural hair."

"I can't just cut my hair," she said.

"Relaxing your hair is like being in prison. You're caged in. Your hair rules you. You didn't go running with Curt today because you don't want to sweat out this straightness. That picture you sent me, you had your hair covered on the boat. You're always battling to make your hair do what it wasn't meant to do. If you go natural and take good care of your hair, it won't fall off like it's doing now. I can help you cut it right now. No need to think about it too much."

Wambui was so sure, so convincing. Ifemelu found a pair of scissors. Wambui cut her hair, leaving only two inches, the new growth since her last relaxer. Ifemelu looked in the mirror. She was all big eyes and big head. At best, she looked like a boy; at worst, like an insect.

"I look so ugly I'm scared of myself."

"You look beautiful. Your bone structure shows so well now. You're just not used to seeing yourself like this. You'll get used to it," Wambui said.

Ifemelu was still staring at her hair. What had she done? She looked unfinished, as though the hair itself, short and stubby, was asking for attention, for something to be done to it, for *more.* After Wambui left, she went to the drugstore, Curt's baseball hat pulled over her head. She bought oils and pomades, applying one and then the other, on wet hair and then on dry hair, willing an unknown miracle to happen. Something, anything, that would make her like her hair. She thought of buying a wig, but wigs brought anxiety, the always-present possibility of flying off your head. She thought of a texturizer to loosen her hair's springy coils, stretch out the kinkiness a little, but a texturizer was really a relaxer, only milder, and she would still have to avoid the rain.

Curt told her, "Stop stressing, babe. It's a really cool and brave look."

"I don't want my hair to be *brave.*"

"I mean like stylish, chic." He paused. "You look beautiful."

"I look like a boy."

Curt said nothing. There was, in his expression, a veiled amusement, as though he did not see why she should be so upset but was better off not saying so.

The next day, she called in sick, and climbed back into bed.

"You didn't call in sick so we could stay a day longer in Bermuda but you call in sick because of your hair?" Curt asked, propped up by pillows, stifling laughter.

"I can't go out like this." She was burrowing under the covers as though to hide.

"It's not as bad as you think," he said.

"At least you finally accept that it's bad."

Curt laughed. "You know what I mean. Come here."

He hugged her, kissed her, and then slid down and began to massage her feet; she liked the warm pressure, the feel of his fingers. Yet she could not relax. In the bathroom mirror, her hair had startled her, dull and shrunken from sleep, like a mop of wool sitting on her head. She reached for her phone and sent Wambui a text: *I hate my hair. I couldn't go to work today.*

Wambui's reply came minutes later: *Go online. HappilyKinkyNappy .com. It's this natural hair community. You'll find inspiration.*

She showed the text to Curt. "What a silly name for the website."

"I know, but it sounds like a good idea. You should check it out sometime."

"Like now," Ifemelu said, getting up. Curt's laptop was open on the desk. As she went to it, she noticed a change in Curt. A sudden tense quickness. His ashen, panicked move towards the laptop.

"What's wrong?" she asked.

"They mean nothing. The e-mails mean nothing."

She stared at him, forcing her mind to work. He had not expected her to use his computer, because she hardly ever did. He was cheating on her. How odd, that she had never considered that. She picked up the laptop, held it tightly, but he didn't try to reach for it. He just stood and watched. The Yahoo mail page was minimized, next to a page about college basketball. She read some of the e-mails. She looked at attached photographs. The woman's e-mails—her address was SparklingPaola123—were strongly suggestive, while Curt's were just suggestive enough to make sure she continued. *I'm going to cook you dinner in a tight red dress and sky-high heels,* she wrote, *and you just bring yourself and a bottle of wine.* Curt replied: *Red would look great on you.* The woman was about his age, but there was, in the photos she sent, an air of hard desperation, hair dyed a brassy blonde, eyes burdened by too much blue make-up, top too low-cut. It surprised Ifemelu that Curt found her attractive. His white ex-girlfriend had been fresh-faced and preppy.

"I met her in Delaware," Curt said. "Remember the conference thing I wanted you to come to? She started hitting on me right away. She's been after me since. She won't leave me alone. She knows I have a girlfriend."

Ifemelu stared at one of the photos, a profile shot in black-and-white, the woman's head thrown back, her long hair flowing behind her. A woman who liked her hair and thought Curt would too.

"Nothing happened," Curt said. "At all. Just the e-mails. She's really after me. I told her about you, but she just won't stop."

She looked at him, wearing a T-shirt and shorts, so certain in his self-justifications. He was entitled in the way a child was: blindly.

"You wrote to her too," she said.

"But that's because she wouldn't stop."

"No, it's because you wanted to."

"Nothing happened."

"That is not the point."

"I'm sorry. I know you're already upset and I hate to make it worse."

"All your girlfriends had long flowing hair," she said, her tone thick with accusation.

"What?"

She was being absurd, but knowing that did not make her any less so. Pictures she had seen of his ex-girlfriends goaded her, the slender Japanese with straight hair dyed red, the olive-skinned Venezuelan with corkscrew hair that fell to her shoulders, the white girl with waves and waves of russet hair. And now this woman, whose looks she did not care for, but who had long straight hair. She shut the laptop. She felt small and ugly. Curt was talking. "I'll ask her never to contact me. This will never happen again, babe, I promise," he said, and she thought he sounded as though it was somehow the woman's responsibility, rather than his.

She turned away, pulled Curt's baseball hat over her head, threw things in a bag and left.

CURT CAME BY LATER, holding so many flowers she hardly saw his face when she opened the door. She would forgive him, she knew, because she believed him. Sparkling Paola was one more small adventure of his. He would not have gone further with her, but he would have kept encouraging her attention, until he was bored. Sparkling Paola was like the silver stars that his teachers pasted on the pages of his elementary school homework, sources of a shallow, fleeting pleasure.

She did not want to go out, but she did not want to be with him in the intimacy of her apartment; she still felt too raw. So she covered her hair in a headwrap and they took a walk, Curt solicitous and full of promises, walking side by side but not touching, all the way to the corner of Charles and University Parkway, and then back to her apartment.

FOR THREE DAYS, she called in sick. Finally, she went to work, her hair a very short, overly combed and overly oiled Afro. "You look different," her co-workers said, all of them a little tentative.

"Does it mean anything? Like, something political?" Amy asked, Amy who had a poster of Che Guevara on her cubicle wall.

"No," Ifemelu said.

At the cafeteria, Miss Margaret, the bosomy African American woman who presided over the counter—and, apart from two security guards, the only other black person in the company—asked, "Why did you cut your hair, hon? Are you a lesbian?"

"No, Miss Margaret, at least not yet."

Some years later, on the day Ifemelu resigned, she went into the cafeteria for a last lunch. "You leaving?" Miss Margaret asked, downcast. "Sorry, hon. They need to treat folk better around here. You think your hair was part of the problem?"

HAPPILYKINKYNAPPY.COM HAD a bright yellow background, message boards full of posts, thumbnail photos of black women blinking at the top. They had long trailing dreadlocks, small Afros, big Afros, twists, braids, massive raucous curls and coils. They called relaxers "creamy crack". They were done with pretending that their hair was what it was not, done with running from the rain and flinching from sweat. They complimented each other's photos and ended comments with "hugs". They complained about black magazines never having natural-haired women in their pages, about drugstore products so poisoned by mineral oil that they could not moisturize natural hair. They traded recipes. They sculpted for themselves a virtual world where their coily, kinky, nappy, woolly hair was normal. And Ifemelu fell into this world with a tumbling gratitude. Women with hair as short as hers had a name for it: TWA, Teeny Weeny Afro. She learned, from women who posted long instructions, to avoid shampoos with silicones, to use a leave-in conditioner on wet hair, to sleep in a satin scarf. She ordered products from women who made them in their kitchens and shipped them with clear instructions: BEST TO REFRIGERATE IMMEDIATELY, DOES NOT CONTAIN PRESERVATIVES. Curt would open the fridge, hold up a container labelled "hair butter" and ask, "Okay to spread this on my toast?" Curt thrummed with fascination about it all. He read posts on HappilyKinkyNappy.com. "I think it's great!" he said. "It's like this *movement* of black women."

One day, at the farmers' market, as she stood hand in hand with Curt in front of a tray of apples, a black man walked past and muttered, "You ever wonder why he likes you looking all jungle like that?" She stopped, unsure for a moment whether she had imagined those words, and then she looked back at the man. He walked with too much rhythm in his step, which suggested to her a certain fickleness of character. A man not worth paying any attention to. Yet his words bothered her, prised open the door for new doubts.

"Did you hear what that guy said?" she asked Curt.

"No, what did he say?"

She shook her head. "Nothing."

She felt dispirited and, while Curt watched a game that evening, she drove to the beauty supply store and ran her fingers through small bundles of silky straight weaves. Then she remembered a post by Jamilah1977—*I love the sistas who love their straight weaves, but I'm never putting horse hair on my head again*—and she left the store, eager to get back and log on and post on the boards about it. She wrote: *Jamilah's words made me remember that there is nothing more beautiful than what God gave me.* Others wrote responses, posting thumbs-up signs, telling her how much they liked the photo she had put up. She had never talked about God so much. Posting on the website was like giving testimony in church; the echoing roar of approval revived her.

On an unremarkable day in early spring—the day was not bronzed with special light, nothing of any significance happened, and it was perhaps merely that time, as it often does, had transfigured her doubts—she looked in the mirror, sank her fingers into her hair, dense and spongy and glorious, and could not imagine it any other way. That simply, she fell in love with her hair.

Why Dark-Skinned Black Women—
Both American and Non-American—Love Barack Obama

Many American blacks proudly say they have some "Indian." Which means Thank God We Are Not Full-Blooded Negroes. Which means they are not too dark. (To clarify, when white people say dark they mean Greek or Italian but when black people say dark they mean Grace Jones.) American black men like their black women to have some exotic quota, like half-Chinese or splash of Cherokee. They like their women light. But beware what American blacks consider "light." Some of these "light" people, in countries of Non-American Blacks, would simply be called white. (Oh, and dark American black men resent light men, for having it too easy with the ladies.)

Now, my fellow Non-American Blacks, don't get smug. Because this bullshit also exists in our Caribbean and African countries. Not as bad as with American blacks, you say? Maybe. But there nonetheless. By the way, what is it with Ethiopians thinking they are not that black? And Small Islanders eager to say their ancestry is "mixed"? But we must not digress. So light skin is valued in the community of American blacks. But everyone pretends this is no longer so. They say the days of the paper-bag test (look this up) are gone and let's move forward. But today most of the American blacks who are successful as entertainers and as public figures, are light. Especially women. Many successful American black men have white wives. Those who deign to have black wives have light (otherwise known as high yellow) wives. And this is the reason dark women love Barack Obama. He broke the mold! He married one of their own. He knows what the world doesn't seem to know: that dark black women totally rock. They want Obama to win because maybe finally somebody will cast a beautiful chocolate babe in a big-budget rom-com that opens in theaters all over the country, not just three artsy theaters in New York City. You see, in American pop culture, beautiful dark women are invisible. (The other group just as invisible is Asian men. But at least they get to be super smart.) In movies, dark black women get to be the fat nice mammy or the strong, sassy, sometimes scary sidekick standing by supportively. They get to dish out wisdom and attitude while the white woman finds love. But they never get to be the hot woman, beautiful and desired and all. So dark black women hope Obama will change that. Oh, and dark black women are also for cleaning up Washington and getting out of Iraq and whatnot.

CHAPTER 21

It was a Sunday morning, and Aunty Uju called, agitated and strained. "Look at this boy! Come and see the nonsense he wants to wear to church. He has refused to wear what I brought out for him. You know that if he does not dress properly, they will find something to say about us. If they are shabby, it's not a problem, but if we are, it is another thing. This is the same way I have been telling him to tone it down at school. The other day, they said he was talking in class and he said he was talking because he had finished his work. He has to tone it down, because his own will always be seen as different, but the boy doesn't understand. Please talk to your cousin!"

Ifemelu asked Dike to take the phone to his room.

"Mom wants me to wear this really ugly shirt." His tone was flat, dispassionate.

"I know how uncool that shirt is, Dike, but wear it for her, okay? Just to church. Just for today."

She did know the shirt, a striped, humourless shirt that Bartholomew had bought for Dike. It was the sort of shirt Bartholomew would buy. It reminded her of his friends she had met one weekend, a Nigerian couple visiting from Maryland, their two boys sitting next to them on the sofa, both buttoned-up and stiff, caged in the airlessness of their parents' immigrant aspirations. She did not want Dike to be like them, but she understood Aunty Uju's anxieties, making her way in unfamiliar terrain as she was.

"You'll probably not see anybody you know in church," Ifemelu said. "And I'll talk to your mum about not making you wear it again." She cajoled until finally Dike agreed, as long as he could wear sneakers, not the lace-ups his mother wanted.

"I'm coming up this weekend," she told him. "I'm bringing my boyfriend, Curt. You'll finally get to meet him."

WITH AUNTY UJU, Curt was solicitous and charming in that well-oiled way that slightly embarrassed Ifemelu. At dinner the other night with Wambui and some friends, Curt had reached out and refilled a wineglass here, a water glass there. Charming, was what one of the girls said later: Your boyfriend is so charming. And the thought occurred to Ifemelu that she did not like charm. Not Curt's kind, with its need to dazzle, to perform. She wished Curt were quieter and more inward. When he started conversations with people in elevators, or lavishly complimented strangers, she held her breath, certain that they could see what an attention-loving person he was. But they always smiled back and responded and allowed themselves to be wooed. As Aunty Uju did. "Curt, won't you try the soup? Ifemelu has never cooked this soup for you? Have you tried fried plantain?"

Dike watched, saying little, speaking politely and properly, even though Curt joked with him and talked sports and tried so hard to win his affection that Ifemelu feared he might do somersaults. Finally, Curt asked, "Want to shoot some hoops?"

Dike shrugged. "Okay."

Aunty Uju watched them leave.

"Look at the way he behaves as if anything you touch starts smelling like perfume. He really likes you," Aunty Uju said, and then, face wrinkling, she added, "And even with your hair like that."

"Aunty, *biko*, leave my hair alone," Ifemelu said.

"It is like jute." Aunty Uju plunged a hand into Ifemelu's Afro.

Ifemelu drew her head away. "What if every magazine you opened and every film you watched had beautiful women with hair like jute? You would be admiring my hair now."

Aunty Uju scoffed. "Okay, you can speak English about it but I am just saying what is true. There is something scruffy and untidy about natural hair." Aunty Uju paused. "Have you read the essay your cousin wrote?"

"Yes."

"How can he say he does not know what he is? Since when is he conflicted? And even that his name is difficult?"

"You should talk to him, Aunty. If that is how he feels, then that is how he feels."

"I think he wrote that because that is the kind of thing they teach them here. Everybody is conflicted, identity this, identity that. Somebody will commit murder and say it is because his mother did not hug him when he was three years old. Or they will do something wicked and say it is a disease that they are struggling with." Aunty Uju looked out of the window. Curt and Dike were dribbling a basketball in the backyard, and farther away was the beginning of thick woods. On Ifemelu's last visit, she had woken up to see, through the kitchen window, a pair of gracefully galloping deer.

"I am tired," Aunty Uju said in a low voice.

"What do you mean?" Ifemelu knew, though, that it would only be more complaints about Bartholomew.

"Both of us work. Both of us come home at the same time and do you know what Bartholomew does? He just sits in the living room and turns on the TV and asks me what we are eating for dinner." Aunty Uju scowled and Ifemelu noticed how much weight she had put on, the beginning of a double chin, the new flare of her nose. "He wants me to give him my salary. Imagine! He said that it is how marriages are since he is the head of the family, that I should not send money home to Brother without his permission, that we should make his car payments from my salary. I want to look at private schools for Dike, with all this nonsense happening in that public school, but Bartholomew said it is too expensive. Too expensive! Meanwhile, his children went to private schools in California. He is not even bothered with all the rubbish going on in Dike's school. The other day I went there, and a teacher's assistant shouted at me across the hall. Imagine. She was so rude. I noticed she did not shout across the hall to the other parents. So I went over and told her off. These people, they make you become aggressive just to hold your dignity." Aunty Uju shook her head. "Bartholomew is not even bothered that Dike still calls him Uncle. I told him to encourage Dike to call him Dad but it doesn't bother him. All he wants is for me to hand over my salary to him and cook peppered gizzard for him on Saturdays while he watches European League on satellite. Why should I give him my salary? Did he pay my fees in medical school? He wants to start a business but they won't give him a loan and he says he will sue them for discrimination because his credit is not bad and he found out a man who goes to our church got a loan with much worse credit. Is it my fault that he cannot get the loan? Did anybody force him to come here? Did he not know we would be the only black people here? Did he not come here because he felt it would benefit him? Everything is money, money, money. He keeps wanting to make my work decisions for me. What does an accountant know about medicine? I just want to be comfortable. I just want to be able to pay for my child's college. I don't need to work longer hours just to accumulate money. It's not as if I am planning to buy a boat like Americans." Aunty Uju moved away from the window and sat down at the kitchen table. "I don't even know why I came to this place. The other day the pharmacist said my accent was incomprehensible. Imagine, I called in a medicine and she actually told me that my accent was incomprehensible. And that same day, as if somebody sent them, one patient, a useless layabout with tattoos all over his body, told me to go back to where I came from. All because I knew he was lying about being in pain and I refused to give him more pain medicine. Why do I have to take this rubbish? I blame Buhari and Babangida and Abacha, because they destroyed Nigeria."

It was strange, how Aunty Uju often spoke about the former heads of state, invoking their names with poisoned blame, but never mentioning The General.

Curt and Dike came back into the kitchen. Dike was bright-eyed, slightly sweaty and talkative; he had, out there in the basketball space, swallowed Curt's star.

"Do you want some water, Curt?" he asked.

"Call him Uncle Curt," Aunty Uju said.

Curt laughed. "Or Cousin Curt. How about Coz Curt?"

"You're not my cousin," Dike said, smiling.

"I would be if I married your cousin."

"Depends on how much you are offering us!" Dike said.

They all laughed. Aunty Uju looked pleased.

"Do you want to get that drink and meet me outside, Dike?" Curt asked. "We've got some unfinished business!"

Curt touched Ifemelu's shoulder gently, asked if she was okay, before going back outside.

"O *na-eji gi ka akwa,*" Aunty Uju said, her tone charged with admiration.

Ifemelu smiled. Curt did indeed hold her like an egg. With him, she felt breakable, precious. Later, as they left, she slipped her hand into his and squeezed; she felt proud—to be with him, and of him.

ONE MORNING, Aunty Uju woke up and went to the bathroom. Bartholomew had just brushed his teeth. Aunty Uju reached for her toothbrush and saw, inside the sink, a thick blob of toothpaste. Thick enough for a full mouth-cleaning. It sat there, far from the drain, soft and melting. It disgusted her. How exactly did a person clean their teeth and end up leaving so much toothpaste in the sink? Had he not seen it? Had he, when it fell into the sink, pressed more onto his toothbrush? Or did he just go ahead and brush anyway with an almost-dry brush? Which meant his teeth were not clean. But his teeth did not concern Aunty Uju. The blob of toothpaste left in the sink did. On so many other mornings, she had cleaned off toothpaste, rinsed out the sink. But not this morning. This morning, she was done. She shouted his name, again and again. He asked her what was wrong. She told him the toothpaste in the sink was wrong. He looked at her and mumbled that he had been in a hurry, he was already late for work, and she told him that she, too, had work to go to, and she earned more than he did, in case he had forgotten. She was paying for his car, after all. He stormed off and went downstairs. At this point in the story, Aunty Uju paused, and Ifemelu imagined Bartholomew in his contrast-collar shirt and his trousers pulled too high up, the unflattering pleats at the front, his K-leg walk as he stormed off. Aunty Uju's voice was unusually calm over the phone.

"I've found a condo in a town called Willow. A very nice gated place near the university. Dike and I are leaving this weekend," Aunty Uju said.

"Ahn-ahn! Aunty, so quickly?"

"I've tried. It is enough."

"What did Dike say?"

"He said he never liked living in the woods. He didn't even say one word about Bartholomew. Willow will be so much better for him."

Ifemelu liked the name of the town, Willow; it sounded to her like freshly squeezed beginnings.

To My Fellow Non-American Blacks: In America, You Are Black, Baby

Dear Non-American Black, when you make the choice to come to America, you become black. Stop arguing. Stop saying I'm Jamaican or I'm Ghanaian. America doesn't care. So what if you weren't "black" in your country? You're in America now. We all have our moments of initiation into the Society of Former Negroes. Mine was in a class in undergrad when I was asked to give the black perspective, only I had no idea what that was. So I just made something up. And admit it—you say "I'm not black" only because you know black is at the bottom of America's race ladder. And you want none of that. Don't deny now. What if being black had all the privileges of being white? Would you still say "Don't call me black, I'm from Trinidad"? I didn't think so. So you're black, baby. And here's the deal with becoming black: You must show that you are offended when such words as "watermelon" or "tar baby" are used in jokes, even if you don't know what the hell is being talked about—and since you are a Non-American Black, the chances are that you won't know. (In undergrad a white classmate asks if I like watermelon, I say yes, and another classmate says, Oh my God that is so racist, and I'm confused. "Wait, how?") You must nod back when a black person nods at you in a heavily white area. It is called the black nod. It is a way for black people to say "You are not alone, I am here too." In describing black women you admire, always use the word "STRONG" because that is what black women are supposed to be in America. If you are a woman, please do not speak your mind as you are used to doing in your country. Because in America, strong-minded black women are SCARY. And if you are a man, be hyper-mellow, never get too excited, or somebody will worry that you're about to pull a gun. When you watch television and hear that a "racist slur" was used, you must immediately become offended. Even though you are thinking "But why won't they tell me exactly what was said?" Even though you would like to be able to decide for yourself how offended to be, or whether to be offended at all, you must nevertheless be very offended.

When a crime is reported, pray that it was not committed by a black person, and if it turns out to have been committed by a black person, stay well away from the crime area for weeks, or you might be stopped for fitting the profile. If a black cashier gives poor service to the non-black person in front of you, compliment that person's shoes or something, to make up for the bad service, because you're just as guilty for the cashier's crimes. If you are in an Ivy League college, and a Young Republican tells you that you got in only because of Affirmative Action, do not whip out your perfect grades from high school. Instead, gently point out that the biggest beneficiaries of Affirmative Action are white women. If you go to eat in a restaurant, please tip generously. Otherwise the next black person who comes in will get awful service, because waiters groan when they get a black table. You see, black people have a gene that makes them not tip, so please overpower that gene. If you're telling a non-black person about something racist that happened to you, make sure you are not bitter. Don't complain. Be forgiving. If possible, make it funny. Most of all, do not be angry. Black people are not supposed to be angry about racism. Otherwise you get no sympathy. This applies only for white liberals, by the way. Don't even bother telling a white conservative about anything racist that happened to you. Because the conservative will tell you that YOU are the real racist and your mouth will hang open in confusion.

CHAPTER 22

One Saturday at the mall in White Marsh, Ifemelu saw Kayode DaSilva. It was raining. She was standing inside, by the entrance, waiting for Curt to bring the car around, and Kayode almost bumped into her.

"Ifemsco!" he said.

"Oh my God. Kayode!"

They hugged, looked at each other, said all the things people said who had not seen each other in many years, both lapsing into their Nigerian voices and their Nigerian selves, louder, more heightened, adding "o" to their sentences. He had left right after secondary school to attend university in Indiana and had graduated years ago.

"I was working in Pittsburgh but I just moved to Silver Spring to start a new job. I love Maryland. I run into Nigerians at the grocery store and in the mall, everywhere. It's like being back home. But I guess you know that already."

"Yes," she said, even though she did not. Her Maryland was a small, circumscribed world of Curt's American friends.

"I was planning to come and find you, by the way." He was looking at her, as though absorbing her details, memorizing her, for when he would tell the story of their meeting.

"Really?"

"So my guy The Zed and I were talking the other day and you came up and he said he'd heard you were living in Baltimore and since I was close by could I just find you and see that you were okay and tell him what you look like now."

A numbness spread swiftly through her. She mumbled, "Oh, you're still in touch?"

"Yes. We got back in touch when he moved to England last year."

England! Obinze was in England. She had created the distance, ignoring him, changing her e-mail address and phone number, and yet she felt deeply betrayed by this news. Changes had been made in his life that she did not know about. He was in England. Only a few months ago, she and Curt had gone to England for the Glastonbury Festival, and later spent two days in London. Obinze might have been there. She might have run into him as she walked down Oxford Street.

"So what happened now? Honestly, I couldn't believe it when he said you guys were not in touch. Ahn-ahn! All of us were just waiting for the wedding invitation card o!" Kayode said.

Ifemelu shrugged. There were things scattered inside of her that she needed to gather together.

"So how have you been? How is life?" Kayode asked.

"Fine," she said coldly. "I'm waiting for my boyfriend to pick me up. Actually, I think that's him."

There was, in Kayode's demeanour, a withdrawal of spirit, a pulling back of his army of warmth, because he sensed very well that she had made the choice to shut him out. She was already walking away. Over her shoulder, she said to him, "Take care." She was supposed to exchange phone numbers, talk for longer, behave in all the expected ways. But emotions were rioting inside her. And she found Kayode guilty for knowing about Obinze, for bringing Obinze back.

"I just ran into an old friend from Nigeria. I haven't seen him since high school," she told Curt.

"Oh, really? That's nice. He live here?"

"In DC."

Curt was watching her, expecting more. He would want to ask Kayode to have drinks with them, want to be friends with her friend, want to be as gracious as he always was. And this, his expectant expression, irritated her. She wanted silence. Even the radio was bothering her. What would Kayode tell Obinze? That she was dating a handsome white man in a BMW coupé, her hair an Afro, a red flower tucked behind her ear. What would Obinze make of this? What was he doing in England? A clear memory came to her, of a sunny day—the sun was always shining in her memories of him and she distrusted this—when his friend Okwudiba brought a video cassette to his house, and

Obinze said, "A British film? Waste of time." To him, only American films were worth watching. And now he was in England.

Curt was looking at her. "Seeing him upset you?"

"No."

"Was he like a boyfriend or something?"

"No," she said, looking out of the window.

Later that day she would send an e-mail to Obinze's Hotmail address: *Ceiling, I don't even know how to start. I ran into Kayode today at the mall. Saying sorry for my silence sounds stupid even to me but I am so sorry and I feel so stupid. I will tell you everything that happened. I have missed you and I miss you.* And he would not reply.

"I booked the Swedish massage for you," Curt said.

"Thank you," she said. Then, in a lower voice, she added, to make up for her peevishness, "You are such a sweetheart."

"I don't want to be a sweetheart. I want to be the fucking love of your life," Curt said with a force that startled her.

Part 3

CHAPTER 23

In London, night came too soon, it hung in the morning air like a threat, and then in the afternoon a blue-grey dusk descended, and the Victorian buildings all wore a mournful air. In those first weeks, the cold startled Obinze with its weightless menace, drying his nostrils, deepening his anxieties, making him urinate too often. He would walk fast on the pavement, turned tightly into himself, hands deep in the coat his cousin had lent him, a grey wool coat whose sleeves nearly swallowed his fingers. Sometimes he would stop outside a tube station, often by a flower or a newspaper vendor, and watch the people brushing past him. They walked so quickly, these people, as though they had an urgent destination, a purpose to their lives, while he did not. His eyes would follow them, with a lost longing, and he would think: *You can work, you are legal, you are visible, and you don't even know how fortunate you are.*

It was at a tube station that he met the Angolans who would arrange his marriage, exactly two years and three days after he arrived in England; he kept count.

"We'll talk in the car," one of them had said earlier over the phone. Their old-model black Mercedes was fussily maintained, the floor mats wavy from vacuuming, the leather seats shiny with polish. The two men looked alike, with thick eyebrows that almost touched, although they had told him they were just friends, and they were dressed alike, too, in leather jackets and long gold chains. Their tabletop haircuts that sat on their heads like tall hats surprised him, but perhaps it was part of their hip image, to have retro haircuts. They spoke to him with the authority of people who had done this before, and also with a slight condescension; his fate was, after all, in their hands.

"We decided on Newcastle because we know people there and London is too hot right now, too many marriages happening in London, yeah, so we don't want trouble," one of them said. "Everything is going to work out. Just make sure you keep a low profile, yeah? Don't attract any attention to yourself until the marriage is done. Don't fight in the pub, yeah?"

"I've never been a very good fighter," Obinze said drily, but the Angolans did not smile.

"You have the money?" the other one asked.

Obinze handed over two hundred pounds, all in twenty-pound notes that he had taken out of the cash machine over two days. It was a deposit, to prove he was serious. Later, after he met the girl, he would pay two thousand pounds.

"The rest has to be up front, yeah? We'll use some of it to do the running around and the rest goes to the girl. Man, you know we're not making anything from this. We usually ask for much more but we're doing this for Iloba," the first one said.

Obinze did not believe them, even then. He met the girl, Cleotilde, a few days later, at a shopping centre, in a McDonald's whose windows looked out onto the dank entrance of a tube station across the street. He sat at a table with the Angolans, watching people hurry past, and wondering which of them was her, while the Angolans both whispered into their phones; perhaps they were arranging other marriages.

"Hello there!" she said.

She surprised him. He had expected somebody with pockmarks smothered under heavy make-up, somebody tough and knowing. But here she was, dewy and fresh, bespectacled, olive-skinned, almost childlike, smiling shyly at him and sucking a milkshake through a straw. She looked like a university freshman who was innocent or dumb, or both.

"I just wanted to know that you're sure about doing this," he told her, and then, worried that he might frighten her away, he added, "I'm very grateful and it won't take too much from you—in a year I'll have my papers and we'll do the divorce. But I just wanted to meet you first and make sure you are okay to do this."

"Yes," she said.

He watched her, expecting more. She played with her straw, shyly, not meeting his eyes, and it took him a while to realize that she was reacting more to him than to the situation. She was attracted to him.

"I want to help my mum out. Things are tight at home," she said, a trace of a non-British accent underlining her words.

"She's with us, yeah," one of the Angolans said, impatiently, as though Obinze had dared to question what they had already told him.

"Show him your details, Cleo," the other Angolan said.

His calling her Cleo rang false: Obinze sensed this from the way he said it, and from the way she heard it, the slight surprise on her face. It was a forced intimacy; the Angolan had never called her Cleo before. Perhaps he had never even called her anything before. Obinze wondered how the Angolans knew her. Did they have a list of young women with European Union passports who needed money? Cleotilde pushed at her hair, a mass of tight coils, and adjusted her glasses, as though first preparing herself before she presented her passport and licence. Obinze examined them. He would have thought her younger than twenty-three.

"Can I have your number?" Obinze asked.

"Just call us for anything," the Angolans said, almost at the same time. But Obinze wrote his number on a napkin and pushed it across to her. The Angolans gave him a sly look. Later, on the phone, she told him that she had been living in London for six years and was saving money to go to fashion school, even though the Angolans had told him she lived in Portugal.

"Would you like to meet?" he asked. "It will be much easier if we try to get to know each other a little."

"Yes," she said without hesitation.

They ate fish and chips in a pub, a thin crust of grime on the sides of the wood table, while she talked about her love of fashion and asked him about Nigerian traditional dress. She seemed a little more mature; he noticed the shimmer on her cheeks, the more defined curl of her hair, and knew she had made an effort with her appearance.

"What will you do after you get your papers?" she asked him. "Will you bring your girlfriend from Nigeria?"

He was touched by her obviousness. "I don't have a girlfriend."

"I've never been to Africa. I'd love to go." She said "Africa" wistfully, like an admiring foreigner, loading the word with exotic excitement. Her black Angolan father had left her white Portuguese mother when she was only three years old, she told him, and she had not seen him since, nor had she ever been to Angola. She said this with a shrug and a cynical raise of her eyebrows, as though it had never bothered her, an effort so out of character, so jarring, that it showed him just how deeply it did bother her. There were difficulties in her life that he wanted to know more about, parts of her thick shapely body that he longed to touch, but he was wary of complicating things. He would wait until after the marriage, until the business side of their relationship was finished. She seemed to understand this without their talking about it. And so as they met and talked in the following weeks, sometimes practising how they would answer questions during their immigration interview and other times just talking about football, there was, between them, the growing urgency of restrained desire. It was there in their standing close to each other, not touching, as they waited at the tube station, in their teasing each other about his support of Arsenal and her support of Manchester United, in their lingering gazes. After he had paid the Angolans two thousand pounds in cash, she told him that they had given her only five hundred pounds.

"I'm just telling you. I know you don't have any more money. I want to do this for you," she said.

She was looking at him, her eyes liquid with things unsaid, and she made him feel whole again, made him remember how starved he was for something simple and pure. He wanted to kiss her, her upper lip pinker and shinier with lip gloss than the lower, to hold her, to tell her how deeply, irrepressibly grateful he was. She would never stir his cauldron of worries, never wave her power in his face. One Eastern European woman, Iloba had told him, had asked the Nigerian man, an hour before their court wedding, to give her a thousand pounds extra or she would walk away. In panic, the man had begun to call all his friends, to raise the money.

"Man, we gave you a good deal" was all one of the Angolans said when Obinze asked how much they had given Cleotilde, in that tone of theirs, the tone of people who knew how much they were needed. It was they, after all, who took him to a lawyer's office, a low-voiced Nigerian in a swivel chair, sliding backwards to reach a filing cabinet as he said, "You can still get married even though your visa is expired.

In fact, getting married is now your only choice." It was they who provided water and gas bills, going back six months, with his name and a Newcastle address, they who found a man who would "sort out" his driving licence, a man cryptically called Brown. Obinze met Brown at the train station in Barking; he stood near the gate as agreed, amid the bustle of people, looking around and waiting for his phone to ring because Brown had refused to give him a phone number.

"Are you waiting for somebody?" Brown stood there, a slight man, his winter hat pulled down to his eyebrows.

"Yes. I'm Obinze," he said, feeling like a character in a spy novel who had to speak in silly code. Brown led him to a quiet corner, handed over an envelope, and there it was, his licence, with his photo and the genuine, slightly worn look of something owned for a year. A slight plastic card, but it weighed down his pocket. A few days later, he walked with it into a London building which, from the outside, looked like a church, steepled and grave, but inside was shabby, harried, knotted with people. Signs were scrawled on whiteboards: BIRTHS AND DEATHS THIS WAY. MARRIAGE REGISTRATION THIS WAY. Obinze, his expression carefully frozen in neutrality, handed the licence over to the registrar behind the desk.

A woman was walking towards the door, talking loudly to her companion. "Look how crowded this place is. It's all sham marriages, all of them, now that Blunkett is after them."

Perhaps she had come to register a death, and her words merely the lonely lashings-out of grief, but he felt the familiar tightening of panic in his chest. The registrar was examining his licence, taking too long. The seconds lengthened and curdled. *All sham marriages, all of them* rang in Obinze's head. Finally the registrar looked up and pushed across a form.

"Getting married, are we? Congratulations!" The words came out with the mechanical good cheer of frequent repetition.

"Thank you," Obinze said, and tried to unfreeze his face.

Behind the desk, a whiteboard was propped on a wall, venues and dates of intended marriages written on it in blue; a name at the bottom caught his eye. *Okoli Okafor and Crystal Smith.* Okoli Okafor was his classmate from secondary school and university, a quiet boy who had been teased for having a surname for a first name, who later joined a vicious cult in university, and then left Nigeria during one of the long strikes. Now here he was, a ghost of a name, about to get married in England. Perhaps it was also a marriage for papers. Okoli Okafor. Everyone called him Okoli Paparazzi in university. On the day Princess Diana died, a group of students had gathered before a lecture, talking about what they had heard on the radio that morning, repeating "paparazzi" over and over, all sounding knowing and cocksure, until, in a lull, Okoli Okafor quietly asked, "But who exactly are the paparazzi? Are they motorcyclists?" and instantly earned himself the nickname Okoli Paparazzi.

The memory, clear as a light beam, took Obinze back to a time when he still believed the universe would bend according to his will. Melancholy descended on him as he left the building. Once, during his final year in the university, the year that people danced in the streets because General Abacha had died, his mother had said, "One day, I will look up and all the people I know will be dead or abroad." She had spoken wearily, as they sat in the living room, eating boiled corn and ube. He sensed, in her voice, the sadness of defeat, as though her friends who were leaving for teaching positions in Canada and America had confirmed to her a great personal failure. For a moment he felt as if he, too, had betrayed her by having his own plan: to get a postgraduate degree in America, to work in America, to live in America. It was a plan he had had for a long time. Of course he knew how unreasonable the American embassy could be—the vice chancellor, of all people, had once been refused a visa to attend a conference—but he had never doubted his plan. He would wonder, later, why he had been so sure. Perhaps it was because he had never simply wanted to go *abroad*, as many others did; some people were now going to South Africa, which amused him. It had always been America, only America. A longing nurtured and nursed over many years. The advertisement on NTA for *Andrew Checking Out*, which he had watched as a child, had given shape to his longings. "Men, I'm checkin' out," the character Andrew had said, staring cockily at the camera. "No good roads, no light, no water. Men, you can't even get a bottle of soft drink!" While Andrew was checking out, General Buhari's soldiers were flogging adults in the streets, lecturers were striking for better pay, and his mother had decided that he could no longer have Fanta whenever he wanted but only on Sundays, with permission. And so, America became a place where bottles and bottles of Fanta were to be had, without permission. He would stand in front of the mirror and repeat Andrew's words: "Men, I'm checkin' out!" Later, seeking out magazines and books and films and second-hand stories about America, his longing took on a minor mystical quality and America became where he was destined to be. He saw himself walking the streets of Harlem, discussing the merits of Mark Twain with his American friends, gazing at Mount Rushmore. Days after he graduated from university, bloated with knowledge about America, he applied for a visa at the American embassy in Lagos.

He already knew that the best interviewer was the blond-bearded man, and as he moved in the line, he hoped he would not be interviewed by the horror story, a pretty white woman famous for screaming into her microphone and insulting even grandmothers. Finally, it was his turn and the blond-bearded man said, "Next person!" Obinze walked up and slid his forms underneath the glass. The man glanced at the forms and said, kindly, "Sorry, you don't qualify. Next person!" Obinze was stunned. He went three more times over the next few months. Each time he was told, without a glance at his documents, "Sorry, you don't qualify," and each time he emerged from the air-conditioned cool of the embassy building and into the harsh sunlight, stunned and unbelieving.

"It's the terrorism fears," his mother said. "The Americans are now averse to foreign young men."

She told him to find a job and try again in a year. His job applications yielded nothing. He travelled to Lagos and to Port Harcourt and to Abuja to take assessment tests, which he found easy, and he attended interviews, answering questions fluidly, but then a long empty silence would follow. Some friends were getting jobs, people who did not have his second-class upper degree and did not speak as well as he did. He wondered whether employers could smell his America-pining on his breath, or sense how obsessively he still looked at the websites of American universities. He was living with his mother, driving her car, sleeping with impressionable young students, browsing overnight at Internet cafés with all-night specials, and sometimes spending days in his room reading and avoiding his mother. He disliked her calm good cheer, how hard she tried to be positive, telling him that now

President Obasanjo was in power, things were changing, the mobile phone companies and banks were growing and recruiting, even giving young people car loans. Most of the time, though, she left him alone. She did not knock on his door. She simply asked the house help, Agnes, to leave some food in the pot for him and to clear away dirty plates from his room. One day, she left him a note on the bathroom sink: *I have been invited to an academic conference in London. We should speak.* He was puzzled. When she came home from her lecture, he was in the living room waiting for her.

"Mummy, *nno*," he said.

She acknowledged his greeting with a nod and put down her bag on the centre table. "I'm going to put your name on my British visa application as my research assistant," she said quietly. "That should get you a six-month visa. You can stay with Nicholas in London. See what you can do with your life. Maybe you can get to America from there. I know that your mind is no longer here."

He stared at her.

"I understand this sort of thing is done nowadays," she said, sitting down on the sofa beside him, trying to sound offhand, but he sensed her discomfort in the uncommon briskness of her words. She was from the generation of the bewildered, who did not understand what had happened to Nigeria but allowed themselves to be swept along. She was a woman who kept to herself and asked no favours, who would not lie, who would not accept even a Christmas card from her students because it might compromise her, who accounted for every single kobo spent on any committee she was on, and here she was, behaving as though truth-telling had become a luxury that they could no longer afford. It went against everything she had taught him, yet he knew that truth had indeed, in their circumstance, become a luxury. She lied for him. If anybody else had lied for him, it would not have mattered as much or even at all, but she lied for him and he got the six-month visa to the United Kingdom and he felt, even before he left, like a failure. He did not contact her for months. He did not contact her because there was nothing to tell her and he wanted to wait until he had something to tell her. He was in England for three years and spoke to her only a few times, strained conversations during which he imagined she was wondering why he had made nothing of himself. But she never asked for details; she only waited to hear what he was willing to tell. Later, when he returned home, he would feel disgusted with his own entitlement, his blindness to her, and he spent a lot of time with her, determined to make amends, to return to their former relationship, but first to attempt to map the boundaries of their estrangement.

CHAPTER 24

Everyone joked about people who went abroad to clean toilets, and so Obinze approached his first job with irony: he was indeed abroad cleaning toilets, wearing rubber gloves and carrying a pail, in an estate agent's office on the second floor of a London building. Each time he opened the swinging door of a stall, it seemed to sigh. The beautiful woman who cleaned the ladies' toilet was Ghanaian, about his age, with the shiniest dark skin he had ever seen. He sensed, in the way she spoke and carried herself, a background similar to his, a childhood cushioned by family, by regular meals, by dreams in which there was no conception of cleaning toilets in London. She ignored his friendly gestures, saying only "Good evening" as formally as she could, but she was friendly with the white woman who cleaned the offices upstairs, and once he saw them in the deserted café, drinking tea and talking in low tones. He stood watching them for a while, a great grievance exploding in his mind. It was not that she did not want friendship, it was rather that she did not want his. Perhaps friendship in their present circumstances was impossible because she was Ghanaian and he, a Nigerian, was too close to what she was; he knew her nuances, while she was free to reinvent herself with the Polish woman, to be whoever she wanted to be.

The toilets were not bad, some urine outside the urinal, some unfinished flushing; cleaning them was much easier than it must have been for the cleaners of the campus toilets back in Nsukka, with the streaks of shit smeared on the walls that had always made him wonder why anybody would go to all that trouble. And so he was shocked, one evening, to walk into a stall and discover a mound of shit on the toilet lid, solid, tapering, centred as though it had been carefully arranged and the exact spot had been measured. It looked like a puppy curled on a mat. It was a performance. He thought about the famed repression of the English. His cousin's wife, Ojiugo, had once said, "English people will live next to you for years but they will never greet you. It is as if they have buttoned themselves up." There was, in this performance, something of an unbuttoning. A person who had been fired? Denied a promotion? Obinze stared at that mound of shit for a long time, feeling smaller and smaller as he did so, until it became a personal affront, a punch on his jaw. And all for three quid an hour. He took off his gloves, placed them next to the mound of shit and left the building. That evening, he received an e-mail from Ifemelu. *Ceiling, I don't even know how to start. I ran into Kayode today at the mall. Saying sorry for my silence sounds stupid even to me but I am so sorry and I feel so stupid. I will tell you everything that happened. I have missed you and I miss you.*

He stared at the e-mail. This was what he had longed for, for so long. To hear from her. When she first stopped contacting him, he had worried himself into weeks of insomnia, roaming the house in the middle of the night, wondering what had happened to her. They had not fought, their love was as sparkling as always, their plan intact, and suddenly there was silence from her, a silence so brutal and complete. He had called and called until she changed her phone number, he had sent e-mails, he had contacted her mother, Aunty Uju, Ginika. Ginika's tone, when she said, "Ifem needs some time, I think she has depression," had felt like ice pressed against his body. Ifemelu was not crippled or blinded from an accident, not suddenly suffering amnesia. She was in touch with Ginika and other people but not with him. She did not *want* to keep in touch with *him*. He wrote her e-mails, asking that she at least tell him why, what had happened. Soon, his e-mails bounced back, undeliverable; she had closed the account. He missed her, a longing that tore deep into him. He resented her. He wondered endlessly what might have happened. He changed, curled more inwardly into himself. He was, by turns, inflamed by anger, twisted by confusion, withered by sadness.

And now here was her e-mail. Her tone the same, as though she had not wounded him, left him bleeding for more than five years. Why was she writing to him now? What was there to tell her, that he cleaned toilets and had only just today encountered a curled turd? How did she know he was still alive? He could have died during their silence and she would not have known. An angry sense of betrayal overwhelmed him. He clicked Delete and Empty Trash.

HIS COUSIN NICHOLAS had the jowly face of a bulldog, yet still somehow managed to be very attractive, or perhaps it was not his features but his aura that appealed, the tall, broad-shouldered, striding masculinity of him. In Nsukka, he had been the most popular student on campus; his beat-up Volkswagen Beetle parked outside a beer parlour lent the drinkers there an immediate cachet. Two Big Chicks once famously fought over him in Bello Hostel, tearing each other's blouses, but he remained roguishly unattached until he met Ojiugo. She was Obinze's mother's favourite student, the only one good enough to be a research assistant, and had stopped by their house one Sunday to discuss a book. Nicholas had stopped by, too, on his weekly ritual, to eat Sunday rice. Ojiugo wore orange lipstick and ripped jeans, spoke bluntly, and smoked in public, provoking vicious gossip and dislike from other girls, not because she did these things but because she dared to without having lived abroad, or having a foreign parent, those qualities that would have made them forgive her lack of conformity. Obinze remembered how dismissive she first was of Nicholas, ignoring him while he, unused to a girl's indifference, talked more and more loudly. But in the end, they left together in his Volkswagen. They would speed around campus in that Volkswagen, Ojiugo driving and Nicholas's arm hanging from the front window, music blaring, bends taken sharply, and once with a friend lodged in the open front boot. They smoked and drank publicly together. They created glamorous myths. Once they were seen at a beer parlour, Ojiugo wearing Nicholas's large white shirt and nothing below, and Nicholas wearing a pair of jeans and nothing above. "Things are hard, so we are sharing one outfit," they said nonchalantly to friends.

That Nicholas had lost his youthful outrageousness did not surprise Obinze; what surprised him was the loss of even the smallest memory of it. Nicholas, husband and father, homeowner in England, spoke with a soberness so forbidding that it was almost comical. "If you come to England with a visa that does not allow you to work," Nicholas told him, "the first thing to look for is not food or water, it is an NI number so you can work. Take all the jobs you can. Spend nothing. Marry an EU citizen and get your papers. Then your life can begin." Nicholas seemed to feel that he had done his part, delivered words of wisdom, and in the following months, he hardly spoke to Obinze at all. It was as if he was no longer the big cousin who had offered Obinze, at fifteen, a cigarette to try, who had drawn diagrams on a piece of paper to show Obinze what to do when his fingers were between a girl's legs. On weekends Nicholas walked around the house in a tense cloud of silence, nursing his worries. Only during Arsenal matches did he relax a little, a can of Stella Artois in hand, shouting "Go, Arsenal!" with Ojiugo and their children, Nna and Nne. After the game, his face would congeal once again. He would come home from work, hug his children and Ojiugo, and ask, "How are you? What did you people do today?" Ojiugo would list what they had done. Cello. Piano. Violin. Homework. Kumon. "Nne is really improving her sight-reading," she would add. Or "Nna was careless with his Kumon and he got two wrong." Nicholas would praise or reprimand each child, Nna who had a chubby bulldog-like face and Nne who had her mother's dark broad-faced beauty. He spoke to them only in English, careful English, as though he thought that the Igbo he shared with their mother would infect them, perhaps make them lose their precious British accents. Then he would say, "Ojiugo, well done. I'm hungry."

"Yes, Nicholas."

She would serve his food, a plate on a tray taken to him in his study or in front of the TV in the kitchen. Obinze sometimes wondered if she bowed while putting it down or whether the bowing was merely in her demeanour, in the slump of her shoulders and curve of her neck. Nicholas spoke to her in the same tone as he spoke to his children. Once Obinze heard him say to her, "You people have scattered my study. Now please leave my study, all of you."

"Yes, Nicholas," she said, and took the children out. "Yes, Nicholas" was her response to almost everything he said. Sometimes, from behind Nicholas, she would catch Obinze's eye and make a funny face, inflating her cheeks into small balloons, or pushing her tongue out of the corner of her mouth. It reminded Obinze of the gaudy theatrics of Nollywood films.

"I keep thinking of how you and Nicholas were in Nsukka," Obinze said one afternoon as he helped her cut up a chicken.

"Ahn-ahn! Do you know we used to fuck in public? We did it at the Arts Theatre. Even in the engineering building one afternoon, in a quiet corner of the corridor!" She laughed. "Marriage changes things. But this country is not easy. I got my papers because I did postgraduate school here, but you know he only got his papers two years ago and so for so long he was living in fear, working under other people's names. That thing can do wonders to your head, *eziokwu*. It has not been easy at all for him. This job he has now is very good but he's on contract. He never knows if they will renew. He got a good offer in Ireland, you know Ireland is seriously booming now and computer programmers do well there, but he doesn't want us to move there. Education for the kids is much better here."

Obinze selected some spice bottles from the cupboard, sprinkled them on the chicken and put the pot on the stove.

"You put nutmeg in chicken?" Ojiugo asked.

"Yes," Obinze said. "Don't you?"

"Me, what do I know? Whoever marries you will win a lottery, honestly. By the way, what did you say happened to you and Ifemelu? I so liked her."

"She went to America and her eyes opened and she forgot me."

Ojiugo laughed.

The phone rang. Because Obinze was all the time willing a call from his job agency, each time the phone did ring, a mild panic would seize his chest, and Ojiugo would say, "Don't worry, The Zed, things will work out for you. Look at my friend Bose. Do you know she applied for asylum, was denied and went through hell before she finally got her papers? Now she owns two nurseries and has a holiday home in Spain. It will happen for you, don't worry, *rapuba*." There was a certain vapidity to her reassurance, an automatic way of expressing goodwill, which did not require any concrete efforts on her part to help him. Sometimes he wondered, not resentfully, whether she truly wanted him to find a job, because he would no longer be able to watch the children while she popped out to Tesco to buy milk, no longer be able to make their breakfast while she supervised their practice before school, Nne on the piano or violin and Nna on the cello. There was something about those days that Obinze would come to miss, buttering toast in the weak light of morning while the sounds of music floated through the house, and sometimes, too, Ojiugo's voice, raised in praise or impatience, saying, "Well done! Try once more!" or "What rubbish are you doing?"

Later that afternoon, after Ojiugo brought the children home from school, she told Nna, "Your Uncle Obinze cooked the chicken."

"Thank you for helping Mummy, Uncle, but I don't think I'll be having any chicken." He had his mother's playful manner.

"Look at this boy," Ojiugo said. "Your uncle is a better cook than I am."

Nna rolled his eyes. "Okay, Mummy, if you say so. Can I watch TV? Just for ten minutes?"

"Okay, ten minutes."

It was the half-hour break after their homework and before their French tutor arrived, and Ojiugo was making jam sandwiches, carefully cutting off the crusts. Nna turned on the television, to a music performance by a man wearing many large shiny chains around his neck.

"Mummy, I've been thinking about this," Nna said. "I want to be a rapper."

"You can't be a rapper, Nna."

"But I want to, Mummy."

"You are not going to be a rapper, sweetheart. We did not come to London for you to become a rapper." She turned to Obinze, stifling laughter. "You see this boy?"

Nne came into the kitchen, a Capri-Sun in hand. "Mummy? May I have one please?"

"Yes, Nne," she said, and, turning to Obinze, repeated her daughter's words in an exaggerated British accent. "Mummy, may I have one please? You see how she sounds so posh? Ha! My daughter will go places. That is why all our money is going to Brentwood School." Ojiugo gave Nne a loud kiss on her forehead and Obinze realized, watching her idly straighten a stray braid on Nne's head, that Ojiugo was a wholly contented person. Another kiss on Nne's forehead. "How are you feeling, Oyinneya?" she asked.

"Fine, Mummy."

"Tomorrow, remember not to read only the line they ask you to read. Go further, okay?"

"Okay, Mummy." Nne had the solemn demeanour of a child determined to please the adults in her life.

"You know her violin exam is tomorrow, and she struggles with sight-reading," Ojiugo said, as though Obinze could possibly have forgotten, as though it were possible to forget when Ojiugo had been talking about it for so long. The past weekend, he had gone with Ojiugo and the children to a birthday party in an echo-filled rented hall, Indian and Nigerian children running around, while Ojiugo whispered to him about some of the children, who was clever at maths but could not spell, who was Nne's biggest rival. She knew the recent test scores of all the clever children. When she could not remember what an Indian child, Nne's close friend, had scored on a recent test, she called Nne to ask her.

"Ahn-ahn, Ojiugo, let her play," Obinze said.

Now, Ojiugo planted a third loud kiss on Nne's forehead. "My precious. We still have to get a dress for the party."

"Yes, Mummy. Something red, no, burgundy."

"Her friend is having a party, this Russian girl, they became friends because they have the same violin tutor. The first time I met the girl's mother, I think she was wearing something illegal, like the fur of an extinct animal, and she was trying to pretend that she did not have a Russian accent, being more British than the British!"

"She's nice, Mummy," Nne said.

"I didn't say she wasn't nice, my precious," Ojiugo said.

Nna had increased the television volume.

"Turn that down, Nna," Ojiugo said.

"Mummy!"

"Turn down the volume right now!"

"But I can't hear anything, Mummy!"

He didn't turn down the volume and she didn't say anything else to him; instead she turned to Obinze to continue talking.

"Speaking of accents," Obinze asked. "Would Nna get away with that if he didn't have a foreign accent?"

"What do you mean?"

"You know last Saturday when Chika and Bose brought their children, I was just thinking that Nigerians here really forgive so much from their children because they have foreign accents. The rules are different."

"*Mba,* it is not about accents. It is because in Nigeria, people teach their children fear instead of respect. We don't want them to fear us but that does not mean we take rubbish from them. We punish them. The boy knows I will slap him if he does any nonsense. Seriously slap him."

"The lady doth protest too much, methinks."

"Oh, but she'll keep her word." Ojiugo smiled. "You know I haven't read a book in ages. No time."

"My mother used to say you would become a leading literary critic."

"Yes. Before her brother's son got me pregnant." Ojiugo paused, still smiling. "Now it is just these children. I want Nna to go to the City of London School. And then by God's grace to Marlborough or Eton. Nne is already an academic star, and I know she'll get scholarships to all the good schools. Everything is about them now."

"One day they will be grown and leave home and you will just be a source of embarrassment or exasperation for them and they won't take your phone calls or won't call you for weeks," Obinze said, and as soon as he said it, he wished he had not. It was petty, it had not come out as he intended. But Ojiugo was not offended. She shrugged and said, "Then I will just carry my bag and go and stand in front of their house."

It puzzled him that she did not mourn all the things she could have been. Was it a quality inherent in women, or did they just learn to shield their personal regrets, to suspend their lives, subsume themselves in child care? She browsed online forums about tutoring and music and schools, and she told him what she had discovered as though she truly felt the rest of the world should be as interested as she was in how music improved the mathematics skills of nine-year-olds. Or she would spend hours on the phone talking to her friends, about which violin teacher was good and which tutorial was a waste of money.

One day, after she had rushed off to take Nna to his piano lesson, she called Obinze to say, laughing, "Can you believe I forgot to brush my teeth?" She came home from Weight Watchers meetings to tell him how much she had lost or gained, hiding Twix bars in her handbag and then asking him, with laughter, if he wanted one. Later she joined another weight-loss programme, attended two morning meetings and came home to tell him, "I'm not going there again. They treat you as if you have a mental problem. I said no, I don't have any internal issues, please, I just like the taste of food, and the smug woman tells me that I have something internal that I am repressing. Rubbish. These white people think that everybody has their mental problems." She was twice the size she had been in university, and while her clothes back then had never been polished, they had the edge of a calculated style, jeans folded away from her ankles, slouchy blouses pulled off one shoulder. Now, they merely looked sloppy. Her jeans left a mound of pulpy flesh above her waist that disfigured her T-shirts, as though something alien were growing underneath.

Sometimes, her friends visited and they would sit in the kitchen talking until they all dashed off to pick up their children. In those weeks of willing the phone to ring, Obinze came to know their voices well. He could hear clearly from the tiny bedroom upstairs where he lay in bed reading.

"I met this man recently," Chika said. "He is nice o, but he is so bush. He grew up in Onitsha and so you can imagine what kind of bush accent he has. He mixes up *ch* and *sh*. I want to go to the chopping centre. Sit down on a sheer."

They laughed.

"Anyway, he told me he was willing to marry me and adopt Charles. Willing! As if he was doing charity work. Willing! Imagine that. But it's not his fault, it's because we are in London. He is the kind of man I would never even look at in Nigeria, not to talk of going out with. The problem is that water never finds its different levels here in London."

"London is a leveller. We are now all in London and we are now all the same, what nonsense," Bose said.

"Maybe he should go and find a Jamaican woman," Amara said. Her husband had left her for a Jamaican woman, with whom it turned out he had a secret four-year-old child, and she somehow managed to veer every conversation towards the subject of Jamaicans. "These West Indian women are taking our men and our men are stupid enough to follow them. Next thing, they will have a baby and they don't want the men to marry them o, they just want child support. All they do is spend their money doing their hair and nails."

"Yes," Bose, Chika and Ojiugo all agreed. A routine, automatic agreement: Amara's emotional well-being was more important than what they actually believed.

The phone rang. Ojiugo took the call and came back to say, "This woman who just called, she is a character. Her daughter and Nne belong to the same orchestra. I met her when Nne took her first exam. She came in her Bentley, a black woman, with a driver and everything. She asked me where we lived and when I told her, I just knew what was on her mind: how can somebody in Essex be thinking of the National Children's Orchestra? So I decided to look for trouble and I told her, My daughter goes to Brentwood, and you should have seen her face! You know people like us are not supposed to be talking about private school and music. The most we should want is a good grammar school. I just looked at the woman and I was laughing inside. Then she started telling me that music for children is very expensive. She kept telling me how expensive it is, as if she had seen my empty bank account. Imagine o! She is one of those black people who want to be the only black person in the room, so any other black person is an immediate threat to her. She just called now to tell me that she read online about an eleven-year-old girl who got grade five distinction and did not get into the National Children's Orchestra. Why would she call just to tell me that negative story?"

"Enemy of progress!" Bose said.

"Is she a Jamaican?" Amara asked.

"She is Black British. I don't know where her people came from."

"It must be Jamaica," Amara said.

CHAPTER 25

Sharp, the word everyone used to describe Emenike in secondary school. Sharp, full of the poisoned admiration they felt for him. Sharp Guy. Sharp Man. If exam questions leaked, Emenike knew how to get them. He knew, too, which girl had had an abortion, what property the parents of the wealthy students owned, which teachers were sleeping together. He always spoke quickly, pugnaciously, as though every conversation was an argument, the speed and force of his words suggesting authority and discouraging dissent. He knew, and he was full of an eagerness to know. Whenever Kayode returned from a London vacation, flush with relevance, Emenike would ask him about the latest music and films, and then examine his shoes and clothes. "Is this one designer? What is the name of this one?" Emenike would ask, his eyes feral with longing. He had told everyone that his father was the igwe of his hometown, and had sent him to Lagos to live with an uncle until he turned twenty-one, to avoid the pressures of princely life. But one day, an old man arrived at school, wearing trousers with a mended patch near the knee, his face gaunt, his body bowed with the humility that poverty had forced on him. All the boys laughed after they discovered that he was really Emenike's father. The laughter was soon forgotten, perhaps because nobody had ever fully believed the prince story—Kayode, after all, always called Emenike Bush Boy behind his back. Or perhaps because they needed Emenike, who had information that nobody else did. This, the audacity of him, had drawn Obinze. Emenike was one of the few people for whom "to read" did not mean "to study" and so they would spend hours talking about books, bartering knowledge for knowledge and playing Scrabble. Their friendship grew. At university, when Emenike lived with him in the boys' quarters of his mother's house, people had sometimes mistaken him for a relative. "What of your brother?" people would ask Obinze. And Obinze would say, "He's fine," without bothering to explain that he and Emenike were not related at all. But there were many things he did not know about Emenike, things he knew not to ask about. Emenike often left school for weeks, only vaguely saying that he had "gone home", and he spoke endlessly of people who were "making it" abroad. His was the coiled, urgent restlessness of a person who believed that fate had mistakenly allotted him a place below his true destiny. When he left for England during a strike in their second year, Obinze never knew how he got a visa. Still, he was pleased for him. Emenike was ripe, bursting, with his ambition, and Obinze thought of his visa as a mercy: that ambition would finally find a release. It seemed to, quite quickly, as Emenike sent news only of progress: his postgraduate work completed, his job at the housing authority, his marriage to an Englishwoman who was a solicitor in the city.

Emenike was the first person Obinze called after he arrived in England.

"The Zed! Good to hear from you. Let me call you back, I'm just going into a managerial meeting," Emenike said. The second time Obinze called, Emenike sounded a little harried. "I'm at Heathrow. Georgina and I are going to Brussels for a week. I'll call you when I get back. I can't wait to catch up, man!" Emenike's e-mail response to Obinze had been similar: *So happy you are coming this way, man, can't wait to see you!* Obinze had imagined, foolishly, that Emenike would take him in, show him the way. He knew of the many stories of friends and relatives who, in the harsh glare of life abroad, became unreliable, even hostile, versions of their former selves. But what was it about the stubbornness of hope, the need to believe in your own exceptionality, that these things happened to other people whose friends were not like yours? He called other friends. Nosa, who had left right after graduation, picked him up at the tube station and drove him to a pub where other friends soon gathered. They shook hands and slapped backs and drank draught beer. They laughed about memories from school. They said little about the details of their present lives. When Obinze said he needed to get a National Insurance number, and asked, "Guys, how I go take do?" they all shook their heads vaguely.

"Just keep your ear to the ground, man," Chidi said.

"The thing is to come closer to central London. You're too far away from things, in Essex," Wale said.

As Nosa drove him back to the station later, Obinze asked, "So where do you work, guy?"

"Underground. A serious hustle, but things will get better," Nosa said. Although Obinze knew he meant the tube, the word "underground" made him think of doomed tunnels that fed into the earth and went on forever, ending nowhere.

"What of Mr Sharp Guy Emenike?" Nosa asked, his tone alive with malice. "He's doing very well and he lives in Islington, with his oyinbo wife who is old enough to be his mother. He has become posh o. He doesn't talk to ordinary people any more. He can help sort you out."

"He's been travelling a lot, we haven't yet seen," Obinze said, hearing too clearly the limpness of his own words.

"How is your cousin Iloba?" Nosa asked. "I saw him last year at Emeka's brother's wedding."

Obinze had not even remembered that Iloba now lived in London; he had last seen him days before graduation. Iloba was merely from his mother's hometown, but he had been so enthusiastic about their kinship that everyone on campus assumed they were cousins. Iloba would often pull up a chair, smiling and uninvited, and join Obinze and his friends at a roadside bar, or appear at Obinze's door on Sunday afternoons when Obinze was tired from the languor of Sunday afternoons. Once, Iloba had stopped Obinze at the General Studies quad, cheerfully calling out "Kinsman!" and then giving him a rundown of marriages and deaths of people from his mother's hometown whom he hardly knew. "Udoakpuanyi died some weeks ago. Don't you know him? Their homestead is next to your mother's." Obinze nodded and made appropriate sounds, humouring Iloba, because Iloba's manner was always so pleasant and oblivious, his trousers always too tight and too short, showing his bony ankles; they had earned him the nickname "Iloba Jump Up", which soon morphed to "Loba Jay You".

Obinze got his phone number from Nicholas and called him.

"The Zed! Kinsman! You did not tell me you were coming to London!" Iloba said. "How is your mother? What of your uncle, the one who married from Abagana? How is Nicholas?" Iloba sounded full of a simple happiness. There were people who were born with an inability to be tangled up in dark emotions, in complications, and Iloba was one of them. For such people, Obinze felt both admiration and boredom. When Obinze asked if Iloba might be able to help him find a National Insurance number, he would have understood a little resentment, a little churlishness—after all, he was contacting Iloba only because he needed something—but it surprised him how sincerely eager to help Iloba was.

"I would let you use mine but I am working with it and it is risky," Iloba said.

"Where do you work?"

"In central London. Security. It's not easy, this country is not easy, but we are managing. I like the night shifts because it gives me time to read for my course. I'm doing a master's in management at Birkbeck College." Iloba paused. "The Zed, don't worry, we will put our heads together. Let me ask around and let you know."

Iloba called back two weeks later to say he had found somebody. "His name is Vincent Obi. He is from Abia State. A friend of mine did the connection. He wants to meet you tomorrow evening."

They met in Iloba's flat. A claustrophobic feel pervaded the flat, the concrete neighbourhood with no trees, the scarred walls of the building. Everything seemed too small, too tight.

"Nice place, Loba Jay You," Obinze said, not because the flat was nice but because Iloba had a flat in London.

"I would have told you to come and stay with me, The Zed, but I live with two of my cousins." Iloba placed bottles of beer and a small plate of fried chin-chin on the table. It seared a sharp homesickness in Obinze, this ritual of hospitality. He was reminded of going back to the village with his mother at Christmas, aunties offering him plates of chin-chin.

Vincent Obi was a small round man submerged in a large pair of jeans and an ungainly coat. As Obinze shook hands with him, they sized each other up. In the set of Vincent's shoulders, in the abrasiveness of his demeanour, Obinze sensed that Vincent had learned very early on, as a matter of necessity, to solve his own problems. Obinze imagined his Nigerian life: a community secondary school full of barefoot children, a polytechnic paid for with help from a number of uncles, a family of many children and a crowd of dependants in his hometown who, whenever he visited, would expect large loaves of bread and pocket money carefully distributed to each of them. Obinze saw himself through Vincent's eyes: a university staff child who grew up eating butter and now needed his help. At first Vincent affected a British accent, saying "innit" too many times.

"This is business, innit, but I'm helping you. You can use my NI number and pay me forty per cent of what you make," Vincent said. "It's business, innit. If I don't get what we agree on, I will report you."

"My brother," Obinze said. "That's a little too much. You know my situation. I don't have anything. Please try and come down."

"Thirty-five per cent is the best I can do. This is business." He had lost his accent and now spoke Nigerian English. "Let me tell you, there are many people in your situation."

Iloba spoke up in Igbo. "Vincent, my brother here is trying to save money and do his papers. Thirty-five is too much, *o rika, biko.* Please just try and help us."

"You know that some people take half. Yes, he is in a situation but all of us are in a situation. I am helping him but this is business." Vincent's Igbo had a rural accent. He put the National Insurance card on the table and was already writing his bank account number on a piece of paper. Iloba's mobile phone began to ring. That evening, as dusk fell, the sky muting to a pale violet, Obinze became Vincent.

CHAPTER 26

Obinze-as-Vincent informed his agency, after his experience with the curled shit on the toilet lid, that he would not be returning to that job. He scoured the newspaper job pages, made calls and hoped, until the agency offered him another job, cleaning wide passages in a detergent-packing warehouse. A Brazilian man, sallow and dark-haired, cleaned the building next to his. "I'm Vincent," Obinze said, when they met in the back room.

"I'm Dee." A pause. "No, you're not English. You can pronounce it. My real name is Duerdinhito, but the English, they cannot pronounce, so they call me Dee."

"Duerdinhito," Obinze repeated.

"Yes!" A delighted smile. A small bond of foreignness. They talked, while emptying their vacuum cleaners, about the 1996 Olympics, Obinze gloating about Nigeria beating Brazil and then Argentina.

"Kanu was good, I give him that," Duerdinhito said. "But Nigeria had luck."

Every evening, Obinze was covered in white chemical dust. Gritty things lodged in his ears. He tried not to breathe too deeply as he cleaned, wary of dangers floating in the air, until his manager told him he was being fired because of a downsizing. The next job was a temporary replacement with a company that delivered kitchens, week after week of sitting beside white drivers who called him "labourer", of endless construction sites full of noises and helmets, of carrying wooden planks up long stairs, unaided and unsung. In the silence with which they drove, and the tone with which they said "labourer!", Obinze sensed the drivers' dislike. Once, when he tripped and landed on his knee, a fall so heavy that he limped back to the truck, the driver told the others at the warehouse, "His knee is bad because he's a knee-grow!" They laughed. Their hostility rankled, but only slightly; what mattered to him was that he earned four pounds an hour, more with overtime, and when he was sent to a new delivery warehouse in West Thurrock, he worried that he might not have opportunities for overtime.

The new warehouse chief looked like the Englishman archetype Obinze carried in his mind, tall and spare, sandy-haired and blue-eyed. But he was a smiling man, and in Obinze's imagination, Englishmen were not smiling men. His name was Roy Snell. He vigorously shook Obinze's hand.

"So, Vincent, you're from Africa?" he asked, as he took Obinze around the warehouse, the size of a football field, much bigger than the last one, and alive with trucks being loaded, flattened cardboard boxes being folded into a deep pit, men talking.

"Yes. I was born in Birmingham and went back to Nigeria when I was six." It was the story he and Iloba had agreed was most convincing.

"Why did you come back? How bad are things in Nigeria?"

"I just wanted to see if I could have a better life here."

Roy Snell nodded. He seemed like a person for whom the word "jolly" would always be apt. "You'll work with Nigel today, he's our youngest," he said, gesturing towards a man with a pale doughy body, spiky dark hair and an almost cherubic face. "I think you'll like working here, Vinny Boy!" It had taken him five minutes to go from Vincent to Vinny Boy and, in the following months, when they played table tennis during lunch break, Roy would tell the men, "I've got to beat Vinny Boy for once!" And they would titter and repeat "Vinny Boy".

It amused Obinze, how keenly the men flipped through their newspapers every morning, stopping at the photo of the big-breasted woman, examining it as though it were an article of great interest, and were any different from the photo on that same page the previous day, the previous week. Their conversations, as they waited for their trucks to be loaded up, were always about cars and football and, most of all, women, each man telling stories that sounded too apocryphal and too similar to a story told the day before, the week before, and each time they mentioned knickers—*the bird flashed her knickers*—Obinze was even more amused, because knickers were, in Nigerian English, shorts rather than underwear, and he imagined these nubile women in ill-fitting khaki shorts, the kind he had worn as a junior student in secondary school.

Roy Snell's morning greeting to him was a jab on his belly. "Vinny Boy! You all right? You all right?" he would ask. He always put Obinze's name up for the outside work that paid better, always asked if he wanted to work weekends, which was double time, always asked about girls. It was as if Roy held a special affection for him, which was both protective and kind.

"You haven't had a shag since you came to the UK, have you, Vinny Boy? I could give you this bird's number," he said once.

"I have a girlfriend back home," Obinze said.

"So what's wrong with a little shag then?"

A few men nearby laughed.

"My girlfriend has magical powers," Obinze said.

Roy found this funnier than Obinze thought it was. He laughed and laughed. "She's into witchcraft, is she? All right then, no shags for you. I've always wanted to go to Africa, Vinny Boy. I think I'll take a holiday and go to Nigeria when you're back there for a visit. You can show me around, find me some Nigerian birds, Vinny Boy, but no witchcraft!"

"Yes, I could do that."

"Oh, I know you could! You look like you know what to do with the birds," Roy said, with another jab at Obinze's belly.

Roy often assigned Obinze to work with Nigel, perhaps because they were the youngest men in the warehouse. That first morning, Obinze noticed that the other men, drinking coffee from paper cups and checking the board to see who would be working with whom, were laughing at Nigel. Nigel had no eyebrows; the patches of slightly pink skin where his eyebrows should have been gave his plump face an unfinished, ghostly look.

"I got pissed at the pub and my mates shaved off my eyebrows," Nigel told Obinze, almost apologetically, as they shook hands.

"No shagging for you until you grow your eyebrows back, mate," one of the men called out as Nigel and Obinze headed for the truck. Obinze secured the washing machines at the back, tightening the straps until they were snug, and then climbed in and studied the map to find the shortest routes to their delivery addresses. Nigel took bends sharply and muttered about how people drove these days. At a traffic light, Nigel brought out a bottle of cologne from the bag he placed at his feet, sprayed it on his neck and then offered it to Obinze.

"No thanks," Obinze said. Nigel shrugged. Days later, he offered it again. The truck interior was dense with the scent of his cologne and Obinze would, from time to time, take deep gulps of fresh air through the open window.

"You're just new from Africa. You haven't seen the London sights, have you, mate?" Nigel asked.

"No," Obinze said.

And so, after early deliveries in central London, Nigel would take him for a drive, showing him Buckingham Palace, the Houses of Parliament, Tower Bridge, all the while talking about his mother's arthritis, and about his girlfriend Haley's knockers. It took a while to completely understand what Nigel said, because of his accent, which was only a deeper version of the accents of the people Obinze had worked with, each word twisted and stretched until it came out of their mouths having become something else. Once Nigel said "male" and Obinze thought he had said "mile", and when Obinze finally understood what Nigel meant, Nigel laughed and said, "You talk kind of posh, don't you? African posh."

One day, months into his job, after they delivered a new fridge to an address in Kensington, Nigel said, about the elderly man who had come into the kitchen, "He's a real gent, he is." Nigel's tone was admiring, slightly cowed. The man had looked dishevelled and hung-over, his hair tousled, his robe open at the chest, and he had said archly, "You do know how to put it all together," as though he did not think they did. It amazed Obinze that, because Nigel thought the man was a "real gent", he did not complain about the dirty kitchen, as he ordinarily would have done. And if the man had spoken with a different accent, Nigel would have called him miserly for not giving them a tip.

They were approaching their next delivery address in South London, and Obinze had just called the homeowner to say that they were almost there, when Nigel blurted out, "What do you say to a girl you like?"

"What do you mean?" Obinze asked.

"Truth is, I'm not really shagging Haley. I like her but I don't know how to tell her. The other day I went round her house and there was another bloke there." Nigel paused. Obinze tried to keep his face expressionless. "You look like you know what to say to the birds, mate," Nigel added.

"Just tell her you like her," Obinze said, thinking how seamlessly Nigel, at the warehouse with other men, often contributed stories of his shagging Haley, and once of shagging her friend while Haley was away on holiday. "No games and no lines. Just say, Look, I like you and I think you're beautiful."

Nigel gave him a wounded glance. It was as if he had convinced himself that Obinze was skilled in the art of women and expected some profundity, which Obinze wished, as he loaded the dishwasher onto a trolley and wheeled it to the door, that he had. An Indian woman opened the door, a portly, kindly housewife who offered them tea. Many people offered tea or water. Once, a sad-looking woman had offered Obinze a small pot of home-made jam, and he had hesitated, but he sensed that whatever deep unhappiness she had would be compounded if he said no, and so he had taken the jam home and it was still languishing in the fridge, unopened.

"Thank you, thank you," the Indian woman said as Obinze and Nigel installed the new dishwasher and rolled away the old.

At the door, she gave Nigel a tip. Nigel was the only driver who split the tips down the middle with Obinze; the others pretended not to remember to share. Once, when Obinze was working with another driver, an old Jamaican woman had pushed ten pounds into his pocket when the driver was not looking. "Thank you, brother," she said, and it made him want to call his mother in Nsukka and tell her about it.

CHAPTER 27

A glum dusk was settling over London when Obinze walked into the bookshop café and sat down to a mocha and a blueberry scone. The soles of his feet ached pleasantly. It was not very cold; he had been sweating in Nicholas's wool coat, which now hung on the back of his chair. This was his weekly treat: to visit the bookshop, buy an overpriced caffeinated drink, read as much as he could for free, and become Obinze again. Sometimes he asked to be dropped off in central London after a delivery and he would wander about and end up in a bookshop and sink to the floor at a corner, away from the clusters of people. He read contemporary American fiction, because he hoped to find a resonance, a shaping of his longings, a sense of the America that he had imagined himself a part of. He wanted to know about day-to-day life in America, what people ate and what consumed them, what shamed them and what attracted them, but he read novel after novel and was disappointed: nothing was grave, nothing serious, nothing urgent, and most dissolved into ironic nothingness. He read American newspapers and magazines, but only skimmed the British newspapers, because there were more and more articles about immigration, and each one stoked new panic in his chest. *Schools Swamped by Asylum Seekers.* He still hadn't found someone. Last week, he had met two Nigerian men, distant friends of a friend, who said they knew an Eastern European woman, and he had paid them a hundred pounds. Now, they did not return his calls and their mobile phones went directly to voicemail. His scone was half-eaten. He did not realize how quickly the café had filled up. He was comfortable, cosy even, and absorbed in a magazine article when a woman and a little boy came up to ask if they could share his table.

They were nut-coloured and dark-haired. He imagined that they were Bangladeshi or Sri Lankan.

"Of course," he said, and shifted his pile of books and magazines, even though it had not been on the side of the table that they would use. The boy looked eight or nine years old, wearing a Mickey Mouse sweater and clutching a blue Game Boy. The woman was wearing a nose ring, a tiny glasslike thing that glittered as she moved her head this way and that. She asked if he had enough room for his magazines, if he wanted her to move her chair a little. Then she told her son, in a laughing tone that was clearly intended for Obinze, that she had never been very sure if those narrow wooden sticks next to the packets of sugar were for stirring.

"I'm not a baby!" her son said when she wanted to cut his muffin.

"I just thought it would be easier for you."

Obinze looked up and saw that she was talking to her son but she was watching him, with something wistful in her eyes. It filled him with possibility, this chance meeting with a stranger, and the thought of the paths on which it might lead him.

The little boy had a delightful curious face. "Do you live in London?" he asked Obinze.

"Yes," Obinze said, but that yes did not tell his story, that he lived in London indeed but invisibly, his existence like an erased pencil sketch; each time he saw a policeman, or anyone in a uniform, anyone with the faintest scent of authority, he would fight the urge to run.

"His father passed away last year," the woman said, in a lower voice. "This is our first vacation in London without him. We used to do it every year before Christmas." The woman nodded continuously as she spoke and the boy looked annoyed, as if he had not wanted Obinze to know that.

"I'm sorry," Obinze said.

"We went to the Tate," the boy said.

"Did you like it?" Obinze asked.

He scowled. "It was boring."

His mother stood up. "We should go. We're going to see a play." She turned to her son and added, "You're not taking that Game Boy in, you know that."

The boy ignored her, said "Bye" to Obinze and turned towards the door. The mother gave Obinze a long look, even more wistful than before. Perhaps she had deeply loved her husband and this, her first awareness of feeling attraction again, was a startling revelation. He watched them leave, wondering whether to get up and ask for her contact information and yet knowing he would not. There was something about the woman that made him think of love, and, as always, Ifemelu came to his mind when he thought of love. Then, quite suddenly, a sexual urge overcame him. A tide of lust. He wanted to fuck somebody. He would text Tendai. They had met at a party Nosa took him to, and he ended up, that night, in her bed. Wise and large-hipped and Zimbabwean Tendai who had a habit of soaking in baths for too long. She stared at him in shock the first time he cleaned her flat and cooked jollof rice for her. She was so unused to being treated well by a man that she watched him endlessly, anxiously, her eyes veiled, as though holding her breath and waiting for the abuse to emerge. She knew he didn't have his papers. "Or you would be the kind of Nigerian working in IT and driving a BMW," she said. She had a British stay, and would have a passport in a year, and she hinted that she might be willing to help him. But he did not want the complication of marrying her for his papers; one day she would wake up and convince herself that it had never been merely for papers.

Before he left the bookshop, he sent Tendai a text: *Are you home? Was thinking of stopping by.* A freezing drizzle was falling as he walked to the tube station, tiny raindrops splattering his coat, and when he got there, he was absorbed by how many blobs of saliva were on the stairs. Why did people not wait until they left the station to spit? He sat on the stained seat of the noisy train, opposite a woman reading the evening paper. *Speak English at home, Blunkett tells immigrants.* He imagined the article she was reading. There were so many of them now published in the newspapers, and they echoed the radio and television, even the chatter of some of the men in the warehouse. The wind blowing across the British Isles was odorous with fear of asylum seekers, infecting everybody with the panic of impending doom, and so articles were written and read, simply and stridently, as though the writers lived in a world in which the present was unconnected to the past, and they had never considered this to be the normal course of history: the influx into Britain of black and brown people from countries created by Britain. Yet he understood. It had to be comforting, this denial of history. The woman closed the newspaper and looked at him. She had stringy brown hair and hard, suspicious eyes. He wondered what she was thinking. Was she wondering whether he was one of those illegal immigrants who were overcrowding an already crowded island? Later, on the train to Essex, he noticed that all the people around him were Nigerians, loud conversations in Yoruba and Pidgin filled the carriage, and for a moment he saw the unfettered non-white foreignness of this scene through the suspicious eyes of the white woman on the tube. He thought again of the Sri Lankan or Bangladeshi woman and the shadow of grief from which she was only just emerging, and he thought of his mother and of Ifemelu, and the life he had imagined for himself, and the life he now had, lacquered as it was by work and reading, by panic and hope. He had never felt so lonely.

CHAPTER 28

One morning in early summer, a renewing warmth in the air, Obinze arrived at the warehouse and knew right away that something was amiss. The men avoided his eyes, an unnatural stiffness in their movements, and Nigel turned swiftly, too swiftly, towards the toilet when he saw Obinze. They knew. It had to be that they had somehow found out. They saw the headlines about asylum seekers draining the National Health Service, they knew of the hordes further crowding a crowded island, and now they knew that he was one of the damned, working with a name that was not his. Where was Roy Snell? Had he gone to call the police? Was it the police that one called? Obinze tried to remember details from the stories of people who had been caught and deported but his mind was numb. He felt naked. He wanted to turn and run but his body kept moving, against his will, towards the loading area. Then he sensed a movement behind him, quick and violent and too close, and before he could turn around, a paper hat had been pushed onto his head. It was Nigel, and with him a gathering of grinning men.

"Happy birthday, Vinny Boy!" they all said.

Obinze froze, frightened by the complete blankness of his mind. Then he realized what it was. Vincent's birthday. Roy must have told the men. Even he had not remembered to remember Vincent's date of birth.

"Oh!" was all he said, nauseous from relief.

Nigel asked him to come into the coffee room, where all the men were trooping in, and as Obinze sat with them, all of them white except for Patrick from Jamaica, passing around the muffins and Coke they had bought with their own money in honour of a birthday they believed was his, a realization brought tears to his eyes: he felt safe.

Vincent called him that evening, and Obinze was mildly surprised, because Vincent had called him only once, months ago, when he changed his bank and wanted to give him the new account number. He wondered whether to say "Happy birthday" to Vincent, whether indeed the call was somehow related to the occasion of the birthday.

"Vincent, *kedu*?" he said.

"I want a raise."

Had Vincent learned that from a film? Those words "I want a raise" sounded contrived and comical. "I want forty-five per cent. I know you are working more now."

"Vincent, ahn-ahn. How much am I making? You know I am saving money to do this marriage thing."

"Forty-five per cent," Vincent said, and hung up.

Obinze decided to ignore him. He knew Vincent's type; they would push to see how far they could go and then they would step back. If he called and tried to negotiate, it might embolden Vincent to make more demands. That he walked in every week to Vincent's bank to deposit money into his account was something Vincent would not risk losing entirely. And so when, a week later, in the morning bustle of drivers and trucks, Roy said, "Vinny Boy, step into my office for a minute," Obinze thought nothing of it. On Roy's desk was a newspaper, folded at the page with the photo of the big-breasted woman. Roy slowly put his cup of coffee on top of the newspaper. He seemed uncomfortable, not looking directly at Obinze.

"Somebody called yesterday. Said you're not who you say you are, that you're illegal and working with a Brit's name." There was a pause. Obinze was stung with surprise. Roy picked up the coffee cup again. "Why don't you just bring in your passport tomorrow and we'll clear it up, all right?"

Obinze mumbled the first words that came to him. "Okay. I'll bring my passport tomorrow." He walked out of the office knowing that he would never remember what he had felt moments ago. Was Roy merely asking him to bring his passport to make the dismissal easier for him, to give him an exit, or did Roy really believe that the caller had been wrong? Why would anybody call about such a thing unless it was true?

Obinze had never made as much of an effort as he did the rest of the day to seem normal, to tame the rage that was engulfing him. It was not the thought of the power that Vincent had over him that infuriated him, but the recklessness with which Vincent had exercised it. He left the warehouse that evening, for the final time, wishing more than anything that he had told Nigel and Roy his real name.

Some years later in Lagos, after Chief told him to find a white man whom he could present as his General Manager, Obinze called Nigel. His mobile number had not changed.

"This is Vinny Boy."

"Vincent! Are you all right, mate?"

"I'm fine, how are you?" Obinze said. Then, later, he said, "Vincent is not my real name, Nigel. My name is Obinze. I have a job offer for you in Nigeria."

CHAPTER 29

The Angolans told him how things had "gone up", or were more "tough", opaque words that were supposed to explain each new request for more money.

"This is not what we agreed to," Obinze would say, or "I don't have any extra cash right now," and they would reply, "Things have gone up, yeah," in a tone that he imagined was accompanied by a shrug. A silence would follow, a wordlessness over the phone line that told him that it was his problem, not theirs. "I'll pay it in by Friday," he would say finally, before hanging up.

Cleotilde's gentle sympathy assuaged him. She told him, "They've got my passport," and he thought this vaguely sinister, almost a hostage holding.

"Otherwise we could just do this on our own," she added. But he did not want to do it on his own, with Cleotilde. It was too important and he needed the weight of the Angolans' expertise, their experience, to make sure all went well. Nicholas had already lent him some money; he had been loath enough to ask at all, because of the judgement in Nicholas's unsmiling eyes, as though he was thinking that Obinze was soft, spoilt, and many people did not have a cousin who could lend them money. Emenike was the only other person he could ask. The last time they spoke, Emenike had told him, "I don't know if you've seen this play in the West End, but Georgina and I have just been and we loved it," as though Obinze, in his delivery job, saving austerely, consumed by immigration worries, would ever even think of seeing a West End play. Emenike's obliviousness had upset him, because it suggested a disregard and, even worse, an indifference to him, and to his present life. He called Emenike and said, speaking quickly, pushing the words out, that he needed five hundred pounds, which he would pay back as soon as he could find another job, and then, more slowly, he told Emenike about the Angolans, and how close he was to finally doing the marriage ceremony, but there were so many extra costs that he had not budgeted for.

"No problem. Let's meet Friday," Emenike said.

Now, Emenike sat across from Obinze in a dimly lit restaurant, after shrugging off his jacket to reveal a tan cashmere sweater that looked faultless. He had not put on weight like most of his other friends now living abroad, didn't look different from the last time Obinze had seen him in Nsukka.

"Man, The Zed, you look well!" he said, his words aflame with dishonesty. Of course Obinze did not look well, shoulders hunched from stress, in clothes borrowed from his cousin. "Abeg, sorry I haven't had time to see you. My work schedule is crazy and we've also been travelling a lot. I would have asked you to come and stay with us but it's not a decision I can take alone. Georgina won't understand. You know these oyinbo people don't behave like us." His lips moved, forming something that looked like a smirk. He was making fun of his wife, but Obinze knew, from the muted awe in his tone, that it was mockery coloured by respect, mockery of what he believed, despite himself, to be inherently superior. Obinze remembered how Kayode had often said about Emenike in secondary school: He can read all the books he wants but the bush is still in his blood.

"We've just come back from America. Man, you need to go to America. No other country like it in the world. We flew to Denver and then drove to Wyoming. Georgina had just finished a really tough case, you remember I told you when I was going to Hong Kong? She was there for work and I flew over for a long weekend. So I thought we should go to America, she needed the holiday." Emenike's phone beeped. He took it out of his pocket, glanced at it and grimaced, as though he wanted to be asked what the text was about, but Obinze did not ask. He was tired; Iloba had given him his own National Insurance card, even though it was risky for both of them to work at the same time, but all the job agencies Obinze had tried so far wanted to see a passport and not just the card. His beer tasted flat, and he wished Emenike would just give him the money. But Emenike resumed talking, gesturing, his movements fluid and sure, his manner still that of a person convinced they knew things that other people would never know. And yet there was something different in him that Obinze could not name. Emenike talked for a long time, often prefacing a story with "The thing you have to understand about this country is this." Obinze's mind strayed to Cleotilde. The Angolans said at least two people from her side had to come to Newcastle, to avoid any suspicion, but she had called him yesterday to suggest that she bring only one friend, so he would not have to pay for the train and hotel bills of two extra people. He had found it sweet, but he asked her to bring the two anyway; he would take no chances.

Emenike was talking about something that had happened at work. "I had actually arrived at the meeting first, kept my files, and then I went to the loo, only to come back and for this stupid oyinbo man to tell me, Oh, I see you are keeping to African time. And you know what? I just told him off. Since then he has been sending me e-mails to go for a drink. Drink for what?" Emenike sipped his beer. It was his third and he had become looser and louder. All his stories about work had the same arc: somebody would first underestimate or belittle him, and he would then end up victorious, with the final clever word or action.

"I miss Naija. It's been so long but I just haven't had the time to travel back home. Besides, Georgina would not survive a visit to Nigeria!" Emenike said, and laughed. He had cast home as the jungle and himself as interpreter of the jungle.

"Another beer?" Emenike asked.

Obinze shook his head. A man trying to get to the table behind them brushed Emenike's jacket down from behind his chair.

"Ha, look at this man. He wants to ruin my Aquascutum. It was my last birthday present from Georgina," Emenike said, hanging the jacket back behind his chair. Obinze did not know the brand but he knew from the stylish smirk on Emenike's face that he was supposed to be impressed.

"Sure you don't want another beer?" Emenike asked, looking around for the waitress. "She is ignoring me. Did you notice how rude she was earlier? These Eastern Europeans just don't like serving black people."

After the waitress had taken his order, Emenike brought out an envelope from his pocket. "Here it is, man. I know you asked for five hundred but it's one thousand. You want to count it?"

Count it? Obinze nearly said, but the words did not leave his mouth. To be given money in the Nigerian manner was to have it pushed into your hands, fists closed, eyes averted from yours, your effusive thanks—and it had to be effusive—waved away, and you certainly did not count the money, sometimes did not even look at it until you were alone. But here was Emenike asking him to count the money. And so he did, slowly, deliberately, moving each note from one hand to the other, wondering if Emenike had hated him all those years in secondary school and university. He had not laughed at Emenike as Kayode and the other boys did, but he had not defended Emenike either. Perhaps Emenike had despised his neutrality.

"Thanks, man," Obinze said. Of course it was a thousand pounds. Did Emenike think a fifty-pound note might have slipped out on his way to the restaurant?

"It's not a loan," Emenike said, leaning back on his seat, smiling thinly.

"Thanks, man," Obinze said again, and despite it all he was grateful and relieved. It had worried him, how many things he still had to pay for before the wedding, and if this was what it took, counting a cash gift while Emenike watched with power in his gaze, then so be it.

Emenike's phone rang. "Georgina," he said happily before he took the call. His voice was slightly raised, for Obinze's benefit. "It's fantastic to see him again after so long." Then, after a pause, "Of course, darling, we should do that."

He put his phone down and told Obinze, "Georgina wants to come and meet us in the next half hour so we can all go to dinner. Is that okay?"

Obinze shrugged. "I never say no to food."

Just before Georgina arrived, Emenike told him, in a lowered tone, "Don't mention this marriage thing to Georgina."

He had imagined Georgina, from the way Emenike spoke of her, as a fragile innocent, a successful lawyer who nonetheless did not truly know the evils of the world, but when she arrived, square-faced with a big square body, brown hair crisply cut, giving her an air of efficiency, he could see right away that she was frank, knowing, even world-weary. He imagined her clients instantly trusting her ability. This was a woman who would check up on the finances of charities she gave to. This was a woman who could certainly survive a visit to Nigeria. Why had Emenike portrayed her as a hapless English rose? She pressed her lips to Emenike's, then turned to shake Obinze's hand.

"Do you fancy anything in particular?" she asked Obinze, unbuttoning her brown suede coat. "There's a nice Indian place nearby."

"Oh, that's a bit tatty," Emenike said. He had changed. His voice had taken on an unfamiliar modulation, his delivery slower, the temperature of his entire being much lower. "We could go to that new place in Kensington, it's not that far."

"I'm not sure Obinze will find it very interesting, darling," Georgina said.

"Oh, I think he'll like it," Emenike said. Self-satisfaction, that was the difference in him. He was married to a British woman, lived in a British home, worked at a British job, travelled on a British passport, said "exercise" to refer to a mental rather than a physical activity. He had longed for this life, and never quite believed he would have it. Now his backbone was stiff with self-satisfaction. He was sated. In the restaurant in Kensington, a candle glowed on the table, and the blond waiter, who seemed too tall and handsome to be a waiter, served tiny bowls of what looked like green jelly.

"Our new lemon and thyme aperitif, with the compliments of the chef," he said.

"Fantastic," Emenike said, instantly sinking into one of the rituals of his new life: eyebrows furrowed, concentration sharp, sipping sparkling water and studying a restaurant menu. He and Georgina discussed the starters. The waiter was called to answer a question. It struck Obinze, how seriously Emenike took this initiation into the voodoo of fine dining, because when the waiter brought him what looked like three elegant bits of green weed, for which he would pay thirteen pounds, Emenike rubbed his palms together in delight. Obinze's burger was served in four pieces, arranged in a large martini glass. When Georgina's order arrived, a pile of red raw beef, an egg sunnily splayed on top of it, Obinze tried not to look at it as he ate, otherwise he might be tempted to vomit.

Emenike did most of the talking, telling Georgina about their time together at school, barely letting Obinze say anything. In the stories he told, he and Obinze were the popular rogues who always got into glamorous trouble. Obinze watched Georgina, only now becoming aware of how much older than Emenike she was. At least eight years. Her manly facial contours were softened by frequent brief smiles, but they were thoughtful smiles, the smiles of a natural sceptic, and he wondered how much she believed of Emenike's stories, how much love had suspended her reason.

"We're having a dinner party tomorrow, Obinze," Georgina said. "You must come."

"Yes, I forgot to mention it," Emenike said.

"You really must come. We're having a few friends over and I think you'll enjoy meeting them," Georgina said.

"I would love to," Obinze said.

THEIR TERRACED HOME in Islington, with its short flight of well-preserved steps that led to the green front door, smelled of roasting food when Obinze arrived. Emenike let him in. "The Zed! You're early, we're just finishing up in the kitchen. Come and stay in my study until the others come." Emenike led him upstairs, and into the study, a clean, bright room made brighter by the white bookshelves and white curtains. The windows ate up large chunks of the walls, and Obinze imagined the room in the afternoon, flooded gloriously with light, and himself sunk in the armchair by the door, lost in a book.

"I'll come and call you in a bit," Emenike said.

There were, on a window ledge, photos of Emenike squinting in front of the Sistine Chapel, making a peace sign at the Acropolis, standing at the Colosseum, his shirt the same nutmeg colour as the wall of the ruin. Obinze imagined him, dutiful and determined, visiting the places he was supposed to visit, thinking, as he did so, not of the things he was seeing but of the photos he would take of them and of the people who would see those photos. The people who would know that he had participated in these triumphs. On the bookshelf, Graham Greene caught his eye. He took *The Heart of the Matter* down and began to read the first chapter, suddenly nostalgic for his teenage years when his mother would reread it every few months.

Emenike came in. "Is that Waugh?"

"No." He showed him the book cover. "My mother loves this book. She was always trying to get me to love her English novels."

"Waugh is the best of them. *Brideshead* is the closest I've read to a perfect novel."

"I think Waugh is cartoonish. I just don't get those so-called comic English novels. It's as if they can't deal with the real and deep complexity of human life and so they resort to doing this comic business. Greene is the other extreme, too morose."

"No, man, you need to go and read Waugh again. Greene doesn't really do it for me, but the first part of *The End of the Affair* is terrific."

"This study is the dream," Obinze said.

Emenike shrugged. "Do you want any books? Take anything you want."

"Thanks, man," Obinze said, knowing that he would not take any.

Emenike looked around, as though seeing the study through new eyes. "We found this desk in Edinburgh. Georgina already had some good pieces but we found some new things together."

Obinze wondered if Emenike had so completely absorbed his own disguise that even when they were alone, he could talk about "good furniture", as though the idea of "good furniture" was not alien in their Nigerian world, where new things were supposed to look new. Obinze might have said something to Emenike about it but not now; too much had already shifted in their relationship. Obinze followed him downstairs. The dining table was a riot of colour, bright mismatched ceramic plates, some of them chipped at the edges, red wine goblets, deep blue napkins. In a silver bowl at the centre of the table, delicate milky flowers floated in water. Emenike made the introductions.

"This is Georgina's old friend Mark, and this is his wife, Hannah, who by the way is completing her PhD on the female orgasm, or the Israeli female orgasm."

"Well, it isn't quite that singularly focused," Hannah said, to general laughter, warmly shaking Obinze's hand. She had a tanned, broad-featured succouring face, the face of a person who could not abide conflict. Mark, pale-skinned and rumpled, squeezed her shoulder but did not laugh along with the others. He said "How do you do" to Obinze in an almost formal manner.

"This is our dear friend Phillip, who is the best solicitor in London, after Georgina of course," Emenike said.

"Are all the men in Nigeria as gorgeous as you and your friend?" Phillip asked Emenike, swooning mockingly as he shook Obinze's hand.

"You'll have to come to Nigeria and see," Emenike said, and winked, in what seemed to be a continuous flirtatiousness with Phillip.

Phillip was slender and elegant, his red silk shirt open at the neck. His mannerisms, supple gestures of his wrists, fingers swirling in the air, reminded Obinze of the boy in secondary school—his name was Hadome—who was said to pay junior students to suck his dick. Once, Emenike and two other boys had lured Hadome into the toilet and beaten him up, Hadome's eye swelling so quickly that, just before school was dismissed, it looked grotesque, like a big purple eggplant. Obinze had stood outside the toilet with other boys, boys who did not join in the beating but who laughed along, boys who taunted and goaded, boys who shouted "Homo! Homo!"

"This is our friend Alexa. Alexa's just moved into a new place in Holland Park, after years in France, and so, lucky us, we'll be seeing much more of her. She works in music publishing. She's also a fantastic poet," Emenike said.

"Oh, stop it," Alexa said, and then turning to Obinze, she asked, "So where are you from, darling?"

"Nigeria."

"No, no, I mean in London, darling."

"I live in Essex, actually," he said.

"I see," she said, as though disappointed. She was a small woman with a very pale face and tomato-red hair. "Shall we eat, boys and girls?" She picked up one of the plates and examined it.

"I love these plates. Georgina and Emenike are never boring, are they?" Hannah said.

"We bought them from this bazaar in India," Emenike said. "Handmade by rural women, just so beautiful. See the detail at the edges?" He raised one of the plates.

"Sublime," Hannah said, and looked at Obinze.

"Yes, very nice," Obinze mumbled. Those plates, with their amateur finishing, the slight lumpiness of the edges, would never be shown in the presence of guests in Nigeria. He still was not sure whether Emenike had become a person who believed that something was beautiful because it was handmade by poor people in a foreign country, or whether he had simply learned to pretend so. Georgina poured the drinks. Emenike served the starter, crab with hard-boiled eggs. He had taken on a careful and calibrated charm. He said "Oh dear" often. When Phillip complained about the French couple building a house next to his in Cornwall, Emenike asked, "Are they between you and the sunset?"

Are they between you and the sunset? It would never occur to Obinze, or to anybody he had grown up with, to ask a question like that.

"So how was America?" Phillip asked.

"A fascinating place, really. We spent a few days with Hugo in Jackson, Wyoming. You met Hugo last Christmas, didn't you, Mark?"

"Yes. So what's he doing there?" Mark seemed unimpressed by the plates; he had not, like his wife, picked one up to look at it.

"It's a ski resort, but it's not pretentious. In Jackson, they say people who go to Aspen expect somebody to tie their ski boots up for them," Georgina said.

"The thought of skiing in America makes me quite ill," Alexa said.

"Why?" Hannah asked.

"Have they got a Disney station in the resort, with Mickey Mouse in ski gear?" Alexa asked.

"Alexa has only been to America once, when she was in school, but she loves to hate it from afar," Georgina said.

"I've loved America from afar my whole life," Obinze said. Alexa turned to him in slight surprise, as though she had not expected him to speak. Under the chandelier light, her red hair took on a strange, unnatural glow.

"What I've noticed being here is that many English people are in awe of America but also deeply resent it," Obinze added.

"Perfectly true," Phillip said, nodding at Obinze. "Perfectly true. It's the resentment of a parent whose child has become far more beautiful and with a far more interesting life."

"But the Americans love us Brits, they love the accent and the

Queen and the double-decker," Emenike said. There, it had been said: the man considered himself British.

"And the great revelation Emenike had while we were there?" Georgina said, smiling. "The difference between the American and British 'bye'."

"Bye?" Alexa asked.

"Yes. He says the Brits draw it out much more, while Americans make it short."

"That was a great revelation. It explained everything about the difference between both countries," Emenike said, knowing that they would laugh, and they did. "I was also thinking about the difference in approaching foreignness. Americans will smile at you and be extremely friendly but if your name is not Cory or Chad, they make no effort at saying it properly. The Brits will be surly and will be suspicious if you're too friendly but they will treat foreign names as though they are actually valid names."

"That's interesting," Hannah said.

Georgina said, "It's a bit tiresome to talk about America being insular, not that we help that much, since if something major happens in America, it is the headline in Britain; something major happens here, it is on the back page in America, if at all. But I do think the most troubling thing was the garishness of the nationalism, don't you think so, darling?" Georgina turned to Emenike.

"Absolutely," Emenike said. "Oh, and we went to a rodeo. Hugo thought we might fancy a bit of culture."

There was a general, tittering laughter.

"And we saw this quite unbelievable parade of little children with heavily made-up faces and then there was a lot of flag-waving and a lot of 'God Bless America'. I was terrified that it was the sort of place where you did not know what might happen to you if you suddenly said, 'I don't like America.'"

"I found America quite jingoistic, too, when I did my fellowship training there," Mark said.

"Mark is a paediatric surgeon," Georgina said to Obinze.

"One got the sense that people—progressive people, that is, because American conservatives come from an entirely different planet, even to this Tory—felt that they could very well criticize their country but they didn't like it at all when you did," Mark said.

"Where were you?" Emenike asked, as if he knew America's smallest corners.

"Philadelphia. A specialty hospital called the Children's Hospital. It was quite a remarkable place and the training was very good. It might have taken me two years in England to see the rare cases that I had in a month there."

"But you didn't stay," Alexa said, almost triumphantly.

"I hadn't planned on staying." Mark's face never quite dissolved into any expression.

"Speaking of which, I've just got involved with this fantastic charity that's trying to stop the UK from hiring so many African health workers," Alexa said. "There are simply no doctors and nurses left on that continent. It's an absolute tragedy! African doctors should stay in Africa."

"Why shouldn't they want to practise where there is regular electricity and regular pay?" Mark asked, his tone flat. Obinze sensed that he did not like Alexa at all. "I'm from Grimsby and I certainly don't want to work in a district hospital there."

"But it isn't quite the same thing, is it? We're speaking of some of the world's poorest people. The doctors have a responsibility as Africans," Alexa said. "Life isn't fair, really. If they have the privilege of that medical degree, then it comes with a responsibility to help their people."

"I see. I don't suppose any of us should have that responsibility for the blighted towns in the north of England?" Mark said.

Alexa's face reddened. In the sudden tense silence, the air wrinkling between them all, Georgina got up and said, "Everyone ready for my roast lamb?"

They all praised the meat, which Obinze wished had stayed a little longer in the oven; he carefully cut around his slice, eating the sides that had greyed from cooking and leaving on his plate the bits stained with pinkish blood. Hannah led the conversation, as though to smooth the air, her voice calming, bringing up subjects they would all agree on, changing to something else if she sensed a looming disagreement. Their conversation was symphonic, voices flowing into one another, in agreement: how atrocious to treat those Chinese cockle pickers like that, how absurd, the idea of fees for higher education, how preposterous that fox-hunting supporters had stormed Parliament. They laughed when Obinze said, "I don't understand why fox hunting is such a big issue in this country. Aren't there more important things?"

"What could possibly be more important?" Mark asked drily.

"Well, it's the only way we know how to fight our class warfare," Alexa said. "The landed gentry and the aristocrats hunt, you see, and we liberal middle classes fume about it. We want to take their silly little toys away."

"We certainly do," Phillip said. "It's monstrous."

"Did you read about Blunkett saying he doesn't know how many immigrants there are in the country?" Alexa asked, and Obinze immediately tensed, his chest tightening.

"'Immigrant', of course, is code for Muslim," Mark said.

"If he really wanted to know, he would go to all the construction sites in this country and do a head count," Phillip said.

"It was quite interesting to see how this plays out in America," Georgina said. "They're kicking up a fuss about immigration as well. Although, of course, America has always been kinder to immigrants than Europe."

"Well, yes, but that is because countries in Europe were based on exclusion and not, as in America, on inclusion," Mark said.

"But it's also a different psychology, isn't it?" Hannah said. "European countries are surrounded by countries that are similar to one another, while America has Mexico, which is really a developing country, and so it creates a different psychology about immigration and borders."

"But we don't have immigrants from Denmark. We have immigrants from Eastern Europe, which is our Mexico," Alexa said.

"Except, of course, for race," Georgina said. "Eastern Europeans are white. Mexicans are not."

"How did you see race in America, by the way, Emenike?" Alexa asked. "It's an iniquitously racist country, isn't it?"

"He doesn't have to go to America for that, Alexa," Georgina said.

"It seemed to me that in America blacks and whites work together but don't play together and here blacks and whites play together but don't work together," Emenike said.

The others nodded thoughtfully, as though he had said something profound, but Mark said, "I'm not sure I quite understand that."

"I think class in this country is in the air that people breathe. Everyone knows their place. Even the people who are angry about class have somehow accepted their place," Obinze said. "A white boy and a black girl who grow up in the same working-class town in this country can get together and race will be secondary, but in America, even if the white boy and black girl grow up in the same neighbourhood, race would be primary."

Alexa gave him another surprised look.

"A bit simplified but yes, that's sort of what I meant," Emenike said, slowly, leaning back on his chair, and Obinze sensed a rebuke. He should have been quiet; this, after all, was Emenike's stage.

"But you haven't really had to deal with any racism here, have you, Emenike?" Alexa asked, and her tone implied that she already knew the answer to the question was no. "Of course people are prejudiced, but aren't we all prejudiced?"

"Well, no," Georgina said firmly. "You should tell the story of the cabbie, darling."

"Oh, that story," Emenike said, as he got up to serve the cheese plate, murmuring something in Hannah's ear that made her smile and touch his arm. How thrilled he was, to live in Georgina's world.

"Do tell," Hannah said.

And so Emenike did. He told the story of the taxi that he had hailed one night, on Upper Street; from afar the cab light was on but as the cab approached him, the light went off, and he assumed the driver was not on duty. After the cab passed him by, he looked back idly and saw that the cab light was back on and that, a little way up the street, it stopped for two white women.

Emenike had told Obinze this story before and he was struck now by how differently Emenike told it. He did not mention the rage he had felt standing on that street and looking at the cab. He was shaking, he had told Obinze, his hands trembling for a long time, a little frightened by his own feelings. But now, sipping the last of his red wine, flowers floating in front of him, he spoke in a tone cleansed of anger, thick only with a kind of superior amusement, while Georgina interjected to clarify: *Can you believe that?*

Alexa, flush with red wine, her eyes red below her scarlet hair, changed the subject. "Blunkett must be sensible and make sure this country remains a refuge. People who have survived frightful wars must absolutely be allowed in!" She turned to Obinze. "Don't you agree?"

"Yes," he said, and felt alienation run through him like a shiver.

Alexa, and the other guests, and perhaps even Georgina, all understood the fleeing from war, from the kind of poverty that crushed human souls, but they would not understand the need to escape from the oppressive lethargy of choicelessness. They would not understand why people like him, who were raised well-fed and watered but mired in dissatisfaction, conditioned from birth to look towards somewhere else, eternally convinced that real lives happened in that somewhere else, were now resolved to do dangerous things, illegal things, so as to leave, none of them starving, or raped, or from burned villages, but merely hungry for choice and certainty.

CHAPTER 30

Nicholas gave Obinze a suit for the wedding. "It's a good Italian suit," he said. "It's small for me so it should fit you." The trousers were big and bunched up when Obinze tightened his belt, but the jacket, also big, shielded this unsightly pleat of cloth at his waist. Not that he minded. So focused was he on getting through the day, on finally beginning his life, that he would have swaddled his lower parts in a baby's nappy if that were required. He and Iloba met Cleotilde near the Civic Centre. She was standing under a tree with her friends, her hair pushed back with a white band, her eyes boldly lined in black; she looked like an older, sexier person. Her ivory dress was tight at her hips. He had paid for the dress. "I haven't got any proper going-out dress," she had said in apology when she called to tell him that she had nothing that looked convincingly bridal. She hugged him. She looked nervous, and he tried to deflect his own nervousness by thinking about them together after this, how in less than an hour, he would be free to walk with surer steps on Britain's streets, and free to kiss her.

"You have the rings?" Iloba asked her.

"Yes," Cleotilde said.

She and Obinze had bought them the week before, plain matching cheap rings from a side-street shop, and she had looked so delighted, laughingly slipping different rings on and then off her finger, that he wondered if she wished it were a real wedding.

"Fifteen minutes to go," Iloba said. He had appointed himself the organizer. He took pictures, his digital camera held away from his face, saying, "Move closer! Okay, one more!" His sprightly good spirits annoyed Obinze. On the train up to Newcastle the previous day, while Obinze had spent his time looking out of the window, unable even to read, Iloba had talked and talked, until his voice became a distant murmur, perhaps because he was trying to keep Obinze from worrying too much. Now, he talked to Cleotilde's friends with an easy friendliness, about the new Chelsea coach, about *Big Brother*, as if they were all there for something ordinary and normal.

"Time to go," Iloba said. They walked towards the Civic Centre. The afternoon was bright with sunshine. Obinze opened the door and stood aside for the others to go ahead, into the sterile hallway, where they paused to get their bearings, to be sure which way to go towards the register office. Two policemen stood behind the door, watching them with stony eyes. Obinze quieted his panic. There was nothing to worry about, nothing at all, he told himself, the Civic Centre probably had policemen present as a matter of routine; but he sensed in the sudden smallness of the hallway, the sudden thickening of doom in the air, that something was wrong, before he noticed another man approaching him, his shirtsleeves rolled up, his cheeks so red he looked as though he was wearing terrible make-up.

"Are you Obinze Maduewesi?" the red-cheeked man asked. In his hands was a sheaf of papers and Obinze could see a photocopy of his passport page.

"Yes," Obinze said quietly, and that word, yes, was an acknowledgement to the red-cheeked immigration officer, to Iloba and to Cleotilde, and to himself that it was over.

"Your visa is expired and you are not allowed to be present in the UK," the red-cheeked man said.

A policeman clamped handcuffs around his wrists. He felt himself watching the scene from far away, watching himself walk to the police car outside, and sink into the too-soft seat in the back. There had been so many times in the past when he had feared that this would happen, so many moments that had become one single blur of panic, and now it felt like the dull echo of an aftermath. Cleotilde had flung herself on the ground and begun to cry. She might never have visited her father's country, but he was convinced at that moment of her Africanness; how else would she be able to fling herself to the ground with that perfect dramatic flourish? He wondered if her tears were for him or for herself or for what might have been between them. She had no need to worry, though, since she was a European citizen; the policemen barely glanced at her. It was he who felt the heaviness of the handcuffs during the drive to the police station, who silently handed over his watch and his belt and his wallet, and watched the policeman take his phone and switch it off. Nicholas's large trousers were slipping down his hips.

"Your shoes too. Take off your shoes," the policeman said.

He took off his shoes. He was led to a cell. It was small, with brown walls, and the metal bars, so thick his hand could not go around one, reminded him of the chimpanzee's cage at Nsukka's dismal, forgotten zoo. From the very high ceilings, a single bulb burned. There was an emptying, echoing vastness in that tiny cell.

"Were you aware that your visa had expired?"

"Yes," Obinze said.

"Were you about to have a sham marriage?"

"No. Cleotilde and I have been dating for a while."

"I can arrange for a lawyer for you, but it's obvious you'll be deported," the immigration officer said evenly.

When the lawyer came, puffy-faced, darkened arcs under his eyes, Obinze remembered all the films in which the state lawyer is distracted and exhausted. He came with a bag but did not open it, and he sat across from Obinze, holding nothing, no file, no paper, no pen. His demeanour was pleasant and sympathetic.

"The government has a strong case and we can appeal, but to be honest it will only delay the case and you will eventually be removed from the UK," he said, with the air of a man who had said those same words, in that same tone, more times than he wished to, or could, remember.

"I'm willing to go back to Nigeria," Obinze said. The last shard of his dignity was like a wrapper slipping off that he was desperate to retie.

The lawyer looked surprised. "Okay, then," he said, and got up a little too hastily, as though grateful that his job had been made easier. Obinze watched him leave. He was going to tick on a form that his client was willing to be removed. "Removed." That word made Obinze feel inanimate. A thing to be removed. A thing without breath and mind. A thing.

HE HATED the cold heaviness of the handcuffs, the mark he imagined they left on his wrists, the glint of the interlinking circles of metal that robbed him of movement. There he was, in handcuffs, being led through the hall of Manchester Airport, and in the coolness and din of that airport, men and women and children, travellers and cleaners and security guards, watched him, wondering what evil he had done. He kept his gaze on a tall white woman hurrying ahead, hair flying behind her, knapsack hunched on her back. She would not understand his story, why he was now walking through the airport with metal clamped around his wrists, because people like her did not approach travel with anxiety about visas. She might worry about money, about a place to stay, about safety, perhaps even about visas, but never with an anxiety that wrenched at her spine.

He was led into a room, bunk beds pushed forlornly against the walls. Three men were already there. One, from Djibouti, said little, lying and staring at the ceiling as though retracing the journey of how he had ended up at a holding facility in Manchester Airport. Two were Nigerian. The younger sat up on his bed eternally cracking his fingers. The older paced the small room and would not stop talking.

"Bros, how did they get you?" he asked Obinze, with an instant familiarity that Obinze resented. Something about him reminded Obinze of Vincent. Obinze shrugged and said nothing to him; there was no need for courtesies simply because they shared a cell.

"Is there anything I could have to read, please?" Obinze asked an immigration officer when she came to lead the man from Djibouti out to see a visitor.

"Read," she repeated, eyebrows raised.

"Yes. A book or a magazine or a newspaper," Obinze said.

"You want to read," she said, and on her face, a contemptuous amusement. "Sorry. But we've got a TV room and you're allowed to go there and watch telly after lunchtime."

In the TV room, there was a group of men, many of them Nigerians, talking loudly. The other men sat around slumped into their own sorrows, listening to the Nigerians trade their stories, sometimes laughing, sometimes self-pitying.

"Ah this na my second time. The first time I come with different passport," one of them said.

"Na for work wey they get me o."

"E get one guy wey they deport, him don come back get him paper. Na him wey go help me," another said.

Obinze envied them for what they were, men who casually changed names and passports, who would plan and come back and do it over again because they had nothing to lose. He didn't have their savoir faire; he was soft, a boy who had grown up eating cornflakes and reading books, raised by a mother during a time when truth-telling was not yet a luxury. He was ashamed to be with them, among them. They did not have his shame and even this, too, he envied.

IN DETENTION, he felt raw, skinned, the outer layers of himself stripped off. His mother's voice on the phone was almost unfamiliar, a woman speaking a crisp Nigerian English, telling him, calmly, to be strong, that she would be in Lagos to receive him, and he remembered how, years ago, when General Buhari's government stopped giving essential commodities, and she no longer came home with free tins of milk, she had begun to grind soya beans at home to make milk. She said soya milk was more nutritious than cow milk and although he refused to drink the grainy fluid in the morning, he watched her do so with an uncomplaining common sense. It was what she showed now, over the phone, telling him she would come and pick him up, as though she had always nursed the possibility of this, her son in detention, waiting to be removed from a country overseas.

He thought a lot about Ifemelu, imagining what she was doing, how her life had changed. She had once told him, in university, "You know what I admired most about you in secondary school? That you never had a problem saying 'I don't know.' Other boys pretended to know what they didn't know. But you just had this confidence and you could always admit that you didn't know something." He had thought it an unusual compliment, and had cherished this image of himself, perhaps because he knew it was not entirely true. He wondered what she would think if she knew where he was now. She would be sympathetic, he was sure, but would she also, in a small way, be disappointed? He almost asked Iloba to contact her. It would not be difficult to find her; he already knew she lived in Baltimore. But he did not ask Iloba. When Iloba visited him, he talked about lawyers. They both knew that there was no point, but still Iloba talked about lawyers. He would sit across from Obinze, rest his head on his hand and talk about lawyers. Obinze wondered if some of the lawyers existed only in Iloba's mind. "I know one lawyer in London, a Ghanaian, he represented this man with no papers, the man was almost on a plane home, and the next thing we knew, the man was free. He now works in IT." Other times, Iloba took comfort in stating what was obvious. "If only the marriage was just done before they came," he said. "You know if they had come even one second after you were pronounced man and wife, they would not touch you?" Obinze nodded. He knew, and Iloba knew that he knew. On Iloba's last visit, after Obinze told him that he was being moved to Dover the next day, Iloba began to cry. "Zed, this was not supposed to happen like this."

"Iloba, why are you talking rubbish? Stop crying, my friend," Obinze said, pleased to be in a position to pretend strength.

And yet when Nicholas and Ojiugo visited, he disliked how strenuously they tried to be positive, to pretend, almost, as though he was merely ill in hospital and they had come to visit him. They sat across from him, the bare cold table between them, and talked about the mundane, Ojiugo speaking a little too quickly, and Nicholas saying more in an hour than Obinze had heard him say in weeks: Nne had been accepted into the National Children's Orchestra, Nna had won yet another prize. They brought him money, novels, a bag of clothes. Nicholas had shopped for him, and most of the clothes were new and in his size. Ojiugo often asked, "But are they treating you well? Are they treating you well?" as though the treatment was what mattered, rather than the blighted reality of it all, that he was in a holding centre, about to be deported. Nobody behaved normally. They were all under the spell of his misfortune.

"They are waiting for seats on a flight to Lagos," Obinze said. "They'll keep me in Dover until there's a seat available."

Obinze had read about Dover in a newspaper. A former prison. It felt surreal, to be driven past the electronic gates, the high walls, the wires. His cell was smaller, colder, than the cell in Manchester and his cellmate, another Nigerian, told him that he was not going to allow himself to be deported. He had a hardened, fleshless face. "I will take off my shirt and my shoes when they try to board me. I will seek asylum," he told Obinze. "If you take off your shirt and your shoes, they will not board you." He repeated this often, like a mantra. From time to time he farted loudly, wordlessly, and from time to time he sank to his knees in the middle of their tiny cell, hands raised up to the heavens, and prayed. "Father Lord, I praise your name! Nothing is too much for you! I bless your name!" His palms were deeply etched with lines. Obinze wondered what atrocities those hands had seen. He felt suffocated in that cell, let out only to exercise and to eat, food that brought to mind a bowl of boiled worms. He could not eat; he felt his body slackening, his flesh disappearing. By the day he was led into a van one early morning, a fuzz of hair, like carpet grass, had covered his entire jaw. It was not yet dawn. He was with two women and five men, all handcuffed, all bound for Nigeria, and they were marched, at Heathrow Airport, through security and immigration and onto the plane, while other passengers stared. They were seated at the very back, in the last row of seats, closest to the toilet. Obinze sat unmoving throughout the flight. He did not want his tray of food. "No, thank you," he said to the flight attendant.

The woman next to him said eagerly, "Can I have his own?" She had been at Dover too. She had very dark lips and a buoyant, undefeated manner. She would, he was sure, get another passport with another name and try again.

As the plane began its descent into Lagos, a flight attendant stood above them and said loudly, "You cannot leave. An immigration officer will come to take charge of you." Her face tight with disgust, as though they were all criminals bringing shame on upright Nigerians like her. The plane emptied out. Obinze looked through the window, at an old jet standing in the mild late afternoon sun, until a uniformed man came walking down the aisle. His belly was large; it must have been a struggle to button up his shirt.

"Yes, yes, I have come to take charge of you! Welcome home!" he said humorously, and he reminded Obinze of that Nigerian ability to laugh, to so easily reach for amusement. He had missed that. "We laugh too much," his mother once said. "Maybe we should laugh less and solve our problems more."

The uniformed man led them to an office, and handed out forms. Name. Age. Country you have come from.

"Did they treat you well?" the man asked Obinze.

"Yes," Obinze said.

"So do you have anything for the boys?"

Obinze looked at him for a moment, his open face, his simple view of the world; deportations happened every day and the living went on living. Obinze brought from his pocket a ten-pound note, part of the money Nicholas had given him. The man took it with a smile.

Outside, it was like breathing steam; he felt light-headed. A new sadness blanketed him, the sadness of his coming days, when he would feel the world slightly off-kilter, his vision unfocused. At the cordoned-off area near Arrivals, standing apart from the other expectant people, his mother was waiting for him.

Part 4

CHAPTER 31

After Ifemelu broke up with Curt, she told Ginika, "There was a feeling I wanted to feel that I did not feel."

"What are you talking about? You cheated on him!" Ginika shook her head as though Ifemelu were mad. "Ifem, honestly, sometimes I don't understand you."

It was true, she had cheated on Curt with a younger man who lived in her apartment building in Charles Village and played in a band. But it was also true that she had longed, with Curt, to hold emotions in her hand that she never could. She had not entirely believed herself while with him—happy, handsome Curt, with his ability to twist life into the shapes he wanted. She loved him, and the spirited easy life he gave her, and yet she often fought the urge to create rough edges, to squash his sunniness, even if just a little.

"I think you are a self-sabotager," Ginika said. "That's why you cut off Obinze like that. And now you cheat on Curt because at some level you don't think you deserve happiness."

"Now you are going to suggest some pills for Self-Sabotage Disorder," Ifemelu said. "That's absurd."

"So why did you do it?"

"It was a mistake. People make mistakes. People do stupid things."

She had done it, in truth, because she was curious, but she would not tell Ginika this, because it would seem flippant; Ginika would not understand, Ginika would prefer a grave and important reason like self-sabotage. She was not even sure she liked him, Rob, who wore dirty ripped jeans, grimy boots, rumpled flannel shirts. She did not understand grunge, the idea of looking shabby because you could afford not to be shabby; it mocked true shabbiness. The way he dressed made him seem superficial to her, and yet she was curious about him, about how he would be, naked in bed with her. The sex was good the first time, she was on top of him, gliding and moaning and grasping the hair on his chest, and feeling faintly and glamorously theatrical as she did so. But the second time, after she arrived at his apartment and he pulled her into his arms, a great torpor descended on her. He was already breathing heavily, and she was extracting herself from his embrace and picking up her handbag to leave. In the elevator, she was overcome with the frightening sense that she was looking for something solid, flailing, and all she touched dissolved into nothingness. She went to Curt's apartment and told him.

"It meant nothing. It happened once and I am so sorry."

"Stop playing," he said, but she knew, from the unbelieving horror that was deepening the blue of his eyes, that he knew she was not playing. It took hours of sidestepping each other, of drinking tea and putting on music and checking e-mail, of Curt lying face up on the couch, still and silent, before he asked, "Who is he?"

She told him the man's name. Rob.

"He's white?"

She was surprised that he would ask her this, and so soon. "Yes." She had first seen Rob months before, in the elevator, with his unkempt clothes and unwashed hair, and he had smiled at her and said, "I see you around." After that, whenever she saw him, he looked at her with a kind of lazy interest, as though they both knew that something would happen between them and it was only a matter of when.

"Who the fuck is he?" Curt asked.

She told him that he lived on the floor above hers, that they said hello to each other and nothing else until that evening when she saw him coming back from the liquor store and he asked if she'd like to have a drink with him and she did a stupid, impulsive thing.

"You gave him what he wanted," Curt said. The planes of his face were hardening. It was an odd thing for Curt to say, the sort of thing Aunty Uju, who thought of sex as something a woman gave a man at a loss to herself, would say.

In a sudden giddy fit of recklessness, she corrected Curt. "I took what I wanted. If I gave him anything, then it was incidental."

"Listen to yourself, just fucking listen to yourself!" Curt's voice had hoarsened. "How could you do this to me? I was so good to you."

He was already looking at their relationship through the lens of the past tense. It puzzled her, the ability of romantic love to mutate, how quickly a loved one could become a stranger. Where did the love go? Perhaps real love was familial, somehow linked to blood, since love for children did not die as romantic love did.

"You won't forgive me," she said, a half question.

"Bitch," he said.

He wielded the word like a knife; it came out of his mouth sharp with loathing. To hear Curt say "bitch" so coldly felt surreal, and tears gathered in her eyes, knowing that she had turned him into a man who could say "bitch" so coldly, and wishing he was a man who would not have said "bitch" no matter what. Alone in her apartment, she cried and cried, crumpled on her living room rug that was so rarely used it still smelled of the store. Her relationship with Curt was what she wanted, a crested wave in her life, and yet she had taken an axe and hacked at it. Why had she destroyed it? She imagined her mother saying it was the devil. She wished she believed in the devil, in a being outside of yourself that invaded your mind and caused you to destroy that which you cared about.

She spent weeks calling Curt, waiting in front of his building until he came out, saying over and over how sorry she was, how much she wanted to work through things. On the day she woke up and finally accepted that Curt would not return her calls, would not open the door of his apartment no matter how hard she knocked, she went alone to their favourite bar downtown. The bartender, the one who knew them, gave her a gentle smile, a sympathy smile. She smiled back and ordered another mojito, thinking that perhaps the bartender was better suited for Curt, with her brown hair blow-dried to satin, her thin arms and tight black clothes and her ability always to be seamlessly, harmlessly chatty. She would also be seamlessly, harmlessly faithful; if she had a man like Curt, she would not be interested in a curiosity copulation with a stranger who played unharmonious music. Ifemelu stared into her glass. There was something wrong with her. She did not know what it was but there was something wrong with her. A hunger, a restlessness. An incomplete knowledge of herself. The sense of something farther away, beyond her reach. She got up and left a big tip on the counter. For a long time afterwards, her memory of the end with Curt was this: speeding down Charles Street in a taxi, a little drunk and a little relieved and a little lonely, with a Punjabi driver who was proudly telling her that his children did better than American children at school.

SOME YEARS LATER, at a dinner party in Manhattan, a day after Barack Obama became the Democratic Party's candidate for President of the United States, surrounded by guests, all fervent Obama supporters who were dewy-eyed with wine and victory, a balding white man said, "Obama will end racism in this country," and a large-hipped, stylish poet from Haiti agreed, nodding, her Afro bigger than Ifemelu's, and said she had dated a white man for three years in California and race was never an issue for them.

"That's a lie," Ifemelu said to her.

"What?" the woman asked, as though she could not have heard properly.

"It's a lie," Ifemelu repeated.

The woman's eyes bulged. "You're telling me what my own experience was?"

Even though Ifemelu by then understood that people like the woman said what they said to keep others comfortable, and to show they appreciated How Far We Have Come; even though she was by then happily ensconced in a circle of Blaine's friends, one of whom was the woman's new boyfriend, and even though she should have left it alone, she did not. She could not. The words had, once again, overtaken her; they overpowered her throat, and tumbled out.

"The only reason you say that race was not an issue is because you wish it was not. We all wish it was not. But it's a lie. I came from a country where race was not an issue; I did not think of myself as black and I only became black when I came to America. When you are black in America and you fall in love with a white person, race doesn't matter when you're alone together because it's just you and your love. But the minute you step outside, race matters. But we don't talk about it.

We don't even tell our white partners the small things that piss us off and the things we wish they understood better, because we're worried they will say we're overreacting, or we're being too sensitive. And we don't want them to say, Look how far we've come, just forty years ago it would have been illegal for us to even be a couple blah blah blah, because you know what we're thinking when they say that? We're thinking why the fuck should it ever have been illegal anyway? But we don't say any of this stuff. We let it pile up inside our heads and when we come to nice liberal dinners like this, we say that race doesn't matter because that's what we're supposed to say, to keep our nice liberal friends comfortable. It's true. I speak from experience."

The host, a Frenchwoman, glanced at her American husband, a slyly pleased smile on her face; the most unforgettable dinner parties happened when guests said unexpected, and potentially offensive, things.

The poet shook her head and said to the host, "I'd love to take some of that wonderful dip home if you have any left," and looked at the others as though she could not believe they were actually listening to Ifemelu. But they were, all of them hushed, their eyes on Ifemelu as though she was about to give up a salacious secret that would both titillate and implicate them. Ifemelu had been drinking too much white wine; from time to time she had a swimming sensation in her head, and she would later send apology e-mails to the host and the poet. But everyone was watching her, even Blaine, whose expression she could not, for once, read clearly. And so she began to talk about Curt.

It was not that they avoided race, she and Curt. They talked about it in the slippery way that admitted nothing and engaged nothing and ended with the word "crazy", like a curious nugget to be examined and then put aside. Or as jokes that left her with a small and numb discomfort that she never admitted to him. And it was not that Curt pretended that being black and being white were the same in America; he knew they were not. It was, instead, that she did not understand how he grasped one thing but was completely tone-deaf about another similar thing, how he could easily make one imaginative leap, but be crippled in the face of another. Before his cousin Ashleigh's wedding, for example, he dropped her off at a small spa near his childhood home, to get her eyebrows shaped. Ifemelu walked in and smiled at the Asian woman behind the counter.

"Hi. I'd like to get my eyebrows waxed."

"We don't do curly," the woman said.

"You don't do curly?"

"No. Sorry."

Ifemelu gave the woman a long look; it was not worth an argument. If they did not do curly, then they did not do curly, whatever curly was. She called Curt and asked him to turn around and come back for her because the salon did not do curly. Curt walked in, his blue eyes bluer, and said he wanted to talk to the manager right away. "You are going to fucking do my girlfriend's eyebrows or I'll shut down this fucking place. You don't deserve to have a licence."

The woman transformed into a smiling, solicitous coquette. "I'm so sorry, it was a misunderstanding," she said. Yes, they could do the eyebrows. Ifemelu did not want to, worried that the woman might scald her, rip her skin off, pinch her, but Curt was too outraged on her behalf, his anger smouldering in the closed air of the spa, and so she sat, tensely, as the woman waxed her eyebrows.

As they drove back, Curt asked, "How is the hair of your eyebrows curly anyway? And how is that hard to fucking wax?"

"Maybe they've never done a black woman's eyebrows and so they think it's different, because our hair *is* different, after all, but I guess now she knows the eyebrows are not that different."

Curt scoffed, reaching across to take her hand, his palm warm. At the cocktail reception, he kept his fingers meshed with hers. Young females in tiny dresses, their breaths and bellies sucked in, trooped across to say hello to him and to flirt, asking if he remembered them, Ashleigh's friend from high school, Ashleigh's room-mate in college. When Curt said, "This is my girlfriend, Ifemelu," they looked at her with surprise, a surprise that some of them shielded and some of them did not, and in their expressions was the question "Why her?" It amused Ifemelu. She had seen that look before, on the faces of white women, strangers on the street, who would see her hand clasped in Curt's and instantly cloud their faces with that look. The look of people confronting a great tribal loss. It was not merely because Curt was white, it was the kind of white he was, the untamed golden hair and handsome face, the athlete's body, the sunny charm and the smell, around him, of money. If he were fat, older, poor, plain, eccentric, or dreadlocked, then it would be less remarkable, and the guardians of the tribe would be mollified. And it did not help that although she might be a pretty black girl, she was not the kind of black that they could, with an effort, imagine him with: she was not light-skinned, she was not biracial. At that party, as Curt held on to her hand, kissed her often, introduced her to everyone, her amusement curdled into exhaustion. The looks had begun to pierce her skin. She was tired even of Curt's protection, tired of needing protection.

Curt leaned in and whispered, "That one, the one with the bad spray tan? She can't even see her fucking boyfriend's been checking you out since we walked in here."

So he had noticed, and understood, the "Why her?" looks. It surprised her. Sometimes, in the middle of floating on his bubbly exuberance, he would have a flash of intuition, of surprising perception, and she would wonder if there were other more primal things she was missing about him. Such as when he told his mother, who had glanced at the Sunday newspaper and mumbled that some people were still looking for reasons to complain even though America was now colour-blind, "Come on, Mother. What if ten people who look like Ifemelu suddenly walked in here to eat? You realize our fellow diners will be less than pleased?"

"Maybe," his mother said, noncommittal, and shot an eyebrow-raise of accusation at Ifemelu, as though to say she knew very well who had turned her son into a pathetic race warrior. Ifemelu smiled a small, victorious smile.

And yet. Once, they visited his aunt, Claire, in Vermont, a woman who had an organic farm and walked around barefoot and talked about how connected to the earth it made her feel. Did Ifemelu have such an experience in Nigeria? she asked, and looked disappointed when Ifemelu said her mother would slap her if she ever stepped outside without shoes. Claire talked, throughout the visit, about her Kenyan safari, about Mandela's grace, about her adoration for Harry Belafonte, and Ifemelu worried that she would lapse into Ebonics or Swahili. As they left her rambling house, Ifemelu said, "I bet she's an interesting woman if she'd just be herself. I don't need her to over-assure me that she likes black people."

And Curt said it was not about race, it was just that his aunt was hyper-aware of difference, any difference.

"She would have done the exact same thing if I had turned up with a blonde Russian," he said.

Of course his aunt would not have done the same thing with a blonde Russian. A blonde Russian was white, and his aunt would not feel the need to prove that she liked people who looked like the blonde Russian. But Ifemelu did not tell Curt this because she wished it were obvious to him.

When they walked into a restaurant with linen-covered tables, and the host looked at them and asked Curt, "Table for one?" Curt hastily told her the host did not mean it "like that". And she wanted to ask him, "How else could the host have meant it?" When the strawberry-haired owner of the bed-and-breakfast in Montreal refused to acknowledge her as they checked in, a steadfast refusal, smiling and looking only at Curt, she wanted to tell Curt how slighted she felt, worse because she was unsure whether the woman disliked black people or liked Curt. But she did not, because he would tell her she was overreacting or tired or both. There were, simply, times that he saw and times that he was unable to see. She knew that she should tell him these thoughts, that not telling him cast a shadow over them both. Still, she chose silence. Until the day they argued about her magazine. He had picked up a copy of *Essence* from the pile on her coffee table, on a rare morning that they spent in her apartment, the air still thick with the aroma of the omelettes she had made.

"This magazine's kind of racially skewed," he said.

"What?"

"Come on. Only black women featured?"

"You're serious," she said.

He looked puzzled. "Yeah."

"We're going to the bookstore."

"What?"

"I need to show you something. Don't ask."

"Okay," he said, unsure what this new adventure was but eager, with that childlike delight of his, to participate.

She drove to the bookstore in the Inner Harbor, took down copies of the different women's magazines from the display shelf and led the way to the café.

"Do you want a latte?" he asked.

"Yes, thanks."

After they settled down on the chairs, paper cups in front of them, she said, "Let's start with the covers." She spread the magazines on the table, some on top of the others. "Look, all of them are white women. This one is supposed to be Hispanic, we know this because they wrote two Spanish words here, but she looks exactly like this white woman, no difference in her skin tone and hair and features. Now, I'm going to flip through, page by page, and you tell me how many black women you see."

"Babe, come on," Curt said, amused, leaning back, paper cup to his lips.

"Just humour me," she said.

And so he counted. "Three black women," he said, finally. "Or maybe four. *She* could be black."

"So three black women in maybe two thousand pages of women's magazines, and all of them are biracial or racially ambiguous, so they could also be Indian or Puerto Rican or something. Not one of them is dark. Not one of them looks like me, so I can't get clues for make-up from these magazines. Look, this article tells you to pinch your cheeks for colour because all their readers are supposed to have cheeks you can pinch for colour. This tells you about different hair products for *everyone*—and 'everyone' means blondes, brunettes and redheads. I am none of those. And this tells you about the best conditioners—for straight, wavy and curly. No kinky. See what they mean by curly? My hair could never do that. This tells you about matching your eye colour and eyeshadow—blue, green and hazel eyes. But my eyes are black so I can't know what shadow works for me. This says that this pink lipstick is universal, but they mean universal if you are white because I would look like a golliwog if I tried that shade of pink. Oh, look, here is some progress. An advertisement for foundation. There are seven different shades for white skin and one generic chocolate shade, but that is progress. Now, let's talk about what is racially skewed. Do you see why a magazine like *Essence* even exists?"

"Okay, babe, okay, I didn't mean for it to be such a big deal," he said.

That evening, Ifemelu wrote a long e-mail to Wambui about the bookstore, the magazines, the things she didn't tell Curt, things unsaid and unfinished. It was a long e-mail, digging, questioning, unearthing. Wambui replied to say, "This is so raw and true. More people should read this. You should start a blog."

Blogs were new, unfamiliar to her. But telling Wambui what happened was not satisfying enough; she longed for other listeners, and she longed to hear the stories of others. How many other people chose silence? How many other people had become black in America? How many had felt as though their world was wrapped in gauze? She broke up with Curt a few weeks after that, and she signed on to WordPress, and her blog was born. She would later change the name, but at first she called it *Raceteenth or Curious Observations by a Non-American Black on the Subject of Blackness in America.* Her first post was a better-punctuated version of the e-mail she had sent to Wambui. She referred to Curt as "The Hot White Ex". A few hours later, she checked her blog stats. Nine people had read it. Panicked, she took down the post. The next day, she put it up again, modified and edited, ending with words she still so easily remembered. She recited those words now, at the dinner table of the French and American couple, while the Haitian poet stared, arms folded.

The simplest solution to the problem of race in America? Romantic love. Not friendship. Not the kind of safe, shallow love where the objective is that both people remain comfortable. But real deep romantic love, the kind that twists you and wrings you out and makes you breathe through the nostrils of your beloved. And because that real deep romantic love is so rare, and because American society is set up to make it even rarer between American Black and American White, the problem of race in America will never be solved.

"Oh! What a wonderful story!" the French host said, her palm placed dramatically on her chest, looking around the table, as though to seek a response. But everyone else remained silent, their eyes averted and unsure.

A Michelle Obama Shout-Out Plus Hair as Race Metaphor

White Girlfriend and I are Michelle Obama groupies. So the other day I say to her—I wonder if Michelle Obama has a weave, her hair looks fuller today, and all that heat every day must damage it. And she says—you mean her hair doesn't grow like that? So is it me or is that the perfect metaphor for race in America right there? Hair. Ever notice makeover shows on TV, how the black woman has natural hair (coarse, coily, kinky, or curly) in the ugly "before" picture, and in the pretty "after" picture, somebody's taken a hot piece of metal and singed her hair straight? Some black women, AB and NAB, would rather run naked in the street than come out in public with their natural hair. Because, you see, it's not professional, sophisticated, whatever, it's just not damn normal. (Please, commenters, don't tell me it's the same as a white woman who doesn't color her hair.) When you DO have natural Negro hair, people think you "did" something to your hair. Actually, the folk with the Afros and dreads are the ones who haven't "done" anything to their hair. You should be asking Beyoncé what she's done. (We all love Bey but how about she show us, just once, what her hair looks like when it grows from her scalp?) I have natural kinky hair. Worn in cornrows, Afros, braids. No, it's not political. No, I am not an artist or poet or singer. Not an earth mother either. I just don't want relaxers in my hair—there are enough sources of cancer in my life as it is. (By the way, can we ban Afro wigs at Halloween? Afro is not costume, for God's sake.) Imagine if Michelle Obama got tired of all the heat and decided to go natural and appeared on TV with lots of woolly hair, or tight spirally curls. (There is no knowing what her texture will be. It is not unusual for a black woman to have three different textures on her head.) She would totally rock but poor Obama would certainly lose the independent vote, even the undecided Democrat vote.

UPDATE: ZoraNeale22, who's transitioning, asked me to post my regimen. Pure shea butter as a leave-in conditioner works for many naturals. Not for me, though. Anything with lots of shea butter leaves my hair grayish and dryish. And dry is my hair's biggest problem. I wash once a week with a silicone-free hydrating shampoo. I use a hydrating conditioner. I do not towel-dry my hair. I leave it wet, divide it in sections, and apply a creamy leave-in product (present favorite is Qhemet Biologics, other preferred brands are Oyin Handmade, Shea Moisture, Bask Beauty, and Darcy's Botanicals). Then I put my hair in three or four big cornrows, and knot my satin scarf around my head (satin is good, it preserves moisture. Cotton is bad, it soaks up moisture). I go to sleep. The next morning, I take out the cornrows and voilà, a lovely fluffy 'fro! Key is to add product while hair is wet. And I never, ever comb my hair when it's dry. I comb only when wet, or damp, or totally drenched in a creamy moisturizer. This plait-while-wet regimen can even work for our Seriously Curly White Girlfriends who are tired of flatirons and keratin treatments. Any AB and NAB naturals out there who want to share their regimen?

CHAPTER 32

For weeks, Ifemelu stumbled around, trying to remember the person she was before Curt. Their life together had happened to her, she would not have been able to imagine it if she had tried, and so, surely, she could return to what was before. But before was a slate-toned blur and she no longer knew who she had been then, what she had enjoyed, disliked, wanted. Her job bored her: she did the same bland things, writing press releases, editing press releases, copy-editing press releases, her movements rote and numbing. Perhaps it had always been so and she had not noticed, because she was blinded by the brightness of Curt. Her apartment felt like a stranger's home. On weekends, she went to Willow. Aunty Uju's condo was in a cluster of stucco buildings, the neighbourhood carefully landscaped, boulders placed at corners, and in the evenings, friendly people walked their handsome dogs. Aunty Uju had taken on a new light-heartedness; she wore a tiny anklet in the summer, a hopeful flash of gold on her leg. She had joined African Doctors for Africa, volunteering her time on two-week medical missions, and on her trip to Sudan, she met Kweku, a divorced Ghanaian doctor. "He treats me like a princess. Just like Curt treated you," she told Ifemelu.

"I'm trying to forget him, Aunty. Stop talking about him!"

"Sorry," Aunty Uju said, not looking sorry at all. She had told Ifemelu to do everything to save the relationship, because she would not find another man who would love her as Curt had. When Ifemelu told Dike that she had broken up with Curt, he said, "He was pretty cool, Coz. Are you going to be okay?"

"Yes, of course."

Perhaps he sensed otherwise, and knew of the slight unsteadiness of her spirit; most nights she lay in bed and cried, berating herself for what she had destroyed, then telling herself that she had no reason to be crying, and crying all the same. Dike brought up a tray to her room, on which he had placed a banana and a can of peanuts.

"Snack time!" he said, with a teasing grin; he still did not understand why anybody would want to eat both together. While Ifemelu ate, he sat on the bed and told her about school. He was playing basketball now, his grades had improved, he liked a girl called Autumn.

"You're really settling in here."

"Yeah," he said, and his smile reminded her of what it used to be in Brooklyn, open, unguarded.

"Remember the character Goku in my Japanese anime?" he asked.

"Yes."

"You kind of look like Goku with your Afro," Dike said, laughing.

Kweku knocked and waited for her to say "Come in" before he poked his head in. "Dike, are you ready?" he asked.

"Yes, Uncle." Dike got up. "Let's roll!"

"We're going to the community centre, would you like to join us?" Kweku asked Ifemelu, tentatively, almost formally; he, too, knew she was suffering from a break-up. He was small and bespectacled, a gentleman and a gentle man; Ifemelu liked him because he liked Dike.

"No, thank you," Ifemelu said. He lived in a house not far away, but some of his shirts were in Aunty Uju's closet, and Ifemelu had seen a face wash for men in Aunty Uju's bathroom, and cartons of organic yogurt in the fridge, which she knew Aunty Uju did not eat. He looked at Aunty Uju with translucent eyes, those of a man who wanted the world to know how much he loved. It reminded Ifemelu of Curt, and made her feel, again, a wistful sadness.

Her mother heard something in her voice over the phone. "Are you sick? Did anything happen?"

"I'm fine. Just work," she said.

Her father, too, asked why she sounded different and if all was well. She told him that all was well, that she was spending much of her time after work blogging; she was about to explain this new pastime of hers, but he said, "I'm fairly familiar with the concept. We have been undergoing a rigorous computer literacy training in the office."

"They have confirmed your father's application. He can take his leave when my school vacates," her mother said. "So we should apply for our visa quickly."

Ifemelu had long dreamed of, and talked about, when they would be able to visit her. She could afford it now, and her mother wanted it now, but she wished it could be another time. She wanted to see them, but the thought of their visit exhausted her. She was not sure she would be able to be their daughter, the person they remembered.

"Mummy, things are very busy at work now."

"Ahn-ahn. Are we coming to disturb your work?"

And so she sent them invitation letters, bank statements, a copy of her green card. The American embassy was better now; the staff was still rude, her father said, but you no longer had to fight and shove outside to get in line. They were given six-month visas. They came for three weeks. They seemed like strangers. They looked the same, but the dignity she remembered was gone, and left instead something small, a provincial eagerness. Her father marvelled at the industrial carpeting in the hallway of her apartment building; her mother hoarded faux-leather handbags at Kmart, paper napkins from the mall food court, even plastic shopping bags. They both posed for photos in front of JC Penney, asking Ifemelu to make sure she got the entire sign of the store. She watched them with a sneer, and for this she felt guilty; she had guarded their memories so preciously and yet, finally seeing them, she watched them with a sneer.

"I do not understand Americans. They say 'job' and you think they have said 'jab'," her father declared, spelling both words. "One finds the British manner of speaking much preferable."

Before they left, her mother asked her quietly, "Do you have a friend?" She said "friend" in English; the tame word parents used because they could not desecrate their tongues with "boyfriend", even though it was exactly what they meant: somebody romantic, a marriage prospect.

"No," Ifemelu said. "I have been very busy with work."

"Work is good, Ifem. But you should also keep your eyes open. Remember that a woman is like a flower. Our time passes quickly."

Before, she might have laughed dismissively, and told her mother that she did not at all feel like a flower, but now she was too tired, it felt too much of an effort. On the day they left for Nigeria, she collapsed onto her bed, crying uncontrollably, and thinking: What is wrong with me? She was relieved that her parents had gone, and she felt guilty for feeling relief. After work, she wandered around the centre of Baltimore, aimlessly, interested in nothing. Was this what the novelists meant by ennui? On a slow Wednesday afternoon, she handed in her resignation. She had not planned to resign, but it suddenly seemed to be what she had to do, and so she typed the letter on her computer and took it to her manager's office.

"You were making such progress. Is there anything we can do to make you change your mind?" her manager asked, very surprised.

"It's personal, family reasons," Ifemelu said vaguely. "I really appreciate all the opportunities you've given me."

So What's the Deal?

They tell us race is an invention, that there is more genetic variation between two black people than there is between a black person and a white person. Then they tell us black people have a worse kind of breast cancer and get more fibroids. And white folk get cystic fibrosis and osteoporosis. So what's the deal, doctors in the house? Is race an invention or not?

CHAPTER 33

The blog had unveiled itself and shed its milk teeth; by turns, it surprised her, pleased her, left her behind. Its readers increased, by the thousands from all over the world, so quickly that she resisted checking the stats, reluctant to know how many new people had clicked to read her that day, because it frightened her. And it exhilarated her. When she saw her posts reposted on another site, she flushed with accomplishment, and yet she had not imagined any of this, had never nursed any firm ambition. E-mails came from readers who wanted to support the blog. Support. That word made the blog even more apart from her, a separate thing that could thrive or not, sometimes without her and sometimes with her. So she put up a link to her PayPal account. Credits appeared, many small and one so large that when she saw it, she let out an unfamiliar sound, a blend of a gasp and a scream. It began to appear every month, anonymously, as regular as a pay cheque, and each time it did, she felt abashed, as though she had picked up something valuable on the street and kept it for herself. She wondered if it was from Curt, just as she wondered if he followed the blog, and what he thought of being referred to as The Hot White Ex. It was a half-hearted wondering; she missed what could have been, but she no longer missed him.

She checked her blog e-mail too often, like a child eagerly tearing open a present she is not sure she wants, and read mail from people asking for a drink, telling her she was a racist, giving her ideas to blog about. A fellow blogger who made hair butters first suggested advertising and, for a token fee, Ifemelu put up the image of a bounteous-haired woman on the top right side of the blog page; clicking on it led to the hair butter website. Another reader offered more money for a blinking graphic that showed, first, a long-necked model in a tight dress, then the same model in a floppy hat. Clicking on the image led to an online boutique. Soon there were e-mails about advertising Pantene shampoos and Covergirl make-up. Then an e-mail from the director of multicultural life at a prep school in Connecticut, so formal she imagined it typed on hand-cut paper with a silver crest, asking if she would speak to the students on diversity. Another e-mail came from a corporation in Pennsylvania, less formally written, telling her a local professor had identified her as a provocative race blogger and asking if she would lead their annual diversity workshop. An editor from *Baltimore Living* e-mailed to say that they wanted to include her in a Ten People to Watch feature; she was photographed next to her laptop, her face doused in shadow, under the caption "The Blogger". Her readers tripled. More invitations came. To receive phone calls, she wore her most serious pair of trousers, her most muted shade of lipstick, and she spoke sitting upright at her desk, legs crossed, her voice measured and sure. Yet a part of her always stiffened with apprehension, expecting the person on the other end to realize that she was play-acting this professional, this negotiator of terms, to see that she was, in fact, an unemployed person who wore a rumpled nightshirt all day, to call her "Fraud!" and hang up. But more invitations came. Hotel and travel were covered and the fees varied. Once she said, on an impulse, that she wanted twice what she had been offered the previous week, and was shocked when the man calling from Delaware said, "Yeah, we could do that."

Most of the people who attended her first diversity talk, in a small company in Ohio, wore sneakers. They were all white. Her presentation was titled "How to talk about race with colleagues of other races", but who, she wondered, would they be talking to, since they were all white? Perhaps the janitor was black.

"I'm no expert so don't quote me," she started, and they laughed, warm encouraging laughter, and she told herself that this would go well, she need not have worried about talking to a roomful of strangers in the middle of Ohio. (She had read, with mild worry, that openly sundown towns still existed here.) "The first step to honest communication about race is to realize that you cannot equate all racisms," she said, and then launched into her carefully prepared speech. When, at the end, she said, "Thank you," pleased with the fluidness of her delivery, the faces around her were frozen. The leaden clapping deflated her. Afterwards, she was left only with the director of human resources, drinking oversweet iced tea in the conference room, and talking about soccer, which he knew Nigeria played well, as though keen to discuss anything but the talk she had just given. That evening she received an e-mail: *YOUR TALK WAS BALONEY. YOU ARE A RACIST. YOU SHOULD BE GRATEFUL WE LET YOU INTO THIS COUNTRY.*

That e-mail, written in all capital letters, was a revelation. The point of diversity workshops, or multicultural talks, was not to inspire any real change but to leave people feeling good about themselves. They did not want the content of her ideas; they merely wanted the gesture of her presence. They had not read her blog but they had heard that she was a "leading blogger" about race. And so, in the following weeks, as she gave more talks at companies and schools, she began to say what they wanted to hear, none of which she would ever write on her blog, because she knew that the people who read her blog were not the same people who attended her diversity workshops. During her talks, she said: "America has made great progress for which we should be very proud." In her blog she wrote: *Racism should never have happened and so you don't get a cookie for reducing it.* Still more invitations came. She hired a student intern, a Haitian American, her hair worn in elegant twists, who was nimble on the Internet, looking up whatever information Ifemelu needed, and deleting inappropriate comments almost as soon as they were posted.

Ifemelu bought a small condominium. She had been startled, when she first saw the listing in the real estate section of the paper, to realize she could afford the down payment in cash. Signing her name above the word "homeowner" had left her with a frightening sense of being grown-up, and also with a small astonishment, that this was possible because of her blog. She converted one of the two bedrooms into a study and wrote there, standing often by the window to look down at her new Roland Park neighbourhood, the restored row homes shielded by old trees. It surprised her, which blog posts got attention and which were hardly clicked on. Her post about trying to date online, "What's Love Got to Do with It?" continued to draw comments, like something sticky, after many months.

So, still a bit sad about the break-up with The Hot White Ex, not into the bar scene, and so I signed up for online dating. And I looked at lots of profiles. So here's the thing. In that category where you choose the ethnicity you are interested in? White men tick white women, and the braver ones tick Asian and Hispanic. Hispanic men tick white and Hispanic. Black men are the only men likely to tick "all", but some don't even tick Black. They tick White, Asian, Hispanic. I wasn't feeling the love. But what's love got to do with all that ticking, anyway? You could walk into a grocery store and bump into someone and fall in love and that someone would not be the race you tick online. So after browsing, I cancelled my membership, thankfully still on trial, got a refund, and will be walking around blindly in the grocery store instead.

Comments came from people with similar stories and people saying she was wrong, from men asking her to put up a photo of herself, from black women sharing success stories of online dating, from people angry and from people thrilled. Some comments amused her, because they were wildly unconnected to the subject of the post. *Oh fuck off,* one wrote. *Black people get everything easy. You can't get anything in this country unless you're black. Black women are even allowed to weigh more.* Her recurring post "Mish Mash Friday", a jumble of thoughts, drew the most clicks and comments each week. Sometimes she wrote some posts expecting ugly responses, her stomach tight with dread and excitement, but they would draw only tepid comments. Now that she was asked to speak at round-tables and panels, on public radio and community radio, always identified simply as The Blogger, she felt subsumed by her blog. She had become her blog. There were times, lying awake at night, when her growing discomforts crawled out from the crevices, and the blog's many readers became, in her mind, a judgemental angry mob waiting for her, biding their time until they could attack her, unmask her.

Open Thread: For All the Zipped-Up Negroes

This is for the Zipped-Up Negroes, the upwardly mobile American and Non-American Blacks who don't talk about Life Experiences That Have to Do Exclusively with Being Black. Because they want to keep everyone comfortable. Tell your story here. Unzip yourself. This is a safe space.

CHAPTER 34

Her blog brought Blaine back into her life. At the Blogging While Brown convention in Washington, DC, during the meet-and-greet on the first day, the hotel foyer crowded with people saying hello to others in nervously over-bright voices, she had been talking to a make-up blogger, a thin Mexican American woman wearing neon eyeshadow, when she looked up and felt herself still and quake, because standing a few delicate feet from her, in a small circle of people, was Blaine. He was unchanged, except for the black-framed glasses. Just as she remembered him on the train: tall and easy-limbed. The make-up blogger was talking about beauty companies always sending free stuff to *Bellachicana*, and the ethics of it, and Ifemelu was nodding, but was truly alert only to the presence of Blaine, and to him easing himself away from his circle, and moving towards her.

"Hi!" he said, peering at her name tag. "So you're the Non-American Black? I love your blog."

"Thank you," she said. He didn't remember her. But why should he? It had been so long since the meeting on the train, and neither of them knew then what the word "blog" meant. It would amuse him to know how much she had idealized him, how he had become a person made not of flesh but of little crystals of perfection, the American man she would never have. He turned to say hello to the make-up blogger and she saw, from his name tag, that he wrote a blog about the "intersection of academia and popular culture".

He turned back to her. "So are your mall visits in Connecticut still going okay? Because I still grow my own cotton."

For a moment, her breath stalled, and then she laughed, a dizzying, exhilarating laugh, because her life had become a charmed film in which people found each other again. "You remember!"

"I've been watching you from the other end of the room. I couldn't believe it when I saw you."

"Oh my God, what has it been, like ten years?"

"About that. Eight?"

"You never called me back," she said.

"I was in a relationship. It was troubled even then, but it lasted much longer than it should have." He paused, with an expression that she would come to know well, a virtuous narrowing of his eyes that announced the high-mindedness of their owner.

E-mails and phone calls between Baltimore and New Haven followed, playful comments posted on each other's blogs, heavy flirting during late-night calls, until the day in winter when he came to her door, his hands sunk into the pockets of his tin-coloured peacoat and his collar sprinkled with snow like magic dust. She was cooking coconut rice, her apartment thick with spices, a bottle of cheap merlot on her counter, and Nina Simone playing loudly on her CD. The song "Don't Let Me Be Misunderstood" guided them, only minutes after he arrived, across the bridge from flirting friends to lovers. Afterwards, he propped himself up on his elbow to watch her. There was something fluid, almost epicene, about his lean body, and it made her remember that he had told her he did yoga. Perhaps he could stand on his head, twist himself into unlikely permutations. When she mixed the rice, now cold, in the coconut sauce, she told him that cooking bored her, and that she had bought all these spices only the day before, and had cooked because he was visiting. She had imagined them both with ginger on their lips, yellow curry licked off her body, bay leaves crushed beneath them, but instead they had been so responsible, kissing in the living room and then her leading him to her bedroom.

"We should have done things more improbably," she said.

He laughed. "I like cooking, so there will be many opportunities for the improbable." But she knew that he was not the sort of person to do things improbably. Not with his slipping on of the condom with such slow and clinical concentration. Later, when she came to know of the letters he wrote to Congress about Darfur, the teenagers he tutored at the high school on Dixwell, the shelter he volunteered at, she thought of him as a person who did not have a normal spine but had, instead, a firm reed of goodness.

IT WAS AS IF because of their train meeting years ago, they could bypass several steps, ignore several unknowns, and slide into an immediate intimacy. After his first visit, she went back to New Haven with him. There were weeks that winter, cold and sunny weeks, when New Haven seemed lit from within, frosted snow clinging on shrubs, a festive quality to a world that seemed inhabited fully only by her and Blaine. They would walk to the falafel place on Howe Street for hummus, and sit in a dark corner talking for hours, and finally emerge, tongues smarting with garlic. Or she would meet him at the library after his class, where they sat in the café, drinking chocolate that was too rich, eating croissants that were too grainily whole wheat, his clutch of books on the table. He cooked organic vegetables and grains whose names she could not pronounce—bulgur, quinoa—and he swiftly cleaned up as he cooked, a splatter of tomato sauce wiped up as soon as it appeared, a spill of water immediately dabbed at. He frightened her, telling her about the chemicals that were sprayed on crops, the chemicals fed to chickens to make them grow quickly, and the chemicals used to give fruits perfect skin. Why did she think people were dying of cancer? And so before she ate an apple, she scrubbed it at the sink, even though Blaine only bought organic fruit. He told her which grains had protein, which vegetables had carotene, which fruits were too sugary. He knew about everything; she was intimidated by this and proud of this and slightly repelled by this. Little domesticities with him, in his apartment on the twentieth floor of a high-rise near the campus, became gravid with meaning—the way he watched her moisturize with cocoa butter after an evening shower, the whooshing sound his dishwasher made when it started—and she imagined a cot in the bedroom, a baby inside it, and Blaine carefully blending organic fruits for the baby. He would be a perfect father, this man of careful disciplines.

"I can't eat tempeh, I don't understand how you like it," she told him.

"I don't like it."

"Then why eat it?"

"It's good for me."

He ran every morning and flossed every night. It seemed so American to her, flossing, that mechanical sliding of a string between teeth, inelegant and functional. "You should floss every day," Blaine told her. And she began to floss, as she began to do other things that he did—going to the gym, eating more protein than carbohydrates—and she did them with a kind of grateful contentment, because they improved her. He was like a salutary tonic; with him, she could only inhabit a higher level of goodness.

HIS BEST FRIEND, Araminta, came up to visit him, and hugged Ifemelu warmly, as though they had met previously. "Blaine hasn't really dated since he broke up with Paula. And now, he's with a sister, and a chocolate sister at that. We're making progress!" Araminta said.

"Mint, stop it," Blaine said, but he was smiling. That his best friend was a woman, an architect with a long straight weave who wore high heels and tight jeans and coloured contact lenses, said something about Blaine that Ifemelu liked.

"Blaine and I grew up together. In high school, we were the only black kids in our class. All our friends wanted us to date, you know how they think the two black kids just have to be together, but he so wasn't my type," Araminta said.

"You wish," Blaine said.

"Ifemelu, can I just say how happy I am that you're not an academic? Have you heard his friends talk? Nothing is just what it is. Everything has to mean something else. It's ridiculous. The other day Marcia was talking about how black women are fat because their bodies are sites of anti-slavery resistance. Yes, that's true, if burgers and sodas are anti-slavery resistance."

"Anybody can see through that whole anti-intellectual pose thing, Miss Drinks at Harvard Club," Blaine said.

"Come on. A good education isn't the same thing as making the whole damn world something to be explained! Even Shan makes fun of you guys. She does a great imitation of you and Grace: *canon formation and topography of the spatial and historical consciousness.*" Araminta turned to Ifemelu. "You haven't met his sister Shan?"

"No."

Later, when Blaine was in the bedroom, Araminta said, "Shan's an interesting character. Don't take her too seriously when you meet her."

"What do you mean?"

"She's great, she's very seductive, but if you think she slights you or anything like that, it's not you, it's just the way she is." And then she said, in a lower voice, "Blaine's a really good guy, a really good guy."

"I know." Ifemelu sensed, in Araminta's words, something that was either a warning or a plea.

Blaine asked her to move in after a month, but it took a year before she did, even though by then she was spending most of her time in New Haven, and had a Yale gym pass as a professor's partner, and wrote her blogs from his apartment, at a desk he had placed for her near the bedroom window. At first, thrilled by his interest, graced by his intelligence, she let him read her blog posts before she put them up. She did not ask for his edits, but slowly she began to make changes, to add and remove, because of what he said. Then she began to resent it. Her posts sounded too academic, too much like him. She had written a post about inner cities—"Why Are the Dankest, Drabbest Parts of American Cities Full of American Blacks?"—and he told her to include details about government policy and redistricting. She did, but after rereading it, she took down the post.

"I don't want to explain, I want to observe," she said.

"Remember people are not reading you as entertainment, they're reading you as cultural commentary. That's a real responsibility. There are kids writing college essays about your blog," he said. "I'm not saying you have to be academic or boring. Keep your style but add more depth."

"It has enough depth," she said, irritated, but with the niggling thought that he was right.

"You're being lazy, Ifem."

He used that word, "lazy", often, for his students who did not hand in work on time, black celebrities who were not politically active, ideas that did not match his own. Sometimes she felt like his apprentice;

when they wandered through museums, he would linger at abstract paintings, which bored her, and she would drift to the bold sculptures or the naturalistic paintings, and sense in his tight smile his disappointment that she had not yet learned enough from him. When he played selections from his complete John Coltrane, he would watch her as she listened, waiting for a rapture he was sure would glaze over her, and then at the end, when she remained untransported, he would quickly avert his eyes. She blogged about two novels she loved, by Ann Petry and Gayl Jones, and Blaine said, "They don't push the boundaries." He spoke gently, as though he did not want to upset her, but it still had to be said. His positions were firm, so thought-through and fully realized in his own mind that he sometimes seemed surprised that she, too, had not arrived at them herself. She felt a step removed from the things he believed, and the things he knew, and she was eager to play catch-up, fascinated by his sense of rightness. Once, as they walked down Elm Street, on their way to get a sandwich, they saw the plump black woman who was a fixture on campus: always standing near the coffee shop, a woollen hat squashed on her head, offering single plastic red roses to passers-by and asking "You got any change?" Two students were talking to her, and then one of them gave her a cappuccino in a tall paper cup. The woman looked thrilled; she threw her head back and drank from the cup.

"That's so disgusting," Blaine said, as they walked past.

"I know," Ifemelu said, although she did not quite understand why he felt so strongly about the homeless woman and her cappuccino gift. Weeks before, an older white woman standing in line behind them at the grocery store had said, "Your hair is so beautiful, can I touch it?" and Ifemelu said yes. The woman sank her fingers into her Afro. She sensed Blaine tense, saw the pulsing at his temples. "How could you let her do that?" he asked afterwards. "Why not? How else will she know what hair like mine feels like? She probably doesn't know any black people."

"And so you have to be her guinea pig?" Blaine asked. He expected her to feel what she did not know how to feel. There were things that existed for him that she could not penetrate. With his close friends, she often felt vaguely lost. They were youngish and well-dressed and righteous, their sentences filled with "sort of", and "the ways in which";

they gathered at a bar every Thursday, and sometimes one of them had a dinner party, where Ifemelu mostly listened, saying little, looking at them in wonder: were they serious, these people who were so enraged about imported vegetables that ripened in trucks? They wanted to stop child labour in Africa. They would not buy clothes made by underpaid workers in Asia. They looked at the world with an impractical, luminous earnestness that moved her, but never convinced her. Surrounded by them, Blaine hummed with references unfamiliar to her, and he would seem far away, as though he belonged to them, and when he finally looked at her, his eyes warm and loving, she felt something like relief.

SHE TOLD her parents about Blaine, that she was leaving Baltimore and moving to New Haven to live with him. She could have lied, invented a new job, or simply said she wanted to move. "His name is Blaine," she said. "He's an American."

She heard the symbolism in her own words, travelling thousands of miles to Nigeria, and she knew what her parents would understand. She and Blaine had not talked about marriage, but the ground beneath her feet felt firm. She wanted her parents to know of him, and of how good he was. She used that word in describing him: "good".

"An American Negro?" her father asked, sounding baffled.

Ifemelu burst out laughing. "Daddy, nobody says Negro any more."

"But why a Negro? Is there a substantive scarcity of Nigerians there?"

She ignored him, still laughing, and asked him to give her mother the phone. Ignoring him, even telling him that she was moving in with a man to whom she was not married, was something she could do only because she lived in America. Rules had shifted, fallen into the cracks of distance and foreignness.

Her mother asked, "Is he a Christian?"

"No. He is a devil-worshipper."

"Blood of Jesus!" her mother shrieked.

"Mummy, yes, he is a Christian," she said.

"Then no problem," her mother said. "When will he come to introduce himself? You can plan it so that we do everything at the same time—door-knocking, bride price and wine-carrying—it will cut costs and that way he does not have to keep coming and going. America is far . . ."

"Mummy, please, we are taking things slowly for now."

After Ifemelu hung up, still amused, she decided to change the title of her blog to *Raceteenth or Various Observations About American Blacks (Those Formerly Known as Negroes) by a Non-American Black.*

Job Vacancy in America—National Arbiter in Chief of "Who Is Racist"

In America, racism exists but racists are all gone. Racists belong to the past. Racists are the thin-lipped mean white people in the movies about the civil rights era. Here's the thing: the manifestation of racism has changed but the language has not. So if you haven't lynched somebody then you can't be called a racist. If you're not a bloodsucking monster, then you can't be called a racist. Somebody has to be able to say that racists are not monsters. They are people with loving families, regular folk who pay taxes. Somebody needs to get the job of deciding who is racist and who isn't. Or maybe it's time to just scrap the word "racist." Find something new. Like Racial Disorder Syndrome. And we could have different categories for sufferers of this syndrome: mild, medium, and acute.

CHAPTER 35

Ifemelu woke up one night to go to the bathroom, and heard Blaine in the living room, talking on the phone, his tone gentle and solacing. "I'm sorry, did I wake you? That was my sister, Shan," he said when he came back to bed. "She's back in New York, from France. Her first book is about to be published and she's having a small meltdown about it." He paused. "Another small meltdown. Shan has lots of meltdowns. Will you go down to the city this weekend with me to see her?"

"Sure. What does she do again?"

"What doesn't Shan do? She used to work at a hedge fund. Then she left and travelled all over the world and did a bit of journalism. She met this Haitian guy and moved to Paris to live with him. Then he got sick and died. It happened very quickly. She stayed for a while, and even after she decided to move back to the States, she kept the flat in Paris. She's been with this new guy, Ovidio, for about a year now. He's the first real relationship she's had since Jerry died. Pretty decent cat. He's away this week, on assignment in California, so Shan's alone. She likes to have these gatherings, she calls them salons. She has an amazing group of friends, mostly artists and writers, and they get together at her place and have really good conversations." He paused. "She's a really special person."

WHEN SHAN WALKED into a room, all the air disappeared. She did not breathe deeply; she did not need to: the air simply floated towards her, drawn by her natural authority, until there was nothing left for others. Ifemelu imagined Blaine's airless childhood, running after

Shan to impress her, to remind her of his existence. Even now, as an adult, he was still the little brother full of desperate love, trying to win an approval that he feared he never would. They arrived at Shan's apartment early in the afternoon, and Blaine stopped to chat with the doorman, as he had chatted with their taxi driver from Penn Station, in that unforced manner that he had, forming alliances with janitors, with cleaning staff, with bus drivers. He knew how much they made and how many hours they worked; he knew they didn't have health insurance.

"Hey, Jorge, how's it going?" Blaine pronounced it the Spanish way: *Hor-hay.*

"Pretty good. How are your students over at Yale?" the doorman asked, looking pleased to see him and pleased that he taught at Yale.

"Driving me crazy as usual," Blaine said. Then he pointed at the woman standing by the elevator with her back to them, cradling a pink yoga mat. "Oh, there's Shan." Shan was tiny and beautiful, with an oval face and high cheekbones, an imperious face.

"Hey!" she said, and hugged Blaine. She did not look once at Ifemelu. "I'm so glad I went to my Pilates class. It leaves you if you leave it. Did you go running today?"

"Yep."

"I just talked to David again. He says he'll send me alternative covers this evening. Finally they seem to be hearing me." She rolled her eyes. The elevator's doors slid open and she led the way in, still talking to Blaine, who now seemed uncomfortable, as though he was waiting for a moment to make introductions, a moment that Shan was not willing to give.

"The marketing director called me this morning. She had that really unbearable politeness that is worse than any insult, you know? And so she tells me how booksellers love the cover already and blah blah blah. It's ridiculous," Shan said.

"It's the herd instinct of corporate publishing. They do what everyone else does," Blaine said.

The elevator stopped at her floor, and she turned to Ifemelu. "Oh, sorry, I'm so stressed," she said. "It's nice to meet you. Blaine won't stop talking about you." She looked at Ifemelu, a frank sizing-up that was not shy to be a frank sizing-up. "You're very pretty."

"*You're* very pretty," Ifemelu said, surprising herself, because those were not the words she would have ordinarily said, but she felt already co-opted by Shan; Shan's compliment had made her strangely happy. Shan is special, Blaine had said, and Ifemelu understood now what he meant. Shan had the air of a person who was somehow *chosen*. The gods had placed a wand on her. If she did ordinary things, they became enigmatic.

"Do you like the room?" Shan asked Ifemelu, with a sweep of her hand, taking in the dramatic furnishing: a red rug, a blue sofa, an orange sofa, a green armchair.

"I know it's supposed to mean something but I don't get it."

Shan laughed, short sounds that seemed cut off prematurely, as though more were supposed to follow but did not, and because she merely laughed, not saying anything, Ifemelu added, "It's interesting."

"Yes, *interesting*." Shan stood by the dining table and raised her leg onto it, leaning over to grasp her foot in her hand. Her body was a collection of graceful small curves, her buttocks, her breasts, her calves, and there was in her movement the entitlement of the chosen; she could stretch her leg on her dining table whenever she wanted, even with a guest in her apartment.

"Blaine introduced me to *Raceteenth*. It's a great blog," she said.

"Thank you," Ifemelu said.

"I have a Nigerian friend who is a writer. Do you know Kelechi Garuba?"

"I've read his work."

"We talked about your blog the other day and he said he was sure the Non-American Black was a Caribbean because Africans don't care about race. He'll be shocked when he meets you!" Shan paused to exchange the leg on the table, leaning in to grasp her foot.

"He's always fretting about how his books don't do well. I've told him he needs to write terrible things about his own people if he wants to do well. He needs to say Africans alone are to blame for African problems, and Europeans have helped Africa more than they've hurt Africa, and he'll be famous and people will say he's so *honest*!"

Ifemelu laughed.

"Interesting picture," she said, gesturing to a photo on a side table, of Shan holding two bottles of champagne high above her head, surrounded by tattered, smiling, brown children in what looked like a Latin American slum, shacks with patched-up tin walls behind her. "I mean interesting literally."

"Ovidio didn't want it displayed but I insisted. It's supposed to be ironic, obviously."

Ifemelu imagined the insisting, a simple sentence, which would not need to be repeated and which would have Ovidio scrambling.

"So do you go home to Nigeria often?" Shan asked.

"No. Actually I haven't been home since I came to the States."

"Why?"

"At first I couldn't afford to. Then I had work and just never seemed to make the time."

Shan was facing her now, her arms stretched out and pushed back like wings.

"Nigerians call us *acata*, right? And it means wild animal?"

"I don't know that it means wild animal, I really don't know what it means, and I don't use it." Ifemelu found herself almost stammering. It was true and yet in the directness of Shan's gaze, she felt guilty. Shan dripped power, a subtle and devastating kind.

Blaine emerged from the kitchen with two tall glasses of a reddish liquid.

"Virgin cocktails!" Shan said, with a childish delight, as she took a glass from Blaine.

"Pomegranate, sparkling water and a bit of cranberry," Blaine said, giving Ifemelu the other glass. "So when are you going to have the next salon, Shan? I was telling Ifemelu about them."

When Blaine had told Ifemelu about Shan calling her gatherings "salons", he had underlined the word with mockery, but now he said it with an earnestly French pronunciation: *sa-lon.*

"Oh, soon, I guess." Shan shrugged, fond and offhand, sipped from her glass and then leaned sideways in a stretch, like a tree bent by wind.

Shan's cell phone rang. "Where did I put that phone? It's probably David."

The phone was on the table. "Oh, it's Luc. I'll call him back later."

"Who's Luc?" Blaine asked, coming out of the kitchen.

"This French guy, rich guy. It's funny, I met him at the airport for fuck's sake. I tell him I have a boyfriend and he goes 'Then I will admire from afar and bide my time.' He actually said 'bide'." Shan sipped her drink. "It's nice how in Europe, white men look at you like a woman, not a black woman. Now I don't want to date them, hell no, I just want to know the possibility is there."

Blaine was nodding, agreeing. If anybody else had said what Shan did, he would instantly comb through the words in search of nuance, and he would disagree with their sweep, their simplicity. Ifemelu had once told him, as they watched a news item about a celebrity divorce, that she did not understand the unbending, unambiguous honesties that Americans required in relationships. "What do you mean?" he asked her, and she heard a looming disagreement in his voice; he, too, believed in unbending, unambiguous honesties.

"It's different for me and I think it's because I'm from the Third World," she said. "To be a child of the Third World is to be aware of the many different constituencies you have and how honesty and truth must always depend on context." She had felt clever to have thought of this explanation but Blaine shook his head even before she finished speaking and said, "That is so lazy, to use the Third World like that."

Now he was nodding as Shan said, "Europeans are just not as conservative and uptight about relationships as Americans are. In Europe the white men are thinking 'I just want a hot woman.' In America the white men are thinking 'I won't touch a black woman but I could maybe do Halle Berry.'"

"That's funny," Blaine said.

"Of course, there's the niche of white men in this country who will only date black women, but that's a kind of fetish and it's nasty," Shan said, and then turned her glowing gaze on Ifemelu.

Ifemelu was almost reluctant to disagree; it was strange, how much she wanted Shan to like her. "Actually my experience has been the opposite. I get a lot more interest from white men than from African American men."

"Really?" Shan paused. "I guess it's your exotic credential, that whole Authentic African thing."

It stung her, the rub of Shan's dismissal, and then it became a prickly resentment directed at Blaine, because she wished he would not agree so heartily with his sister.

Shan's phone rang again. "Oh, that had better be David!" She took the phone into the bedroom.

"David is her editor. They want to put this sexualized image, a black torso, on her cover and she's fighting it," Blaine said.

"Really." Ifemelu sipped her drink and flipped through an art magazine, still irritated with him.

"Are you okay?" he asked.

"I'm fine."

Shan was back. Blaine looked at her. "All okay?"

She nodded. "They're not using it. Everyone seems to be on the same page now."

"That's great," Blaine said.

"You should be my guest blogger for a couple of days when your book comes out," Ifemelu said. "You would be amazing. I would love to have you."

Shan raised her eyebrows, an expression Ifemelu could not read, and she feared that she had been too gushing.

"Yes, I guess I could," Shan said.

Obama Can Win Only If He Remains the Magic Negro

His pastor is scary because it means maybe Obama is not the Magic Negro after all. By the way, the pastor is pretty melodramatic, but have you been to an old school American Black church? Pure theater. But this guy's basic point is true: that American Blacks (certainly those his age) know an America different from American Whites; they know a harsher, uglier America. But you're not supposed to say that, because in America everything is fine and everyone is the same. So now that the pastor's said it, maybe Obama thinks so too, and if Obama thinks so then he isn't the Magic Negro and only a Magic Negro can win an American election. And what's a Magic Negro, you ask? The black man who is eternally wise and kind. He never reacts under great suffering, never gets angry, is never threatening. He always forgives all kinds of racist shit. He teaches the white person how to break down the sad but understandable prejudice in his heart. You see this man in many films. And Obama is straight from central casting.

CHAPTER 36

It was a surprise birthday party in Hamden, for Marcia, Blaine's friend.

"Happy birthday, Marcia!" Ifemelu said in a chorus with the other friends, standing beside Blaine. Her tongue a little heavy in her mouth, her excitement a little forced. She had been with Blaine for more than a year, but she did not quite belong with his friends.

"You bastard!" Marcia said to her husband, Benny, laughing, tears in her eyes.

Marcia and Benny both taught history, they came from the South and they even looked alike, with their smallish bodies and honey complexions and long locs grazing their necks. They wore their love like a heavy perfume, exuding a transparent commitment, touching each other, referring to each other. Watching them, Ifemelu imagined this life for her and Blaine, in a small house on a quiet street, batiks hung on the walls, African sculptures glowering in corners, and both of them existing in a steady hum of happiness.

Benny was pouring drinks. Marcia was walking around, still stunned, looking into the trays of catered food spread on the dining table, and then up at the mass of balloons bobbing against the ceiling. "When did you do all this, baby? I was just gone an hour!"

She hugged everyone, while wiping the tears from her eyes. Before she hugged Ifemelu, a wrinkle of worry flickered on her face, and Ifemelu knew that Marcia had forgotten her name. "*So* good to see you again, thank you for coming," she said, with an extra dose of sincerity, the "so" emphasized, as though to make up for forgetting Ifemelu's name.

"Chile!" she said to Blaine, who hugged her and lifted her slightly off the floor, both of them laughing.

"You're lighter than you were on your last birthday!" Blaine said.

"And she looks younger every day!" Paula, Blaine's ex-girlfriend, said.

"Marcia, are you going to bottle your secret?" a woman whom Ifemelu did not know asked, her bleached hair bouffant like a platinum helmet.

"Her secret is good sex," Grace said seriously, a Korean American woman who taught African American studies, tiny and slender, always in stylishly loose-fitting clothes, so that she seemed to float in a swish of silks. "I'm that rare thing, a Christian left-wing nut," she had told Ifemelu when they first met.

"Did you hear that, Benny?" Marcia asked. "Our secret is good sex."

"That's right!" Benny said, and winked at her. "Hey, anybody see Barack Obama's announcement this morning?"

"Yes, it's been on the news all day," Paula said. She was short and blonde, with a clear pinkish complexion, outdoorsy and healthy, that made Ifemelu wonder if she rode horses.

"I don't even have a television," Grace said, with a self-mocking sigh. "I only recently sold out and got a cell phone."

"They'll replay it," Benny said.

"Let's eat!" It was Stirling, the wealthy one, who Blaine told her came from Boston old money; he and his father had been legacy students at Harvard. He was left-leaning and well-meaning, crippled by his acknowledgement of his own many privileges. He never allowed himself to have an opinion. "Yes, I see what you mean," he said often.

The food was eaten with a lot of praise and wine, the fried chicken, the greens, the pies. Ifemelu took tiny portions, pleased she had snacked on some nuts before they left; she did not like soul food.

"I haven't had corn bread this good in years," Nathan said, seated beside her. He was a literature professor, neurotic and blinky behind his glasses, who Blaine once said was the only person at Yale that he trusted completely. Nathan had told her, some months earlier, in a voice filled with hauteur, that he did not read any fiction published after 1930. "It all went downhill after the thirties," he said.

She had told Blaine about it later, and there was an impatience in her tone, almost an accusation, as she added that academics were not intellectuals; they were not curious, they built their stolid tents of specialized knowledge and stayed securely in them.

Blaine said, "Oh, Nathan just has his issues. It's not about being an academic." A new defensiveness had begun to creep into Blaine's tone when they talked about his friends, perhaps because he sensed her discomfort with them. When she attended a talk with him, he would make sure to say it could have been better, or that the first ten minutes were boring, as though to pre-empt her own criticisms. The last talk they had attended was his ex-girlfriend Paula's, at a college in Middletown, Paula standing in front of the classroom, in a dark-green wrap dress and boots, sounding fluid and convinced, provoking and charming her audience at the same time; the young pretty political scientist who would certainly get tenure. She had glanced often at Blaine, like a student at a professor, gauging her performance from his expression. As she spoke, Blaine nodded continuously, and once even sighed aloud as though her words had brought to him a familiar and exquisite epiphany. They had remained good friends, Paula and Blaine, had kept in the same circle after she cheated on him with a woman also named Paula, and now called Pee to distinguish them from each other. "Our relationship had been in trouble for a while. She said she was just experimenting with Pee but I could tell it was much more, and I was right because they're still together," Blaine told Ifemelu, and it all seemed to her to be too tame, too civil. Even Paula's friendliness towards her seemed too scrubbed clean.

"How about we ditch him and go and have one drink?" Paula had said to Ifemelu that evening after her talk, her cheeks flushed from the excitement and relief of having done well.

"I'm exhausted," Ifemelu had said.

Blaine said, "And I need to prep for class tomorrow. Let's do something this weekend, okay?" And he hugged her goodbye.

"It wasn't too bad, was it?" Blaine asked Ifemelu on their drive back to New Haven.

"I was sure you were going to have an orgasm," she said, and Blaine laughed. She had thought, watching Paula speak, that Paula was comfortable with Blaine's rhythms in a way that she was not, and she thought so now, as she watched Paula eat her third helping of collard greens, sitting next to her girlfriend Pee and laughing at something Marcia had said.

The woman with the helmetlike hair was eating her collard greens with her fingers.

"We humans are not supposed to eat with utensils," she said.

Michael, seated beside Ifemelu, snorted loudly. "Why don't you just go on and live in a cave?" he asked, and they all laughed, but Ifemelu was not sure he had been joking. He had no patience for fey talk. She liked him, cornrows running down the length of his scalp, and his expression always wry, scornful of sentimentality. "Michael's a good cat but he tries so hard to keep it real that he can seem full of negativity," Blaine had said when she first met Michael. Michael had been in prison for a carjacking when he was nineteen and he was fond of saying "Some black folk don't appreciate education until after they go to prison." He was a photographer on a fellowship and the first time Ifemelu saw his photographs, in black-and-white, in dances of shadow, their delicacy and vulnerability had surprised her. She had expected grittier imagery. Now one of those photographs hung on the wall in Blaine's apartment, opposite her writing desk.

From across the table, Paula asked, "Did I tell you I'm having my students read your blog, Ifemelu? It's interesting how safe their thinking is and I want to push them out of their comfort zone. I loved the last post, 'Friendly Tips for the American Non-Black: How to React to an American Black Talking About Blackness.'"

"That is funny!" Marcia said. "I'd love to read that."

Paula brought out her phone and fiddled with it and then began to read aloud.

Dear American Non-Black, if an American Black person is telling you about an experience about being black, please do not eagerly bring up examples from your own life. Don't say "It's just like when I . . ." You have suffered. Everyone in the world has suffered. But you have not suffered precisely because you are an American Black. Don't be quick to find alternative explanations for what happened. Don't say "Oh, it's not really race, it's class. Oh, it's not race, it's gender. Oh, it's not race, it's the cookie monster." You see, American Blacks actually don't WANT it to be race. They would rather not have racist shit happen. So maybe when they say something is about race, it's maybe because it actually is? Don't say "I'm color-blind," because if you are color-blind, then you need to see a doctor and it means that when a black man is shown on TV as a crime suspect in your neighborhood, all you see is a blurry purplish-grayish-creamish figure. Don't say "We're tired of talking about race" or "The only race is the human race." American Blacks, too, are tired of talking about race. They wish they didn't have to. But shit keeps happening. Don't preface your response with "One of my best friends is black" because it makes no difference and nobody cares and you can have a black best friend and still do racist shit and it's probably not true anyway, the "best" part, not the "friend" part. Don't say your grandfather was Mexican so you can't be racist (please click here for more on There Is No United League of the Oppressed). Don't bring up your Irish great-grandparents' suffering. Of course they got a lot of shit from established America. So did the Italians. So did the Eastern Europeans. But there was a hierarchy. A hundred years ago, the white ethnics hated being hated, but it was sort of tolerable because at least black people were below them on the ladder. Don't say your grandfather was a serf in Russia when slavery happened because what matters is you are American now and being American means you take the whole shebang, America's assets and America's debts, and Jim Crow is a big-ass debt. Don't say it's just like antisemitism. It's not. In the hatred of Jews, there is also the possibility of envy—they are so clever, these Jews, they control everything, these Jews—and one must concede that a certain respect, however grudging, accompanies envy. In the hatred of American Blacks, there is no possibility of envy—they are so lazy, these blacks, they are so unintelligent, these blacks.

Don't say "Oh, racism is over, slavery was so long ago." We are talking about problems from the 1960s, not the 1860s. If you meet an elderly American black man from Alabama, he probably remembers when he had to step off the curb because a white person was walking past. I bought a dress from a vintage shop on eBay the other day, made in 1960, in perfect shape, and I wear it a lot. When the original owner wore it, black Americans could not vote because they were black. (And maybe the original owner was one of those women, in the famous sepia photographs, standing by in hordes outside schools shouting "Ape!" at young black children because they did not want them to go to school with their young white children. Where are those women now? Do they sleep well? Do they think about shouting "Ape"?) Finally, don't put on a

Let's Be Fair tone and say "But black people are racist too." Because of course we're all prejudiced (I can't even stand some of my blood relatives, grasping, selfish folks), but racism is about the power of a group and in America it's white folks who have that power. How? Well, white folks don't get treated like shit in upper-class African American communities and white folks don't get denied bank loans or mortgages precisely because they are white and black juries don't give white criminals worse sentences than black criminals for the same crime and black police officers don't stop white folk for driving while white and black companies don't choose not to hire somebody because their name sounds white and black teachers don't tell white kids that they're not smart enough to be doctors and black politicians don't try some tricks to reduce the voting power of white folks through gerrymandering and advertising agencies don't say they can't use white models to advertise glamorous products because they are not considered "aspirational" by the "mainstream."

So after this listing of don'ts, what's the do? I'm not sure. Try listening, maybe. Hear what is being said. And remember that it's not about you. American Blacks are not telling you that you are to blame. They are just telling you what is. If you don't understand, ask questions. If you're uncomfortable about asking questions, say you are uncomfortable about asking questions and then ask anyway. It's easy to tell when a question is coming from a good place. Then listen some more. Sometimes people just want to feel heard. Here's to possibilities of friendship and connection and understanding.

Marcia said, "I love the part about the dress!"

"It's cringe-funny," Nathan said.

"So you must be raking in the speaking fees from that blog," Michael said.

"Only most of it goes to my hungry relatives back in Nigeria," Ifemelu said.

"It must be good to have that," he said.

"To have what?"

"To know where you're from. Ancestors going way back, that kind of thing."

"Well," she said. "Yes."

He looked at her, with an expression that made her uncomfortable, because she was not sure what his eyes held, and then he looked away.

Blaine was telling Marcia's friend with the helmetlike hair, "We need to get over that myth. There was nothing Judaeo-Christian about American history. Nobody liked Catholics and Jews. It's Anglo-Protestant values, not Judaeo-Christian values. Even Maryland very quickly stopped being so Catholic-friendly." He stopped abruptly and brought his phone out of his pocket and got up. "Excuse me, folks," he said, and then in a lower voice to Ifemelu, "It's Shan. I'll be right back," and walked into the kitchen to take the call.

Benny turned on the TV and they watched Barack Obama, a thin man in a black coat that looked a size too big, his demeanour slightly uncertain. As he spoke, puffs of cloudy steam left his mouth, like smoke, in the cold air. *"And that is why, in the shadow of the Old State Capitol, where Lincoln once called on a divided house to stand together, where common hopes and common dreams still live, I stand before you today to announce my candidacy for president of the United States of America."*

"I can't believe they've talked him into this. The guy has potential, but he needs to grow first. He needs some heft. He'll ruin it for black people because he won't come close and a black person won't be able to run for the next fifty years in this country," Grace said.

"He just makes me feel good!" Marcia said, laughing. "I love that, the idea of building a more hopeful America."

"I think he stands a chance," Benny said.

"Oh, he can't win. They'd shoot his ass first," Michael said.

"It's so refreshing to see a politician who gets nuance," Paula said.

"Yes," Pee said. She had overly toned arms, thin and bulging with muscles, a pixie haircut and an air of intense anxiety; she was the sort of person whose love would suffocate. "He sounds so smart, so articulate."

"*You* sound like my mother," Paula said in the barbed tone of a private fight being continued, words meaning other things. "Why is it so remarkable that he's articulate?"

"Are we hormonal, Pauly?" Marcia asked.

"She is!" Pee said. "Did you see she's eaten all the fried chicken?"

Paula ignored Pee, and, as though in defiance, reached out to have another slice of pumpkin pie.

"What do you think of Obama, Ifemelu?" Marcia asked, and Ifemelu guessed that Benny or Grace had whispered her name in Marcia's ear, and now Marcia was eager to unleash her new knowledge.

"I like Hillary Clinton," Ifemelu said. "I don't really know anything about this Obama guy."

Blaine came back into the room. "What did I miss?"

"Shan okay?" Ifemelu asked. Blaine nodded.

"It doesn't matter what anybody thinks of Obama. The real question is whether white people are ready for a black president," Nathan said.

"I'm ready for a black president. But I don't think the nation is," Pee said.

"Seriously, have you been talking to my mom?" Paula asked her. "She said the exact same thing. If you're ready for a black president, then who exactly is this vague country that isn't ready? People say that when they can't say that *they* are not ready. And even the idea of being ready is ridiculous."

Ifemelu borrowed those words months later, in a blog post written during the final, frenzied lap of the presidential campaign: "Even the Idea of Being Ready Is Ridiculous." *Does nobody see how absurd it is to ask people if they are ready for a black president? Are you ready for Mickey Mouse to be president? How about Kermit the Frog? And Rudolph the Red-Nosed Reindeer?*

"My family has impeccable liberal credentials, we've ticked all the right boxes," Paula said, lips turned down in irony, twirling the stem of her empty wineglass. "But my parents were always quick to tell their friends that Blaine was at Yale. As if they were saying he's one of the few good ones."

"You're being too hard on them, Pauly," Blaine said.

"No, really, didn't you think so?" she asked. "Remember that awful Thanksgiving at my parents' house?"

"You mean how I wanted mac and cheese?"

Paula laughed. "No, that's not what I mean." But she did not say what she meant and so the memory was left unaired, wrapped in their shared privacy.

Back in Blaine's apartment, Ifemelu told him, "I was jealous."

It *was* jealousy, the twinge of unease, the unsettledness in her stomach. Paula had the air of a real ideologue; she could, Ifemelu imagined, slip easily into anarchy, stand at the forefront of protests, defying the clubs of policemen and the taunts of unbelievers. To sense this about Paula was to feel wanting, compared to her.

"There's nothing to be jealous about, Ifem," Blaine said.

"The fried chicken you eat is not the fried chicken I eat, but it's the fried chicken that Paula eats."

"What?"

"For you and Paula, fried chicken is battered. For me, fried chicken has no batter. I just thought about how you both have a lot in common."

"We have fried chicken in common? Do you realize how loaded fried chicken is as a metaphor here?" Blaine was laughing, a gentle, affectionate laugh. "Your jealousy is kind of sweet, but there is no chance at all of anything going on."

She knew there was nothing going on. Blaine would not cheat on her. He was too sinewy with goodness. Fidelity came easily to him; he did not turn to glance at pretty women on the street because it did not occur to him. But she was jealous of the emotional remnants that existed between him and Paula, and by the thought that Paula was like him, good like him.

Traveling While Black

A friend of a friend, a cool AB with tons of money, is writing a book called Traveling While Black. Not just black, he says, but recognizably black because there's all kinds of black and no offense but he doesn't mean those black folk who look Puerto Rican or Brazilian or whatever, he means recognizably black. Because the world treats you differently. So here's what he says: "I got the idea for the book in Egypt. So I get to Cairo and this Egyptian Arab guy calls me a black barbarian. I'm like, hey, this is supposed to be Africa! So I started thinking about other parts of the world and what it would be like to travel there if you're black. I'm as black as they get. White folk in the South today would look at me and think there goes a big black buck. They tell you in the guidebooks what to expect if you're gay or if you're a woman. Hell, they need to do it for if you're recognizably black. Let traveling black folk know what the deal is. It's not like anybody is going to shoot you but it's great to know where to expect that people will stare at you. In the German Black Forest, it's pretty hostile staring. In Tokyo and Istanbul, everyone was cool and indifferent. In Shanghai the staring was intense, in Delhi it was nasty. I thought, 'Hey, aren't we kind of in this together? You know, people of color and all?' I'd been reading that Brazil is the race mecca and I go to Rio and nobody looks like me in the nice restaurants and the nice hotels. People act funny when I'm walking to the first-class line at the airport. Kind of nice funny, like you're making a mistake, you can't look like that and fly first class. I go to Mexico and they're staring at me. It's not hostile at all, but it just makes you know you stick out, kind of like they like you but you're still King Kong." And at this point my Professor Hunk says, "Latin America as a whole has a really complicated relationship with blackness, which is overshadowed by that whole 'we are all mestizo' story that they tell themselves. Mexico isn't as bad as places like Guatemala and Peru, where the white privilege is so much more overt, but then those countries have a much more sizable black population." And then another friend says, "Native blacks are always treated worse than non-native blacks everywhere in the world. My friend who was born and raised in France of Togolese parents pretends to be Anglophone when she goes shopping in Paris, because the shop attendants are nicer to black people who don't speak French. Just like American Blacks get a lot of respect in African countries." Thoughts? Please post your own Traveling Tales.

CHAPTER 37

It seemed to Ifemelu as though she had glanced away for a moment, and looked back to find Dike transformed; her little cousin was gone, and in his place a boy who did not look like a boy, six feet tall with lean muscles, playing basketball for Willow High School, and dating the nimble blonde girl Page, who wore tiny skirts and Converse sneakers. Once, when Ifemelu asked, "So how are things going with Page?" Dike replied, "We're not yet having sex, if that's what you want to know."

In the evenings, six or seven friends converged in his room, all of them white except for Min, the tall Chinese boy whose parents taught at the university. They played computer games and watched videos on YouTube, needling and jousting, all of them enclosed in a sparkling arc of careless youth, and at their centre was Dike. They all laughed at Dike's jokes, and looked to him for agreement, and in a delicate, unspoken way, they let him make their collective decisions: ordering pizza, going down to the community centre to play Ping-Pong. With them, Dike changed; he took on a swagger in his voice and in his gait, his shoulders squared, as though in a high-gear performance, and sprinkled his speech with "ain't" and "y'all".

"Why do you talk like that with your friends, Dike?" Ifemelu asked.

"Yo, Coz, how you gonna treat me like that?" he said, with an exaggerated funny face that made her laugh.

Ifemelu imagined him in college; he would be a perfect student guide, leading a pack of would-be students and their parents, showing them the wonderful things about the campus and making sure to add one thing he personally disliked, all the time being relentlessly funny and bright and bouncy, and the girls would have instant crushes on him, the boys would be envious of his panache, and the parents would wish their kids were like him.

SHAN WORE a sparkly gold top, her breasts unbound, swinging as she moved. She flirted with everyone, touching an arm, hugging too closely, lingering over a cheek kiss. Her compliments were clotted with an extravagance that made them seem insincere, yet her friends smiled and bloomed under them. It did not matter what was said; it mattered that it was Shan who said it. Her first time at Shan's salon, and Ifemelu was nervous. There was no need to be, it was a mere gathering of friends, but still she was nervous. She had agonized about what to wear, tried on and discarded nine outfits before she decided on a teal dress that made her waist look small.

"Hey!" Shan said, when Blaine and Ifemelu arrived, exchanging hugs.

"Is Grace coming?" she asked Blaine.

"Yes. She's taking the later train."

"Great. I haven't seen her in ages." Shan lowered her voice and said to Ifemelu, "I heard Grace steals her students' research."

"What?"

"Grace. I heard she steals her students' research. Did you know that?"

"No," Ifemelu said. She found it strange, Shan telling her this about Blaine's friend, and yet it made her feel special, admitted into Shan's intimate cave of gossip. Then, suddenly ashamed that she had not been strong enough in her defence of Grace, whom she liked, she said, "I don't think that's true at all."

But Shan's attention was already elsewhere.

"I want you to meet the sexiest man in New York, Omar," Shan said, introducing Ifemelu to a man as tall as a basketball player, whose hairline was too perfectly shaped, a sharp curve sweeping his forehead, sharp angles dipping near his ears. When Ifemelu reached out to shake his hand, he bowed slightly, hand on his chest, and smiled.

"Omar doesn't touch women to whom he is not related," Shan said. "Which is very sexy, no?" And she tilted her head to look up suggestively at Omar.

"This is the beautiful and utterly original Maribelle, and her girlfriend Joan, who is just as beautiful. They make me feel bad!" Shan said, while Maribelle and Joan giggled, smallish white women in dark-framed oversize glasses. They both wore short dresses, one in red polka-dot, the other lace-fringed, with the slightly faded, slightly ill-fitting look of vintage-shop finds. It was, in some ways, costume. They ticked the boxes of a certain kind of enlightened, educated middle-classness, the love of dresses that were more interesting than pretty, the love of the eclectic, the love of what they were supposed to love. Ifemelu imagined them when they travelled: they would collect unusual things and fill their homes with them, unpolished evidence of their polish.

"Here's Bill!" Shan said, hugging the muscular dark man in a fedora. "Bill is a writer but unlike the rest of us, he has oodles of money." Shan was almost cooing. "Bill has this great idea for a travel book called *Traveling While Black.*"

"I'd love to hear about it," Ashanti said.

"By the way, Ashanti, girl, I adore your hair," Shan said.

"Thank you!" Ashanti said. She was a vision in cowries: they rattled from her wrists, were strung through her curled dreadlocks, and looped around her neck. She said "motherland" and "Yoruba religion" often, glancing at Ifemelu as though for confirmation, and it was a parody of Africa that Ifemelu felt uncomfortable about and then felt bad for feeling so uncomfortable.

"You finally have a book cover you like?" Ashanti asked Shan.

"'Like' is a strong word," Shan said. "So, everyone, this book is a memoir, right? It's about tons of stuff, growing up in this all-white town, being the only black kid in my prep school, my mom's passing, all that stuff. My editor reads the manuscript and says, 'I understand that race is important here but we have to make sure the book transcends race, so that it's not just about race.' And I'm thinking, But why do I have to transcend race? You know, like race is a brew best served mild, tempered with other liquids, otherwise white folk can't swallow it."

"That's funny," Blaine said.

"He kept flagging the dialogue in the manuscript and writing on the margins: 'Do people actually say this?' And I'm thinking, Hey, how many black people do you know? I mean know as equals, as friends. I don't mean the receptionist in the office and maybe the one black couple whose kid goes to your kid's school and you say hi to. I mean really know know. None. So how are you telling me how black people talk?"

"Not his fault. There aren't enough middle-class black folks to go around," Bill said. "Lots of liberal white folks are looking for black friends. It's almost as hard as finding an egg donor who is a tall blonde eighteen-year-old at Harvard."

They all laughed.

"I wrote this scene about something that happened in grad school, about a Gambian woman I knew. She loved to eat baking chocolate. She always had a pack of baking chocolate in her bag. Anyway, she lived in London and she was in love with this white English guy and he was leaving his wife for her. So we were at a bar and she was telling a few of us about it, me and this other girl, and this guy Peter. Short guy from Wisconsin. And you know what Peter said to her? He said, 'His wife must feel worse knowing you're black.' He said it like it was pretty obvious. Not that the wife would feel bad about another woman, period, but that she would feel bad because the woman was black. So I put it in the book and my editor wants to change it because he says it's not *subtle*. Like life is always fucking subtle. And then I write about my mom being bitter at work, because she felt she'd hit a ceiling and they wouldn't let her get further because she was black, and my editor says, 'Can we have more nuance? Did your mom have a bad rapport with someone at work, maybe? Or had she already been diagnosed with cancer?' He thinks we should complicate it, so it's not race alone. And I say, But it *was* race. She was bitter because she thought if everything was the same, except for her race, she would have been made vice-president. And she talked about it a lot until she died. But somehow my mom's experience is suddenly unnuanced. 'Nuance' means keep people comfortable so everyone is free to think of themselves as *individuals* and everyone got where they are because of their *achievement*."

"Maybe you should turn it into a novel," Maribelle said.

"Are you kidding me?" Shan asked, slightly drunk, slightly dramatic, and now sitting yoga-style on the floor. "You can't write an honest novel about race in this country. If you write about how people are really affected by race, it'll be too *obvious*. Black writers who do literary fiction in this country, all three of them, not the ten thousand who write those bullshit ghetto books with the bright covers, have two choices: they can do precious or they can do pretentious. When you do neither, nobody knows what to do with you. So if you're going to write about race, you have to make sure it's so lyrical and subtle that the reader who doesn't read between the lines won't even know it's about race. You know, a Proustian meditation, all watery and fuzzy, that at the end just leaves you feeling watery and fuzzy."

"Or just find a white writer. White writers can be blunt about race and get all activist because their anger isn't threatening," Grace said.

"What about this recent book, *Monk Memoirs*?" Mirabelle said.

"It's a cowardly, dishonest book. Have you read it?" Shan asked.

"I read a review," Mirabelle said.

"That's the problem. You read more about books than you read actual books."

Maribelle blushed. She would, Ifemelu sensed, take this quietly only from Shan.

"We are very ideological about fiction in this country. If a character is not familiar, then that character becomes unbelievable," Shan said. "You can't even read American fiction to get a sense of how actual life is lived these days. You read American fiction to learn about dysfunctional white folk doing things that are weird to normal white folks."

Everyone laughed. Shan looked delighted, like a little girl showing off her singing to her parents' eminent friends.

"The world just doesn't look like this room," Grace said.

"But it can," Blaine said. "We prove that the world can be like this room. It can be a safe and equal space for everyone. We just need to dismantle the walls of privilege and oppression."

"There goes my flower child brother," Shan said.

There was more laughter.

"You should blog about this, Ifemelu," Grace said.

"You know why Ifemelu can write that blog, by the way?" Shan said. "Because she's African. She's writing from the outside. She doesn't really feel all the stuff she's writing about. It's all quaint and curious to her. So she can write it and get all these accolades and get invited to give talks. If she were African American, she'd just be labelled angry and shunned."

The room was, for a moment, swollen in silence.

"I think that's fair enough," Ifemelu said, disliking Shan, and herself, too, for bending to Shan's spell. It was true that race was not embroidered in the fabric of her history; it had not been etched on her soul. Still, she wished Shan had said this to her when they were alone, instead of saying it now, so jubilantly, in front of friends, and leaving Ifemelu with an embittered knot, like bereavement, in her chest.

"A lot of this is relatively recent. Black and pan-African identities were actually strong in the early nineteenth century. The Cold War forced people to choose, and it was either you became an internationalist, which of course meant communist to Americans, or you became a part of American capitalism, which was the choice the African American elite made," Blaine said, as though in Ifemelu's defence, but she thought it too abstract, too limp, too late.

Shan glanced at Ifemelu and smiled and in that smile was the possibility of great cruelty. When, months later, Ifemelu had the fight with Blaine, she wondered if Shan had fuelled his anger, an anger she never fully understood.

Is Obama Anything but Black?

So lots of folk—mostly non-black—say Obama's not black, he's biracial, multiracial, black-and-white, anything but just black. Because his mother was white. But race is not biology; race is sociology. Race is not genotype; race is phenotype. Race matters because of racism. And racism is absurd because it's about how you look. Not about the blood you have. It's about the shade of your skin and the shape of your nose and the kink of your hair. Booker T. Washington and Frederick Douglass had white fathers. Imagine them saying they were not black.

Imagine Obama, skin the color of a toasted almond, hair kinky, saying to a census worker—I'm kind of white. Sure you are, she'll say. Many American Blacks have a white person in their ancestry, because white slave owners liked to go a-raping in the slave quarters at night. But if you come out looking dark, that's it. (So if you are that blond, blue-eyed woman who says "My grandfather was Native American and I get discrimination too" when black folk are talking about shit, please stop it already.) In America, you don't get to decide what race you are. It is decided for you. Barack Obama, looking as he does, would have had to sit in the back of the bus fifty years ago. If a random black guy commits a crime today, Barack Obama could be stopped and questioned for fitting the profile. And what would that profile be? "Black Man."

CHAPTER 38

Blaine did not like Boubacar, and perhaps this mattered or perhaps it did not matter in the story of their fight, but Blaine did not like Boubacar and her day began with visiting Boubacar's class. She and Blaine had met Boubacar at a university-hosted dinner party in his honour, a sable-skinned Senegalese professor who had just moved to the US to teach at Yale. He was blistering in his intelligence and blistering in his self-regard. He sat at the head of the table, drinking red wine and talking drily of French presidents whom he had met, of the French universities that had offered him jobs.

"I came to America because I want to choose my own master," he said. "If I must have a master, then better America than France. But I will never eat a cookie or go to McDonald's. How barbaric!"

Ifemelu was charmed and amused by him. She liked his accent, his English drenched in Wolof and French.

"I thought he was great," she told Blaine later.

"It's interesting how he says ordinary things and thinks they are pretty deep," Blaine said.

"He has a bit of an ego, but so did everyone at that table," Ifemelu said. "Aren't you Yale people supposed to, before you get hired?"

Blaine did not laugh, as he ordinarily would have. She sensed, in his reaction, a territorial dislike that was foreign to his nature; it surprised her. He would put on a bad French accent and mimic Boubacar. "'Francophone Africans break for coffee, Anglophone Africans break for tea. It is impossible to get real café au lait in this country!'"

Perhaps he resented how easily she had drifted to Boubacar that day, after desserts were served, as though to a person who spoke the same silent language as she did. She had teased Boubacar about Francophone Africans, how battered their minds were by the French and how thin-skinned they had become, too aware of European slights, and yet too enamoured of Europeanness. Boubacar laughed, a familial laugh; he would not laugh like that with an American, he would be cutting if an American dared say the same thing. Perhaps Blaine resented this mutuality, something primally African from which he felt excluded. But her feelings for Boubacar were fraternal, free of desire. They met often for tea in Atticus Bookstore and talked—or she listened since he did most of the talking—about West African politics and family and home and she left, always, with the feeling of having been fortified.

BY THE TIME Boubacar told her about the new humanities fellowship at Princeton, she had begun to gaze at her past. A restlessness had taken hold of her. Her doubts about her blog had grown.

"You must apply. It would be perfect for you," he said.

"I'm not an academic. I don't even have a graduate degree."

"The current fellow is a jazz musician, very brilliant, but he has only a high school diploma. They want people who are doing new things, pushing boundaries. You must apply, and please use me as a reference. We need to get into these places, you know. It is the only way to change the conversation."

She was touched, sitting across from him in a café and feeling between them the warm affinities of something shared.

Boubacar had often invited her to visit his class, a seminar on contemporary African issues. "You might find something to blog about," he said. And so, on the day that began the story of her fight with Blaine, she visited Boubacar's class. She sat at the back, by the window. Outside, the leaves were falling from grand old trees, people with scarf-bundled necks hurried along the sidewalk holding paper cups, the women, particularly the Asian women, pretty in slender skirts and high-heeled boots. Boubacar's students all had laptops open in front of them, the screens bright with e-mail pages, Google searches, celebrity photos. From time to time they would open a Word file and type a few words from Boubacar. Their jackets were hung behind their chairs and their body language, slouching, slightly impatient, said this: We already know the answers. After class they would go to the café in the library and buy a sandwich with zhou from North Africa, or a curry from India, and on their way to another class, a student group would give them condoms and lollipops, and in the evening they would attend tea in a master's house where a Latin American president or a Nobel laureate would answer their questions as though they mattered.

"Your students were all browsing the Internet," she told Boubacar as they walked back to his office.

"They do not doubt their presence here, these students. They believe they should be here, they have earned it and they are paying for it. *Au fond*, they have bought us all. It is the key to America's greatness, this hubris," Boubacar said, a black felt beret on his head, his hands sunk into his jacket pockets. "That is why they do not understand that they should be grateful to have me stand before them."

They had just arrived at his office when there was a knock on the half-open door.

"Come in," Boubacar said.

Kavanagh came in. Ifemelu had met him a few times, an assistant professor of history who had lived in Congo as a child. He was curly-haired and foul-humoured, and seemed better suited for covering dangerous wars in far-flung countries than for teaching history to undergraduates. He stood at the door and told Boubacar that he was leaving on a sabbatical and the department was ordering sandwiches the next day as a going-away lunch for him, and he had been told they were fancy sandwiches with such things as alfalfa sprouts.

"If I am bored enough, I will stop by," Boubacar said.

"You should come," Kavanagh said to Ifemelu. "Really."

"I'll come," she said. "Free lunch is always a good idea."

As she left Boubacar's office, Blaine sent her a text: *Did you hear about Mr White at the library?*

Her first thought was that Mr White had died; she did not feel any great sadness, and for this she felt guilty. Mr White was a security guard at the library who sat at the exit and checked the back flap of each book, a rheumy-eyed man with skin so dark it had an undertone of blueberries. She was so used to seeing him seated, a face and a torso, that the first time she saw him walking, his gait saddened her:

his shoulders stooped, as though burdened by lingering losses. Blaine had befriended him years ago, and sometimes during his break, Blaine would stand outside talking to him. "He's a history book," Blaine told her. She had met Mr White a few times. "Does she have a sister?" Mr White would ask Blaine, gesturing to her. Or he would say "You look tired, my man. Somebody keep you up late?" in a way Ifemelu thought inappropriate. Whenever they shook hands, Mr White squeezed her fingers, a gesture thick with suggestion, and she would pull her hand free and avoid his eyes until they left. There was, in that handshake, a claiming, a leering, and for this she had always harboured a small dislike, but she had never told Blaine because she was also sorry about her dislike. Mr White was, after all, an old black man beaten down by life and she wished she could overlook the liberties he took.

"Funny how I've never heard you speak Ebonics before," she told Blaine, the first time she heard him talking to Mr White. His syntax was different, his cadences more rhythmic.

"I guess I've become too used to my White People Are Watching Us voice," he said. "And you know, younger black folk don't really do code-switching any more. The middle-class kids can't speak Ebonics and the inner-city kids speak only Ebonics and they don't have the fluidity that my generation has."

"I'm going to blog about that."

"I knew you would say that."

She sent Blaine a text back: *No, what happened? Is Mr White okay? Are you done? Want to get a sandwich?*

Blaine called her and asked her to wait for him on the corner of Whitney, and soon she saw him walking towards her, a quick-moving trim figure in a grey sweater.

"Hey," he said, and kissed her.

"You smell nice," she said, and he kissed her again.

"You survived Boubacar's class? Even though there were no proper croissants or pain au chocolat?"

"Stop it. What happened to Mr White?"

As they walked hand in hand to the bagel sandwich store, he told her how Mr White's friend, a black man, came by yesterday evening and the two stood outside the library. Mr White gave his friend his car keys, because the friend wanted to borrow his car, and the friend gave Mr White some money, which Mr White had lent him earlier. A white library employee, watching them, assumed that the two black men were dealing drugs and called a supervisor. The supervisor called the police. The police came and led Mr White away to be questioned.

"Oh my God," Ifemelu said. "Is he okay?"

"Yes. He's back at his desk." Blaine paused. "I think he expects this sort of thing to happen."

"That's the actual tragedy," Ifemelu said, and realized she was using Blaine's own words; sometimes she heard in her voice the echo of his. The actual tragedy of Emmett Till, he had told her once, was not the murder of a black child for whistling at a white woman but that some black people thought: But why did you whistle?

"I talked to him for a bit. He just shrugged the whole thing off and said it wasn't a big deal and instead he wanted to talk about his daughter, who he's really worried about. She's talking about dropping out of high school. So I'm going to step in and tutor her. I'm going to meet her Monday."

"Blaine, that's the seventh kid you'll be tutoring," she said. "Are you going to tutor the whole of inner-city New Haven?"

It was windy and he was squinting, cars driving past them on Whitney Avenue, and he turned to glance at her with narrowed eyes.

"I wish I could," he said quietly.

"I just want to see more of you," she said, and slipped an arm around his waist.

"The university's response is total bullshit. A simple mistake that wasn't racial at all? Really? I'm thinking of organizing a protest tomorrow, get people to come out and say this is not okay. Not in our backyard."

He had already decided, she could tell, he was not merely thinking about it. He sat down at a table by the door while she went up to the counter to order, seamlessly ordering for him, because she was so used to him, to what he liked. When she came back with a plastic tray—her turkey sandwich and his veggie wrap lying beside two bags of baked unsalted chips—his head was bent to his phone. By evening, he had made calls and sent e-mails and texts and the news had been passed on, and his phone jingled and rang and beeped, with responses from people saying they were on board. A student called to ask him for suggestions about what to write on placards; another student was contacting the local TV stations.

The next morning, before he left for class, Blaine said, "I'm teaching back to back so I'll see you at the library? Text me when you're on your way."

They had not discussed it, he had simply assumed that she would be there, and so she said, "Okay."

But she did not go. And she did not forget. Blaine might have been more forgiving if she had simply forgotten, if she had been so submerged in reading or blogging that the protest had slipped from her mind. But she did not forget. She merely preferred to go to Kavanagh's going-away lunch instead of standing in front of the university library holding a placard. Blaine would not mind too much, she told herself. If she felt any discomfort, she was not conscious of it until she was seated in a classroom with Kavanagh and Boubacar and other professors, sipping a bottle of cranberry juice, listening to a young woman talk about her upcoming tenure review, when Blaine's texts flooded her phone. *Where are you? You okay? Great turnout, looking for you. Shan just surprised me and turned up! You okay?* She left early and went back to the apartment and, lying in bed, sent Blaine a text to say she was so sorry, she was just up from a nap that had gone on too long. *Okay. On my way home.*

He walked in and wrapped her in his arms, with a force and an excitement that had come through the door with him.

"I missed you. I really wanted you to be there. I was so happy Shan came," he said, a little emotional, as though it had been a personal triumph of his. "It was like a mini-America. Black kids and white kids and Asian kids and Hispanic kids. Mr White's daughter was there, taking pictures of his photos on the placard, and I felt as if that finally gave him some real dignity back."

"That's lovely," she said.

"Shan says hello. She's getting on the train back now."

It would have been easy for Blaine to find out, perhaps a casual mention from someone who had been at the lunch, but she never knew exactly how he did. He came back the next day and looked at her, a glare like silver in his eyes, and said, "You lied." It was said with a kind of horror that baffled her, as though he had never considered it possible that she could lie. She wanted to say, "Blaine, people lie." But she said, "I'm sorry."

"Why?" He was looking at her as though she had reached in and torn away his innocence, and for a moment she hated him, this man who ate her apple cores and turned even that into something of a moral act.

"I don't know why, Blaine. I just didn't feel up to it. I didn't think you would mind too much."

"You just didn't feel up to it?"

"I'm sorry. I should have told you about the lunch."

"How is this lunch suddenly so important? You hardly even know this Boubacar's colleague!" he said, incredulous. "You know, it's not just about writing a blog, you have to live like you believe it. That blog is a game that you don't really take seriously, it's like choosing an *interesting* elective evening class to complete your credits." She recognized, in his tone, a subtle accusation, not merely about her laziness, her lack of zeal and conviction, but also about her Africanness; she was not sufficiently furious because she was African, not African American.

"It's unfair of you to say that," she said. But he had turned away from her, icy, silent.

"Why won't you talk to me?" she asked. "I don't understand why this matters so much."

"How can you not understand? It's the principle of it," he said, and at that moment, he became a stranger to her.

"I'm really sorry," she said.

He had walked into the bathroom and shut the door.

She felt withered in his wordless rage. How could principle, an abstract thing floating in the air, wedge itself so solidly between them, and turn Blaine into somebody else? She wished it were an uncivil emotion, a passion like jealousy or betrayal.

She called Araminta. "I feel like the confused wife calling her sister-in-law to explain her husband to her," she said.

"In high school, I remember there was some fund-raiser, and they put out a table with cookies and whatever, and you were supposed to put some money in the jar and take a cookie, and you know, I'm feeling rebellious so I just take a cookie and don't put any money in, and Blaine was furious with me. I remember thinking, Hey, it's just a cookie. But I think for him it was the principle of it. He can be ridiculously high-minded sometimes. Give him a day or two, he'll get over this."

But a day passed, then two, and Blaine remained caged in his frozen silence. On the third day of his not saying a single word to her, she packed a small bag and left. She could not go back to Baltimore—her condo was rented out and her furniture in storage—and so she went to Willow.

What Academics Mean by White Privilege, or Yes It Sucks to Be Poor and White but Try Being Poor and Non-White

So this guy said to Professor Hunk, "White privilege is nonsense. How can I be privileged? I grew up fucking poor in West Virginia. I'm an Appalachian hick. My family is on welfare." Right. But privilege is always relative to something else. Now imagine someone like him, as poor and as fucked up, and then make that person black. If both are caught for drug possession, say, the white guy is more likely to be sent to treatment and the black guy is more likely to be sent to jail. Everything else the same except for race. Check the stats. The Appalachian hick guy is fucked up, which is not cool, but if he were black, he'd be fucked up plus. He also said to Professor Hunk: Why must we always talk about race anyway? Can't we just be human beings? And Professor Hunk replied—that is exactly what white privilege is, that you can say that. Race doesn't really exist for you because it has never been a barrier. Black folks don't have that choice. The black guy on the street in New York doesn't want to think about race, until he tries to hail a cab, and he doesn't want to think about race when he's driving his Mercedes under the speed limit, until a cop pulls him over. So Appalachian hick guy doesn't have class privilege but he sure as hell has race privilege. What do you think? Weigh in, readers, and share your experiences, especially if you are non-black.

PS—Professor Hunk just suggested I post this, a test for White Privilege, copyright a pretty cool woman called Peggy McIntosh. If you answer mostly no, then congratulations, you have white privilege. What's the point of this you ask? Seriously? I have no idea. I guess it's just good to know. So you can gloat from time to time, lift you up when you're depressed, that sort of thing. So here goes:

When you want to join a prestigious social club, do you wonder if your race will make it difficult for you to join?

When you go shopping alone at a nice store, do you worry that you will be followed or harassed?

When you turn on mainstream TV or open a mainstream newspaper, do you expect to find mostly people of another race?

Do you worry that your children will not have books and school materials that are about people of their own race?

When you apply for a bank loan, do you worry that, because of your race, you might be seen as financially unreliable?

If you swear, or dress shabbily, do you think that people might say this is because of the bad morals or the poverty or the illiteracy of your race?

If you do well in a situation, do you expect to be called a credit to your race? Or to be described as "different" from the majority of your race?

If you criticize the government, do you worry that you might be seen as a cultural outsider? Or that you might be asked to "go back to X," X being somewhere not in America?

If you receive poor service in a nice store and ask to see "the person in charge," do you expect that this person will be a person of another race?

If a traffic cop pulls you over, do you wonder if it is because of your race?

If you take a job with an Affirmative Action employer, do you worry that your co-workers will think you are unqualified and were hired only because of your race?

If you want to move to a nice neighborhood, do you worry that you might not be welcome because of your race?

If you need legal or medical help, do you worry that your race might work against you?

When you use the "nude" color of underwear and Band-Aids, do you already know that it will not match your skin?

CHAPTER 39

Aunty Uju had taken up yoga. She was on her hands and knees, back arched high, on a bright blue mat on the basement floor, while Ifemelu lay on the couch, eating a chocolate bar and watching her.

"How many of those things have you eaten? And since when do you eat regular chocolate? I thought you and Blaine eat only organic, fair trade."

"I bought them at the train station."

"Them? How many?"

"Ten."

"Ahn-ahn! Ten!"

Ifemelu shrugged. She had already eaten them all, but she would not tell Aunty Uju that. It had given her pleasure, buying chocolate bars from the news-stand, cheap bars filled with sugar and chemicals and other genetically modified ghastly things.

"Oh, so because you are quarrelling with Blaine, you are now eating the chocolate he doesn't like?" Aunty Uju laughed.

Dike came downstairs and looked at his mother, her arms now up in the air, warrior position. "Mom, you look ridiculous."

"Didn't your friend say that your mother was hot, the other day? This is why."

Dike shook his head. "Coz, I need to show you something on YouTube, this hilarious video."

Ifemelu got up.

"Has Dike told you about the computer incident at school?" Aunty Uju asked.

"No, what?" Ifemelu asked.

"The principal called me on Monday to say that Dike hacked into the school's computer network on Saturday. This is a boy who was with me all day on Saturday. We went to Hartford to visit Ozavisa. We were there the whole day and the boy did not go near a computer. When I asked why they thought it was him, they said they got information. Imagine, you just wake up and blame my son. The boy is not even good with computers. I thought we had left them behind in that bush town. Kweku wants us to lodge a formal complaint, but I don't think it's worth the time. They have now said they no longer suspect him."

"I don't even know *how* to hack," Dike said drily.

"Why would they do this sort of rubbish?" Ifemelu asked.

"You have to blame the black kid first," he said, and laughed.

Later, he told her how his friends would say, "Hey, Dike, got some weed?" and how funny it was. He told her about the pastor at church, a white woman, who had said hello to all the other kids but when she came to him, she said, "What's up, bro?" "I feel like I have vegetables instead of ears, like large broccoli sticking out of my head," he said, laughing. "So of course it had to be me that hacked into the school network."

"Those people in your school are fools," Ifemelu said.

"So funny how you say that word, Coz, *fools*." He paused and then repeated her words, "Those people in your school are fools," in a good mimicry of a Nigerian accent. She told him the story of the Nigerian pastor who, while giving a sermon in a church in America, said something about a beach but because of his accent, his parishioners thought he had said "bitch" and they wrote to his bishop to complain. Dike laughed and laughed. It became one of their stock jokes. "Hey, Coz, I just want to spend a summer day at the bitch," he would say.

FOR NINE DAYS, Blaine did not take her calls. Finally he answered the phone, his voice muffled.

"Can I come this weekend so we can cook coconut rice? I'll do the cooking," she said. Before he said "Okay," she sensed an intake of breath and she wondered if he was surprised that she dared to suggest coconut rice.

SHE WATCHED BLAINE cutting the onions, watched his long fingers and recalled them on her body, tracing lines on her collarbone, and on the darkened skin below her navel. He looked up and asked if the slices were a good size and she said, "The onion is fine," and thought how he had always known the right size for onions, slicing them so precisely, how he had always steamed the rice although she was going to do it now. He broke the coconut against the sink and let the water out before he began to nudge the white meat off the shell with a knife. Her hands shook as she poured rice into the boiling water and, as she watched the narrow basmati grains begin to swell, she wondered if they were failing at this, their reconciliatory meal. She checked the chicken on the stove. The spices wafted up when she opened the pot—ginger and curry and bay leaves—and she told him, unnecessarily, that it looked good.

"I didn't over-spice it like you do," he said. She felt a momentary anger and wanted to say that it was unfair of him to hold out forgiveness like this but instead she asked if he thought she should add some water. He kept grating the coconuts and said nothing. She watched the coconut crumble into white dust; it saddened her to think that it would never be a whole coconut again, and she reached out and held Blaine from the back, wrapped her arms around his chest, felt the warmth through his sweatshirt, but he eased away and said he had to finish before the rice got too soft. She walked across the living room to look out of the window, at the clock tower, high and regal, imposing itself on the other buildings of the Yale campus below, and saw the first snow flurries swirling through the late evening air, as though flung from above, and she remembered her first winter with him, when everything had seemed burnished and unendingly new.

Understanding America for the Non-American Black: A Few Explanations of What Things Really Mean

1. Of all their tribalisms, Americans are most uncomfortable with race. If you are having a conversation with an American, and you want to discuss something racial that you find interesting, and the American

says, "Oh, it's simplistic to say it's race, racism is so complex," it means they just want you to shut up already. Because of course racism is complex. Many abolitionists wanted to free the slaves but didn't want black people living nearby. Lots of folk today don't mind a black nanny or black limo driver. But they sure as hell mind a black boss. What is simplistic is saying "It's so complex." But shut up anyway, especially if you need a job/favor from the American in question.

2. Diversity means different things to different folks. If a white person is saying a neighborhood is diverse, they mean nine percent black people. (The minute it gets to ten percent black people, the white folks move out.) If a black person says diverse neighborhood, they are thinking forty percent black.

3. Sometimes they say "culture" when they mean race. They say a film is "mainstream" when they mean "white folks like it or made it." When they say "urban" it means black and poor and possibly dangerous and potentially exciting. "Racially charged" means we are uncomfortable saying "racist."

CHAPTER 40

They did not fight again until the relationship ended, but in the time of Blaine's stoniness, when Ifemelu burrowed into herself and ate whole chocolate bars, her feelings for him changed. She still admired him, his moral fibre, his life of clean lines, but now it was admiration for a person separate from her, a person far away. And her body had changed. In bed, she did not turn to him full of a raw wanting as she used to do, and when he reached for her, her first instinct was to roll away. They kissed often, but always with her lips firmly pursed; she did not want his tongue in her mouth. Their union was leached of passion, but there was a new passion, outside of themselves, that united them in an intimacy they had never had before, an unfixed, unspoken, intuitive intimacy: Barack Obama. They agreed, without any prodding, without the shadows of obligation or compromise, on Barack Obama.

At first, even though she wished America would elect a black man as president, she thought it impossible, and she could not imagine Obama as president of the United States; he seemed too slight, too skinny, a man who would be blown away by the wind. Hillary Clinton was sturdier. Ifemelu liked to watch Clinton on television, in her square trouser suits, her face a mask of resolve, her prettiness disguised, because that was the only way to convince the world that she was able. Ifemelu liked her. She wished her victory, willed good fortune her way, until the morning she picked up Barack Obama's book, *Dreams from My Father*, which Blaine had just finished and left lying on the bookshelf, some of its pages folded in. She examined the photographs on the cover, the young Kenyan woman staring befuddled at the camera, arms enclosing her son, and the young American man, jaunty of manner, holding his daughter to his chest. Ifemelu would later remember the moment she decided to read the book. Just to see. She might not have read it if Blaine had recommended it, because she more and more avoided the books he liked. But he had not recommended it, he had merely left it on the shelf, next to a pile of other books he had finished but meant to go back to. She read *Dreams from My Father* in a day and a half, sitting up on the couch, Nina Simone playing on Blaine's iPod speaker. She was absorbed and moved by the man she met in those pages, an enquiring and intelligent man, a kind man, a man so utterly, helplessly, winningly humane. He reminded her of Obinze's expression for people he liked. *Obi ocha.* A clean heart. She believed Barack Obama. When Blaine came home, she sat at the dining table, watching him chop fresh basil in the kitchen, and said, "If only the man who wrote this book could be the president of America."

Blaine's knife stopped moving. He looked up, eyes lit, as though he had not dared hope she would believe the same thing that he believed, and she felt between them the first pulse of a shared passion. They clutched each other in front of the television when Barack Obama won the Iowa caucuses. The first battle, and he had won. Their hope was radiating, exploding into possibility: Obama could actually win this thing. And then, as though choreographed, they began to worry. They worried that something would derail him, crash his fast-moving train. Every morning, Ifemelu woke up and checked to make sure that Obama was still alive. That no scandal had emerged, no story dug up from his past. She would turn on her computer, her breath still, her heart frantic in her chest, and then, reassured that he was alive, she would read the latest news about him, quickly and greedily, seeking information and reassurance, multiple windows minimized at the bottom of the screen. Sometimes, in chat rooms, she wilted as she read the posts about Obama, and she would get up and move away from her computer, as though the laptop itself were the enemy, and stand by the window to hide her tears even from herself. *How can a monkey be president? Somebody do us a favor and put a bullet in this guy. Send him back to the African jungle. A black man will never be in the white house, dude, it's called the white house for a reason.* She tried to imagine the people who wrote those posts, under monikers like SuburbanMom231 and NormanRockwellRocks, sitting at their desks, a cup of coffee beside them, and their children about to come home on the school bus in a glow of innocence. The chat rooms made her blog feel inconsequential, a comedy of manners, a mild satire about a world that was anything but mild. She did not blog about the vileness that seemed to have multiplied each morning she logged on, more chat rooms springing up, more vitriol flourishing, because to do so would be to spread the words of people who abhorred not the man that Barack Obama was, but the idea of him as president. She blogged, instead, about his policy positions, in a recurring post titled "This Is Why Obama Will Do It Better", often adding links to his website, and she blogged, too, about Michelle Obama. She gloried in the off-beat dryness of Michelle Obama's humour, the confidence in her long-limbed carriage, and then she mourned when Michelle Obama was clamped, flattened, made to sound tepidly wholesome in interviews. Still, there was, in Michelle Obama's overly arched eyebrows and in her belt worn higher on her waist than tradition would care for, a glint of her old self. It was this that drew Ifemelu, the absence of apology, the promise of honesty.

"If she married Obama then he can't be that bad," she joked often with Blaine, and Blaine would say, "True that, true that."

SHE GOT an e-mail from a princeton.edu address and before she read it, her hands shook from excitement. The first word she saw was "pleased". She had received the research fellowship. The pay was good, the requirements easy: she was expected to live in Princeton and use the library and give a public talk at the end of the year. It seemed too good to be true, an entry into a hallowed American kingdom. She and Blaine took the train to Princeton to look for an apartment, and she was struck by the town itself, the greenness, the peace and grace of it. "I got into Princeton for undergrad," Blaine told her. "It was almost bucolic then. I visited and thought it was beautiful but I just couldn't see myself actually going there."

Ifemelu knew what he meant, even now that it had changed and become, in Blaine's words, when they walked past the rows of shiny stores, "aggressively consumer capitalist". She felt admiration and disorientation. She liked her apartment, off Nassau Street; the bedroom window looked out to a grove of trees, and she walked the empty room thinking of a new beginning for herself, without Blaine, and yet unsure if this was truly the new beginning she wanted.

"I'm not moving here until after the election," she said.

Blaine nodded before she finished speaking; of course she would not move until they had seen Barack Obama through to his victory. He became a volunteer for the Obama campaign and she absorbed all of his stories about the doors he knocked on and the people behind them. One day he came home and told her about an old black woman, face shrivelled like a prune, who stood holding on to her door as though she might fall otherwise, and told him, "I didn't think this would happen even in my grandbaby's lifetime."

Ifemelu blogged about this story, describing the silver streaks in the woman's grey hair, the fingers quivering from Parkinson's, as though she herself had been there with Blaine. All of his friends were Obama supporters, except for Michael, who always wore a Hillary Clinton pin on his breast, and at their gatherings, Ifemelu no longer felt excluded. Even that nebulous unease when she was around Paula, part churlishness and part insecurity, had melted away. They gathered at bars and apartments, discussing details of the campaign, mocking the silliness of the news stories. Will Hispanics vote for a black man? Can he bowl? Is he patriotic?

"Isn't it funny how they say 'blacks want Obama' and 'women want Hillary', but what about black women?" Paula said.

"When they say 'women', they automatically mean 'white women', of course," Grace said.

"What I don't understand is how anybody can say that Obama is benefiting because he's a black man," Paula said.

"It's complicated, but he is, and also to the extent that Clinton is benefiting because she's a white woman," Nathan said, leaning forward and blinking even more quickly. "If Clinton were a black woman, her star would not shine so brightly. If Obama were a white man, his star might or might not shine so brightly, because some white men have become president who had no business being president, but that doesn't change the fact that Obama doesn't have a lot of experience and people are excited by the idea of a black candidate who has a real chance."

"Although if he wins, he will no longer be black, just as Oprah is no longer black, she's Oprah," Grace said. "So she can go where black people are loathed and be fine. He'll no longer be black, he'll just be Obama."

"To the extent that Obama is benefiting, and that idea of benefiting is very problematic, by the way, but to the extent that he is, it's not because he's black, it's because he's a different kind of black," Blaine said. "If Obama didn't have a white mother and wasn't raised by white grandparents and didn't have Kenya and Indonesia and Hawaii and all of the stories that make him somehow a bit like everyone, if he was just a plain black guy from Georgia, it would be different. America will have made real progress when an ordinary black guy from Georgia becomes president, a black guy who got a C average in college."

"I agree," Nathan said. And it struck Ifemelu anew, how much everyone agreed. Their friends, like her and Blaine, were believers. True believers.

ON THE DAY Barack Obama became the nominee of the Democratic Party, Ifemelu and Blaine made love, for the first time in weeks, and Obama was there with them, like an unspoken prayer, a third emotional presence. She and Blaine drove hours to hear him speak, holding hands in a thick crowd, raising placards, CHANGE written on them in a bold white print. A black man nearby had hoisted his son onto his shoulders, and the son was laughing, his mouth full of milky teeth, one missing from the upper row. The father was looking up, and Ifemelu knew that he was stunned by his own faith, stunned to find himself believing in things he did not think he ever would. When the crowd exploded in applause, clapping and whistling, the man could not clap, because he was holding his son's legs, and so he just smiled and smiled, his face suddenly young with joyfulness. Ifemelu watched him, and the other people around them, all glowing with a strange phosphorescence, all treading a single line of unbroken emotion. They believed. They truly believed. It often came to her as a sweet shock, the knowledge that there were so many people in the world who felt exactly as she and Blaine did about Barack Obama.

On some days their faith soared. On other days, they despaired.

"This is not good," Blaine muttered as they went back and forth between different television channels, each showing the footage of Barack Obama's pastor giving a sermon, and his words "God Damn America" seared their way into Ifemelu's dreams.

SHE FIRST READ, on the Internet, the breaking news that Barack Obama would give a speech on race, in response to the footage of his pastor, and she sent a text to Blaine, who was teaching a class. His reply was simple: *Yes!* Later, watching the speech, seated between Blaine and Grace on their living room couch, Ifemelu wondered what Obama was truly thinking and what he would feel as he lay in bed that night, when all was quiet and empty. She imagined him, the boy who knew his grandmother was afraid of black men, now a man telling that story to the world to redeem himself. She felt a small sadness at this thought. As Obama spoke, compassionate and cadenced, American flags fluttering behind him, Blaine shifted, sighed, leaned back on the couch. Finally, Blaine said, "It's immoral to equate black grievance and white fear like this. It's just *immoral.*"

"This speech was not done to open up a conversation about race but actually to close it. He can win only if he avoids race. We all know that," Grace said. "But the important thing is to get him into office first. The guy's gotta do what he's gotta do. At least now this pastor business is closed."

Ifemelu, too, felt pragmatic about the speech, but Blaine took it personally. His faith cracked, and for a few days he lacked his bounce, coming back from his morning run without his usual sweaty high, walking around heavy-footed. It was Shan who unknowingly pulled him out of his slump.

"I have to go to the city for a few days to be with Shan," he told Ifemelu. "Ovidio just called me. She's not functioning."

"She is not functioning?"

"A nervous breakdown. I dislike that expression, it has a very old wives' tale vibe to it. But that's what Ovidio called it. She's been in bed for days. She's not eating. She won't stop crying."

Ifemelu felt a flash of irritation; even this, it seemed to her, was yet another way for Shan to demand attention.

"She's had a really hard time," Blaine said. "The book not getting any attention and all."

"I know," Ifemelu said, and yet she could feel no real sympathy, which frightened her. Perhaps it was because she held Shan responsible, at some level, for the fight with Blaine, for not wielding her power over Blaine to let him know he was overreacting.

"She'll be fine," Ifemelu said. "She's a strong person."

Blaine looked at her with surprise. "Shan is one of the most fragile people in the world. She's not strong, she's never been. But she's special."

The last time Ifemelu had seen Shan, about a month ago, Shan had said, "I just knew you and Blaine would get back together." Hers was the tone of a person talking about a beloved sibling who had returned to psychedelic drugs.

"Isn't Obama exciting?" Ifemelu had asked, hoping that this would, at least, be something she and Shan could talk about without an underlying prick of pins.

"Oh, I'm not following this election," Shan had said dismissively.

"Have you read his book?" Ifemelu asked.

"No." Shan shrugged. "It would be good if somebody read *my* book."

Ifemelu swallowed her words. *It's not about you. For once, it's not about you.*

"You should read *Dreams from My Father.* The other books are campaign documents," Ifemelu said. "He's the real deal."

But Shan was not interested. She was talking about a panel she had done the week before, at a writers' festival. "So they ask me who my favourite writers are. Of course I know they expected mostly black writers and no way am I going to tell them that Robert Hayden is the love of my life, which he is. So I didn't mention anybody black or remotely of colour or politically inclined or alive. And so I name, with insouciant aplomb, Turgenev and Trollope and Goethe, but so as not to be too indebted to dead white males because that would be a little too unoriginal, I added Selma Lagerlöf. And suddenly they don't know what to ask me, because I'd thrown the script out the window."

"That's so funny," Blaine said.

ON THE EVE of Election Day, Ifemelu lay sleepless in bed.

"You awake?" Blaine asked her.

"Yes."

They held each other in the dark, saying nothing, their breathing regular until finally they drifted into a state of half sleep and half wakefulness. In the morning, they went to the high school; Blaine wanted to be one of the first to vote. Ifemelu watched the people already there, in line, waiting for the door to open, and she willed them all to vote for Obama. It felt to her like a bereavement, that she could not vote. Her application for citizenship had been approved but the oath-taking was still weeks away. She spent a restless morning, checking all the news sites, and when Blaine came back from class he asked her to turn off the computer and television so they could take a break, breathe deeply, eat the risotto he had made. They had barely finished eating before Ifemelu turned her computer back on. Just to make sure Barack Obama was alive and well. Blaine made virgin cocktails for their friends. Araminta arrived first, straight from the train station, holding two phones, checking for updates on both. Then Grace arrived, in her swishy silks, a golden scarf at her neck, saying, "Oh my God, I can't breathe for nervousness!" Michael came with a bottle of prosecco. "I wish my mama was alive to see this day no matter what happens," he said.

Paula and Pee and Nathan arrived together, and soon they were all seated, on the couch and the dining chairs, eyes on the television, sipping tea and Blaine's virgin cocktails and repeating the same things they had said before. *If he wins Indiana and Pennsylvania, then that's it. It's looking good in Florida. The news from Iowa is conflicting.*

"There's a huge black voter turnout in Virginia, so it's looking good," Ifemelu said.

"Virginia is unlikely," Nathan said.

"He doesn't need Virginia," Grace said, and then she screamed. "Oh my God, Pennsylvania!"

A graphic had flashed on the television screen, a photo of Barack Obama. He had won the states of Pennsylvania and Ohio.

"I don't see how McCain can do this now," Nathan said.

Paula was sitting next to Ifemelu a short while later when the flash of graphics appeared on the screen: Barack Obama had won the state of Virginia.

"Oh my God," Paula said. Her hand trembling at her mouth. Blaine was sitting straight and still, staring at the television, and then came the deep voice of Keith Olbermann, whom Ifemelu had watched so obsessively on MSNBC in the past months, the voice of a searing, sparkling liberal rage; now that voice was saying "Barack Obama is projected to be the next president of the United States of America."

Blaine was crying, holding Araminta, who was crying, and then holding Ifemelu, squeezing her too tight, and Pee was hugging Michael and Grace was hugging Nathan and Paula was hugging Araminta and Ifemelu was hugging Grace and the living room became an altar of disbelieving joy.

Her phone beeped with a text from Dike.

I can't believe it. My president is black like me. She read the text a few times, her eyes filling with tears.

On television, Barack Obama and Michelle Obama and their two young daughters were walking onto a stage. They were carried by the wind, bathed in incandescent light, victorious and smiling.

"Young and old, rich and poor, Democrat and Republican, black, white, Hispanic, Asian, Native American, gay, straight, disabled and not disabled, Americans have sent a message to the world that we have never been just a collection of

red states and blue states. We have been and always will be the United States of America."

Barack Obama's voice rose and fell, his face solemn, and around him the large and resplendent crowd of the hopeful. Ifemelu watched, mesmerized. And there was, at that moment, nothing that was more beautiful to her than America.

Understanding America for the Non-American Black: Thoughts on the Special White Friend

One great gift for the Zipped-Up Negro is The White Friend Who Gets It. Sadly, this is not as common as one would wish, but some are lucky to have that white friend who you don't need to explain shit to. By all means, put this friend to work. Such friends not only get it, but also have great bullshit-detectors and so they totally understand that they can say stuff that you can't. So there is, in much of America, a stealthy little notion lying in the hearts of many: that white people earned their place at jobs and school while black people got in because they were black. But in fact, since the beginning of America, white people have been getting jobs because they are white. Many whites with the same qualifications but Negro skin would not have the jobs they have. But don't ever say this publicly. Let your white friend say it. If you make the mistake of saying this, you will be accused of a curiosity called "playing the race card." Nobody quite knows what this means.

When my father was in school in my NAB country, many American Blacks could not vote or go to good schools. The reason? Their skin color. Skin color alone was the problem. Today, many Americans say that skin color cannot be part of the solution. Otherwise it is referred to as a curiosity called "reverse racism." Have your white friend point out how the American Black deal is kind of like you've been unjustly imprisoned for many years, then all of a sudden you're set free, but you get no bus fare. And, by the way, you and the guy who imprisoned you are now automatically equal. If the "slavery was so long ago" thing comes up, have your white friend say that lots of white folks are still inheriting money that their families made a hundred years ago. So if that legacy lives, why not the legacy of slavery?

And have your white friend say how funny it is, that American pollsters ask white and black people if racism is over. White people in general say it is over and black people in general say it is not. Funny indeed. More suggestions for what you should have your white friend say? Please post away. And here's to all the white friends who get it.

CHAPTER 41

Aisha pulled out her phone from her pocket and then slipped it back with a frustrated sigh.

"I don't know why Chijioke not call to come," she said.

Ifemelu said nothing. She and Aisha were alone in the salon; Halima had just left. Ifemelu was tired and her back throbbed and the salon had begun to nauseate her, with its stuffy air and rotting ceiling. Why couldn't these African women keep their salon clean and ventilated? Her hair was almost finished, only a small section, like a rabbit's tail, was left at the front of her head. She was eager to leave.

"How you get your papers?" Aisha asked.

"What?"

"How you get your papers?"

Ifemelu was startled into silence. A sacrilege, that question; immigrants did not ask other immigrants how they got their papers, did not burrow into those layered, private places; it was sufficient simply to admire that the papers had been got, a legal status acquired.

"Me, I try an American when I come, to marry. But he bring many problems, no job, and every day he say give me money, money, money," Aisha said, shaking her head. "How you get your own?"

Suddenly, Ifemelu's irritation dissolved, and in its place, a gossamered sense of kinship grew, because Aisha would not have asked if she were not an African, and in this new bond, she saw yet another augury of her return home.

"I got mine from work," she said. "The company I worked for sponsored my green card."

"Oh," Aisha said, as though she had just realized that Ifemelu belonged to a group of people whose green cards simply fell from the sky. People like her could not, of course, get theirs from an employer.

"Chijioke get his papers with lottery," Aisha said. She slowly, almost lovingly, combed the section of hair she was about to twist.

"What happened to your hand?" Ifemelu asked.

Aisha shrugged. "I don't know. It just come and after it go."

"My aunt is a doctor. I'll take a picture of your arm and ask her what she thinks," Ifemelu said.

"Thank you."

Aisha finished a twist in silence.

"My father die, I don't go," she said.

"What?"

"Last year. My father die and I don't go. Because of papers. But maybe, if Chijioke marry me, when my mother die, I can go. She is sick now. But I send her money."

For a moment, Ifemelu did not know what to say. Aisha's wan tone, her expressionless face, magnified her tragedy.

"Sorry, Aisha," she said.

"I don't know why Chijioke not come. So you talk to him."

"Don't worry, Aisha. It will be okay."

Then, just as suddenly as she had spoken, Aisha began to cry. Her eyes melted, her mouth caved and a terrifying thing happened to her face: it collapsed into despair. She kept twisting Ifemelu's hair, her hand movements unchanged, while her face, as though it did not belong to her body, continued to crumple, tears running from her eyes, her chest heaving.

"Where does Chijioke work?" Ifemelu asked. "I will go there and talk to him."

Aisha stared at her, the tears still sliding down her cheeks.

"I will go and talk to Chijioke tomorrow," Ifemelu repeated. "Just tell me where he works and what time he goes on break."

What was she doing? She should get up and leave, and not be dragged further into Aisha's morass, but she could not get up and leave. She was about to go back home to Nigeria, and she would see her parents, and she could come back to America if she wished, and here was Aisha, hoping but not really believing that she would ever see her mother again. She would talk to this Chijioke. It was the least she could do.

She brushed the hair from her clothes and gave Aisha a thin roll of dollars. Aisha spread it out on her palm, counting briskly, and Ifemelu wondered how much would go to Mariama and how much to Aisha. She waited for Aisha to put the money into her pocket before she gave her the tip. Aisha took the single twenty-dollar bill, her eyes now dried of tears, her face back to its expressionlessness. "Thank you."

The room was dense with awkwardness, and Ifemelu, as though to dilute it, once again examined her hair in the mirror, patting it lightly as she turned this way and that.

"I will go and see Chijioke tomorrow and I'll call you," Ifemelu said. She brushed at her clothes for any stray bits of hair and looked around to make sure she had taken everything.

"Thank you." Aisha moved towards Ifemelu, as though to embrace her, then stopped, hesitant. Ifemelu gripped her shoulder gently before turning to the door.

On the train, she wondered just how she would persuade a man who didn't seem keen to marry to do so. Her head was aching and the hair at her temples, even though Aisha had not twisted too tightly, still caused a tugging discomfort, a disturbance of her neck and nerves. She longed to get home and have a long, cold shower, put her hair up in a satin bonnet, and lie down on her couch with her laptop. The train had just stopped at Princeton station when her phone rang. She stopped on the platform to fumble in her bag for it and, at first, because Aunty Uju was incoherent, talking and sobbing at the same time, Ifemelu thought she said that Dike was dead. But what Aunty Uju was saying was *o nwuchagokwa, Díke anwuchagokwa.* Dike had nearly died.

"He took an overdose of pills and went down to the basement and lay down on the couch there!" Aunty Uju said, her voice cracked with her own disbelief. "I never go to the basement when I come back. I only do my yoga in the morning. It was God that told me to go down today to defrost the meat in the freezer. It was God! I saw him lying there looking so sweaty, sweat all over his body, and immediately I panicked. I said these people have given my son drugs."

Ifemelu was shaking. A train whooshed past and she pressed her finger into her other ear to hear Aunty Uju's voice better. Aunty Uju was saying "signs of liver toxicity" and Ifemelu felt choked by those words, *liver toxicity*, by her confusion, by the sudden darkening of the air.

"Ifem?" Aunty Uju asked. "Are you there?"

"Yes." The word had travelled up a long tunnel. "What happened? What exactly happened, Aunty? What are you saying?"

"He swallowed a whole bottle of Tylenol. He is in the ICU now and he will be fine. God was not ready for him to die, that is all," Aunty Uju said. The sound of her nose-blowing was loud over the phone. "Do you know he also took anti-nausea so that the medicine would stay in his stomach? God was not ready for him to die."

"I am coming tomorrow," Ifemelu said. She stood on the platform for a long time, and wondered what she had been doing while Dike was swallowing a bottle of pills.

Part 5

CHAPTER 42

Obinze checked his BlackBerry often, too often, even when he got up at night to go to the toilet, and although he mocked himself, he could not stop checking. Four days, four whole days, passed before she replied. This dampened him. She was never coy, and she would have ordinarily replied much sooner. She might be busy, he told himself, although he knew very well how convenient and unconvincing a reason "busy" was. Or she might have changed and become the kind of woman who waited four whole days so that she would not seem too eager, a thought that dampened him even more. Her e-mail was warm, but too short, telling him she was excited and nervous about leaving her life and moving back home, but there were no specifics. When was she moving back exactly? And what was it that was so difficult to leave behind? He Googled the black American again, hoping perhaps to find a blog post about a break-up, but the blog only had links to academic papers. One of them was on early hip-hop music as political activism—how American, to study hip-hop as a viable subject—and he read it hoping it would be silly, but it was interesting enough for him to read all the way to the end and this soured his stomach. The black American had become, absurdly, a rival. He tried Facebook. Kosi was active on Facebook, she put up photos and kept in touch with people, but he had deleted his account a while ago. He had at first been excited by Facebook, ghosts of old friends suddenly morphing to life with wives and husbands and children, and photos trailed by comments. But he began to be appalled by the air of unreality, the careful manipulation of images to create a parallel life, pictures that people had taken with Facebook in mind, placing in the background the things of which they were proud. Now, he reactivated his account to search for Ifemelu, but she did not have a Facebook profile. Perhaps she was as unenchanted with Facebook as he was. This pleased him vaguely, another example of how similar they were. Her black American was on Facebook, but his profile was visible only to his friends, and for a crazed moment, Obinze considered sending him a friend request, just to see if he had posted pictures of Ifemelu. He wanted to wait a few days before replying to her but he found himself that night in his study writing her a long e-mail about the death of his mother. *I never thought that she would die until she died. Does this make sense?* He had discovered that grief did not dim with time; it was instead a volatile state of being. Sometimes the pain was as abrupt as it was on the day her house help called him sobbing to say she was lying unbreathing on her bed; other times, he forgot that she had died and would make cursory plans about flying to the east to see her. She had looked askance at his new wealth, as though she did not understand a world in which a person could make so much so easily. After he bought her a new car as a surprise, she told him her old car was perfectly fine, the Peugeot 505 she had been driving since he was in secondary school. He had the car delivered to her house, a small Honda that she would not think too ostentatious, but each time he visited, he saw it parked in the garage, coated in a translucent haze of dust. He remembered very clearly his last conversation with her over the phone, three days before she died, her growing despondence with her job and with life on the campus.

"Nobody publishes in international journals," she had said. "Nobody goes to conferences. It's like a shallow muddy pond that we are all wallowing in."

He wrote this in his e-mail to Ifemelu, how his mother's sadness with her job had also made him sad. He was careful not to be too heavy-handed, writing about how the church in his hometown had made him pay many dues before her funeral, and how the caterers had stolen meat at the burial, wrapping chunks of beef in fresh banana leaves and throwing them across the compound wall to their accomplices, and how his relatives had become preoccupied with the stolen meat. Voices were raised, accusations flung back and forth, and an aunt had said, "Those caterers must return every last bit of the stolen goods!" Stolen goods. His mother would have been amused about meat being a stolen good, and even by her funeral ending up a brawl about stolen meat. Why, he wrote to Ifemelu, do our funerals become so quickly about other things that are not about the person who died? Why do the villagers wait for a death before they proceed to avenge past wrongs, those real and those imagined, and why do they dig deep to the bone in their bid to get their pound of flesh?

Ifemelu's reply came an hour later, a rush of heartbroken words. *I am crying as I write this. Do you know how often I wished that she was my mother? She was the only adult—except for Aunty Uju—who treated me like a person with an opinion that mattered. You were so fortunate to be raised by her. She was everything I wanted to be. I am so sorry, Ceiling. I can imagine how ripped apart you must have felt and still sometimes feel. I am in Massachusetts with Aunty Uju and Dike and I am going through something right now that gives me a sense of that kind of pain, but only a small sense. Please give me a number so I can call—if it's okay.*

Her e-mail made him happy. Seeing his mother through her eyes made him happy. And it emboldened him. He wondered what pain she was referring to and hoped that it was the break-up with the black American, although he did not want the relationship to have mattered so much to her that the break-up would throw her into a kind of mourning. He tried to imagine how changed she would be now, how Americanized, especially after being in a relationship with an American. There was a manic optimism that he noticed in many of the people who had moved back from America in the past few years, a head-bobbing, ever-smiling, over-enthusiastic kind of manic optimism that bored him, because it was like a cartoon, without texture or depth. He hoped she had not become like that. He could not imagine that she would have. She had asked for his number. She could not feel so strongly about his mother if she did not still have feelings for him. So he wrote to her again, giving her all of his phone numbers, his three mobile phones, his office phone and his home landline. He ended his e-mail with these words: *It's strange how I have felt, with every major event that has occurred in my life, that you were the only person who would understand.* He felt giddy, but after he clicked Send, regrets assailed him. It had been too much too soon. He should not have written something so heavy. He checked his BlackBerry obsessively, day after day, and by the tenth day he realized she would not write back.

He composed a few e-mails apologizing to her, but he did not send them because it felt awkward apologizing for something he could not name. He never consciously decided to write her the long, detailed e-mails that followed. His claim, that he had missed her at every major event in his life, was grandiose, he knew, but it was not entirely false. Of course there were stretches of time when he had not actively thought about her, when he was submerged in his early excitement with Kosi, in his new child, in a new contract, but she had never been absent. He had held her always clasped in the palm of his mind. Even through her silence, and his confused bitterness.

He began to write to her about his time in England, hoping she would reply and then later looking forward to the writing itself. He had never told himself his own story, never allowed himself to reflect on it, because he was too disoriented by his deportation and then by the suddenness of his new life in Lagos. Writing to her also became a way of writing to himself. He had nothing to lose. Even if she was reading his e-mails with the black American and laughing at his stupidity, he did not mind.

FINALLY, she replied.

> Ceiling, sorry for the silence. Dike attempted suicide. I didn't want to tell you earlier (and I don't know why). He's doing much better, but it has been traumatic and it's affected me more than I thought it would (you know, "attempted" doesn't mean it happened, but I've spent days crying, thinking about what might have happened). I'm sorry I didn't call to give you my condolences about your mother. I had planned to, and appreciated your giving me your phone number, but I took Dike to his psychiatrist appointment that day and afterwards, I just couldn't get myself to do anything. I felt as if I had been felled by something. Aunty Uju tells me I have depression. You know America has a way of turning everything into an illness that needs medicine. I'm not taking medicines, just spending a lot of time with Dike, watching a lot of terrible films with vampires and spaceships. I have loved your e-mails about England and they have been so good for me, in so many ways, and I cannot thank you

enough for writing them. I hope I will have a chance to fill you in on my own life—whenever that is. I've just finished a fellowship at Princeton and for years I wrote an anonymous blog about race, which then became how I made my living, and you can read the archives here. I've postponed my return home. I'll be in touch. Take care and hope all is well with you and your family.

Dike had tried to kill himself. It was impossible to comprehend. His memory of Dike was of a toddler, a white puff of Pampers at his waist, running around in the house in Dolphin Estate. Now he was a teenager who had tried to kill himself. Obinze's first thought was that he wanted to go to Ifemelu, right away. He wanted to buy a ticket and get on a plane to America and be with her, console her, help Dike, make everything right. Then he laughed at his own absurdity.

"Darling, you're not paying attention," Kosi said to him.

"Sorry, omalicha," he said.

"No work thoughts for now."

"Okay, sorry. What were you saying?"

They were in the car, on their way to a nursery-primary school in Ikoyi, visiting during the open day as guests of Jonathan and Isioma, Kosi's friends from church, whose son went there. Kosi had arranged it all, their second school visit, to help them decide where Buchi would go.

Obinze had spent time with them only once, when Kosi invited them to dinner. He thought Isioma interesting; the few things she allowed herself to say were thoughtful, but she often remained silent, shrinking herself, pretending not to be as intelligent as she was, to salve Jonathan's ego, while Jonathan, a bank CEO whose photos were always in the newspapers, dominated the evening with long-winded stories about his dealings with estate agents in Switzerland, the Nigerian governors he had advised and the various companies he had saved from collapse.

He introduced Obinze and Kosi to the school headmistress, a small round Englishwoman, saying, "Obinze and Kosi are our very close friends. I think their daughter might be joining us next year."

"Many high-level expatriates bring their children here," the headmistress said, her tone pride-tinged, and Obinze wondered if this was something she said routinely. She had probably said it often enough to know how well it worked, how much it impressed Nigerians.

Isioma was asking why their son was not yet doing much of mathematics and English.

"Our approach is more conceptual. We like the children to explore their environment during the first year," the headmistress said.

"But it should not be mutually exclusive. They can also start to learn some maths and English," Isioma said. Then, with an amusement that did not try to shield its underlying seriousness, she added, "My niece goes to a school on the mainland and at age six she could spell 'onomatopoeia'!"

The headmistress smiled tightly; she did not, her smile said, think it worthwhile to address the processes of lesser schools. Later, they sat in a large hall and watched the children's production of a Christmas play, about a Nigerian family who find an orphan on their doorstep on Christmas Day. Halfway through the play, a teacher turned on a fan that blew small bits of white cotton wool around the stage. Snow. It was snowing in the play.

"Why do they have snow falling? Are they teaching children that a Christmas is not a real Christmas unless snow falls like it does abroad?" Isioma said.

Jonathan said, "Ahn-ahn, what is wrong with that? It's just a play!"

"It's just a play, but I also see what Isioma is saying," Kosi said, and then turned to Obinze. "Darling?"

Obinze said, "The little girl that played the angel was very good."

In the car, Kosi said, "Your mind is not here."

HE READ all the archives of *Raceteenth or Various Observations About American Blacks (Those Formerly Known as Negroes) by a Non-American Black.* The blog posts astonished him, they seemed so American and so alien, the irreverent voice with its slanginess, its mix of high and low language, and he could not imagine her writing them. He cringed reading her references to her boyfriends—The Hot White Ex, Professor Hunk. He read "Just This Evening" a few times, because it was the most personal post she had written about the black American, and he searched for clues and subtleties, about what kind of man he was, what kind of relationship they had.

So in NYC, Professor Hunk was stopped by the police. They thought he had drugs. American Blacks and American Whites use drugs at the same rate (look this up), but say the word "drugs" and see what image comes to everyone's mind. Professor Hunk is upset. He says he's an Ivy League professor and he knows the deal, and he wonders what it would feel like if he were some poor kid from the inner city. I feel bad for my baby. When we first met, he told me how he wanted to get straight As in high school because of a white teacher who told him to "focus on getting a basketball scholarship, black people are physically inclined and white people are intellectually inclined, it's not good or bad, just different" (and this teacher went to Columbia, just sayin'). So he spent four years proving her wrong. I couldn't identify with this: wanting to do well to prove a point. But I felt bad then too. So off to make him some tea. And administer some TLC.

Because he had last known her when she knew little of the things she blogged about, he felt a sense of loss, as though she had become a person he would no longer recognize.

Part 6

CHAPTER 43

For the first few days, Ifemelu slept on the floor in Dike's room. *It did not happen. It did not happen.* She told herself this often, and yet endless, elliptical thoughts of what could have happened churned in her head. His bed, this room, would have been empty forever. Somewhere inside her, a gash would have ruptured that would never seal itself back. She imagined him taking the pills. Tylenol, mere Tylenol; he had read on the Internet that an overdose could kill you. What was he thinking? Did he think of her? After he came home from the hospital, his stomach pumped, his liver monitored, she searched his face, his gestures, his words, for a sign, for proof that it had really almost happened. He looked no different from before; there were no shadows under his eyes, no funereal air about him. She made him the kind of jollof rice he liked, flecked with bits of red and green peppers, and as he ate, fork moving from the plate to his mouth, saying, "This is pretty good," as he always had in the past, she felt her tears and her questions gathering. Why? Why had he done it? What was on his mind? She did not ask him because the therapist had said that it was best not to ask him anything yet. The days passed. She clung to him, wary of letting go and wary, also, of suffocating him. She was sleepless at first, refusing the small blue pill Aunty Uju offered her, and she would lie awake at night, thinking and turning, her mind held hostage by thoughts of what could have been, until she fell, finally, into a drained sleep. On some days, she woke up scarred with blame for Aunty Uju.

"Do you remember when Dike was telling you something and he said 'we black folk' and you told him 'you are not black'?" she asked Aunty Uju, her voice low because Dike was still asleep upstairs. They were in the kitchen of the condo, in the soft flare of morning light, and Aunty Uju, dressed for work, was standing by the sink and eating yogurt, scooping from a plastic cup.

"Yes, I remember."

"You should not have done that."

"You know what I meant. I didn't want him to start behaving like these people and thinking that everything that happens to him is because he's black."

"You told him what he wasn't but you didn't tell him what he was."

"What are you saying?" Aunty Uju pressed the lever with her foot, the trash can slid out and she threw in the empty yogurt cup. She had switched to part-time work so that she could spend some time with Dike, and drive him to his therapist appointments herself.

"You never reassured him."

"Ifemelu, his suicide attempt was from depression," Aunty Uju said gently, quietly. "It is a clinical disease. Many teenagers suffer from it."

"Do people just wake up and become depressed?"

"Yes, they do."

"Not in Dike's case."

"Three of my patients have attempted suicide, all of them white teenagers. One succeeded," Aunty Uju said, her tone pacifying and sad, as it had been since Dike came home from the hospital.

"His depression is because of his experience, Aunty!" Ifemelu said, her voice rising, and then she was sobbing, apologizing to Aunty Uju, her own guilt spreading and sullying her. Diké would not have swallowed those pills if she had been more diligent, more awake. She had crouched too easily behind laughter, she had failed to till the emotional soil of Dike's jokes. It was true that he laughed, and that his laughter convinced with its sound and its light, but it might have been a shield, and underneath, there might have been a growing pea plant of trauma.

Now, in the shrill, silent aftermath of his suicide attempt, she wondered how much they had masked with all that laughter. She should have worried more. She watched him carefully. She guarded him. She did not want his friends to visit, although the therapist said it was fine if he wanted them to. Even Page, who had burst out crying a few days ago when she was alone with Ifemelu, saying, "I just can't believe he didn't reach out to me." She was a child, well-meaning and simple, and yet Ifemelu felt a wave of resentment towards her, for thinking that Dike should have reached out to her. Kweku came back from his medical mission in Nigeria, and he spent time with Dike, watching television with him, bringing calm and normalcy back.

The weeks passed. Ifemelu stopped panicking when Dike stayed a little too long in the bathroom. His birthday was days away and she asked what he would like, her tears again gathering, because she imagined his birthday passing not as the day he turned seventeen but as the day he would have turned seventeen.

"How about we go to Miami?" he said, half joking, but she took him to Miami and they spent two days in a hotel, ordering burgers at the thatch-covered bar by the pool, talking about everything but the suicide attempt.

"This is the life," he said, lying with his face to the sun. "That blog of yours was a great thing, had you swimming in the dough and all. Now you've closed it, we won't be able to do more of this stuff!"

"I wasn't swimming, kind of just splattering," she said, looking at him, her handsome cousin, and the curl of wet hair on his chest made her sad, because it implied his new, tender adulthood, and she wished he would remain a child; if he remained a child then he would not have taken pills and lain on the basement couch with the certainty that he would never wake up again.

"I love you, Dike. We love you, you know that?"

"I know," he said. "Coz, you should go."

"Go where?"

"Back to Nigeria, like you were planning to. I'm going to be okay, I promise."

"Maybe you could come and visit me," she said.

After a pause, he said, "Yeah."

Part 7

CHAPTER 44

At first, Lagos assaulted her; the sun-dazed haste, the yellow buses full of squashed limbs, the sweating hawkers racing after cars, the advertisements on hulking billboards (others scrawled on walls—PLUMBER CALL 080177777) and the heaps of rubbish that rose on the roadsides like a taunt. Commerce thrummed too defiantly. And the air was dense with exaggeration, conversations full of over-protestations. One morning, a man's body lay on Awolowo Road. Another morning, The Island flooded and cars became gasping boats. Here, she felt, anything could happen, a ripe tomato could burst out of solid stone. And so she had the dizzying sensation of falling, falling into the new person she had become, falling into the strange familiar. Had it always been like this or had it changed so much in her absence? When she left home, only the wealthy had mobile phones, all the numbers started with 090, and girls wanted to date 090 men. Now, her hair braider had a mobile phone, the plantain seller tending a blackened grill had a mobile phone. She had grown up knowing all the bus stops and the side streets, understanding the cryptic codes of conductors and the body language of street hawkers. Now, she struggled to grasp the unspoken. When had shopkeepers become so rude? Had buildings in Lagos always had this patina of decay? And when did it become a city of people quick to beg and too enamoured of free things?

"Americanah!" Ranyinudo teased her often. "You are looking at things with American eyes. But the problem is that you are not even a real Americanah. At least if you had an American accent we would tolerate your complaining!"

Ranyinudo picked her up from the airport, standing by the Arrivals exit in a billowy bridesmaid's dress, her blusher too red on her cheeks like bruises, the green satin flowers in her hair now askew. Ifemelu was struck by how arresting, how attractive, she was. No longer a ropy mass of gangly arms and gangly legs, but now a big, firm, curvy woman, exulting in her weight and height, and it made her imposing, a presence that drew the eyes.

"Ranyi!" Ifemelu said. "I know my coming back is a big deal but I didn't know it was big enough for a ball gown."

"Idiot. I came straight from the wedding. I didn't want to risk the traffic of going home first to change."

They hugged, holding each other close. Ranyinudo smelled of a floral perfume and exhaust fumes and sweat; she smelled of Nigeria.

"You look amazing, Ranyi," Ifemelu said. "I mean, underneath all that war paint. Your pictures didn't even show you well."

"Ifemsco, see you, beautiful babe, even after a long flight," she said, laughing, dismissing the compliment, playing at her old role of the girl who was not the pretty one. Her looks had changed but the excitable, slightly reckless air about her had not. Unchanged, too, was the eternal gurgle in her voice, laughter just beneath the surface, ready to break free, to erupt. She drove fast, braking sharply and glancing often at the BlackBerry on her lap; whenever the traffic stilled, she picked it up and typed swiftly.

"Ranyi, you should text and drive only when you are alone so that you kill only yourself," Ifemelu said.

"Haba! I don't text and drive o. I text when I'm not driving," she said. "This wedding was something else, the best wedding I've been to. I wonder if you'll remember the bride. She was Funke's very good friend in secondary school. Ijeoma, very yellow girl. She went to Holy Child but she used to come to our WAEC lesson with Funke. We became friends in university. If you see her now, eh, she's a serious babe. Her husband has major money. Her engagement ring is bigger than Zuma Rock."

Ifemelu stared out of the window, half listening, thinking how unpretty Lagos was, roads infested with potholes, houses springing up unplanned like weeds. Of her jumble of feelings, she recognized only confusion.

"Lime and peach," Ranyinudo said.

"What?"

"The wedding colours. Lime and peach. The hall decoration was so nice and the cake was just beautiful. Look, I took some pictures. I'm going to put this one up on Facebook." Ranyinudo gave Ifemelu her BlackBerry. Ifemelu held on to it so that Ranyinudo would focus on her driving.

"And I met someone o. He saw me when I was waiting outside for the mass to end. It was so hot, my foundation was melting on my face and I know I looked like a zombie, but he still came to talk to me! That's a good sign. I think this one is serious husband material. Did I tell you my mother was saying novenas to end my relationship when I was dating Ibrahim? At least she will not have a heart attack with this one. His name is Ndudi. Cool name, *abí*? You can't get more Igbo than that. And you should have seen his watch! He's into oil. His business card has Nigerian and international offices."

"Why were you waiting outside during mass?"

"All the bridesmaids had to wait outside because our dresses were indecent." Ranyinudo rolled "indecent" around her tongue and chuckled. "It happens all the time, especially in Catholic churches. We even had cover-ups but the priest said they were too lacy, so we just waited outside until the mass ended. But thank God for that or I would not have met this guy!"

Ifemelu looked at Ranyinudo's dress, its thin straps, its pleated neckline that showed no cleavage. Before she left, were bridesmaids banished from church services because their dresses had spaghetti straps? She did not think so, but she was no longer sure. She was no longer sure what was new in Lagos and what was new in herself. Ranyinudo parked on a street in Lekki, which was bare reclaimed land when Ifemelu left, but now a cavalcade of large houses encircled by high walls.

"My flat is the smallest, so I don't have parking space inside," Ranyinudo said. "The other tenants park inside, but you should see all the shouting that happens in the morning when somebody does not move their car out of the way, and somebody else is late for work!"

Ifemelu climbed out of the car and into the loud, discordant drone of generators, too many generators; the sound pierced the soft middle of her ears and throbbed in her head.

"No light for the past week," Ranyinudo said, shouting to be heard above the generators.

The gateman had hurried over to help with the suitcases.

"Welcome back, Aunty," he said to Ifemelu.

He had not merely said "welcome" but "welcome *back*", as though he somehow knew that she was truly back. She thanked him, and in the grey of the evening darkness, the air burdened with smells, she ached with an almost unbearable emotion that she could not name. It was nostalgic and melancholy, a beautiful sadness for the things she had missed and the things she would never know. Later, sitting on the couch in Ranyinudo's small stylish living room, her feet sunk into the too-soft carpet, the flat-screen TV perched on the opposite wall, Ifemelu looked unbelievingly at herself. She had done it. She had come back. She turned the TV on and searched for the Nigerian channels. On NTA, the first lady, blue scarf wrapped around her face, was addressing a rally of women, and crawling across the screen were the words "The First Lady is Empowering Women with Mosquito Nets".

"I can't remember the last time I watched that stupid station," Ranyinudo said. "They lie for the government but they can't even lie well."

"So which Nigerian channel do you watch?"

"I don't even really watch any o. I watch Style and E! Sometimes CNN and BBC." Ranyinudo had changed into shorts and a T-shirt. "I have a girl who comes and cooks and cleans for me, but I made this stew myself because you were coming, so you must eat it o. What will you drink? I have malt and orange juice."

"Malt! I'm going to drink all the malt in Nigeria. I used to buy it from a Hispanic supermarket in Baltimore, but it was not the same thing."

"I ate really nice ofada rice at the wedding, I'm not hungry," Ranyinudo said. But, after she served Ifemelu's food on a dinner plate, she ate some rice and chicken stew from a plastic bowl, perched on the arm of the couch, while they gossiped about old friends: Priye was an event planner and had recently gone big time after being introduced to the governor's wife. Tochi had lost her job at a bank after the last bank crisis, but she had married a wealthy lawyer and had a baby.

"Tochi used to tell me how much people had in their accounts," Ranyinudo said. "Remember that guy Mekkus Parara who was dying for Ginika? Remember how he always had smelly yellow patches under his arms? He has major money now, but it is dirty money. You know, all these guys who do fraud in London and America, then run back to Nigeria with the money and build mighty houses in Victoria Garden City. Tochi told me that he never came to the bank himself. He used to send his boys with Ghana Must Go bags to carry ten million today, twenty million tomorrow. Me, I never wanted to work in a bank. The problem with working in a bank is that if you don't get a good branch with high-net customers, you are finished. You will spend all your time attending to useless traders. Tochi was lucky with her job and she worked in a good branch and she met her husband there. Do you want another malt?"

Ranyinudo got up. There was a luxurious, womanly slowness to her gait, a lift, a roll, a toggle of her buttocks with each step. A Nigerian walk. A walk, too, that hinted at excess, as though it spoke of something in need of toning down. Ifemelu took the cold bottle of malt from Ranyinudo and wondered if this would have been her life if she had not left, if she would be like Ranyinudo, working for an advertising company, living in a one-bedroom flat whose rent her salary could not pay, attending a Pentecostal church where she was an usher, and dating a married chief executive who bought her business-class tickets to London. Ranyinudo showed Ifemelu his photographs on her phone. In one, he was bare-chested with the slight swell of a middle-aged belly, reclining on Ranyinudo's bed, smiling the bashful smile of a man just sated from sex. In another, he was looking down in a close-up shot, his face a blurred and mysterious silhouette. There was something attractive, even distinguished, about his grey-speckled hair.

"Is it me or does he look like a tortoise?" Ifemelu said.

"It's you. But Ifem, seriously, Don is a good man o. Not like many of these useless Lagos men running around town."

"Ranyi, you told me it was just a passing thing. But two years is not a passing thing. I worry about you."

"I have feelings for him, I won't deny it, but I want to marry and he knows that. I used to think maybe I should have a child for him but look at Uche Okafor, remember her from Nsukka? She had a child for the managing director of Hale Bank and the man told her to go to hell, that he is not the father, and now she is left with raising a child alone. *Na wa.*"

Ranyinudo was looking at the photograph on her phone with a faint, fond smile. Earlier, on the drive back from the airport, she had said, as she slowed down to sink into, and then climb out of, a large pothole, "I really want Don to change this car. He has been promising for the past three months. I need a jeep. Do you see how terrible the roads are?" And Ifemelu felt something between fascination and longing for Ranyinudo's life. A life in which she waved a hand and things fell from the sky, things that she quite simply expected should fall from the sky.

At midnight, Ranyinudo turned off her generator and opened the windows. "I have been running this generator for one straight week, can you imagine? The light situation has not been this bad in a long time."

The coolness dissipated quickly. Warm, humid air gagged the room, and soon Ifemelu was tossing in the wetness of her own sweat. A painful throbbing had started behind her eyes and a mosquito was buzzing nearby and she felt suddenly, guiltily grateful that she had a blue American passport in her bag. It shielded her from choicelessness. She could always leave; she did not have to stay.

"What kind of humidity is this?" she said. She was on Ranyinudo's bed, and Ranyinudo was on a mattress on the floor. "I can't breathe."

"I can't breathe," Ranyinudo mimicked, her voice laughter-filled. "Haba! Americanah!"

CHAPTER 45

Ifemelu had found the listing on *Nigerian Jobs Online*—"features editor for leading women's monthly magazine". She edited her résumé, invented past experience as a staff writer on a women's magazine ("folded due to bankruptcy" in parentheses), and days after she sent it off by courier, the publisher of *Zoe* called from Lagos. There was, about the mature, friendly voice on the other end of the line, a vague air of inappropriateness. "Oh, call me Aunty Onenu," she said cheerfully when Ifemelu asked who was speaking. Before she offered Ifemelu the job, she said, tone hushed in confidence, "My husband did not support me when I started this, because he thought men would chase me if I went to seek advertising." Ifemelu sensed that the magazine was a hobby for Aunty Onenu, a hobby that meant something, but still a hobby. Not a passion. Not something that consumed her. And when she met Aunty Onenu, she felt this more strongly: here was a woman easy to like but difficult to take seriously.

Ifemelu went with Ranyinudo to Aunty Onenu's home in Ikoyi. They sat on leather sofas that felt cold to the touch, and talked in low voices, until Aunty Onenu appeared. A slim, smiling, well-preserved woman, wearing leggings, a large T-shirt and an overly youthful weave, the wavy hair trailing all the way to her back.

"My new features editor has come from America!" she said, hugging Ifemelu. It was difficult to tell her age, anything between fifty and sixty-five, but it was easy to tell that she had not been born with her light complexion, its sheen was too waxy and her knuckles were dark, as though those folds of skin had valiantly resisted her bleaching cream.

"I wanted you to come around before you start on Monday so I can welcome you personally," Aunty Onenu said.

"Thank you." Ifemelu thought the home visit unprofessional and odd, but this was a small magazine, and this was Nigeria, where boundaries were blurred, where work blended into life, and bosses were called Mummy. Besides, she already imagined taking over the running of *Zoe*, turning it into a vibrant, relevant companion for Nigerian women, and—who knew—perhaps one day buying out Aunty Onenu. And she would not welcome new recruits in her home.

"You are a pretty girl," Aunty Onenu said, nodding, as though being pretty were needed for the job and she had worried that Ifemelu might not be. "I liked how you sounded on the phone. I am sure with you on board our circulation will soon surpass *Glass*. You know we are a much younger publication but already catching up to them!"

A steward in white, a grave, elderly man, emerged to ask what they would drink.

"Aunty Onenu, I've been reading back issues of both *Glass* and *Zoe*, and I have some ideas about what we can do differently," Ifemelu said, after the steward left to get their orange juice.

"You are a real American! Ready to get to work, a no-nonsense person! Very good. First of all, tell me how you think we compare to *Glass*?"

Ifemelu had thought both magazines vapid, but *Glass* was better edited, the page colours did not bleed as badly as they did in *Zoe*, and it was more visible in traffic; whenever Ranyinudo's car slowed, there was a hawker pressing a copy of *Glass* against her window. But because she could already see Aunty Onenu's obsession with the competition, so nakedly personal, she said, "It's about the same, but I think we can do better. We need to cut down the profile interviews and do just one a month and profile a woman who has actually achieved something real on her own. We need more personal columns, and we should introduce a rotating guest column, and do more health and money, have a stronger online presence, and stop lifting foreign magazine pieces. Most of your readers can't go into the market and buy broccoli because we don't have it in Nigeria, so why does this month's *Zoe* have a recipe for cream of broccoli soup?"

"Yes, yes," Aunty Onenu said, slowly. She seemed astonished. Then, as though recovering herself, she said, "Very good. We'll discuss all this on Monday."

In the car, Ranyinudo said, "Talking to your new boss like that, ha! If you had not come from America, she would have fired you immediately."

"I wonder what the story is between her and the *Glass* publisher."

"I read in one of the tabloids that they hate each other. I am sure it is man trouble, what else? Women, eh! I think Aunty Onenu started *Zoe* just to compete with *Glass.* As far as I'm concerned, she's not a publisher, she's just a rich woman who decided to start a magazine, and tomorrow she might close it and start a spa."

"And what an ugly house," Ifemelu said. It was monstrous, with two alabaster angels guarding the gate, and a dome-shaped fountain sputtering in the front yard.

"Ugly *kwa*? What are you talking about? The house is beautiful!"

"Not to me," Ifemelu said, and yet she had once found houses like that beautiful. But here she was now, disliking it with the haughty confidence of a person who recognized kitsch.

"Her generator is as big as my flat and it is completely noiseless!" Ranyinudo said. "Did you notice the generator house on the side of the gate?"

Ifemelu had not noticed. And it piqued her. This was what a true Lagosian should have noticed: the generator house, the generator size.

On Kingsway Road, she thought she saw Obinze drive past in a low-slung black Mercedes and she sat up, straining and peering, but, slowed at a traffic jam, she saw that the man looked nothing like him. There were other imagined glimpses of Obinze over the next weeks, people she knew were not him but could have been: the straight-backed figure in a suit walking into Aunty Onenu's office, the man in the back of a car with tinted windows, his face bent to a phone, the figure behind her in the supermarket line. She even imagined, when she first went to meet her landlord, that she would walk in and discover Obinze sitting there. The estate agent had told her that the landlord preferred expatriate renters. "But he relaxed when I told him you came from America," he added. The landlord was an elderly man in a brown caftan and matching trousers; he had the weathered skin and wounded air of one who had endured much at the hands of others.

"I do not rent to Igbo people," he said softly, startling her. Were such things now said so easily? Had they been said so easily and had she merely forgotten? "That is my policy since one Igbo man destroyed my house at Yaba. But you look like a responsible somebody."

"Yes, I am responsible," she said, and feigned a simpering smile. The other flats she liked were too expensive. Even though pipes poked out under the kitchen sink and the toilet was lopsided and the bathroom tiles shoddily laid, this was the best she could afford. She liked the airiness of the living room, with its large windows, and the narrow flight of stairs that led to a tiny verandah charmed her, but, most of all, it was in Ikoyi. And she wanted to live in Ikoyi. Growing up, Ikoyi had reeked of gentility, a faraway gentility that she could not touch: the people who lived in Ikoyi had faces free of pimples and drivers designated "the children's driver". The first day she saw the flat, she stood on the verandah and looked across at the compound next door, a grand colonial house, now yellowed from decay, the grounds swallowed in foliage, grass and shrubs climbing atop one another. On the roof of the house, a part of which had collapsed and sunk in, she saw a movement, a turquoise splash of feathers. It was a peacock. The estate agent told her that an army officer had lived there during General Abacha's regime; now the house was tied up in court. And she imagined the people who had lived there fifteen years ago while she, in a little flat on the crowded mainland, longed for their spacious, serene lives.

She wrote the cheque for two years' rent. This was why people took bribes and asked for bribes; how else could anyone honestly pay two years' rent in advance? She planned to fill her verandah with white lilies in clay pots, and decorate her living room in pastels, but first, she had to find an electrician to install air conditioners, a painter to redo the oily walls, and somebody to lay new tiles in the kitchen and bathroom. The estate agent brought a man who did tiles. It took him a week and, when the estate agent called her to say that the work was done, she went eagerly to the flat. In the bathroom, she stared in disbelief. The tile edges were rough, tiny spaces gaping at the corners. One tile had an ugly crack across the middle. It looked like something done by an impatient child.

"What is this nonsense? Look at how rough this is! One tile is broken! This is even worse than the old tiles! How can you be happy with this useless work?" she asked the man.

He shrugged; he clearly thought she was making unnecessary trouble. "I am happy with the work, Aunty."

"You want me to pay you?"

A small smile. "Ah, Aunty, but I have finish the work."

The estate agent intervened. "Don't worry, ma, he will repair the broken one."

The tile man looked reluctant. "But I have finish the work. The problem is the tile is breaking very easily. It is the quality of tile."

"You have finished? You do this rubbish job and say you have finished?" Her anger was growing, her voice rising and hardening. "I will not pay you what we agreed, no way, because you have not done what we agreed."

The tile man was staring at her, eyes narrowed.

"And if you want trouble, trust me, you will get it," Ifemelu said. "The first thing I will do is call the commissioner of police and they will lock you up in Alagbon Close!" She was screaming now. "Do you know who I am? You don't know who I am, that is why you can do this kind of rubbish work for me!"

The man looked cowed. She had surprised herself. Where had that come from, the false bravado, the easy resort to threats? A memory came to her, undiminished after so many years, of the day Aunty Uju's General died, how Aunty Uju had threatened his relatives. "No, don't go, just stay there," she had said to them. "Stay there while I go and call my boys from the army barracks."

The estate agent said, "Aunty, don't worry, he will do the work again."

Later, Ranyinudo told her, "You are no longer behaving like an Americanah!" and despite herself, Ifemelu felt pleased to hear this.

"The problem is that we no longer have artisans in this country," Ranyinudo said. "Ghanaians are better. My boss is building a house and he is using only Ghanaians to do his finishing. Nigerians will do rubbish for you. They do not take their time to finish things properly. It's terrible. But Ifem, you should have called Obinze. He would have sorted everything out for you. This is what he does, after all. He must have all kinds of contacts. You should have called him before you even started looking for a flat. He could have given you reduced rent in one of his properties, even a free flat *sef.* I don't know what you are waiting for before you call him."

Ifemelu shook her head. Ranyinudo, for whom men existed only as sources of things. She could not imagine calling Obinze to ask him for reduced rent in one of his properties. Still, she did not know why she had not called him at all. She had thought of it many times, often bringing out her phone to scroll to his number, and yet she had not called. He still sent e-mails, saying he hoped she was fine, or he hoped Dike was doing better, and she replied to a few, always briefly, replies he would assume were sent from America.

CHAPTER 46

She spent weekends with her parents, in the old flat, happy simply to sit and look at the walls that had witnessed her childhood; only when she began to eat her mother's stew, an oil layer floating on top of the pureed tomatoes, did she realize how much she had missed it. The neighbours stopped by to greet her, the daughter back from America. Many of them were new and unfamiliar, but she felt a sentimental fondness for them, because they reminded her of the others she had known, Mama Bomboy downstairs who had once pulled her ear when she was in primary school and said, "You do not greet your elders," Oga Tony upstairs who smoked on his verandah, the trader next door who called her, for reasons she never knew, "champion".

"They are just coming to see if you will give them anything," her mother said, in a whisper, as if the neighbours who had all left might overhear. "They all expected me to buy something for them when we went to America, so I went to the market and bought small-small bottles of perfume and told them it was from America!"

Her parents liked to talk about their visit to Baltimore, her mother about the sales, her father about how he could not understand the news because Americans now used expressions like "divvy up" and "nuke" in serious news.

"It is the final infantilization and informalization of America! It portends the end of the American empire, and they are killing themselves from within!" he pronounced.

Ifemelu humoured them, listening to their observations and memories, and hoped that neither of them would bring up Blaine; she had told them a work issue had delayed his visit.

She did not have to lie to her old friends about Blaine, but she did, telling them she was in a serious relationship and he would join her in Lagos soon. It surprised her how quickly, during reunions with old friends, the subject of marriage came up, a waspish tone in the voices of the unmarried, a smugness in those of the married. Ifemelu wanted to talk about the past, about the teachers they had mocked and the boys they had liked, but marriage was always the preferred topic—whose husband was a dog, who was on a desperate prowl, posting too many dressed-up pictures of herself on Facebook, whose man had disappointed her after four years and left her to marry a small girl he could control. (When Ifemelu told Ranyinudo that she had run into an old classmate, Vivian, at the bank, Ranyinudo's first question was "Is she married?") And so she used Blaine as armour. If they knew of Blaine, then the married friends would not tell her "Don't worry, your own will come, just pray about it," and the unmarried friends would not assume that she was a member of the self-pity party of the single. There was, also, a strained nostalgia in those reunions, some in Ranyinudo's flat, some in hers, some in restaurants, because she struggled to find, in these adult women, some remnants from her past that were often no longer there.

Tochi was unrecognizable now, so fat that even her nose had changed shape, her double chin hanging below her face like a bread roll. She came to Ifemelu's flat with her baby in one hand, her BlackBerry in the other and a house help trailing behind, holding a canvas bag full of bottles and bibs. "Madam America" was Tochi's greeting, and then she spoke, for the rest of her visit, in defensive spurts, as though she had come determined to battle Ifemelu's Americanness.

"I buy only British clothes for my baby because American ones fade after one wash," she said. "My husband wanted us to move to America but I refused, because the education system is so bad. An international agency rated it the lowest in the developed countries, you know."

Tochi had always been perceptive and thoughtful; it was Tochi who had intervened with calm reason whenever Ifemelu and Ranyinudo argued in secondary school. In Tochi's changed persona, in her need to defend against imagined slights, Ifemelu saw a great personal unhappiness. And so she appeased Tochi, putting America down, talking only about the things she, too, disliked about America, exaggerating her non-American accent, until the conversation became an enervating charade. Finally Tochi's baby vomited, a yellowish liquid that the house help hastily wiped, and Tochi said, "We should go, baby wants to sleep." Ifemelu, relieved, watched her leave. People changed, sometimes they changed too much.

Priye had not changed so much as hardened, her personality coated in chrome. She arrived at Ranyinudo's flat with a pile of newspapers, full of photographs of the big wedding she had just planned. Ifemelu imagined how people would talk about Priye. She is doing well, they would say, she is really doing well.

"My phone has not stopped ringing since last week!" Priye said triumphantly, pushing back the auburn straight weave that fell across one eye; each time she raised a hand to push back the hair, which invariably fell back again across her eye since it had been sewn in to do so, Ifemelu was distracted by the brittle pink colour of her nails. Priye had the sure, slightly sinister manner of someone who could get other people to do what she wanted. And she glittered—her yellow-gold earrings, the metal studs on her designer bag, the sparkly bronze lipstick.

"It was a very successful wedding: we had seven governors in attendance, seven!" she said.

"And none of them knew the couple, I'm sure," Ifemelu said drily.

Priye gestured, a shrug, an upward flick of her palm, to show how irrelevant that was.

"Since when has the success of weddings been measured by how many governors attend?" Ifemelu asked.

"It shows you're connected. It shows prestige. Do you know how powerful governors in this country are? Executive power is not a small thing," Priye said.

"Me, I want as many governors as possible to come to my own wedding o. It shows levels, serious levels," Ranyinudo said. She was studying the photographs, turning the newspaper pages slowly. "Priye, you heard Mosope is getting married in two weeks?"

"Yes. She approached me, but their budget was too small for me. That girl never understood the first rule of life in this Lagos. You do not marry the man you love. You marry the man who can best maintain you."

"Amen!" Ranyinudo said, laughing. "But sometimes one man can be both o. This is the season of weddings. When will it be my turn,

Father Lord?" She glanced upwards, raised her hands as though in prayer.

"I've told Ranyinudo that I'll do her wedding at no commission," Priye said to Ifemelu. "And I'll do yours too, Ifem."

"Thank you, but I think Blaine will prefer a governor-free event," Ifemelu said, and they all laughed. "We'll probably do something small on a beach."

Sometimes she believed her own lies. She could see it now, she and Blaine wearing white on a beach in the Caribbean, surrounded by a few friends, running to a makeshift altar of sand and flowers, and Shan watching and hoping one of them would trip and fall.

CHAPTER 47

Onikan was the old Lagos, a slice of the past, a temple to the faded splendour of the colonial years; Ifemelu remembered how houses here had sagged, unpainted and untended, and mould crept up the walls, and gate hinges rusted and atrophied. But developers were renovating and dismantling now, and on the ground floor of a newly refurbished three-storey building, heavy glass doors opened into a reception area painted a terracotta orange, where a pleasant-faced receptionist, Esther, sat, and behind her loomed giant words in silver: ZOE MAGAZINE. Esther was full of small ambitions. Ifemelu imagined her combing through the piles of second-hand shoes and clothes in the side stalls of Tejuosho market, finding the best pieces and then haggling tirelessly with the trader. She wore neatly pressed clothes and scuffed but carefully polished high heels, read books like *Praying Your Way to Prosperity*, and was superior with the drivers and ingratiating with the editors. "This your earring is very fine, ma," she said to Ifemelu. "If you ever want to throw it away, please give it to me to help you throw it away." And she ceaselessly invited Ifemelu to her church.

"Will you come this Sunday, ma? My pastor is a powerful man of God. So many people have testimonies of miracles that have happened in their lives because of him."

"Why do you think I need to come to your church, Esther?"

"You will like it, ma. It is a spirit-filled church."

At first, the "ma" had made Ifemelu uncomfortable, Esther was at least five years older than she was, but status, of course, surpassed age: she was the features editor, with a car and a driver and the spirit of America hanging over her head, and even Esther expected her to play the madam. And so she did, complimenting Esther and joking with Esther, but always in that manner that was both playful and patronizing, and sometimes giving Esther things, an old handbag, an old watch. Just as she did with her driver, Ayo. She complained about his speeding, threatened to fire him for being late again, asked him to repeat her instructions to make sure he had understood. Yet she always heard the unnatural high pitch of her voice when she said these things, unable fully to convince even herself of her own madamness.

Aunty Onenu liked to say, "Most of my staff are foreign graduates while that woman at *Glass* hires riff-raff who cannot punctuate sentences!" Ifemelu imagined her saying this at a dinner party, "most of my staff" making the magazine sound like a large, busy operation, although it was an editorial staff of three, an administrative staff of four, and only Ifemelu and Doris, the editor, had foreign degrees. Doris, thin and hollow-eyed, a vegetarian who announced that she was a vegetarian as soon as she possibly could, spoke with a teenage American accent that made her sentences sound like questions, except for when she was speaking to her mother on the phone; then her English took on a flat, stolid Nigerianness. Her long sisterlocks were sun-bleached a coppery tone, and she dressed unusually—white socks and brogues, men's shirts tucked into pedal pushers—which she considered original, and which everyone in the office forgave her for because she had come back from abroad. She wore no make-up except for bright-red lipstick, and it gave her face a certain shock value, that slash of crimson, which was probably her intent, but her unadorned skin tended towards ashy grey and Ifemelu's first urge, when they met, was to suggest a good moisturizer.

"You went to Wellson in Philly? I went to Temple?" Doris said, as though to establish right away that they were members of the same superior club. "You're going to be sharing this office with me and Zemaye. She's the assistant editor, and she's out on assignment until this afternoon, or maybe longer? She always stays as long as she wants."

Ifemelu caught the malice. It was not subtle; Doris had meant for it to be caught.

"I thought you could, like, just spend this week getting used to things? See what we do? And then next week you can start some assignments?" Doris said.

"Okay," Ifemelu said.

The office itself, a large room with four desks, on each of which sat a computer, looked bare and untested, as though it was everybody's first day at work. Ifemelu was not sure what would make it look otherwise, perhaps pictures of family on the desks, or just more things, more files and papers and staplers, proof of its being inhabited.

"I had a great job in New York, but I decided to move back and settle down here?" Doris said. "Like, family pressure to settle down and stuff, you know? Like I'm the only daughter? When I first got back one of my aunts looked at me and said, 'I can get you a job at a good bank, but you have to cut off that dada hair.'" She shook her head from side to side in mockery as she mimicked a Nigerian accent. "I swear to God this city is full of banks that just want you to be reasonably attractive in a kind of predictable way and you have a job in customer service? Anyway, I took this job because I'm interested in the magazine business? And this is like a good place to meet people, because of all the events we get to go to, you know?" Doris sounded as if she and Ifemelu somehow shared the same plot, the same view of the world. Ifemelu felt a small resentment at this, the arrogance of Doris's certainty that she, too, would of course feel the same way as Doris.

Just before lunchtime, into the office walked a woman in a tight pencil skirt and patent shoes high as stilts, her straightened hair sleekly pulled back. She was not pretty, her facial features created no harmony, but she carried herself as though she was. Nubile. She made Ifemelu think of that word, with her shapely slenderness, her tiny waist and the unexpected high curves of her breasts.

"Hi. You're Ifemelu, right? Welcome to *Zoe.* I'm Zemaye." She shook Ifemelu's hand, her face carefully neutral.

"Hi, Zemaye. It's nice to meet you. You have a lovely name," Ifemelu said.

"Thank you." She was used to hearing it. "I hope you don't like cold rooms."

"Cold rooms?"

"Yes. Doris likes to put the AC on too high and I have to wear a sweater in the office, but now that you are here sharing the office, maybe we can vote," Zemaye said, settling down at her desk.

"What are you talking about? Since when do you have to wear a sweater in the office?" Doris asked.

Zemaye raised her eyebrows and pulled out a thick shawl from her drawer.

"It's the humidity that's just so crazy?" Doris said, turning to Ifemelu, expecting agreement. "I felt like I couldn't breathe when I first came back?"

Zemaye, too, turned to Ifemelu. "I am a Delta girl, home-made, born and bred. So I did not grow up with air conditioners and I can breathe without a room being cold." She spoke in an impassive tone, and everything she said was delivered evenly, never rising or falling.

"Well, I don't know about cold?" Doris said. "Most offices in Lagos have air conditioners?"

"Not turned to the lowest temperature," Zemaye said.

"You've never said anything about it?"

"I tell you all the time, Doris."

"I mean that it actually prevents you from working?"

"It's cold, full stop," Zemaye said.

Their mutual dislike was a smouldering, stalking leopard in the room.

"I don't like cold," Ifemelu said. "I think I would freeze if the AC was turned on to the lowest."

Doris blinked. She looked not merely betrayed but surprised that she had been betrayed. "Well, okay, we can turn it off and on throughout the day? I have a hard time breathing without the AC and the windows are so damn small?"

"Okay," Ifemelu said.

Zemaye said nothing; she had turned to her computer, as though indifferent to this small victory, and Ifemelu felt unaccountably disappointed. She had taken sides, after all, boldly standing with Zemaye, and yet Zemaye remained expressionless, hard to read. Ifemelu wondered what her story was. Zemaye intrigued her.

Later, Doris and Zemaye were looking over photographs spread out on Doris's table, of a portly woman wearing tight ruffled clothes, when Zemaye said, "Excuse me, I'm pressed," and hurried to the door, her supple movements making Ifemelu want to lose weight. Doris's eyes followed her too.

"Don't you just hate it how people say 'I'm pressed' or 'I want to ease myself' when they want to go to the bathroom?" Doris asked.

Ifemelu laughed. "I know!"

"I guess 'bathroom' is very American. But there's 'toilet', 'restroom', 'the ladies'."

"I never liked 'the ladies'. I like 'toilet'."

"Me too!" Doris said. "And don't you just hate it when people here use 'on' as a verb? On the light!"

"You know what I can't stand? When people say 'take' instead of 'drink'. 'I will take wine. I don't take beer.'"

"Oh God, I know!"

They were laughing when Zemaye came back in, and she looked at Ifemelu with her eerily neutral expression and said, "You people must be discussing the next Been-To meeting."

"What's that?" Ifemelu asked.

"Doris talks about them all the time, but she can't invite me because it is only for people who have come from abroad." If there was mockery in Zemaye's tone, and there had to be, she kept it under her flat delivery.

"Oh, please. 'Been-To' is like so outdated? This is not 1960," Doris said. Then to Ifemelu, she said, "I was actually going to tell you about it. It's called the Nigerpolitan Club and it's just a bunch of people who have recently moved back, some from England, but mostly from the US? Really low-key, just like sharing experiences and networking? I bet you'll know some of the people. You should totally come?"

"Yes, I'd like to."

Doris got up and took her handbag. "I have to go to Aunty Onenu's house."

After she left, the room was silent, Zemaye typing at her computer, Ifemelu browsing the Internet, and wondering what Zemaye was thinking.

Finally, Zemaye said, "So you were a famous race blogger in America. When Aunty Onenu told us, I didn't understand."

"What do you mean?"

"Why race?"

"I discovered race in America and it fascinated me."

"Hmm," Zemaye murmured, as though she thought this, discovering race, an exotic and self-indulgent phenomenon. "Aunty Onenu said your boyfriend is a black American and he is coming soon?"

Ifemelu was surprised. Aunty Onenu had asked about her personal life, with a casualness that was also insistent, and she had told her the false story of Blaine, thinking that her boss had no business with her personal life anyway, and now it seemed that personal life had been shared with other staff. Perhaps she was being too American about it, fixating on privacy for its own sake. What did it really matter if Zemaye knew of Blaine?

"Yes. He should be here by next month," she said.

"Why is it only black people that are criminals over there?"

Ifemelu opened her mouth and closed it. Here she was, famous race blogger, and she was lost for words.

"I love *Cops.* It is because of that show that I have DSTV," Zemaye said. "And all the criminals are black people."

"It's like saying every Nigerian is a 419," Ifemelu said finally. She sounded too limp, too insufficient.

"But it is true, all of us have small 419 in our blood!" Zemaye smiled with what seemed to be, for the first time, a real amusement in her eyes. Then she added, "Sorry o. I did not mean that your boyfriend is a criminal. I was just asking."

CHAPTER 48

Ifemelu asked Ranyinudo to come with her and Doris to the Nigerpolitan meeting.

"I don't have energy for you returnees, please," Ranyinudo said. "Besides, Ndudi is finally back from all his travelling up and down and we're going out."

"Good luck choosing a man over your friend, you witch."

"Yes o. Are you the person that will marry me? Meanwhile I told Don I am going out with you, so make sure you don't go anywhere that he might go." Ranyinudo was laughing. She was still seeing Don, waiting to make sure that Ndudi was "serious" before she stopped, and she hoped, too, that Don would get her the new car before then.

The Nigerpolitan Club meeting: a small cluster of people drinking champagne in paper cups, at the poolside of a home in Osborne Estate, chic people, all dripping with savoir faire, each nursing a self-styled quirkiness—a ginger-coloured Afro, a T-shirt with a graphic of Thomas Sankara, oversize handmade earrings that hung like pieces of modern art. Their voices burred with foreign accents. *You can't find a decent smoothie in this city! Oh my God, were you at that conference? What this country needs is an active civil society.* Ifemelu knew some of them. She chatted with Bisola and Yagazie, both of whom had natural hair, worn in a twist-out, a halo of spirals framing their faces. They talked about hair salons here, where the hairdressers struggled and fumbled to comb natural hair, as though it were an alien eruption, as though their own hair was not the same way before it was defeated by chemicals.

"The salon girls are always like, 'Aunty, you don't want to relax your hair?' It's ridiculous that Africans don't value our natural hair in Africa," Yagazie said.

"I know," Ifemelu said, and she caught the righteousness in her voice, in all their voices. They were the sanctified, the returnees, back home with an extra gleaming layer. Ikenna joined them, a lawyer who had lived outside Philadelphia and whom she had met at a Blogging While Brown convention. And Fred joined them too. He had introduced himself to Ifemelu earlier, a pudgy, well-groomed man. "I lived in Boston until last year," he said, in a falsely low-key way, because "Boston" was code for Harvard (otherwise he would say MIT or Tufts or anywhere else), just as another woman said, "I was in New Haven," in that coy manner that pretended not to be coy, which meant that she had been at Yale. Other people joined them, all encircled by a familiarity, because they could reach so easily for the same references. Soon they were laughing and listing the things they missed about America.

"Low-fat soya milk, NPR, fast Internet," Ifemelu said.

"Good customer service, good customer service, good customer service," Bisola said. "Folks here behave as if they are doing you a favour by serving you. The high-end places are okay, not great, but the regular restaurants? Forget it. The other day I asked a waiter if I could get boiled yam with a different sauce than was on the menu and he just looked at me and said no. Hilarious."

"But the American customer service can be so annoying. Someone hovering around and bothering you all the time. *Are you still working on that?* Since when did eating become work?" Yagazie said.

"I miss a decent vegetarian place?" Doris said, and then talked about her new house help who could not make a simple sandwich, about how she had ordered a vegetarian spring roll at a restaurant in Victoria Island, bit in and tasted chicken, and the waiter, when summoned, just smiled and said, "Maybe they put chicken today." There was laughter. Fred said a good vegetarian place would open soon, now that there was so much new investment in the country; somebody would figure out that there was a vegetarian market to cater to.

"A vegetarian restaurant? Impossible. There are only four vegetarians in this country, including Doris," Bisola said.

"You're not vegetarian, are you?" Fred asked Ifemelu. He just wanted to talk to her. She had looked up from time to time to find his eyes on her.

"No," she said.

"Oh, there's this new place that opened on Akin Adesola," Bisola said. "The brunch is really good. They have the kinds of things we can eat. We should go next Sunday."

They have the kinds of things we can eat. An unease crept up on Ifemelu. She was comfortable here, and she wished she were not. She wished, too, that she was not so interested in this new restaurant, did not perk up, imagining fresh green salads and steamed still-firm vegetables. She loved eating all the things she had missed while away, jollof rice cooked with a lot of oil, fried plantains, boiled yams, but she longed, also, for the other things she had become used to in America, even quinoa, Blaine's specialty, made with feta and tomatoes. This was what she hoped she had not become but feared that she had: a "they have the kinds of things we can eat" kind of person.

Fred was talking about Nollywood, speaking a little too loudly. "Nollywood is really public theatre, and if you understand it like that, then it is more tolerable. It's for public consumption, even mass participation, not the kind of individual experience that film is." He was looking at her, soliciting her agreement with his eyes: they were not supposed to watch Nollywood, people like them, and if they did, then only as amusing anthropology.

"I like Nollywood," Ifemelu said, even though she, too, thought Nollywood was more theatre than film. The urge to be contrarian was strong. If she set herself apart, perhaps she would be less of the person she feared she had become. "Nollywood may be melodramatic, but life in Nigeria is very melodramatic."

"Really?" the New Haven woman said, squeezing her paper cup in her hand, as though she thought it a great oddity, that a person at this gathering would like Nollywood. "It is so offensive to my intelligence. I mean, the products are just bad. What does it say about us?"

"But Hollywood makes equally bad movies. They just make them with better lighting," Ifemelu said.

Fred laughed, too heartily, to let her know he was on her side.

"It's not just about the technical stuff," the New Haven woman said. "The industry is regressive. I mean, the portrayal of women? The films are more misogynistic than the society."

Ifemelu saw a man across the pool whose wide shoulders reminded her of Obinze. But he was too tall to be Obinze. She wondered what

Obinze would make of a gathering like this. Would he even come? He had been deported from England, after all, so perhaps he would not consider himself a returnee like them.

"Hey, come back," Fred said, moving closer to her, claiming personal space. "Your mind isn't here."

She smiled thinly. "It is now."

Fred knew things. He had the confidence of a person who knew practical things. He probably had a Harvard MBA and used words like "capacity" and "value" in conversation. He would not dream in imagery, but in facts and figures.

"There's a concert tomorrow at MUSON. Do you like classical music?" he asked.

"No." She had not expected that he would, either.

"Are you willing to like classical music?"

"Willing to like something, it's a strange idea," she said, now curious about him, vaguely interested in him. They talked. Fred mentioned Stravinsky and Strauss, Vermeer and Van Dyck, making unnecessary references, quoting too often, his spirits attuned across the Atlantic, too transparent in his performance, too eager to show how much he knew of the Western world. Ifemelu listened with a wide internal yawn. She had been wrong about him. He was not the MBA type who thought the world was a business. He was an impresario, well oiled and well practised, the sort of man who did a good American accent and a good British accent, who knew what to say to foreigners, how to make foreigners comfortable, and who could easily get foreign grants for dubious projects. She wondered what he was like beneath that practised layer.

"So will you come for this drinks thing?" he asked.

"I'm exhausted," she said. "I think I'll head home. But call me."

CHAPTER 49

The speedboat was gliding on foaming water, past beaches of ivory sand, and trees a bursting, well-fed green. Ifemelu was laughing. She caught herself in mid-laughter, and looked at her present, an orange life jacket strapped around her, a ship in the greying distance, her friends in their sunglasses, on their way to Priye's friend's beach house, where they would grill meat and race barefoot. She thought: I'm really home. I'm home. She no longer sent Ranyinudo texts about what to do—*Should I buy meat in Shoprite or send Iyabo to the market? Where should I buy hangers?* Now she awoke to the sound of the peacocks, and got out of bed, with the shape of her day familiar and her routines unthinking. She had signed up at a gym, but had gone only twice, because after work she preferred to meet her friends, and even though she always planned not to eat, she ended up eating a club sandwich and drinking one or two Chapmans, and then she would decide to postpone the gym. Her clothes felt even tighter now. Somewhere, in a faraway part of her mind, she wanted to lose weight before she saw Obinze again. She had not called him; she would wait until she was back to her slender self.

At work, she felt an encroaching restlessness. *Zoe* stifled her. It was like wearing a scratchy sweater in the cold: she longed to yank it off, but was afraid of what would happen if she did. She thought often of starting a blog, writing about what she cared about, building it up slowly, and finally publishing her own magazine. But it was nebulous, too much of an unknown. Having this job, now that she was home, made her feel anchored. At first, she had enjoyed doing the features, interviewing society women in their homes, observing their lives and relearning old subtleties. But she soon became bored and she would sit through the interviews, half listening and half present. Each time she walked into their cemented compounds, she longed for sand in which to curl her toes. A servant or child would let her in, seat her in a living room of leather and marble that brought to mind a clean airport in a wealthy country. Then Madam would appear, warm and good-humoured, offering her a drink, sometimes food, before settling on a sofa to talk. All of them, the madams she interviewed, boasted about what they owned and where they or their children had been and what they had done, and then they capped their boasts with God. *We thank God. It is God that did it. God is faithful.* Ifemelu thought, as she left, that she could write the features without doing the interviews.

She could, also, cover events without attending them. How common that word was in Lagos, and how popular: event. It could be a product rebranding, a fashion show, an album launch. Aunty Onenu always insisted that an editor go with the photographer. "Please make sure you mingle," Aunty Onenu said. "If they are not advertising with us yet, we want them to start; if they have started, we want them to increase!" To Ifemelu, Aunty Onenu said "mingle" with great emphasis, as though this were something she thought Ifemelu did not do well. Perhaps Aunty Onenu was right. At those events, in halls aflame with balloons, rolls of silky cloth draped in corners, chairs covered in gauze and too many ushers walking around, their faces gaudily bright with make-up, Ifemelu disliked talking to strangers about *Zoe.* She would spend her time exchanging texts with Ranyinudo or Priye or Zemaye, bored, waiting until when it would not be impolite to leave. There were always two or three meandering speeches, and all of them seemed written by the same verbose, insincere person. The wealthy and the famous were recognized—"We wish to recognize in our presence the former governor of . . ." Bottles were uncorked, juice cartons folded open, samosas and chicken satays served. Once, at an event she attended with Zemaye, the launch of a new beverage brand, she thought she saw Obinze walk past. She turned. It was not him, but it very well could have been. She imagined him attending events like this, in halls like this, with his wife by his side. Ranyinudo had told her that his wife, when she was a student, was voted the most beautiful girl at the University of Lagos, and in Ifemelu's imagination, she looked like Bianca Onoh, that beauty icon of her teenage years, high-cheekboned and almond-eyed. And when Ranyinudo mentioned his wife's name, Kosisochukwu, an uncommon name, Ifemelu imagined Obinze's mother asking her to translate it. The thought of Obinze's mother and Obinze's wife deciding which translation was better—God's Will or As It Pleases God—felt like a betrayal. That memory, of Obinze's mother saying "translate it" all those years ago, seemed even more precious now that she had passed away.

As Ifemelu was leaving the event, she saw Don. "Ifemelu," he said. It took her a moment to recognize him. Ranyinudo had introduced them one afternoon, months ago, when Don dropped by Ranyinudo's flat on his way to his club, wearing tennis whites, and Ifemelu had left almost immediately, to give them privacy. He looked dapper in a navy suit, his grey-sprinkled hair burnished.

"Good evening," she said.

"You're looking well, very well," he said, taking in her low-cut cocktail dress.

"Thank you."

"You don't ask about me." As though there was a reason for her to ask about him. He gave her his card. "Call me, make sure you call me, eh. Let's talk. Take care."

He was not interested in her, not particularly; he was simply a big man in Lagos, she attractive and alone, and by the laws of their universe, he had to make a pass, even if a half-hearted pass, even if he was already dating her friend, and he expected, of course, that she would not tell her friend. She slipped his card into her bag and, back home, tore it into tiny bits which she watched float in the toilet water for a while before flushing. She was, strangely, angry with him. His action said something about her friendship with Ranyinudo that she disliked. She called Ranyinudo, and was about to tell her what happened, when Ranyinudo said, "Ifem, I'm so depressed." And so Ifemelu merely listened. It was about Ndudi. "He's such a *child*," Ranyinudo said. "If you say something he doesn't like, he will stop talking and start humming. Seriously humming, loud humming. How does a grown man behave so immaturely?"

IT WAS MONDAY MORNING. Ifemelu was reading *Postbourgie,* her favourite American blog. Zemaye was looking through a stash of glossy photographs. Doris was staring at her computer screen, cradling in her palms a mug that said I ♥ FLORIDA. On her desk, next to her computer, was a tin of loose-leaf tea.

"Ifemelu, I think this feature is too snarky?"

"Your editorial feedback is priceless," Ifemelu said.

"What does 'snarky' mean? Please explain to some of us who did not go to school in America," Zemaye said.

Doris ignored her completely.

"I just don't think Aunty Onenu will want us to run this?"

"Convince her, you're her editor," Ifemelu said. "We need to get this magazine going."

Doris shrugged and got up. "We'll talk about it at the meeting?"

"I am so sleepy," Zemaye said. "I'm going to send Esther to make Nescafé before I fall asleep in the meeting."

"Instant coffee is just awful?" Doris said. "I'm so glad I'm not much of a coffee drinker or I would just die."

"What is wrong with Nescafé?" Zemaye said.

"It shouldn't even be called coffee?" Doris said. "It's like beyond bad."

Zemaye yawned and stretched. "Me, I like it. Coffee is coffee."

Later, as they walked into Aunty Onenu's office, Doris ahead, wearing a loose-fitting blue pinafore and black square-heeled mary janes, Zemaye asked Ifemelu, "Why does Doris wear rubbish to work? She looks like she is cracking a joke with her clothes."

They sat around the oval conference table in Aunty Onenu's large office. Aunty Onenu's weave was longer and more incongruous than the last, high and coiffed in front, with waves of hair floating to her back. She sipped from a bottle of diet Sprite and said she liked Doris's piece "Marrying Your Best Friend".

"Very good and inspirational," she said.

"Ah, but Aunty Onenu, women should not marry their best friend because there is no sexual chemistry," Zemaye said.

Aunty Onenu gave Zemaye the look given to the crazy student whom one could not take seriously, then she shuffled her papers and said she did not like Ifemelu's profile of Mrs Funmi King.

"Why did you say 'she never looks at her steward when she speaks to him'?" Aunty Onenu asked.

"Because she didn't," Ifemelu said.

"But it makes her sound wicked," Aunty Onenu said.

"I think it's an interesting detail," Ifemelu said.

"I agree with Aunty Onenu," Doris said. "Interesting or not, it is judgemental?"

"The idea of interviewing someone and writing a profile is judgemental," Ifemelu said. "It's not about the subject. It's about what the interviewer makes of the subject."

Aunty Onenu shook her head. Doris shook her head.

"Why do we have to play it so safe?" Ifemelu asked.

Doris said, with false humour, "This isn't your American race blog where you provoked everybody, Ifemelu. This is like a wholesome women's magazine?"

"Yes, it is!" Aunty Onenu said.

"But Aunty Onenu, we will never beat *Glass* if we continue like this," Ifemelu said.

Aunty Onenu's eyes widened.

"*Glass* is doing exactly what we are doing," Doris said quickly.

Esther came in to tell Aunty Onenu that her daughter had arrived. Esther's black high heels were shaky, and as she walked past, Ifemelu worried that the shoes would collapse and sprain Esther's ankles. Earlier in the morning, Esther had told Ifemelu, "Aunty, your hair is jaga-jaga," with a kind of sad honesty, about what Ifemelu considered an attractive twist-out style.

"Ehn, she is already here?" Aunty Onenu said. "Girls, please finish the meeting. I am taking my daughter to shop for a dress and I have an afternoon meeting with our distributors."

Ifemelu was tired, bored. She thought, again, of starting a blog. Her phone was vibrating, Ranyinudo calling, and ordinarily she would have waited until the meeting was over to call her back. But she said, "Sorry, I have to take this, international call," and hurried out. Ranyinudo was complaining about Don. "He said I am not the sweet girl I used to be. That I've changed. Meanwhile, I know he has bought the jeep for me and has even cleared it at the port, but now he doesn't want to give it to me."

Ifemelu thought about the expression "sweet girl". Sweet girl meant that, for a long time, Don had moulded Ranyinudo into a malleable shape, or that she had allowed him to think he had.

"What about Ndudi?"

Ranyinudo sighed loudly. "We haven't talked since Sunday. Today he will forget to call me. Tomorrow he will be too busy. And so I told him that it's not acceptable. Why should I be making all the effort? Now he is sulking. He can never initiate a conversation like an adult, or agree that he did something wrong."

Later, back in the office, Esther came in to say that a Mr Tolu wanted to see Zemaye.

"Is that the photographer you did the tailors article with?" Doris asked.

"Yes. He's late. He has been dodging my calls for days," Zemaye said.

Doris said, "You need to handle that and make sure I have the images by tomorrow afternoon? I need everything to get to the printer before three? I don't want a repeat of the printer's delay, especially now that *Glass* is printing in South Africa?"

"Okay." Zemaye shook her mouse. "The server is so slow today. I just need to send this thing. Esther, tell him to wait."

"Yes, ma."

"You are feeling better, Esther?" Doris asked.

"Yes, ma, Thank you, ma." Esther curtsied, Yoruba-style. She had been standing by the door as though waiting to be dismissed, listening in on the conversation. "I am taking the medicine for typhoid."

"You have typhoid?" Ifemelu asked.

"Didn't you notice how she looked on Monday? I gave her some money and told her to go to the hospital, not to a chemist?" Doris said.

Ifemelu wished that *she* had noticed that Esther was unwell.

"Sorry, Esther," Ifemelu said.

"Thank you, ma."

"Esther, sorry o," Zemaye said. "I saw her dull face, but I thought she was just fasting. You know she's always fasting. She will fast and fast until God gives her a husband."

Esther giggled.

"I remember I had this really bad case of typhoid when I was in secondary school," Ifemelu said. "It was terrible, and it turned out I was taking an antibiotic that wasn't strong enough. What are you taking, Esther?"

"Medicine, ma."

"What antibiotic did they give you?"

"I don't know."

"You don't know the name?"

"Let me bring them, ma."

Esther came back with transparent packets of pills, on which instructions, but no names, were written in a crabbed handwriting in blue ink. *Two to be taken morning and night. One to be taken three times daily.*

"We should write about this, Doris. We should have a health column with useful practical information. Somebody should let the health minister know that ordinary Nigerians go to see a doctor and the doctor gives them unnamed medicines. This can kill you. How will anybody know what you have already taken, or what you shouldn't take if you're already taking something else?"

"Ahn-ahn, but that one is a small problem: they do it so that you don't buy the medicine from someone else," Zemaye said. "But what about fake drugs? Go to the market and see what they are selling."

"Okay, let's all calm down? No need to go all activist? We're not doing investigative journalism here?" Doris said.

Ifemelu began then to visualize her new blog, a blue-and-white design, and, on the masthead, an aerial shot of a Lagos scene. Nothing familiar, not a traffic clog of yellow rusted buses or a waterlogged slum of zinc shacks. Perhaps the abandoned house next to her flat would do. She would take the photo herself, in the haunted light of early evening, and hope to catch the male peacock in flight. The blog posts would be in a stark, readable font. An article about health care, using Esther's story, with pictures of the packets of nameless medicine. A piece about the Nigerpolitan Club. A fashion article about clothes that women could actually afford. Posts about people helping others, but nothing like the *Zoe* stories that always featured a wealthy person, hugging children at a motherless babies' home, with bags of rice and tins of powdered milk propped in the background.

"But, Esther, you have to stop all that fasting o," Zemaye said. "You know, some months Esther will give her whole salary to her church, they call it 'sowing a seed', then she will come and ask me to give her three hundred naira for transport."

"But, ma, it is just small help. You are equal to the task," Esther said, smiling.

"Last week she was fasting with a handkerchief," Zemaye continued. "She kept it on her desk all day. She said somebody in her church got promoted after fasting with the handkerchief."

"Is that what that handkerchief on her table was about?" Ifemelu asked.

"But I believe miracles totally work? I know my aunt was cured of cancer in her church?" Doris said.

"With a magic handkerchief, *abi*?" Zemaye scoffed.

"You don't believe, ma? But it is true." Esther was enjoying the camaraderie, reluctant to return to her desk.

"So you want a promotion, Esther? Which means you want my job?" Zemaye asked.

"No, ma! All of us will be promoted in Jesus' name!" Esther said.

They were all laughing.

"Has Esther told you what spirit you have, Ifemelu?" Zemaye asked, walking to the door. "When I first started working here, she kept inviting me to her church and then one day she told me there would be a special prayer service for people with the spirit of seductiveness. People like me."

"That's not like entirely far-fetched?" Doris said and smirked.

"What is my spirit, Esther?" Ifemelu asked.

Esther shook her head, smiling, and left the office.

Ifemelu turned to her computer. The title for the blog had just come to her. *The Small Redemptions of Lagos.*

"I wonder who Zemaye is dating?" Doris said.

"She told me she doesn't have a boyfriend."

"Have you seen her car? Her salary can't pay for the light in that car? It's not like her family is rich or anything. I've been working with her almost a year now and I don't know what she like really does?"

"Maybe she goes home and changes her clothes and becomes an armed robber at night," Ifemelu said.

"Whatever," Doris said.

"We should do a piece about churches," Ifemelu said. "Like Esther's church."

"That's not a good fit for *Zoe*?"

"It makes no sense that Aunty Onenu likes to run three profiles of these boring women who have achieved nothing and have nothing to say. Or the younger women with zero talent who have decided that they are fashion designers."

"You know they pay Aunty Onenu, right?" Doris asked.

"They pay her?" Ifemelu stared. "No, I didn't know. And you know I didn't know."

"Well, they do. Most of them. You have to realize a lot of things happen in this country like that?"

Ifemelu got up to gather her things. "I never know where you stand or if you stand on anything at all."

"And you are such a judgemental bitch?" Doris screamed, her eyes bulging. Ifemelu, alarmed by the suddenness of the change, thought that perhaps Doris was, underneath her retro affectations, one of those women who could transform when provoked, and tear off their clothes and fight in the street.

"You sit there and judge everyone," Doris was saying. "Who do you think you are? Why do you think this magazine should be about you? It isn't yours. Aunty Onenu has told you what she wants her magazine to be and it's either you do it or you shouldn't be working here?"

"You need to get yourself a moisturizer and stop scaring people with that nasty red lipstick," Ifemelu said. "And you need to get a life, and stop thinking that sucking up to Aunty Onenu and helping her publish a god-awful magazine will open doors for you, because it won't."

She left the office feeling common, shamed, by what had just happened. Perhaps this was a sign, to quit now and start her blog.

On her way out, Esther said, her voice earnest and low, "Ma? I think you have the spirit of husband-repelling. You are too hard, ma, you will not find a husband. But my pastor can destroy that spirit."

CHAPTER 50

Dike was seeing a therapist three times a week. Ifemelu called him every other day, and sometimes he spoke about his session, and other times he did not, but always he wanted to hear about her new life. She told him about her flat, and how she had a driver who drove her to work, and how she was seeing her old friends, and how, on Sundays, she loved to drive herself because the roads were empty; Lagos became a gentler version of itself, and the people in their bright church clothes looked, from far away, like flowers in the wind.

"You would like Lagos, I think," she said, and he, eagerly, surprisingly, said, "Can I come visit you, Coz?"

Aunty Uju was reluctant at first. "Lagos? Is it safe? You know what he has been through. I don't think he can handle it."

"But he asked to come, Aunty."

"He asked to come? Since when has he known what is good for him? Is he not the same person who wanted to make me childless?"

But Aunty Uju bought Dike's ticket and now here they were, she and Dike in her car, crawling through the crush of traffic in Oshodi, Dike looking wide-eyed out of the window. "Oh my God, Coz, I've never seen so many black people in the same place!" he said.

They stopped at a fast-food place, where he ordered a hamburger. "Is this horse meat, Coz? Because it isn't a hamburger." Afterwards, he would eat only jollof rice and fried plantain.

It was auspicious, his arrival, a day after she put up her blog and a week after she resigned. Aunty Onenu did not seem surprised by her resignation, nor did she try to make her stay. "Come and give me a hug, my dear," was all she said, smiling vacuously, while Ifemelu's pride soured. But Ifemelu was full of sanguine expectations for *The Small Redemptions of Lagos*, with a dreamy photograph of an abandoned colonial house on its masthead. Her first post was a short interview with Priye, with photographs from weddings Priye had planned. Ifemelu thought most of the décor fussy and overdone, but the post received enthusiastic comments, especially about the décor. *Fantastic decoration. Madam Priye, I hope you will do my own wedding. Great work, carry go.* Zemaye had written, under a pseudonym, a piece about body language and sex, "Can You Tell If Two People Are Doing It Just by Looking at Them Together?" That, too, drew many comments. But the most comments, by far, were for Ifemelu's piece about the Nigerpolitan Club.

> Lagos has never been, will never be, and has never aspired to be like New York, or anywhere else for that matter. Lagos has always been undisputably itself, but you would not know this at the meeting of the Nigerpolitan Club, a group of young returnees who gather every week to moan about the many ways that Lagos is not like New York as though Lagos had ever been close to being like New York. Full disclosure: I am one of them. Most of us have come back to make money in Nigeria, to start businesses, to seek government contracts and contacts. Others have come with dreams in their pockets and a hunger to change the country, but we spend all our time complaining about Nigeria, and even though our complaints are legitimate, I imagine myself as an outsider saying: Go back where you came from! If your cook cannot make the perfect panini, it is not because he is stupid. It is because Nigeria is not a nation of sandwich-eating people and his last oga did not eat bread in the afternoon. So he needs training and practice. And Nigeria is not a nation of people with food allergies, not a nation of picky eaters for whom food is about distinctions and separations. It is a nation of people who eat beef and chicken and cow skin and intestines and dried fish in a single bowl of soup, and it is called assorted, and so get over yourselves and realize that the way of life here is just that, assorted.

The first commenter wrote: *Rubbish post. Who cares?* The second wrote: *Thank God somebody is finally talking about this. Na wa for arrogance of Nigerian returnees. My cousin came back after six years in America and the other morning she came with me to the nursery school at Unilag where I was dropping off my niece and, near the gate, she saw students standing in line for the bus and she said, "Wow, people actually stand in line here!"* Another early commenter wrote: *Why should Nigerians who school abroad have a choice of where to get posted for their national youth service? Nigerians who school in Nigeria are randomly posted so why shouldn't Nigerians who school abroad be treated the same way?* That comment sparked more responses than the original post had. By the sixth day, the blog had one thousand unique visitors.

Ifemelu moderated the comments, deleting anything obscene, revelling in the liveliness of it all, in the sense of herself at the surging forefront of something vibrant. She wrote a long post about the expensive lifestyles of some young women in Lagos, and a day after she put it up, Ranyinudo called her, furious, her breathing heavy over the phone.

"Ifem, how can you do this kind of thing? Anyone who knows me will know it's me!"

"That's not true, Ranyi. Your story is so common."

"What are you saying? It is so obviously me! Look at this!" Ranyinudo paused and then began to read aloud.

> There are many young women in Lagos with Unknown Sources of Wealth. They live lives they can't afford. They have only ever traveled business class to Europe but have jobs that can't even afford them a regular flight ticket. One of them is my friend, a beautiful, brilliant woman who works in advertising. She lives on The Island and is dating a big man banker. I worry that she will end up like many women in Lagos who define their lives by men they can never truly have, crippled by their culture of dependence, with desperation in their eyes and designer handbags on their wrists.

"Ranyi, honestly, nobody will know it's you. All the comments so far have been from people saying that they identify. So many women lose themselves in relationships like that. What I really had in mind was Aunty Uju and The General. That relationship destroyed her. She became a different person because of The General and she couldn't do anything for herself and when he died, she lost herself."

"And who are you to pass judgement? How is it different from you and the rich white guy in America? Would you have your US citizenship today if not for him? How did you get your job in America? You need to stop this nonsense. Stop feeling so superior!"

Ranyinudo hung up on her. For a long time, Ifemelu stared at the silent phone, shaken. Then she took down the post and drove over to Ranyinudo's place.

"Ranyi, I'm sorry. Please don't be angry," she said.

Ranyinudo gave her a long look.

"You're right," Ifemelu said. "It's easy to be judgemental. But it was not personal, and it was not coming from a bad place. Please, *biko.* I will never invade your privacy like that again."

Ranyinudo shook her head. "Ifemelunamma, your problem is emotional frustration. Go and find Obinze, please."

Ifemelu laughed. It was what she least expected to hear.

"I have to lose weight first," she said.

"You're just afraid."

Before Ifemelu left, they sat on the couch and drank malt and watched the latest celebrity news on E!.

DIKE VOLUNTEERED to moderate the blog comments, so that she could take a break.

"Oh my God, Coz, people take this stuff really personal!" he said. Sometimes he laughed aloud on reading a comment. Other times, he asked her what unfamiliar expressions meant. *What's "shine your eye"?* The first time the power went off after he arrived, the buzzing, whirring, piping sounds of her UPS startled him. "Oh my God, is that like a fire alarm?" he asked.

"No, that's just something that makes sure my TV doesn't get destroyed by crazy power cuts."

"*That's* crazy," Dike said, but only days later he was going to the back of the flat to turn on the generator himself when the power went off. Ranyinudo brought her cousins to meet him, girls who were close to his age, skinny jeans clinging to their slender hips, their budding breasts outlined in tight T-shirts. "Dike, you must marry one of them o," Ranyinudo said. "We need fine children in our family." "Ranyi!" her cousins said, abashed, hiding their shyness. They liked Dike. It was so easy to like him, with his charm and his humour and the vulnerability openly lurking underneath. On Facebook, he posted a picture Ifemelu had taken of him standing on the verandah with Ranyinudo's cousins, and he captioned it: *No lions yet to eat me, folks.*

"I wish I spoke Igbo," he told her after they had spent an evening with her parents.

"But you understand perfectly," she said.

"I just wish I spoke."

"You can still learn," she said, suddenly feeling desperate, unsure how much this mattered to him, thinking again of him lying on the couch in the basement, drenched in sweat. She wondered if she should say more or not.

"Yes, I guess so," he said, and shrugged, as though to say it was already too late.

Some days before he left, he asked her, "What was my father really like?"

"He loved you."

"Did you like him?"

She did not want to lie to him. "I don't know. He was a big man in a military government and that does something to you and the way you relate to people. I was worried for your mum because I thought she deserved better. But she loved him, she really did, and he loved you. He used to carry you with such tenderness."

"I can't believe Mom hid from me for so long that she was his mistress."

"She was protecting you," Ifemelu said.

"Can we go see the house in Dolphin Estate?"

"Yes."

She drove him to Dolphin Estate, astounded by how much it had declined. The paint was peeling on buildings, the streets pitted with potholes, and the whole estate resigned to its own shabbiness. "It was so much nicer then," she told him. He stood looking at the house for a while, until the gateman said, "Yes? Any problem?" and they got back into the car.

"Can I drive, Coz?" he asked.

"Are you sure?"

He nodded. She came out of the driver's seat and went around to his. He drove them home, hesitating slightly before he merged onto Osborne Road, and then easing into traffic with more confidence. She knew it meant something to him that she could not name. That night, when the power went off, her generator would not come on, and she suspected that her driver, Ayo, had been sold diesel spiked with kerosene. Dike complained about the heat, about mosquitoes biting him. She opened the windows, made him take off his shirt, and they lay side by side in bed talking, desultory talking, and she reached out and touched his forehead and left her hand there until she heard the gentle even breathing of his sleep.

In the morning, the sky was overcast with slate-grey clouds, the air thick with rains foreboding. From nearby a clutch of birds screeched and flew away. The rain would come down, a sea unleashed from the sky, and DSTV images would get grainy, phone networks would clog, the roads would flood and traffic would gnarl. She stood with Dike on the verandah as the early droplets came down.

"I kind of like it here," he told her.

She wanted to say, "You can live with me. There are good private schools here that you could go to," but she did not.

She took him to the airport, and stayed watching until he went past security, waved and turned the corner. Back home, she heard the hollowness in her steps as she walked from bedroom to living room to verandah and then back again. Later, Ranyinudo told her, "I don't understand how a fine boy like Dike would want to kill himself. A boy living in America with everything. How can? That is very foreign behaviour."

"Foreign behaviour? What the fuck are you talking about? Foreign behaviour? Have you read *Things Fall Apart*?" Ifemelu asked, wishing she had not told Ranyinudo about Dike. She was angrier with Ranyinudo than she had ever been, yet she knew that Ranyinudo meant well, and had said what many other Nigerians would say, which was why she had not told anyone else about Dike's suicide attempt, since she came back.

CHAPTER 51

It had terrified her, the first time she came to the bank, to walk past the armed security guard, and into the beeping door, where she stood in the enclosure, sealed and airless like a standing coffin, until the light changed to green. Had banks always had this ostentatious security? Before she left America, she had wired some money to Nigeria, and Bank of America had made her speak to three different people, each one telling her that Nigeria was a high-risk country; if anything happened to her money, they would not be responsible. Did she understand? The last woman she spoke to made her repeat herself. *Ma'am, I'm sorry, I didn't hear you. I need to know that you understand that Nigeria is a high-risk country.* "I understand!" she said. They read her caveat after caveat, and she began to fear for her money, snaking its way through the air to Nigeria, and she worried even more when she came to the bank and saw the gaudy garlands of security at the entrance. But the money was safely in her account. And now, as she walked into the bank, she saw Obinze at the customer service section. He was standing with his back to her and she knew, from the height and the shape of the head, that it was him. She stopped, sick with apprehension, hoping he would not turn just yet until she had gathered her nerves. Then he turned and it was not Obinze. Her throat felt tight. Her head was filled with ghosts. Back in her car, she turned on the air conditioner and decided to call him, to free herself of the ghosts. His phone rang and rang. He was a big man now; he would not, of course, pick up a call from an unknown number. She sent a text: *Ceiling, it's me.* Her phone rang almost immediately.

"Hello? Ifem?" That voice she had not heard in so long, and it sounded both changed and unchanged.

"Ceiling! How are you?"

"You're back."

"Yes." Her hands were trembling. She should have sent an e-mail first. She should be chatty, ask about his wife and child, tell him that she had in fact been back for a while.

"So," Obinze said, dragging the word. "How are you? Where are you? When can I see you?"

"What about now?" The recklessness that often emerged when she felt nervous had pushed out those words, but perhaps it was best to see him right away and get it over with. She wished she had dressed up a bit more, maybe worn her favourite wrap dress, with its slimming cut, but her knee-length skirt was not too bad, and her high heels always made her feel confident, and her Afro was, thankfully, not yet too shrunken from the humidity.

There was a pause on Obinze's end—something hesitant?—which made her regret her rashness.

"I'm actually running a bit late for a meeting," she added quickly. "But I just wanted to say hi and we can meet up soon . . ."

"Ifem, where are you?"

She told him she was on her way to Jazzhole to buy a book, and would be there in a few minutes. Half an hour later, she was standing in front of the bookshop when a black Range Rover pulled in and Obinze got out from the back.

THERE WAS a moment, a caving of the blue sky, an inertia of stillness, when neither of them knew what to do, he walking towards her, she standing there squinting, and then he was upon her and they hugged. She thumped him on the back, once, twice, to make it a chummy-chummy hug, a platonic and safe chummy-chummy hug, but he pulled her ever so slightly close to him, and held her for a moment too long, as though to say he was not being chummy-chummy.

"Obinze Maduewesi! Long time! Look at you, you haven't changed!" She was flustered, and the new shrillness in her voice annoyed her. He was looking at her, an open unabashed looking, and she would not hold his gaze. Her fingers were shaking of their own accord, which was bad enough, she did not need to stare into his eyes, both of them standing there, in the hot sun, in the fumes of traffic from Awolowo Road.

"It's so good to see you, Ifem," he said. He was calm. She had forgotten what a calm person he was. There was still, in his bearing, a trace of his teenage history: the one who didn't try too hard, the one the girls wanted and the boys wanted to be.

"You're bald," she said.

He laughed and touched his head. "Yes. Mostly by choice."

He had filled out, from the slight boy of their university days to a fleshier, more muscled man, and perhaps because he had filled out, he seemed shorter than she remembered. In her high heels, she was taller than he was. She had not forgotten, but merely remembered anew, how understated his manner was, his plain dark jeans, his leather slippers, the way he walked into the bookshop with no need to dominate it.

"Let's sit down," he said.

The bookshop was dimly cool, its air moody and eclectic, books, CDs and magazines spread out on low shelves. A man standing near the entrance nodded at them in welcome, while adjusting the large headphones around his head. They sat opposite each other in the tiny café at the back and ordered fruit juice. Obinze put his two phones on the table; they lit up often, ringing in silent mode, and he would glance at them and then away. He worked out, she could tell from the firmness of his chest, across which stretched the double front pockets of his fitted shirt.

"You've been back for a while," he said. He was watching her again, and she remembered how she had often felt as if he could see her mind, knew things about her that she might not consciously know.

"Yes," she said.

"So what did you come to buy?"

"What?"

"The book you wanted to buy."

"Actually I just wanted to meet you here. I thought if it turns out that seeing you again is something I'd like to remember, then I want to remember it in Jazzhole."

"I want to remember it in Jazzhole," he repeated, smiling as though only she could have come up with that expression. "You haven't stopped being honest, Ifem. Thank God."

"I already think I'm going to want to remember this." Her nervousness was melting away; they had raced past the requisite moments of awkwardness.

"Do you need to be anywhere right now?" he asked. "Can you stay a while?"

"Yes."

He switched off both his phones. A rare declaration, in a city like Lagos for a man like him, that she had his absolute attention. "How is Dike? How is Aunty Uju?"

"They're fine. He's doing well now. He actually came to visit me here. He only just left."

The waitress served tall cups of mango-orange juice.

"What has surprised you the most about being back?" he asked.

"Everything, honestly. I started wondering if something was wrong with me."

"Oh, it's normal," he said, and she remembered how he had always been quick to reassure her, to make her feel better. "I was away for a much shorter time, obviously, but I was very surprised when I came back. I kept thinking that things should have waited for me but they hadn't."

"I'd forgotten that Lagos is so expensive. I can't believe how much money the Nigerian wealthy spend."

"Most of them are thieves or beggars."

She laughed. "Thieves or beggars."

"It's true. And they don't just spend a lot, they expect to spend a lot. I met this guy the other day, and he was telling me how he started his satellite-dish business about twenty years ago. This was when satellite dishes were still new in the country and so he was bringing in something most people didn't know about. He put his business plan together, and came up with a good price that would fetch him a good profit. Another friend of his, who was already a businessman and was going to invest in the business, took a look at the price and asked him to double it. Otherwise, he said, the Nigerian wealthy would not buy. He doubled it and it worked."

"Crazy," she said. "Maybe it's always been this way and we didn't know, because we couldn't know. It's as if we are looking at an adult Nigeria that we didn't know about."

"Yes." He liked that she had said "we", she could tell, and she liked that "we" had slipped so easily out of her.

"It's such a transactional city," she said. "Depressingly transactional. Even relationships, they're all transactional."

"Some relationships."

"Yes, some," she agreed. They were telling each other something that neither could yet articulate. Because she felt the nervousness creeping up her fingers again, she turned to humour. "And there is a certain bombast in the way we speak that I had also forgotten. I started feeling truly at home again when I started being bombastic!"

Obinze laughed. She liked his quiet laugh. "When I came back, I was shocked at how quickly my friends had all become fat, with big beer bellies. I thought: What is happening? Then I realized that they were the new middle class that our democracy created. They had jobs and they could afford to drink a lot more beer and to eat out, and you know eating out for us here is chicken and chips, and so they got fat."

Ifemelu's stomach clenched. "Well, if you look carefully you'll notice it's not only your friends."

"Oh, no, Ifem, you're not fat. You're being very American about that. What Americans consider fat can just be normal. You need to see my guys to know what I am talking about. Remember Uche Okoye? Even Okwudiba? They can't even button their shirts now." Obinze paused. "You put on some weight and it suits you. *I maka*."

She felt shy, a pleasant shyness, hearing him say she was beautiful.

"You used to tease me about not having an ass," she said.

"I take my words back. At the door, I waited for you to go ahead for a reason."

They laughed and then, laughter tapering off, were silent, smiling at each other in the strangeness of their intimacy. She remembered how, as she got up naked from his mattress on the floor in Nsukka, he would look up and say, "I was going to say shake it but there's nothing to shake," and she would playfully kick him in the shin. The clarity of that memory, the sudden stab of longing it brought, left her unsteady.

"But talk of being surprised, Ceiling," she said. "Look at you. Big Man with your Range Rover. Having money must have really changed things."

"Yes, I guess it has."

"Oh, come on," she said. "How?"

"People treat you differently. I don't just mean strangers. Friends too. Even my cousin Nneoma. Suddenly you're getting all of this sucking-up from people because they think you expect it, all this exaggerated politeness, exaggerated praise, even exaggerated respect that you haven't earned at all, and it's so fake and so garish, it's like a bad over-coloured painting, but sometimes you start believing a little bit of it yourself and sometimes you see yourself differently. One day I went to a wedding in my hometown, and the MC was doing a lot of silly praise-singing when I came in and I realized I was walking differently. I didn't *want* to walk differently but I was."

"What, like a swagger?" she teased. "Show me the walk!"

"You'll have to sing my praises first." He sipped his drink. "Nigerians can be so obsequious. We are a confident people but we are so obsequious. It's not difficult for us to be insincere."

"We have confidence but no dignity."

"Yes." He looked at her, recognition in his eyes. "And if you keep getting that overdone sucking-up, it makes you paranoid. You don't know if anything is honest or true any more. And then people become paranoid for you, but in a different way. My relatives are always telling me: Be careful where you eat. Even here in Lagos my friends tell me to watch what I eat. Don't eat in a woman's house because she'll put something in your food."

"And do you?"

"Do I what?"

"Watch what you eat?"

"I wouldn't in your house." A pause. He was being openly flirtatious and she was unsure what to say.

"But no," he continued. "I like to think that if I wanted to eat in somebody's house, it would be a person who would not think of slipping jazz into my food."

"It all seems really desperate."

"One of the things I've learned is that everybody in this country has the mentality of scarcity. We imagine that even the things that are not scarce are scarce. And it breeds a kind of desperation in everybody. Even the wealthy."

"The wealthy like you, that is," she quipped.

He paused. He often paused before he spoke. She thought this exquisite; it was as though he had such regard for his listener that he wanted his words strung together in the best possible way. "I like to think I don't have that desperation. I sometimes feel as if the money I have isn't really mine, as if I'm holding it for someone else for a while. After I bought my property in Dubai, it was my first property outside Nigeria, I felt almost frightened and when I told Okwudiba how I felt, he said I was crazy and I should stop behaving as if life is one of the novels I read. He was so impressed by what I owned, and I just felt as if my life had become this layer of pretension after pretension and I started to get sentimental about the past. I would think about when I was staying with Okwudiba in his first small flat in Surulere and how we would heat the iron on the stove when NEPA took light. And how his neighbour downstairs used to shout 'Praise the Lord!' whenever the light came back and how even for me there was something so beautiful about the light coming back, when it's out of your control because you don't have a generator. But it's a silly sort of romance, because of course I don't want to go back to that life."

She looked away, worried that the crush of emotions she had felt while he was speaking would now converge on her face. "Of course you don't. You like your life," she said.

"I live my life."

"Oh, how mysterious we are."

"What about you, famous race blogger, Princeton fellow, how have you changed?" he asked, smiling, leaning towards her with his elbows on the table.

"When I was babysitting in undergrad, one day I heard myself telling the kid I was babysitting 'You're such a trouper!' Is there another word more American than 'trouper'?"

Obinze was laughing.

"That's when I thought, yes, I may have changed a little," she said.

"You don't have an American accent."

"I made an effort not to."

"I was surprised when I read the archives of your blog. It didn't sound like you."

"I really don't think I've changed that much, though."

"Oh, you've changed," he said with a certitude that she instinctively disliked.

"How?"

"I don't know. You're more self-aware. Maybe more guarded."

"You sound like a disappointed uncle."

"No." Another one of his pauses, but this time he seemed to be holding back. "But your blog also made me proud. I thought: She's gone, she's learned and she's conquered."

Again, she felt shy. "I don't know about conquering."

"Your aesthetics changed too," he said.

"What do you mean?"

"Did you cure your own meats in America?"

"What?"

"I read a piece about this new movement among the American privileged classes. Where people want to drink milk straight from the cow and that sort of thing. I thought maybe you're into that, now that you wear a flower in your hair."

She burst out laughing.

"But really, tell me how you've changed." His tone was teasing, yet she tensed slightly at his question; it seemed too close to her vulnerable, soft core. And so she said, in a breezy voice, "My taste, I guess. I can't believe how much I find ugly now. I can't stand most of the houses in this city. I'm now a person who has learned to admire exposed wooden rafters." She rolled her eyes and he smiled at her self-mockery, a smile that seemed to her like a prize that she wanted to win over and over again.

"It's really a kind of snobbery," she added.

"It's snobbery, not a kind," he said. "I used to have that about books. Secretly feeling that your taste is superior."

"The problem is I'm not always secret about it."

He laughed. "Oh, we know that."

"You said you used to? What happened?"

"What happened was that I grew up."

"Ouch," she said.

He said nothing; the slight sardonic raise of his eyebrows said that she, too, would have to grow up.

"What are you reading these days?" she asked. "I'm sure you've read every American novel ever published."

"I've been reading a lot more non-fiction, history and biographies. About everything, not just America."

"What, you fell out of love?"

"I realized I could buy America, and it lost its shine. When all I had was my passion for America, they didn't give me a visa, but with my new bank account, getting a visa was very easy. I've visited a few times. I was looking into buying property in Miami."

She felt a pang; he had visited America and she had not known.

"So what did you finally make of your dream country?"

"I remember when you first went to Manhattan and you wrote to me and said 'It's wonderful but it's not heaven.' I thought of that when I took my first cab ride in Manhattan."

She remembered writing that, too, not long before she stopped contacting him, before she pushed him behind many walls. "The best thing about America is that it gives you space. I like that. I like that you buy into the dream, it's a lie but you buy into it and that's all that matters."

He looked down at his glass, uninterested in her philosophizing, and she wondered if what she had seen in his eyes was resentment, if he, too, was remembering how she had so completely shut him out. When he asked, "Are you still friends with your old friends?" she thought it a question about whom else she had shut out all these years. She wondered whether to bring it up herself, whether to wait for him to. She should bring it up, she owed him that, but a wordless fear had seized her, a fear of breaking delicate things.

"With Ranyinudo, yes. And Priye. The others are now people who used to be my friends. Kind of like you and Emenike. You know, when I read your e-mails, I wasn't surprised that Emenike turned out like that. There was always something about him."

He shook his head and finished his drink; he had earlier put the straw aside, sipping from the glass.

"Once I was with him in London and he was mocking this guy he worked with, a Nigerian guy, for not knowing how to pronounce F-e-a-t-h-e-r-s-t-o-n-e-h-a-u-g-h. He pronounced it phonetically like the guy had, which was obviously the wrong way, and he didn't say it the right way. I didn't know how to pronounce it either and he knew I didn't know, and there were these horrible minutes when he pretended we were both laughing at the guy. When of course we weren't. He was laughing at *me too.* I remember it as the moment when I realized he just had never been my friend."

"He's an asshole," she said.

"Asshole. Very American word."

"Is it?"

He half raised his eyebrows as though there was no need to state the obvious. "Emenike didn't contact me at all after I was deported. Then, last year, after somebody must have told him I was now in the game, he started calling me." Obinze said "in the game" in a voice thick with mockery. "He kept asking if there were any deals we could do together, that kind of nonsense. And one day I told him I really preferred his condescension, and he hasn't called me since."

"What of Kayode?"

"We're in touch. He has a child with an American woman."

Obinze looked at his watch and picked up his phones. "I hate to go but I have to."

"Yes, me too." She wanted to prolong this moment, sitting amid the scent of books, discovering Obinze again. Before they got into their separate cars, they hugged, both murmuring, "So good to see you," and she imagined his driver and her driver watching them curiously.

"I'll call you tomorrow," he said, but she had hardly settled into the car when her phone beeped with a new text message from him. *Are you free to have lunch tomorrow?* She was free. It was a Saturday and she should ask why he would not be with his wife and child, and she should initiate a conversation about what they were doing exactly, but they had a history, a connection thick as twine, and it did not have to mean that they were doing anything, or that a conversation was necessary, and so she opened the door when he rang the bell and he came in and admired the flowers on her verandah, the white lilies that rose from the pots like swans.

"I spent the morning reading *The Small Redemptions of Lagos*. Scouring it, actually," he said.

She felt pleased. "What did you think?"

"I liked the Nigerpolitan Club post. A little self-righteous, though."

"I'm not sure how to take that."

"As truth," he said, with that half-raising of an eyebrow that had to be a new quirk; she did not remember him doing it in the past. "But it's a fantastic blog. It's brave and intelligent. I love the layout." There he was again, reassuring her.

She pointed at the compound next door. "Do you recognize that?"

"Ah! Yes."

"I thought it would be just perfect for the blog. Such a beautiful house and in this kind of magnificent ruin. Plus peacocks on the roof."

"It looks a little like a courthouse. I'm always fascinated by these old houses and the stories they carry." He tugged at the thin metal railing of her verandah, as though to check how durable it was, how safe, and she liked that he did that. "Somebody is going to snap it up soon, tear it down, and put up a gleaming block of overpriced luxury flats."

"Somebody like you."

"When I started in real estate, I considered renovating old houses instead of tearing them down, but it didn't make sense. Nigerians don't buy houses because they're old. A renovated two-hundred-year-old mill granary, you know, the kind of thing Europeans like. It doesn't work here at all. But of course it makes sense because we are Third Worlders and Third Worlders are forward-looking, we like things to be new, because our best is still ahead, while in the West their best is already past and so they have to make a fetish of that past."

"Is it me or are you now given to delivering little lectures?" she asked.

"It's just refreshing to have an intelligent person to talk to."

She looked away, wondering if this was a reference to his wife, and disliking him for it.

"Your blog already has such a following," he said.

"I have big plans for it. I'd like to travel through Nigeria and post dispatches from each state, with pictures and human stories, but I have to do things slowly first, establish it, make some money from advertising."

"You need investors."

"I don't want your money," she said, a little sharply, keeping her eyes levelly on the sunken roof of the abandoned house. She was irritated by his comment about an intelligent person because it was, it had to be, about his wife, and she wanted to ask why he was telling her that. Why had he married a woman who was not intelligent only to turn around and tell her that his wife was not intelligent?

"Look at the peacock, Ifem," he said, gently, as though he sensed her irritation.

They watched the peacock walk out of the shadow of a tree, then its lugubrious flight up to its favourite perch on the roof, where it stood and surveyed the decayed kingdom below.

"How many are there?" he asked.

"One male and two females. I've been hoping to see the male do its mating dance but I never have. They wake me up in the morning with their cries. Have you heard them? Almost like a child that doesn't want to do something."

The peacock's slender neck moved this way and that, and then, as though it had heard her, it cawed, its beak parted wide, the sounds pouring out of its throat.

"You were right about the sound," he said, moving closer to her. "Something of a child about it. The compound reminds me of a property I have in Enugu. An old house. It was built before the war, and I bought it to tear it down, but then I decided to keep it. It's very gracious and restful, big verandahs and old frangipani trees in the back. I'm redoing the interior completely, so it will be very modern inside, but the outside has its old look. Don't laugh, but when I saw it, it reminded me of poetry."

There was a boyishness in the way he said "Don't laugh" that made her smile at him, half making fun of him, half letting him know she liked the idea of a house that had reminded him of poetry.

"I imagine one day when I run away from it all, I'll go and live there," he said.

"People really do become eccentric when they become rich."

"Or maybe we all have eccentricity in us, we just don't have the money to show it? I'd love to take you to see the house."

She murmured something, a vague acquiescence.

His phone had been ringing for a while, an endless, dull buzzing in his pocket. Finally he brought it out, glanced at it and said, "Sorry, I have to take this." She nodded and went inside, wondering if it was his wife.

From the living room, she heard snatches of his voice, raised, lowered and then raised again, speaking Igbo, and when he came inside, there was a tightening in his jaw.

"Everything okay?" she asked.

"It's a boy from my hometown. I pay his school fees but he now has a mad sense of entitlement and this morning he sent me a text telling me he needs a mobile phone and could I send it to him by Friday. A fifteen-year-old boy. The gall of it. And then he starts calling me. So I've just told him off and I've told him his scholarship is off, too, just to scare some sense into his head."

"Is he related to you?"

"No."

She waited, expecting more.

"Ifem, I do what rich people are supposed to do. I pay school fees for a hundred students in my village and my mum's village." He spoke with an awkward indifference; this was not a subject that he cared to talk about. He was standing by her bookshelf. "What a beautiful living room."

"Thank you."

"You shipped all your books back?"

"Most of them."

"Ah. Derek Walcott."

"I love him. I finally get some poetry."

"I see Graham Greene."

"I started reading him because of your mother. I love *The Heart of the Matter.*"

"I tried reading it after she died. I wanted to love it. I thought maybe if I could just love it . . ." He touched the book, his voice trailing away.

His wistfulness moved her. "It's real literature, the kind of human story people will read in two hundred years," she said.

"You sound just like my mother," he said.

He felt familiar and unfamiliar at the same time. Through the parted curtains, a crescent of light fell across the living room. They were standing by the bookshelf and she was telling him about the first time she finally read *The Heart of the Matter*, and he was listening, in that intense manner of his, as though swallowing her words like a drink. They were standing by the bookshelf and laughing about how often his mother had tried to get him to read the book. And then they were standing by the bookshelf and kissing. A gentle kiss at first, lips pressed to lips, then their tongues were touching and she felt boneless against him. He pulled away first.

"I don't have condoms," she said, brazen, deliberately brazen.

"I didn't know we needed condoms to have lunch."

She hit him playfully. Her entire body was invaded by millions of uncertainties. She did not want to look at his face. "I have a girl who cleans and cooks so I have a lot of stew in my freezer and jollof rice in my fridge. We can have lunch here. Would you like something to drink?" She turned towards the kitchen.

"What happened in America?" he asked. "Why did you just cut off contact?"

Ifemelu kept walking to the kitchen.

"Why did you just cut off contact?" he repeated quietly. "Please tell me what happened."

Before she sat opposite him at her small dining table and told him about the corrupt-eyed tennis coach in Ardmore, Pennsylvania, she poured them both some mango juice from a carton. She told him small details about the man's office that were still fresh in her mind, the stacks of sports magazines, the smell of damp, but when she got to the part where he took her to his room, she said, simply, "I took off my clothes and did what he asked me to do. I couldn't believe that I got wet. I hated him. I hated myself. I really hated myself. I felt like I had, I don't know, betrayed myself." She paused. "And you."

For many long minutes, he said nothing, his eyes downcast, as though absorbing the story.

"I don't really think about it much," she added. "I remember it, but I don't dwell on it, I don't let myself dwell on it. It's so strange now to actually talk about it. It seems a stupid reason to throw away what we had, but that's why, and as more time passed, I just didn't know how to go about fixing it."

He was still silent. She stared at the framed caricature of Dike that hung on her wall, Dike's ears comically pointed, and wondered what Obinze was feeling.

Finally, he said, "I can't imagine how bad you must have felt, and how alone. You should have told me. I so wish you had told me."

She heard his words like a melody and she felt herself breathing unevenly, gulping at the air. She would not cry, it was ridiculous to cry after so long, but her eyes were filling with tears and there was a boulder in her chest and a stinging in her throat. The tears felt itchy. She made no sound. He took her hand in his, both clasped on the table, and between them silence grew, an ancient silence that they both knew. She was inside this silence and she was safe.

CHAPTER 52

"Let's go and play table tennis. I belong to this small private club in Victoria Island," he said.

"I haven't played in ages."

She remembered how she had always wanted to beat him, even though he was the school champion, and how he would tell her, teasingly, "Try more strategy and less force. Passion never wins any game, never mind what they say." He said something similar now: "Excuses don't win a game. You should try strategy."

He had driven himself. In the car, he turned the engine on, and the music came on too. Bracket's "Yori Yori".

"Oh, I love this song," she said.

He increased the volume and they sang along; there was an exuberance to the song, its rhythmic joyfulness, so free of artifice, that filled the air with lightness.

"Ahn-ahn! How long have you been back and you can already sing this so well?" he asked.

"First thing I did was brush up on all the contemporary music. It's so exciting, all the new music."

"It is. Now clubs play Nigerian music."

She would remember this moment, sitting beside Obinze in his Range Rover, stalled in traffic, listening to "Yori Yori"—*Your love dey make my heart do yori yori. Nobody can love you the way I do*—beside them a shiny Honda, the latest model, and in front of them an ancient Datsun that looked a hundred years old.

After a few games of table tennis, all of which he won, all the time playfully taunting her, they had lunch in the small restaurant, where they were alone except for a woman reading newspapers at the bar. The manager, a round man who was almost bursting out of his ill-fitting black jacket, came over to their table often to say, "I hope everything is fine, sah. It is very good to see you again, sah. How is work, sah."

Ifemelu leaned in and asked Obinze, "Is there a point at which you gag?"

"The man wouldn't come by so often if he didn't think I was being neglected. You're addicted to that phone."

"Sorry. I was just checking the blog." She felt relaxed and happy. "You know, you should write for me."

"Me?"

"Yes, I'll give you an assignment. How about the perils of being young and good-looking and rich?"

"I would be happy to write on a subject with which I can personally identify."

"How about security? I want to do something on security. Have you had any experience on Third Mainland Bridge? Somebody was telling me about leaving a club late and going back to the mainland and their car tyre burst on the bridge and they just kept going, because it's so dangerous to stop on the bridge."

"Ifem, I live in Lekki, and I don't go clubbing. Not any more."

"Okay." She glanced at her phone again. "I just want to have new, vibrant content often."

"You're distracted."

"Do you know Tunde Razaq?"

"Who doesn't? Why?"

"I want to interview him. I want to start this weekly feature of 'Lagos from an Insider', and I want to start with the most interesting people."

"What's interesting about him? That he is a Lagos playboy living off his father's money, said money accumulated from a diesel importation monopoly that they have because of their contact with the president?"

"He's also a music producer, and apparently a champion at chess. My friend Zemaye knows him and he's just written to her to say he will do the interview only if I let him buy me dinner."

"He's probably seen a picture of you somewhere." Obinze stood up and pushed back his chair with a force that surprised her. "The guy is a dog."

"Be nice," she said, amused; his jealousy pleased her. He played "Yori Yori" again on the drive back to her flat, and she swayed and danced with her arms, much to his amusement.

"I thought your Chapman was non-alcoholic," he said. "I want to play another song. It makes me think of you."

Obiwon's "Obi Mu O" started and she sat still and silent as the words filled the car: *This is that feeling that I've never felt . . . and I'm not gonna let it die.* When the male and female voices sang in Igbo, Obinze sang along with them, glancing away from the road to look at her, as though he was telling her that this was really their conversation, he calling her beautiful, she calling him beautiful, both calling each other their true friends. *Nwanyi oma, nwoke oma, omalicha nwa, ezigbo oyi m o.*

When he dropped her off, he leaned across to kiss her cheek, hesitant to come too close or to hold her, as though afraid of being defeated by their attraction. "Can I see you tomorrow?" he asked, and she said yes. They went to a Brazilian restaurant by the lagoon, where the waiter brought skewer after skewer stacked with meat and seafood, until Ifemelu told him that she was about to be sick. The next day, he asked if she would have dinner with him, and he took her to an Italian restaurant, whose overpriced food she found bland, and the bow-tied waiters, doleful and slow-moving, filled her with faint sorrow.

They drove past Obalende on the way back, tables and stalls lining the bustling road, orange flames flickering from the hawkers' lamps.

Ifemelu said, "Let's stop and buy fried plantain!"

Obinze found a spot farther ahead, in front of a beer parlour, and he eased the car in. He greeted the men seated on benches drinking, his manner easy and warm, and they hailed him, "Chief! Carry go! Your car is safe!"

The fried plantain hawker tried to persuade Ifemelu to buy fried sweet potatoes as well.

"No, only plantain."

"What about akara, aunty? I make am now. Very fresh."

"Okay," Ifemelu said. "Put four."

"Why are you buying akara that you don't want?" Obinze asked, amused.

"Because this is real enterprise. She's selling what she makes. She's not selling her location or the source of her oil or the name of the person that ground the beans. She's simply selling what she makes."

Back in the car, she opened the oily plastic bag of plantains, slid a small, perfectly fried yellow slice into her mouth. "This is so much better than that thing drenched in butter that I could hardly finish at the restaurant. And you know we can't get food poisoning because the frying kills the germs," she added.

He was watching her, smiling, and she suspected that she was talking too much. This memory, too, she would store, of Obalende at night, lit as it was by a hundred small lights, the raised voices of drunk men nearby, and the sway of a large madam's hips, walking past the car.

HE ASKED if he could take her to lunch and she suggested a new casual place she had heard of, where she ordered a chicken sandwich and then complained about the man smoking in the corner. "How very American, complaining about smoke," Obinze said, and she could not tell whether he meant it as a rebuke or not.

"The sandwich comes with chips?" Ifemelu asked the waiter.

"Yes, madam."

"Do you have real potatoes?"

"Madam?"

"Are your potatoes the frozen imported ones, or do you cut and fry your potatoes?"

The waiter looked offended. "It is the imported frozen ones."

As the waiter walked away, Ifemelu said, "Those frozen things taste horrible."

"He can't believe you're actually asking for real potatoes," Obinze said drily. "Real potatoes are backward for him. Remember this is our newly middle-class world. We haven't completed the first cycle of prosperity, before going back to the beginning again, to drink milk from the cow's udder."

Each time he dropped her off, he kissed her on the cheek, both of them leaning towards each other, and then pulling back so that she could say "Bye" and climb out of his car. On the fifth day, as he drove into her compound, she asked, "Do you have condoms in your pocket?"

He said nothing for a while. "No, I don't have condoms in my pocket."

"Well, I bought a pack some days ago."

"Ifem, why are you saying this?"

"You're married with a child and we are hot for each other. Who are we kidding with this chaste dating business? So we might as well get it over with."

"You are hiding behind sarcasm," he said.

"Oh, how very lofty of you." She was angry. It was barely a week since she first saw him but already she was angry, furious that he would drop her off and go home to his other life, his real life, and that she could not visualize the details of that life, did not know what kind of bed he slept in, what kind of plate he ate from. She had, since she began to gaze at her past, imagined a relationship with him, but only in faded images and faint lines. Now, faced with the reality of him, and of the silver ring on his finger, she was frightened of becoming used to him, of drowning. Or perhaps she was already drowned, and her fear came from that knowledge.

"Why didn't you call me when you came back?" he asked.

"I don't know. I wanted to settle down first."

"I hoped I would help you settle down."

She said nothing.

"Are you still with Blaine?"

"What does it matter, married man, you?" she said, with an irony that sounded far too caustic; she wanted to be cool, distant, in control.

"Can I come in for a bit? To talk?"

"No, I need to do some research for the blog."

"Please, Ifem."

She sighed. "Okay."

In her flat, he sat on the couch while she sat on her armchair, as far from him as possible. She had a sudden bilious terror about whatever it was he was going to say, which she did not want to hear, and so she said, wildly, "Zemaye wants to write a tongue-in-cheek guide for men who want to cheat. She said her boyfriend was unreachable the other day and when he finally turned up, he told her that his phone had fallen into water. She said it's the oldest story in the book, phone fell into water. I thought that was funny. I've never heard that before. So number one on her guide is never say your phone fell into water."

"This doesn't feel like cheating to me," he said quietly.

"Does your wife know you're here?" She was taunting him. "I wonder how many men say that when they cheat, that it doesn't feel like cheating. I mean, would they actually ever say that it felt like cheating?"

He got up, his movements deliberate, and at first she thought he was coming closer to her, or perhaps wanted the toilet, but he walked to the front door, opened it and left. She stared at the door. She sat still for a long time, and then she got up and paced, unable to focus, wondering whether to call him, debating with herself. She decided not to call him; she resented his behaviour, his silence, his pretence. When her doorbell rang minutes later, a part of her was reluctant to open the door.

She let him in. They sat side by side on her couch.

"I'm sorry I left like that," he said. "I just haven't been myself since you came back and I didn't like the way you talked as if what we have is common. It isn't. And I think you know that. I think you were saying that to hurt me but mostly because *you* feel confused. I know it must be difficult for you, how we've seen each other and talked about so much but still avoided so much."

"You're speaking in code," she said.

He looked stressed, tight-jawed, and she longed to kiss him. It was true that he was intelligent and sure of himself, but there was an innocence about him, too, a confidence without ego, a throwback to another time and place, which she found endearing.

"I haven't said anything because sometimes I am just so happy being with you that I don't want to spoil it," he said. "And also because I want to have something to say first, before I say anything."

"I touch myself thinking of you," she said.

He stared at her, thrown slightly off balance.

"We're not single people who are courting, Ceiling," she said. "We can't deny the attraction between us and maybe we should have a conversation about that."

"You know this isn't about sex," he said. "This has never been about sex."

"I know," she said, and took his hand. There was, between them, a weightless, seamless desire. She leaned in and kissed him, and at first he was slow in his response, and then he was pulling up her blouse, pushing down her bra cups to free her breasts. She remembered clearly the firmness of his embrace, and yet there was, also, a newness to their union; their bodies remembered and did not remember. She touched the scar on his chest, remembering it again. She had always thought the expression "making love" a little maudlin; "having sex" felt truer and "fucking" was more arousing, but lying next to him afterwards, both of them smiling, sometimes laughing, her body suffused with peace, she thought how apt it was, that expression "making love". There was an awakening even in her nails, in those parts of her body that had always been numb. She wanted to tell him, "There is no week that passed that I did not think of you." But was that true? Of course there were weeks during which he was folded under layers of her life, but it *felt* true.

She propped herself up and said, "I always saw the ceiling with other men."

He smiled a long, slow smile. "You know what I have felt for so long? As if I was waiting to be happy."

He got up to go to the bathroom. She found it so attractive, his shortness, his solid firm shortness. She saw, in his shortness, a groundedness; he could weather anything, he would not easily be swayed. He came back and she said she was hungry and he found oranges in her fridge, and peeled them, and they ate the oranges, sitting up next to each other, and then they lay entwined, naked, in a full circle of completeness, and she fell asleep and did not know when he left. She woke up to a dark, overcast rainy morning. Her phone was ringing. It was Obinze.

"How are you?" he asked.

"Groggy. Not sure what happened yesterday. Did you seduce me?"

"I'm glad your door has a dead bolt. I would have hated to wake you up to lock the door."

"So you did seduce me."

He laughed. "Can I come to you?"

She liked the way he said "Can I come to you?"

"Yes. It's raining crazily."

"Really? It's not raining here. I'm in Lekki."

She found this foolishly exciting, that it was raining where she was and it was not raining where he was, only minutes from her, and so she waited, with impatience, with a charged delight, until they could both see the rain together.

CHAPTER 53

And so began her heady days full of cliché: she felt fully alive, her heart beat faster when he arrived at her door, and she viewed each morning like the unwrapping of a gift. She would laugh, or cross her legs or slightly sway her hips, with a heightened awareness of herself. Her nightshirt smelled of his cologne, a muted citrus and wood scent, because she left it unwashed for as long as she could, and she delayed in wiping off a spill of hand cream he had left on her sink, and after they made love, she left untouched the indentation on the pillow, the soft groove where his head had lain, as though to preserve his essence until the next time. They often stood on her verandah and watched the peacocks on the roof of the abandoned house, from time to time slipping their hands into each other's, and she would think of the next time, and the next, that they would do this together. This was love, to be eager for tomorrow. Had she felt this way as a teenager? The emotions seemed absurd. She fretted when he did not respond to her text right away. Her mind was darkened with jealousy about his past. "You are the great love of my life," he told her, and she believed him, but still she was jealous of those women whom he had loved even if fleetingly, those women who had carved out space in his thoughts. She was jealous even of the women who liked him, imagining how much attention he got here in Lagos, good-looking as he was, and now also wealthy. The first time she introduced him to Zemaye, lissome Zemaye in her tight skirt and platform heels, she stifled her discomfort, because she saw in Zemaye's alert appreciative eyes the eyes of all the hungry women in Lagos. It was a jealousy of her imagination, he did nothing to aid it; he was present and transparent in his devotion, She marvelled at what an intense, careful listener he was.

He remembered everything she told him. She had never had this before, to be listened to, to be truly heard, and so he became newly precious; each time he said bye at the end of a telephone call, she felt a sinking panic. It was truly absurd. Their teenage love had been less melodramatic. Or perhaps it was because the circumstances were different, and looming over them now was the marriage he never talked about. Sometimes he said, "I can't come on Sunday until mid-afternoon," or "I have to leave early today," all of which she knew were about his wife, but they did not talk further about it. He did not try to, and she did not want to, or she told herself that she did not want to. It surprised her, that he took her out openly, to lunch and to dinner, to his private club where the waiter called her "madam", perhaps assuming she was his wife; that he stayed with her until past midnight and never showered after they made love; that he went home wearing her touch and her smell on his skin. He was determined to give their relationship as much dignity as he could, to pretend that he was not hiding even though he, of course, was. Once he said cryptically, as they lay entwined on her bed in the undecided light of late evening, "I can stay the night, I would like to stay." She said a quick no and nothing else. She did not want to get used to waking up beside him, did not permit herself to think of why he could stay this night. And so his marriage hung above them, unspoken, unprobed, until one evening when she did not feel like eating out. He said eagerly, "You have spaghetti and onions. Let me cook for you."

"As long as it doesn't give me a stomach ache."

He laughed. "I miss cooking. I can't cook at home." And, in that instant, his wife became a dark spectral presence in the room. It was palpable and menacing in a way it had never been when he said, "I can't come on Sunday until mid-afternoon," or "I have to leave early today." She turned away from him, and flipped open her laptop to check on the blog. A furnace had lit itself deep inside her. He sensed it, too, the sudden import of his words, because he came and stood beside her.

"Kosi never liked the idea of my cooking. She has really basic, mainstream ideas of what a wife should be and she thought my wanting to cook was an indictment of her, which I found silly. So I stopped, just to have peace. I make omelettes but that's it and we both pretend as if my onugbu soup isn't better than hers. There's a lot of pretending in my marriage, Ifem." He paused. "I married her when I was feeling vulnerable; I had a lot of upheaval in my life at the time."

She said, her back turned to him, "Obinze, please just cook the spaghetti."

"I feel a great responsibility for Kosi and that is all I feel. And I want you to know that." He gently turned her around to face him, holding her shoulders, and he looked as if there were other things he wanted to say, but expected her to help him say them, and for this she felt the flare of a new resentment. She turned back to her laptop, choked with the urge to destroy, to slash and burn.

"I'm having dinner with Tunde Razaq tomorrow," she said.

"Why?"

"Because I want to."

"You said the other day that you wouldn't."

"What happens when you go home and climb into bed with your wife? What happens?" she asked, and felt herself wanting to cry. Something had cracked and spoilt between them.

"I think you should go," she said.

"No."

"Obinze, please just go."

He refused to leave, and later she felt grateful that he had not left. He cooked spaghetti and she pushed it around her plate, her throat parched, her appetite gone.

"I'm never going to ask you for anything. I'm a grown woman and I knew your situation when I got into this," she said.

"Please don't say that," he said. "It scares me. It makes me feel dispensable."

"It's not about you."

"I know. I know it's the only way you can feel a little dignity in this."

She looked at him and even his reasonableness began to irritate her.

"I love you, Ifem. We love each other," he said.

There were tears in his eyes. She began to cry, too, a helpless crying, and they held each other. Later, they lay in bed together, and the air was so still and noiseless that the gurgling sound from his stomach seemed loud.

"Was that my stomach or yours?" he asked, teasing.

"Of course it was yours."

"Remember the first time we made love? You had just been standing on me. I loved you standing on me."

"I can't stand on you now. I'm too fat. You would die."

"Stop it."

Finally, he got up and pulled on his trousers, his movements slow and reluctant. "I can't come tomorrow, Ifem. I have to take my daughter—"

She cut him short. "It's okay."

"I'm going to Abuja on Friday," he said.

"Yes, you said." She was trying to push away the sense of a coming abandonment; it would overwhelm her as soon as he left and she heard the click of the door closing.

"Come with me," he said.

"What?"

"Come with me to Abuja. I just have two meetings and we can stay the weekend. It'll be good for us to be in a different place, to talk. And you've never been to Abuja. I can book separate hotel rooms if you want me to. Say yes. Please."

"Yes," she said.

She had not permitted herself to do so earlier, but after he left, she looked at Kosi's photographs on Facebook. Kosi's beauty was startling, those cheekbones, that flawless skin, those perfect womanly curves. When she saw one photo taken at an unflattering angle, she examined it for a while and found in it a small and wicked pleasure.

SHE WAS at the hair salon when he sent her a text: *I'm sorry Ifem but I think I should probably go alone to Abuja. I need some time to think things through. I love you.* She stared at the text and, fingers shaking, she wrote him back a two-word text: *Fucking coward.* Then she turned to the hair braider. "You are going to blow-dry my hair with that brush? You must be joking. Can't you people think?"

The hair braider looked puzzled. "Aunty, sorry o, but that is what I use before in your hair."

By the time Ifemelu drove into her compound, Obinze's Range Rover was parked in front of her flat. He followed her upstairs.

"Ifem, please, I want you to understand. I think it has been a little too fast, everything between us, and I want to take some time to put things in perspective."

"A little too fast," she repeated. "How unoriginal. Not like you at all."

"You are the woman I love. Nothing can change that. But I feel this sense of responsibility about what I need to do."

She flinched from him, the hoarseness of his voice, the nebulous and easy meaninglessness of his words. What did "responsibility about what I need to do" mean? Did it mean that he wanted to continue seeing her but had to stay married? Did it mean that he could no longer continue seeing her? He communicated clearly when he wanted to, but now here he was, hiding behind watery words.

"What are you saying?" she asked him. "What are you trying to tell me?"

When he remained silent, she said, "Go to hell."

She walked into her bedroom and locked the door. From her bedroom window, she watched his Range Rover until it disappeared down the bend in the road.

CHAPTER 54

Abuja had far-flung horizons, wide roads, order; to come from Lagos was to be stunned here by sequence and space. The air smelled of power; here everyone sized everyone else up, wondering how much of a "somebody" each was. It smelled of money, easy money, easily exchanged money. It dripped, too, of sex. Obinze's friend Chidi said he didn't chase women in Abuja because he didn't want to step on a minister's or senator's toes. Every attractive young woman here became mysteriously suspect. Abuja was more conservative than Lagos, Chidi said, because it was more Muslim than Lagos, and at parties women didn't wear revealing clothing, yet you could buy and sell sex so much more easily here. It was in Abuja that Obinze had come close to cheating on Kosi, not with any of the flashy girls in coloured contact lenses and tumbling hair weaves who endlessly propositioned him, but with a middle-aged woman in a caftan who sat next to him at the hotel bar, and said, "I know you are bored." She looked hungry for recklessness, perhaps a repressed, frustrated wife who had broken free on this one night.

For a moment, lust, a quaking raw lust, overcame him, but he thought about how much more bored he would be afterwards, how keen to get her out of his hotel room, and it all seemed too much of an effort.

She would end up with one of the many men in Abuja who lived idle, oily lives in hotels and part-time homes, grovelling and courting connected people so as to get a contract or to be paid for a contract. On Obinze's last trip to Abuja, one such man, whom he hardly knew, had looked for a while at two young women at the other end of the bar and then asked him casually, "Do you have a spare condom?" and he had baulked.

Now, sitting at a white-covered table in Protea Asokoro, waiting for Edusco, the businessman who wanted to buy his land, he imagined Ifemelu next to him, and wondered what she would make of Abuja. She would dislike it, the soullessness of it, or perhaps not. She was not easy to predict. Once, at dinner in a restaurant in Victoria Island, sombre waiters hovering around, she had seemed distant, her eyes on the wall behind him, and he had worried that she was upset about something. "What are you thinking?" he asked.

"I am thinking of how all the paintings in Lagos always look crooked, never hung straight," she said. He laughed, and thought how, with her, he was as he had never been with another woman: amused, alert, alive. Later, as they left the restaurant, he had watched as she briskly sidestepped the puddles of water in the potholes by the gate and felt a desire to smooth all the roads in Lagos, for her.

His mind was overwrought: one minute he thought it was the right decision not to have come to Abuja with her, because he needed to think things through, and the next he was filled with self-reproach. He might have pushed her away. He had called her many times, sent texts asking if they could talk, but she had ignored him, which was perhaps for the better because he did not know what he would say if they did talk.

Edusco had arrived. A loud voice bellowing from the restaurant foyer as he spoke on the phone. Obinze did not know him well—they had done business only once before, introduced by a mutual friend—but Obinze admired men like him, men who did not know any Big Man, who had no connections, and had made their money in a way that did not defy the simple logic of capitalism. Edusco had only a primary school education before he began to apprentice for traders; he had started off with one stall in Onitsha and now owned the second-largest transport company in the country. He walked into the restaurant, bold-stepped and big-bellied, speaking his terrible English loudly; it did not occur to him to doubt himself.

Later, as they discussed the price of the land, Edusco said, "Look, my brother. You won't sell it at that price, nobody will buy. *Ife esíka kita.* The recession is biting everybody."

"Bros, bring up your hand a little, this is land in Maitama we are talking about, not land in your village," Obinze said.

"Your stomach is full. What else do you want? You see, this is the problem with you Igbo people. You don't do brother-brother. That is why I like Yoruba people, they look out for one another. Do you know that the other day I went to the Inland Revenue office near my house and one man there, an Igbo man, I saw his name and spoke to him in Igbo and he did not even answer me! A Hausa man will speak Hausa to his fellow Hausa man. A Yoruba man will see a Yoruba person anywhere and speak Yoruba. But an Igbo man will speak English to an Igbo man. I am even surprised that you are speaking Igbo to me."

"It's true," Obinze said. "It's sad, it's the legacy of being a defeated people. We lost the Biafran war and learned to be ashamed."

"It is just selfishness!" Edusco said, uninterested in Obinze's intellectualizing. "The Yoruba man is there helping his brother, but you Igbo people? *I ga-asikwa*. Look at you now quoting me this price."

"Okay, Edusco, why don't I give you the land for free? Let me go and bring the title and give it to you now."

Edusco laughed. Edusco liked him, he could tell; he imagined Edusco talking about him in a gathering of other self-made Igbo men, men who were brash and striving, who juggled huge businesses and supported vast extended families. *Obinze ma ife,* he imagined Edusco saying. *Obinze is not like some of these useless small boys with money. This one is not stupid.*

Obinze looked at his almost-empty bottle of Gulder. It was strange how lost of lustre everything was without Ifemelu; even the taste of his favourite beer was different. He should have brought her with him to Abuja. It was stupid to claim that he needed time to think things over when all he was doing was hiding from a truth he already knew. She had called him a coward, and there was indeed a cowardliness in his fear of disorder, of disrupting what he did not even want: his life with Kosi, that second skin that had never quite fitted him snugly.

"Okay, Edusco," Obinze said, suddenly feeling drained. "I am not going to eat the land if I don't sell it."

Edusco looked startled. "You mean you agree to my price?"

"Yes," Obinze said.

After Edusco left, Obinze called Ifemelu over and over but she did not answer. Perhaps her ringer was switched off, and she was eating at her dining table, wearing that pink T-shirt she wore so often, with the small hole at the neck, and HEARTBREAKER CAFÉ written across the front; her nipples, when they got hard, would punctuate those words like inverted commas. Thinking of her pink T-shirt aroused him. Or perhaps she was reading in bed, her abada wrapper spread over her like a blanket, wearing plain black boyshorts and nothing else. All her underwear was plain black boyshorts; girly underwear amused her. Once, he had picked up those boyshorts from the floor where he had flung them after rolling them down her legs, and looked at the milky crust on the crotch, and she laughed and said, "Ah, you want to smell it? I've never understood that whole business of smelling underwear." Or perhaps she was on her laptop, working on the blog. Or out with Ranyinudo. Or on the phone with Dike. Or perhaps with some man in her living room, telling him about Graham Greene. A queasiness roiled in him at the thought of her with anybody else. Of course she would not be with anyone else, not so soon. Still, there was that unpredictable stubbornness in her; she might do it to hurt him. When she told him, that first day, "I always saw the ceiling with other men," he wondered how many there had been. He wanted to ask her, but he did not, because he feared she would tell him the truth and he feared he would forever be tormented by it. She knew, of course, that he loved her but he wondered if she knew how it consumed him, how each day was infected by her, affected by her; and how she wielded power over even his sleep. "Kimberly adores her husband, and her husband adores himself. She should leave him but she never will," she said once, about the woman she had worked for in America, the woman with *obi ocha.* Ifemelu's words had been light, free of shadow, and yet he heard in them the sting of other meanings.

When she told him about her American life, he listened with a keenness close to desperation. He wanted to be a part of everything she had done, be familiar with every emotion she had felt. Once she had told him, "The thing about cross-cultural relationships is that you spend so much time explaining. My ex-boyfriends and I spent a lot of time explaining. I sometimes wondered whether we would even have anything at all to say to each other if we were from the same place," and it pleased him to hear that, because it gave his relationship with her a depth, a lack of trifling novelty. They were from the same place and they still had a lot to say to each other.

They were talking about American politics once when she said, "I like America. It's really the only place else where I could live apart from here. But one day a bunch of Blaine's friends and I were talking about kids and I realized that if I ever have children, I don't want them to have American childhoods. I don't want them to say 'Hi' to adults, I want them to say 'Good morning' and 'Good afternoon.' I don't want them to mumble 'Good' when somebody says 'How are you?' to them. Or to raise five fingers when asked how old they are. I want them to say 'I'm fine, thank you' and 'I'm five years old.' I don't want a child who feeds on praise and expects a star for effort and talks back to adults in the name of self-expression. Is that terribly conservative? Blaine's friends said it was and for them, 'conservative' is the worst insult you can get."

He had laughed, wishing he had been there with the "bunch of friends", and he wanted that imaginary child to be his, that conservative child with good manners. He told her, "The child will turn eighteen and paint her hair purple," and she said, "Yes, but by then I would have kicked her out of the house."

At the Abuja airport on his way back to Lagos, he thought of going to the international wing instead, buying a ticket to somewhere improbable, like Malabo. Then he felt a passing self-disgust because he would not, of course, do it; he would instead do what he was expected to do. He was boarding his Lagos flight when Kosi called.

"Is the flight on time? Remember we are taking Nigel out for his birthday," she said.

"Of course I remember."

A pause from her end. He had snapped.

"I'm sorry," he said. "I have a funny headache."

"Darling, *ndo.* I know you're tired," she said. "See you soon."

He hung up and thought about the day their baby, slippery, curly-haired Buchi, was born at the Woodlands Hospital in Houston, how Kosi had turned to him while he was still fiddling with his latex gloves and said, with something like apology, "Darling, we'll have a boy next time." He had recoiled. He realized then that she did not know him. She did not know him at all. She did not know he was indifferent about the gender of their child. And he felt a gentle contempt towards her, for wanting a boy because they were supposed to want a boy, and for being able to say, fresh from birthing their first child, those words "we'll have a boy next time". Perhaps he should have talked more with her, about the baby they were expecting and about everything else, because although they exchanged pleasant sounds and were good friends and shared comfortable silences, they did not really talk. But he had never tried, because he knew that the questions he asked of life were entirely different from hers.

He knew this from the beginning, had sensed it in their first conversation after a friend introduced them at a wedding. She was wearing a satin bridesmaid's dress in fuchsia, cut low to show a cleavage he could not stop looking at, and somebody was making a speech, describing the bride as "a woman of virtue" and Kosi nodded eagerly and whispered to him, "She is a true woman of virtue." It surprised him, that she could use the word "virtue" without the slightest irony, as was done in the badly written articles in the women's section of the weekend newspapers. *The minister's wife is a homely woman of virtue.* Still, he had wanted her, chased her with a lavish single-mindedness. He had never seen a woman with such a perfect incline to her cheekbones that made her entire face seem so alive, so architectural, lifting when she smiled. He was also newly rich and newly disoriented: one week he was broke and squatting in his cousin's flat and the next he had millions of naira in his bank account. Kosi became a touchstone of realness. If he could be with her, so extraordinarily beautiful and yet so ordinary, predictable and domestic and dedicated, then perhaps his life would start to seem believably his. She moved into his house from the flat she shared with a friend and arranged her perfume bottles on his dresser, citrusy scents that he came to associate with home, and she sat in the BMW beside him as though it had always been his car, and she casually suggested trips abroad as though he had always been able to travel, and when they showered together, she scrubbed him with a rough sponge, even between his toes, until he felt reborn. Until he owned his new life. She did not share his interests—she was a literal person who did not read, she was content rather than curious about the world—but he felt grateful to her, fortunate to be with her. Then she told him her relatives were asking what his intentions were. "They just keep asking," she said and stressed the "they", to exclude herself from the marriage clamour. He recognized, and disliked, her manipulation. Still, he married her. They were living together anyway, and he was not unhappy, and he imagined that she would, with time, gain a certain heft. She had not, after four years, except physically, in a way that he thought made her look even more beautiful, fresher, with fuller hips and breasts, like a well-watered houseplant.

IT AMUSED OBINZE, that Nigel had decided to move to Nigeria, instead of simply visiting whenever Obinze needed to present his white General Manager. The money was good, Nigel could now live the kind of life in Essex that he would never have imagined before, but he wanted to live in Lagos, at least for a while. And so Obinze's gleeful waiting commenced, for Nigel to weary of pepper soup and nightclubs and drinking at the shacks in Kuramo Beach. But Nigel was staying put, in his flat in Ikoyi, with a live-in house help and his dog. He no longer said, "Lagos has so much flavour," and he complained more about the traffic and he had finally stopped moping about his last girlfriend, a girl from Benue with a pretty face and dissembling manner, who had left him for a wealthy Lebanese businessman.

"The bloke's completely bald," Nigel had told Obinze.

"The problem with you, my friend, is you love too easily and too much. Anybody could see the girl was a fake, looking for the next bigger thing," Obinze told him.

"Don't say 'bigger thing' like that, mate!" Nigel said.

Now he had met Ulrike, a lean, angular-faced woman with the body of a young man, who worked at an embassy and seemed determined to sulk her way through her Nigerian posting. At dinner, she wiped her cutlery with the napkin before she began eating.

"You don't do that in your country, do you?" Obinze asked coldly. Nigel darted a startled glance at him.

"Actually I do," Ulrike said, squarely meeting his gaze.

Kosi patted his thigh under the table, as though to calm him down, which irritated him. Nigel, too, was irritating him, suddenly talking about the town houses Obinze was planning to build, how exciting the new architect's design was. A timid attempt to end Obinze's conversation with Ulrike.

"Fantastic plan inside, made me think of some of those pictures of fancy lofts in New York," Nigel said.

"Nigel, I'm not using that plan. An open kitchen plan will never work for Nigerians and we are targeting Nigerians because we are selling, not renting. Open kitchen plans are for expats and expats don't buy property here." He had already told Nigel many times that Nigerian cooking was not cosmetic, with all that pounding. It was sweaty and spicy and Nigerians preferred to present the final product, not the process.

"No more work talk!" Kosi said brightly. "Ulrike, have you tried any Nigerian food?"

Obinze got up abruptly and went into the bathroom. He called Ifemelu and felt himself getting enraged when she still did not pick up. He blamed her. He blamed her for making him a person who was not entirely in control of what he was feeling.

Nigel came into the bathroom. "What's wrong, mate?" Nigel's cheeks were bright red, as they always were when he drank. Obinze stood by the sink holding his phone, that drained lassitude spreading over him again. He wanted to tell Nigel, Nigel was perhaps the only friend he fully trusted, but Nigel fancied Kosi. "She's all woman, mate," Nigel had said to him once, and he saw in Nigel's eyes the tender and crushed longing of a man for that which was forever unattainable. Nigel would listen to him, but Nigel would not understand.

"Sorry, I shouldn't have been rude to Ulrike," Obinze said. "I'm just tired. I think I'm coming down with malaria."

That night, Kosi sidled close to him, in offering. It was not a statement of desire, her caressing his chest and reaching down to take his penis in her hand, but a votive offering. A few months ago, she had said she wanted to start seriously "trying for our son". She did not say "trying for our second child", she said "trying for our son", and it was the kind of thing she learned in her church. *There is power in the spoken word. Claim your miracle.* He remembered how, months into trying to get pregnant the first time, she began to say with sulky righteousness, "All my friends who lived very rough lives are pregnant."

After Buchi was born, he had agreed to a thanksgiving service at Kosi's church, a crowded hall full of lavishly dressed people, people who were Kosi's friends, Kosi's kind. And he had thought of them as a sea of simple brutes, clapping, swaying simple brutes, all of them accepting and pliant before the pastor in his designer suit.

"What's wrong, darling?" Kosi asked, when he remained limp in her hand. "Are you feeling well?"

"Just tired."

Her hair was covered in a black hair net, her face coated in a cream that smelled of peppermint, which he had always liked. He turned away from her. He had been turning away since the day he first kissed Ifemelu. He should not compare, but he did. Ifemelu demanded of him. "No, don't come yet, I'll kill you if you come," she would say, or "No, baby, don't move," then she would dig into his chest and move at her own rhythm, and when finally she arched her back and let out a sharp cry, he felt accomplished to have satisfied her. She expected to be satisfied, but Kosi did not. Kosi always met his touch with complaisance, and sometimes he would imagine her pastor telling her that a wife should have sex with her husband, even if she didn't feel like it, otherwise the husband would find solace in a Jezebel.

"I hope you're not getting sick," she said.

"I'm okay." Ordinarily he would hold her, slowly rub her back until she fell asleep. But he could not get himself to do so now. So many times in the past weeks he had started to tell her about Ifemelu but had stopped. What would he say? It would sound like something from a silly film. *I am in love with another woman. There's someone else. I'm leaving you.* That these were words that anybody could say seriously, outside a film and outside the pages of a book, seemed odd. Kosi was wrapping her arms around him. He eased away and mumbled something about his stomach being upset and went into the toilet. She had put a new potpourri, a mix of dried leaves and seeds in a purple bowl, on the cover of the toilet tank. The too-strong lavender scent choked him. He emptied the bowl into the toilet and then instantly felt remorseful. She had meant well. She did not know that the too-strong scent of lavender would be unappealing to him, after all.

The first time he saw Ifemelu at Jazzhole, he had come home and told Kosi, "Ifemelu is in town. I had a drink with her," and Kosi had said, "Oh, your girlfriend in university," with an indifference so indifferent that he did not entirely trust it.

Why had he told her? Perhaps because he had sensed even then the force of what he felt, and he wanted to prepare her, to tell her in stages. But how could she not see that he had changed? How could she not see it on his face? In how much time he spent alone in his study, and in how often he went out, how late he stayed? He had hoped, selfishly, that it might alienate her, provoke her. But she always nodded, glib and accepting nods, when he told her he had been at the club. Or at Okwudiba's. Once he said that he was still chasing the difficult deal with the new Arab owners of Megatel, and he had said "the deal" casually, as if she already knew about it, and she made vague, encouraging sounds. But he was not even involved at all with Megatel.

THE NEXT MORNING, he woke up unrested, his mind furred with a great sadness. Kosi was already up and bathed, sitting in front of her dressing table, which was full of creams and potions so carefully arranged that he sometimes imagined putting his hands under the table and overturning it, just to see how all those bottles would fare.

"You haven't made me eggs in a while, The Zed," she said, coming over to kiss him when she saw that he was awake. And so he made her eggs, and played with Buchi in the living room downstairs, and after Buchi fell asleep, he read the newspapers, all the time his head furred with that sadness. Ifemelu was still not taking his calls. He went upstairs to the bedroom. Kosi was cleaning out a closet. A pile of shoes, high heels sticking up, lay on the floor. He stood by the door and said quietly, "I'm not happy, Kosi. I love somebody else. I want a divorce. I will make sure you and Buchi lack nothing."

"What?" She turned from the mirror to look at him blankly.

"I'm not happy." It was not how he had planned to say it, but he had not even planned what to say. "I'm in love with somebody. I will make sure . . ."

She raised her hand, her open palm facing him, to make him stop talking. Say no more, her hand said. Say no more. And it irked him that she did not want to know more. Her palm was pale, almost diaphanous, and he could see the greenish criss-cross of her veins. She lowered her hand. Then, slowly, she sank to her knees. It was an easy descent for her, sinking to her knees, because she did that often when she prayed, in the TV room upstairs, with the house help and nanny and whoever else was staying with them. "Buchi, shh," she would say in between the words of prayer, while Buchi would continue her toddler talk, but at the end Buchi always squeaked in a high piping voice, "Amen!" When Buchi said "Amen!" with that delight, that gusto, Obinze feared she would grow up to be a woman who, with that word "amen", would squash the questions she wanted to ask of the world. And now Kosi was sinking to her knees before him and he did not want to comprehend what she was doing.

"Obinze, this is a family," Kosi said. "We have a child. She needs you. I need you. We have to keep this family together."

She was kneeling and begging him not to leave and he wished she would be furious instead.

"Kosi, I love another woman. I hate to hurt you like this and . . ."

"It's not about another woman, Obinze," Kosi said, rising to her feet, her voice steeling, her eyes hardening. "It's about keeping this family together! You took a vow before God. I took a vow before God. I am a good wife. We have a marriage. Do you think you can just destroy this family because your old girlfriend came into town? Do you know what it means to be a responsible father? You have a responsibility to that child downstairs! What you do today can ruin her life and make her damaged until the day she dies! And all because your old girlfriend came back from America? Because you have had acrobatic sex that reminded you of your time in university?"

Obinze backed away. So she knew. He left and went into his study and locked the door. He loathed Kosi, for knowing all this time and pretending she didn't know, and for the sludge of humiliation it left in his stomach. He had been keeping a secret that was not even a secret. A multilayered guilt weighed him down, guilt not only for wanting to leave Kosi, but for having married her at all. He could not first marry her, knowing very well that he should not have done so, and now, with a child, want to leave her. She was determined to remain married and it was the least he owed her, to remain married. Panic lanced through him at the thought of remaining married; without Ifemelu, the future loomed as an endless, joyless tedium. Then he told himself that he was being silly and dramatic. He had to think of his daughter. Yet as he sat on his chair and swivelled to look for a book on the shelf, he felt himself already in flight.

BECAUSE HE HAD RETREATED to his study, and slept on the couch there, because they had said nothing else to each other, he thought Kosi would not want to go to his friend Ahmed's child's christening party the next day. But in the morning Kosi laid out, on their bed, her blue lace long skirt, his blue Senegalese caftan, and in between, Buchi's flouncy blue velvet dress. She had never done that before, laid out colour-coordinated outfits for them all. Downstairs, he saw that she had made pancakes, the thick ones he liked, set out on the breakfast table. Buchi had spilled some Ovaltine on her table mat.

"Hezekiah has been calling me," Kosi said musingly, about his cousin in Awka, who called only when he wanted money. "He sent a text to say he can't reach you. I don't know why he pretends not to know that you ignore his calls."

It was an odd thing for her to say, talking about Hezekiah's pretence while immersed in pretence herself; she was putting cubes of fresh pineapple on his plate, as if the previous night had never happened.

"But you should do something for him, no matter how small, otherwise he will not leave you alone," she said.

"Do something for him" meant give him money and Obinze, all of a sudden, hated that tendency of Igbo people to resort to euphemism whenever they spoke of money, to indirect references, to gesturing instead of pointing. Find something for this person. Do something for that person. It riled him. It seemed cowardly, especially for a people who otherwise were blisteringly direct. *Fucking coward,* Ifemelu had called him. There was something cowardly even in his texting and calling her, knowing she would not respond; he could have gone over to her flat and knocked on her door, even if only to have her ask him to leave. And there was something cowardly in his not telling Kosi again that he wanted a divorce, in his leaning back into the ease of Kosi's denial. Kosi took a piece of pineapple from his plate and ate it. She was unfaltering, single-minded, calm.

"Hold Daddy's hand," she told Buchi as they walked into Ahmed's festive compound that afternoon. She wanted to will normalcy back.

She wanted to will a good marriage into being. She was carrying a present wrapped in silver paper, for Ahmed's baby. In the car, she had told him what it was, but already he had forgotten. Canopies and buffet tables dotted the massive compound, which was green and landscaped, with the promise of a swimming pool in the back. A live band was playing. Two clowns were running around. Children dancing and shrieking.

"They are using the same band we used for Buchi's party," Kosi whispered. She had wanted a big party to celebrate Buchi's birth, and he had floated through that day, a bubble of air between him and the party. When the MC said "the new father", he had been strangely startled to realize that the MC meant him, that he was really the new father. A father.

Ahmed's wife, Sike, was hugging him, tugging Buchi's cheeks, people milling about, laughter thick in the air's clasp. They admired the new baby, asleep in the crook of her bespectacled grandmother's arms. And it struck Obinze that, a few years ago, they were attending weddings, now it was christenings and soon it would be funerals. They would die. They would all die after trudging through lives in which they were neither happy nor unhappy. He tried to shake off the morose shadow that was enveloping him. Kosi took Buchi over to the cluster of women and children near the living room entrance; there was some sort of game being played in a circle, at the centre of which was a red-lipped clown. Obinze watched his daughter—her ungainly walk, the blue band, speckled with silk flowers, that sat on her head of thick hair, the way she looked up imploringly at Kosi, her expression reminding him of his mother. He could not bear the thought of Buchi growing up to resent him, to lack something that he should have been for her. But it wasn't whether or not he left Kosi that should matter, it was how often he saw Buchi. He would live in Lagos, after all, and he would make sure he saw her as often as he could. Many people grew up without fathers. He himself had, although he had always had the consoling spirit of his father, idealized, frozen in joyful childhood memories. Since Ifemelu came back, he found himself seeking stories of men who had left their marriages, and willing the stories to end well, the children more contented with separated parents than with married unhappy parents. But most of the stories were of resentful children who were bitter about divorce, children who had wanted even unhappy parents to remain together. Once, at his club, he had perked up as a young man talked to some friends about his own parents' divorce, how he had felt relieved by it, because their unhappiness had been heavy. "Their marriage just blocked the blessings in our life, and the worst part is that they didn't even fight."

Obinze, from the other end of the bar, had said, "Good!" drawing strange looks from everyone.

He was still watching Kosi and Buchi talk to the red-lipped clown, when Okwudiba arrived. "The Zed!"

They hugged, thumped backs.

"How was China?" Obinze asked.

"These Chinese people, ehn. Very wily people. You know the previous idiots in my project had signed a lot of nonsense deals with the Chinese. We wanted to review some of the agreements but these Chinese, fifty of them will come to a meeting and bring papers and just tell you 'Sign here, sign here!' They will wear you down with negotiation until they have your money and also your wallet." Okwudiba laughed. "Come, let's go upstairs. I hear that Ahmed packed bottles of Dom Pérignon there."

Upstairs, in what seemed to be a dining room, the heavy burgundy drapes were drawn, shutting out the daylight, and a bright elaborate chandelier, like a wedding cake made of crystals, hung down from the middle of the ceiling. Men were seated around the large oak table, which was crowded with bottles of wine and liquor, with dishes of rice and meat and salads. Ahmed was in and out, giving instructions to the server, listening in on conversations and adding a line or two.

"The wealthy don't really care about tribe. But the lower you go, the more tribe matters," Ahmed was saying when Obinze and Okwudiba came in. Obinze liked Ahmed's sardonic nature. Ahmed had leased strategic rooftops in Lagos just as the mobile phone companies were coming in, and now he sublet the rooftops for their base stations and made what he wryly referred to as the only clean easy money in the country.

Obinze shook hands with the men, most of whom he knew, and

asked the server, a young woman who had placed a wineglass in front of him, if he could have a Coke instead. Alcohol would sink him deeper into his marsh. He listened to the conversation around him, the joking, the needling, the telling and retelling. Then they began, as he knew they invariably would, to criticize the government—money stolen, contracts uncompleted, infrastructure left to rot.

"Look, it's very hard to be a clean public official in this country. Everything is set up for you to steal. And the worst part is, people want you to steal. Your relatives want you to steal, your friends want you to steal," Olu said. He was thin and slouchy, with the easy boastfulness that came with his inherited wealth, his famous surname. Once, he had apparently been offered a ministerial position and had responded, according to the urban legend, "But I can't live in Abuja, there's no water, I can't survive without my boats." Olu had just divorced his wife, Morenike, Kosi's friend from university. He had often badgered Morenike, who was only slightly overweight, about losing weight, about keeping him interested by keeping herself fit. During their divorce, she discovered a cache of pornographic pictures on the home computer, all of obese women, arms and bellies in rolls of fat, and she had concluded, and Kosi agreed, that Olu had a spiritual problem.

"Why does everything have to be a spiritual problem? The man just has a fetish," Obinze had told Kosi. Now, he sometimes found himself looking at Olu with curious amusement; you could never tell with people.

"The problem is not that public officials steal, the problem is that they steal too much," Okwudiba said. "Look at all these governors. They leave their state and come to Lagos to buy up all the land and they will not touch it until they leave office. That is why nobody can afford to buy land these days."

"It's true! Land speculators are just spoiling prices for everybody. And the speculators are guys in government. We have serious problems in this country," Ahmed said.

"But it's not just Nigeria. There are land speculators everywhere in the world," Eze said. Eze was the wealthiest man in the room, an owner of oil wells, and as many of the Nigerian wealthy were, he was free of angst, an obliviously happy man. He collected art and he told everyone that he collected art. It reminded Obinze of his mother's friend Aunty

Chinelo, a professor of literature who had come back from a short stay at Harvard and told his mother over dinner at their dining table, "The problem is we have a very backward bourgeoisie in this country. They have money but they need to become sophisticated. They need to learn about wine." And his mother had replied, mildly, "There are many different ways to be poor in the world but increasingly there seems to be one single way to be rich." Later, after Aunty Chinelo left, his mother said, "How silly. Why should they learn about wine?" It had struck Obinze—they need to learn about wine—and, in a way, it had disappointed him, too, because he had always liked Aunty Chinelo. He imagined that somebody had told Eze something similar—you need to collect art, you need to learn about art—and so the man had gone after art with the zeal of an invented interest. Every time Obinze saw Eze, and heard him talk fumblingly about his collection, he was tempted to tell Eze to give it all away and free himself.

"Land prices are no problem for people like you, Eze," Okwudiba said.

Eze laughed, a laugh of preening agreement. He had taken off his red blazer and hung it on his chair. He teetered, in the name of style, on dandyism; he always wore primary colours, and his belt buckles were always large and prominent, like buck-teeth.

From the other end of the table, Mekkus was saying, "Do you know that my driver said he passed WAEC, but the other day I told him to write a list and he cannot write at all! He cannot spell 'boy' and 'cat'! Wonderful!"

"Speaking of drivers, my friend was telling me the other day that his driver is an economic homosexual, that the man follows men who give him money, meanwhile he has a wife and children at home," Ahmed said.

"Economic homosexual!" somebody repeated, to loud general laughter. Charlie Bombay seemed particularly amused. He had a rough scarred face, the kind of man who would be most himself in the middle of a pack of loud men, eating peppery meat, drinking beer and watching Arsenal.

"The Zed! You are really quiet today," Okwudiba said, now on his fifth glass of champagne. "*Aru adikwa?*"

Obinze shrugged. "I'm fine. Just tired."

"But The Zed is always quiet," Mekkus said. "He is a gentleman. Is it because he came here to sit with us? The man reads poems and Shakespeare. Correct Englishman." Mekkus laughed loudly at his own non-joke. At university, he had been brilliant with electronics, he fixed CD players that were considered lost causes, and his was the first personal computer Obinze had ever seen. He graduated and went to America, then came back a short while afterwards, very furtive and very wealthy from what many said was a massive credit card fraud. His house was studded with CCTV cameras; his security men had automatic guns. And now, at the merest mention of America in a conversation, he would say, "You know I can never enter America after the deal I did there," as though to take the sting from the whispers that trailed him.

"Yes, The Zed is a serious gentleman," Ahmed said. "Can you imagine Sike was asking me whether I know anybody like The Zed that I can introduce to her sister? I said, Ahn-ahn, you are not looking for somebody like me to marry your sister and instead you are looking for somebody like The Zed, imagine o!"

"No, The Zed is not quiet because he is a gentleman," Charlie Bombay said, in his slow manner, his thick Igbo accent adding extra syllables to his words, halfway through a bottle of cognac that he had put territorially in front of himself. "It is because he doesn't want anybody to know how much money he has!"

They laughed. Obinze had always imagined that Charlie Bombay was a wife beater. There was no reason for him to; he knew nothing of Charlie Bombay's personal life, had never even seen his wife. Still, every time he saw Charlie Bombay, he imagined him beating his wife with a thick leather belt. He seemed full of violence, this swaggering, powerful man, this godfather who had paid for his state governor's campaign and now had a monopoly on almost every business in that state.

"Don't mind The Zed, he thinks we don't know that he owns half the land in Lekki," Eze said.

Obinze produced an obligatory chuckle. He brought out his phone and quickly sent Ifemelu a text: *Please talk to me.*

"We haven't met, I'm Dapo," the man sitting on the other side of Okwudiba said, reaching across to shake Obinze's hand enthusiastically, as though Obinze had just sprung into existence. Obinze enclosed his hand in a half-hearted shake. Charlie Bombay had mentioned his wealth, and suddenly he was interesting to Dapo.

"Are you into oil too?" Dapo asked.

"No," Obinze said shortly. He had heard snatches of Dapo's conversation earlier, his work in oil consulting, his children in London. Dapo was probably one of those who installed their wife and children in England and then came back to Nigeria to chase money.

"I was just saying that the Nigerians who keep complaining about the oil companies don't understand that this economy will collapse without them," Dapo said.

"You must be very confused if you think the oil companies are doing us a favour," Obinze said. Okwudiba gave him an astonished look; the coldness of his tone was out of character. "The Nigerian government basically finances the oil industry with cash calls, and the big oils are planning to withdraw from onshore operations anyway. They want to leave that to the Chinese and focus on offshore operations only. It's like a parallel economy; they keep offshore, only invest in high-tech equipment, pump up oil from thousands of kilometres deep. No local crew. Oil workers flown in from Houston and Scotland. So, no, they are not doing us a favour."

"Yes!" Mekkus said. "And they are all common riff-raff. All those underwater plumbers and deep-sea divers and people who know how to repair maintenance robots underwater. Common riff-raff, all of them. You see them in the British Airways lounge. They have been on the rig for one month with no alcohol and by the time they get to the airport they are already stinking drunk and they make fools of themselves on the flight. My cousin used to be a flight attendant and she said that it got to a point that the airlines had to make these men sign agreements about drinking, otherwise they wouldn't let them fly."

"But The Zed doesn't fly British Airways, so he wouldn't know," Ahmed said. He had once laughed at Obinze's refusal to fly British Airways, because it was, after all, what the big boys flew.

"When I was a regular man in economy, British Airways treated me like shit from a bad diarrhoea," Obinze said.

The men laughed. Obinze was hoping his phone would vibrate, and chafing under his hope. He got up.

"I need to find the toilet."

"It's just straight down," Mekkus said.

Okwudiba followed him out.

"I'm going home," Obinze said. "Let me find Kosi and Buchi."

"The Zed, *o gini*? What is it? Is it just tiredness?"

They were standing by the curving staircase, hemmed by an ornate balustrade.

"You know Ifemelu is back," Obinze said, and just saying her name warmed him.

"I know." Okwudiba meant that he knew more.

"It's serious. I want to marry her."

"Ahn-ahn, have you become a Muslim without telling us?"

"Okwu, I'm not joking. I should never have married Kosi. I knew it even then."

Okwudiba took a deep breath and exhaled, as though to brush aside the alcohol. "Look, The Zed, many of us didn't marry the woman we truly loved. We married the woman that was around when we were ready to marry. So forget this thing. You can keep seeing her, but no need for this kind of white-people behaviour. If your wife has a child for somebody else or if you beat her, that is a reason for divorce. But to get up and say you have no problem with your wife but you are leaving for another woman? *Haba.* We don't behave like that, please."

Kosi and Buchi were standing at the bottom of the stairs. Buchi was crying. "She fell," Kosi said. "She said Daddy must carry her."

Obinze began to descend the stairs. "Buch-Buch! What happened?" Before he got to her, she already had her arms outstretched, waiting for him.

CHAPTER 55

One day, Ifemelu saw the male peacock dance, its feathers fanned out in a giant halo. The female stood by pecking at something on the ground and then, after a while, it walked away, indifferent to the male's great flare of feathers. The male seemed suddenly to totter, perhaps from the weight of its feathers or from the weight of rejection. Ifemelu took a picture for her blog. She wondered what Obinze would think of it; she remembered how he had asked if she had ever seen the male dance. Memories of him so easily invaded her mind; she would, in the middle of a meeting at an advertising agency, remember Obinze pulling out an ingrown hair on her chin with tweezers, her face up on a pillow, and him very close and very keen in examination. Each memory stunned her with its blinding luminosity. Each brought with it a sense of unassailable loss, a great burden hurtling towards her, and she wished she could duck, lower herself so that it would bypass her, so that she would save herself. Love was a kind of grief. This was what the novelists meant by suffering. She had often thought it a little silly, the idea of suffering for love, but now she understood. She carefully avoided the street in Victoria Island where his club was, and she no longer shopped at the Palms and she imagined him, too, avoiding her part of Ikoyi, keeping away from Jazzhole. She had not run into him anywhere.

At first she played "Yori Yori" and "Obi Mu O" endlessly and then she stopped, because the songs brought to her memories a finality, as though they were dirges. She was wounded by the half-heartedness in his texting and calling, the limpness of his efforts. He loved her, she knew, but he lacked a certain strength; his backbone was softened by duty. When she put up the post, written after a visit to Ranyinudo's office, about the government's demolishing of hawkers' shacks, an anonymous commenter wrote, *This is like poetry.* And she knew it was him. She just knew.

It is morning. A truck, a government truck, stops near the tall office building, beside the hawkers' shacks, and men spill out, men hitting and destroying and leveling and trampling. They destroy the shacks, reduce them to flat pieces of wood. They are doing their job, wearing "demolish" like crisp business suits. They themselves eat in shacks like these, and if all the shacks like these disappeared in Lagos, they will go lunchless, unable to afford anything else. But they are smashing, trampling, hitting. One of them slaps a woman, because she does not grab her pot and her wares and run. She stands there and tries to talk to them. Later, her face is burning from the slap as she watches her biscuits buried in dust. Her eyes trace a line towards the bleak sky. She does not know yet what she will do but she will do something, she will regroup and recoup and go somewhere else and sell her beans and rice and spaghetti cooked to a near mush, her Coke and sweets and biscuits.

It is evening. Outside the tall office building, daylight is fading and the staff buses are waiting. Women walk up to them, wearing flat slippers and telling slow stories of no consequence. Their high-heeled shoes are in their bags. From one woman's unzipped bag, a heel sticks out like a dull dagger. The men walk more quickly to the buses. They walk under a cluster of trees which, only hours ago, housed the livelihoods of food hawkers. There, drivers and messengers bought their lunch. But now the shacks are gone. They are erased, and nothing is left, not a stray biscuit wrapper, not a bottle that once held water, nothing to suggest that they were once there.

Ranyinudo urged her, often, to go out more, to date. "Obinze always felt a little too cool with himself anyway," Ranyinudo said, and although Ifemelu knew Ranyinudo was only trying to make her feel better, it still startled her, that everyone else did not think Obinze as near-perfect as she did.

She wrote her blog posts wondering what he would make of them. She wrote of a fashion show she had attended, how the model had twirled around in an ankara skirt, a vibrant swish of blues and greens, looking like a haughty butterfly. She wrote of the woman at the street corner in Victoria Island who joyously said, "Fine Aunty!" when Ifemelu stopped to buy apples and oranges. She wrote about the views from her bedroom window: a white egret drooped on the compound wall, exhausted from heat; the gateman helping a hawker raise her tray to her head, an act so full of grace that she stood watching long after the hawker had walked away. She wrote about the announcers on radio stations, with their accents so fake and so funny. She wrote about the tendency of Nigerian women to give advice, sincere advice dense with sanctimony. She wrote about the waterlogged neighbourhood crammed with zinc houses, their roofs like squashed hats, and of the young women who lived there, fashionable and savvy in tight jeans, their lives speckled stubbornly with hope: they wanted to open hair salons, to go to university. They believed their turn would come. *We are just one step away from this life in a slum, all of us who live air-conditioned middle-class lives,* she wrote, and wondered if Obinze would agree. The pain of his absence did not decrease with time; it seemed instead to sink in deeper each day, to rouse in her even clearer memories. Still, she was at peace: to be home, to be writing her blog, to have discovered Lagos again. She had, finally, spun herself fully into being.

SHE WAS reaching back to her past. She called Blaine to say hello, to tell him she had always thought he was too good, too pure, for her, and he was stilted over the phone, as though resentful of her call, but at the end he said, "I'm glad you called." She called Curt and he sounded upbeat, thrilled to hear from her, and she imagined getting back together, being in a relationship free of depth and pain.

"Was it you, those large amounts of money I used to get for the blog?" she asked.

"No," he said, and she wasn't sure whether to believe him or not. "So you still blogging?"

"Yes."

"About race?"

"No, just about life. Race doesn't really work here. I feel like I got off the plane in Lagos and stopped being black."

"I bet."

She had forgotten how very American he sounded.

"It's not been the same with anybody else," he said. She liked hearing that. He called her late at night, Nigerian time, and they talked about what they used to do together. The memories seemed burnished now. He made vague references to visiting her in Lagos and she made vague sounds of assent.

One evening, while she was walking into Terra Kulture to see a play with Ranyinudo and Zemaye, she ran into Fred. They all sat in the restaurant afterwards, drinking smoothies.

"Nice guy," Ranyinudo whispered to Ifemelu.

At first Fred talked, as before, about music and art, his spirit knotted up with the need to impress.

"I'd like to know what you're like when you're not performing," Ifemelu said.

He laughed. "If you go out with me you'll know."

There was a silence, Ranyinudo and Zemaye looking at Ifemelu expectantly, and it amused her.

"I'll go out with you," she said.

He took her to a nightclub, and when she said she was bored by the too-loud music and the smoke and the barely clothed bodies of strangers too close to hers, he told her sheepishly that he, too, disliked nightclubs; he had assumed she liked them. They watched films together in her flat, and then in his house in Oniru, where arch paintings hung on his wall. It surprised her that they liked the same films. His cook, an elegant man from Cotonou, made a groundnut stew that she loved. Fred played the guitar for her, and sang, his voice husky, and told her how his dream was to be a lead singer in a folksy band. He was attractive, the kind of attractiveness that grew on you. She liked him. He reached out often to push his glasses up, a small push with his finger, and she thought this endearing. As they lay naked on her bed, all pleasant and all warm, she wished it were different. If only she could feel what she wanted to feel.

AND THEN, on a languorous Sunday evening, seven months since she had last seen him, there Obinze was, at the door of her flat. She stared at him.

"Ifem," he said.

It was such a surprise to see him, his shaved-bald head and the beautiful gentleness of his face. His eyes were urgent, intense, and she could see the up-down chest movement of his heavy breathing. He was holding a long sheet of paper dense with writing. "I've written this for you. It's what I would like to know if I were you. Where my mind has been. I've written everything."

He was holding out the paper, his chest still heaving, and she stood there not reaching out for the paper.

"I know we could accept the things we can't be for each other, and even turn it into the poetic tragedy of our lives. Or we could act. I want to act. I want this to happen. Kosi is a good woman and my marriage was a kind of floating-along contentment but I should never have married her. I always knew that something was missing. I want to raise Buchi, I want to see her every day. But I've been pretending all these months and one day she'll be old enough to know I'm pretending. I moved out of the house today. I'll stay in my flat in Parkview for now and I hope to see Buchi every day if I can. I know it's taken me too long and I know you're moving on and I completely understand if you are ambivalent and need time."

He paused, shifted. "Ifem, I'm chasing you. I'm going to chase you until you give this a chance."

For a long time she stared at him. He was saying what she wanted to hear and yet she stared at him.

"Ceiling," she said, finally. "Come in."

Acknowledgements

My deep gratitude to my family, who read drafts, told me stories, said "*jisie ike*" just when I needed to hear it, honoured my need for space and time, and never wavered in that strange and beautiful faith born of love: James and Grace Adichie, Ivara Esege, Ijeoma Maduka, Uche Sonny-Eduputa, Chuks Adichie, Obi Maduka, Sonny Eduputa, Tinuke Adichie, Kene Adichie, Okey Adichie, Nneka Adichie Okeke, Oge Ikemelu, and Uju Egonu.

Three lovely people gave so much of their time and wisdom to this book: Ike Anya, *oyi di ka nwanne*; Louis Edozien; and Chinakueze Onyemelukwe.

For their intelligence and their remarkable generosity in reading the manuscript, sometimes more than once, and letting me see my characters through their eyes, and telling me what worked and what didn't, I am grateful to these dear friends: Aslak Sira Myhre, Binyavanga Wainaina, Chioma Okolie, Dave Eggers, Muhtar Bakare, Rachel Silver, Ifeacho Nwokolo, Kym Nwosu, Colum McCann, Funmi Iyanda, Martin Kenyon (beloved pedant), Ada Echetebu, Thandie Newton, Simi Dosekun, Jason Cowley, Chinazo Anya, Simon Watson, and Dwayne Betts.

My thanks to my editor Robin Desser at Knopf; to Nicholas Pearson, Minna Fry and Michelle Kane at Fourth Estate; to the Wylie Agency staff, especially Charles Buchan, Jackie Ko, and Emma Paterson; to Sarah Chalfant, friend and agent, for that ongoing feeling of safety; and to the Radcliffe Institute for Advanced Study at Harvard, for the small office filled with light.

A NOTE ON THE TYPE

The text of this book was set in Requiem, created in the 1990s by the Hoefler Type Foundry. It was derived from a set of inscriptional capitals appearing in Ludovico Vicentino degli Arrighi's 1523 writing manual, *Il Modo de Temperare le Penne*. A master scribe, Arrighi is remembered as an exemplar of the chancery italic, a style revived in Requiem Italic.